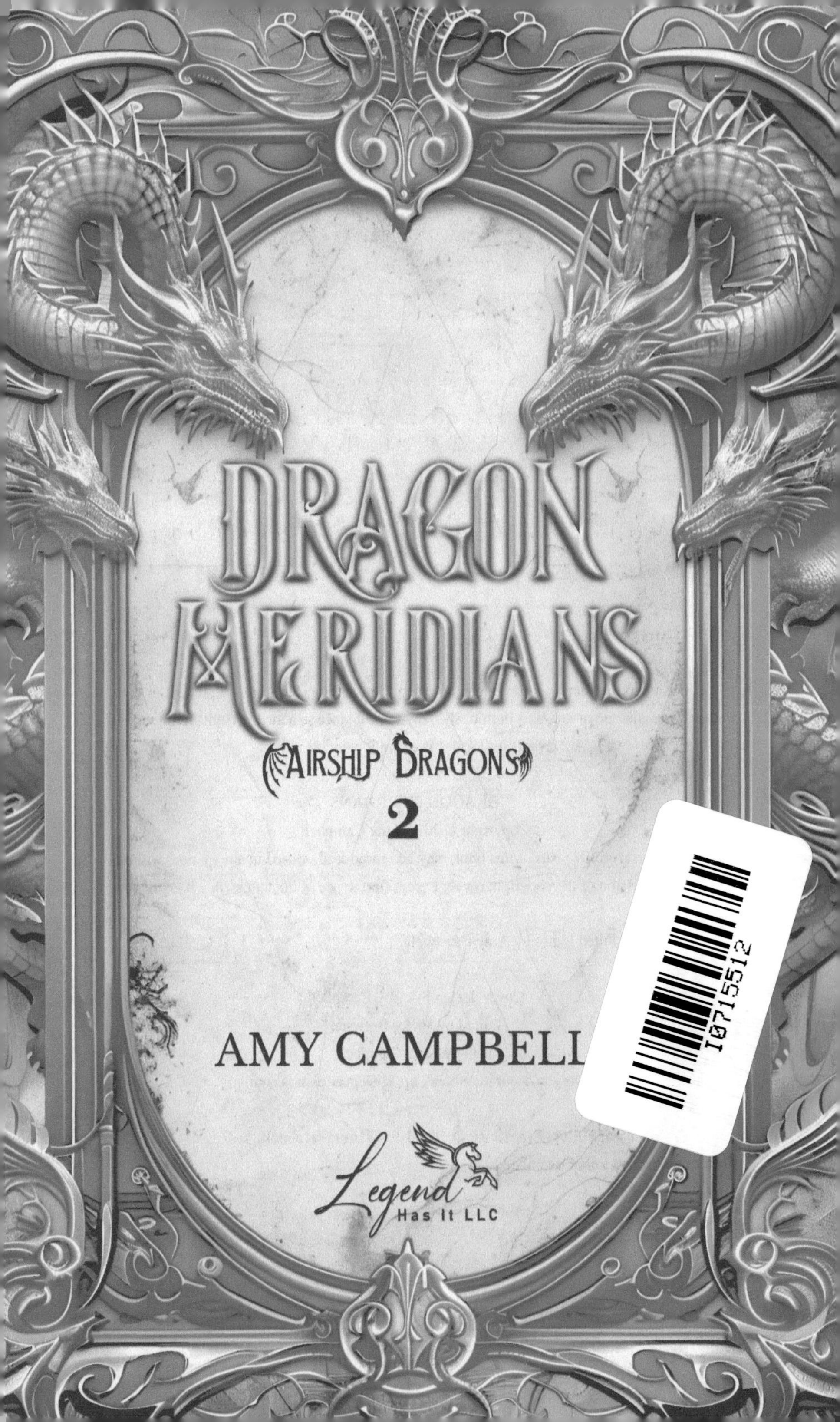

DRAGON MERIDIANS
AIRSHIP DRAGONS
2
AMY CAMPBELL
Legend
Has It LLC

DRAGON MERIDIANS

Published in the United States by Amy Campbell

Cover design by Amy Campbell
Edited by Vicky Brewster
Map by Amy Campbell
Dragon decorative break art © Depositphotos.com.

ISBN-13: 978-1-957816-06-7 (paperback), 978-1-957816-05-0 (ebook)
First paperback edition: December 2024
10 9 8 7 6 5 4 3 2 1
www.amycampbell.info

v101024

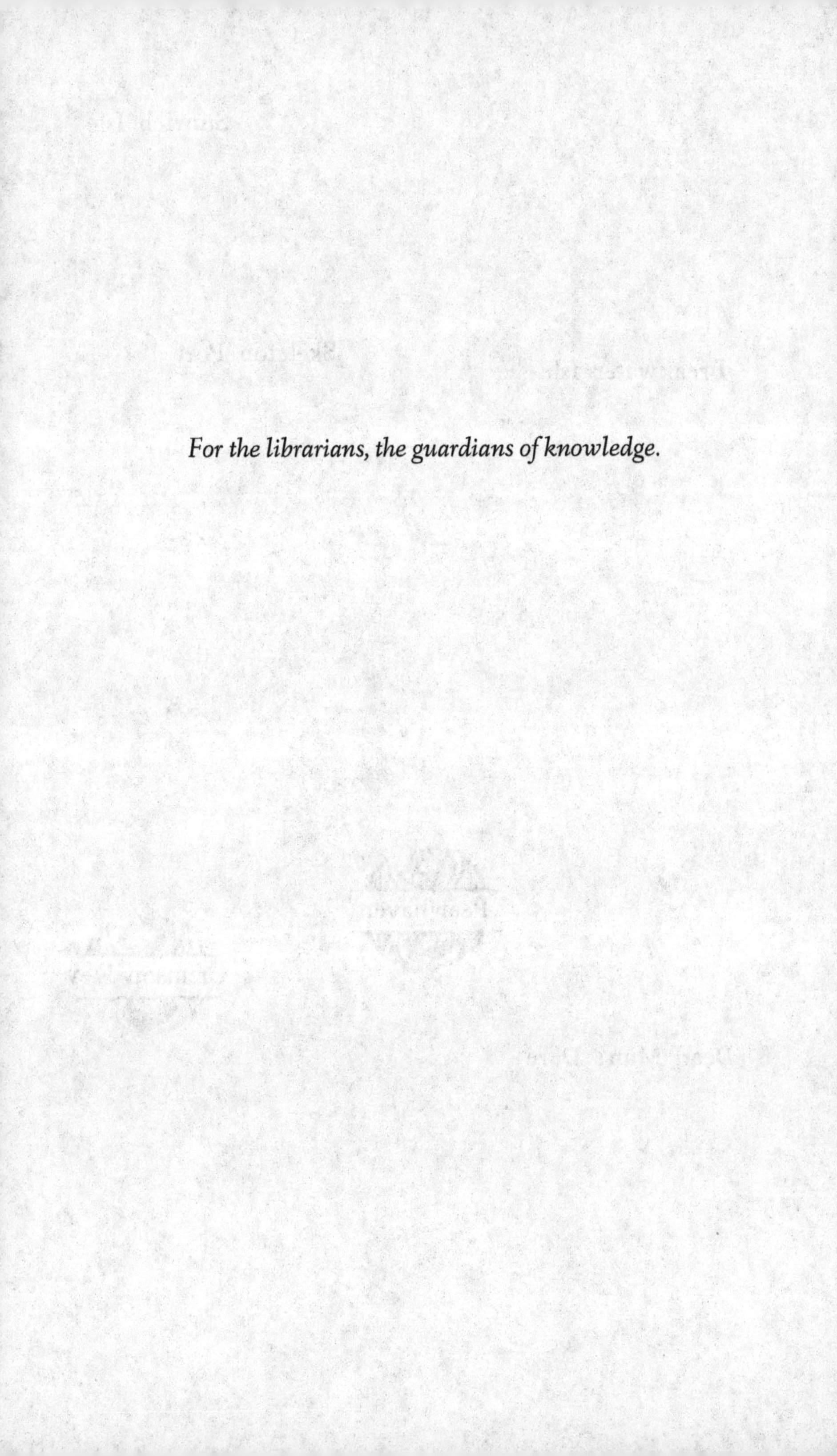

For the librarians, the guardians of knowledge.

Sunrich Isle
Skeleton Port
Breakwater Isle
Dead Man's Dare

Pearlhaven

Crimson Key

Ship's End

Rotgut Bay

Pronunciation Guide

Not sure how to say a name or other unusual word? This guide will help! But if you want to pronounce a word differently than shown below, that's fine. I'm not the boss of you!

Arvena - ar-ven-UH
Belen - Bell-IN
Cailan - KAY-lin
Canen - KAY-nun
Chandra - CHAN-druh
Danelor - DAYN-eh-lor
Elazar - el-uh-SAR
Freyak - FRAY-ak
Halafarin - hal-uh-FAIR-in
Iaxis - EYE-ax-iss
Ilyrana - il-ee-RAH-nuh
Macawi - Muh-caw-EE
Nesbitt - NEZ-bit
Rasmira - Raz-MEER-uh
Selene - suh-LEEN
Skirate - SKY-rit (rhymes with pirate)
Tiberia - Ty-BEER-ee-uh
Vizzy - VIZ-ee

THE PROPHECY

In the Dragon Latitudes far and wide,
A creature unknown and undefined,
Born of fire and shaped by fate,
Destined to tip the scales of hate.

The Dragon Who Isn't, a mystery untold,
A power that lies in stories of old,
Born to be hunted, born to be found,
Destined to change the world around.

With wings of copper and mettle untried,
This dragon's future won't be denied,
But danger and darkness lie in wait,
As the Dragon Who Isn't decides his fate.

1

KEEP AN OPEN MIND

Danelor

The sound of a dog barking echoed through the tunnels of Outcast Island. At first, Dane had almost mistaken it for a sea lion, but as it continued, he realized the error. This had a deeper sound, though it was no doubt reverberating throughout the tunnel system.

"What in the winds is a dog doing here?" Dane murmured.

The island was supposed to be uninhabited. It had been during his stay here in previous migration seasons. And though it had most recently been used to house the prisoners of the Jade Court, all of the survivors had been either relocated to

Jadefire Island or killed after the battle over the Dragon Who Isn't.

The echoing bark came again.

Dane frowned, gripping the hilt of his dagger as he cautiously made his way toward the source. Outcast Island was supposed to be a refuge, a place where he could live in comfort during migration season. The Empress had made sure to clear the island of any potential threats, leaving it empty.

Yet, here was a dog—a sign of life, of habitation. Dane rubbed his jaw as he considered the implications. If there were dogs, then there were likely people as well. And if people were here, it meant trouble.

Carefully, he crept forward, taking a shallow breath to stave off his ever-present pain. The tunnels were dim, the only illumination coming from the hurricane lantern he carried. Normally, Dane preferred the dim interior of the cave system to the too-bright exterior of the island. But now, he found himself wondering what awaited him in the shadows.

As he drew closer to the source of the barking, he heard the faint rumble of a voice. Cursing under his breath, Dane ducked behind a large rock, peering around it to get a better look.

Claws skittered against stone. A moment later, a fluffy white dog appeared, the canine striding forward as if on a mission. No one accompanied the creature. The dog's head roved from side to side, as if tracking a scent, before trotting purposefully over to Dane.

The dog was huge, and Dane took a step back. The beast's head nearly came up to his shoulder! The few dogs Dane had seen in his life were tiny by comparison. Then Dane realized this was no dog at all...it had wings.

"An aralez?" Dane murmured, brow furrowing as he stared at the creature.

The canine gave a soft woof, seemingly in confirmation.

Then the aralez turned, bounding a handful of strides before whirling to stare at Dane as if asking him to follow.

Dane hesitated, his hand tightening around the dagger's hilt, then started after the canine. His never-ending pain flared, a sharp lance of agony that made him wince. Dane gritted his teeth, forcing himself to take a step forward. If this creature meant him harm, he would have to be ready to defend himself. But something about the aralez's gaze seemed almost...pleading.

Dane took another step, then another, following the fluffy white creature down the dark tunnel. The pain in his leg grew worse with each stride, but Dane pushed onward, driven by curiosity.

The tunnel opened into a large cavern, and Dane's breath caught in his throat. There, resting on her side, was a massive, blue dragon. Her scales were dull and dark, caked with long-dried blood. Gooseflesh pebbled Dane's arms—this was one of the dragons the Jade Empress had slain, or so he had been told.

But as Dane watched, the dragon's pale eye slowly opened. She was alive, and very much aware of his presence.

Dane froze, knowing full well what angry, injured dragons were capable of. He eased back a step. The aralez, however, let out a soft, rumbling bark and trotted over to the dragon's side, pawing at one of her forelegs. The dragon's gaze shifted, focusing on the canine-like creature, and Dane could have sworn he saw a glimmer of...recognition?

Dane watched, scarcely daring to breathe, as the aralez settled down next to the dragon, its fluffy tail swishing back and forth. The dragon let out a low, rumbling sigh, and Dane's confusion increased. This was not the behavior of a ferocious predator, but rather that of a wounded, weary creature seeking comfort.

Tentatively, Dane took a step forward, his gaze never leaving the dragon's form. He had to know—how was this possible? How could a dragon that the Jade Empress had supposedly slain be alive and here, on Outcast Island?

The dragon's head lifted, her eyes suddenly seeming to clear. "You are not one of my tormenters." Her voice was a rasp, as if she hadn't used it in ages. Which wasn't far from the truth—two months had passed since the battle. She should have been long dead.

"No," Dane agreed, watching her intently. "They're gone. I live here alone." He saw no reason to explain his contentious relationship with the Jade Court. How his condition made it a struggle to accompany the Jade Court airships during migration season. "You're Chandra, the Seer. How are you here, alive?"

"No fate is so immovable that we cannot change it." Chandra flexed her talons, as if working out cramps from unused muscles. She glanced at the aralez. "And sometimes, salvation comes from those you least expect."

The canine? Dane had heard the mystic creatures were capable of healing, but *this*? He nearly shivered at the thought.

Dane watched, perplexed, as the aralez's ears suddenly flattened. The fluffy white creature's hackles raised, its wings flaring out. But the aggression wasn't directed at Dane—instead, the canine was focused on the dragon.

Chandra, for her part, seemed simply irritated by the aralez's behavior. "Vesper, quiet," she commanded in a low, stern tone.

The aralez, Vesper, immediately fell silent, though his body remained tense, alert. He glanced between Dane and Chandra, an almost uncertain expression in his intelligent eyes.

"Forgive him," Chandra said, her gaze shifting to Dane. "Vesper is...confused after my long convalescence. He is quite protective."

Dane nodded slowly, his mind whirling. He could understand the creature's protectiveness, even if its aggressive display had caught him off guard. But why had it been aimed at the Seer if they were companions?

"If you're not one of my tormentors, then what are you?" Chandra asked, her tone full of curiosity.

Dane forced himself to stand a little taller despite the ache in his leg. "I'm Danelor. I...I live here, on Outcast Island, while the Jade Court is away on migration."

Chandra's brow furrowed slightly. "Hiding, are you?" She sucked in a great breath, then exhaled softly. "Ah, *now* I see why you must hide."

Of course, it was easy for a dragon to discover what he lacked. Dane shook his head. "I'm not *hiding*. But during migration seasons, they travel on airships." He finished the explanation with a shrug, as if it didn't matter to him. Dane hoped the dragon didn't press for more. He didn't want to go into his sensitivity to light and sound. The Jade Court airships, so large and full of so many, were more than he could handle.

The Seer nodded, as if it all made sense to her. "There are dragons who would attack you for what you are."

"There are dragons who would kill me for what I'm not," Dane corrected. And while he was strong, his constant pain in human form would always be seen as a great weakness among dragons. But aside from his pain, he wasn't the only one in this situation. "But there are others like me—though everyone else has gone on migration." He hoped he didn't sound envious. Though his only attempt at migration had revealed he couldn't handle the massive airships, the idea of traveling still appealed to him.

"You are Jade Court," Chandra murmured. She paused, considering his words. "Then you must know of the prophecy regarding the Dragon Who Isn't that the Jade Empress seeks."

One couldn't be a part of the Jade Court and not know the

prophecy. The Jade Empress had become obsessed. "Yes, I know of it." He paused. "The Jade Empress has him."

At that news, the agitated aralez whimpered. Chandra studied Dane with a thoughtful expression, her pale eyes narrowing. "So, the Jade Empress has the Dragon Who Isn't," she murmured, a faint hint of surprise in her voice. Then Chandra's lips curled into a small smile. "Perhaps fate is on my side, after all." She flexed her claws, the motion almost casual.

Dane shifted his weight, wincing as a spike of pain shot through his leg. "What do you mean?"

Chandra's gaze shifted to him, and Dane was unnerved by the intensity of her stare. "I need to ensure the Dragon Who Isn't finds his way to the Forgotten Library," she said, her voice low. "Will you help me, Danelor?"

Dane cocked his head as he considered her words. The Forgotten Library—a place of legend, rumored to hold great and terrible knowledge. And the Dragon Who Isn't, the one the Jade Empress sought... Yes, Dane was Jade Court, but because of his condition he'd never been considered someone who might actively *help* the Court.

But could that change? What if he could prove to everyone that his imperfect form didn't matter?

"Help you how?" Dane asked, his tone guarded. "What exactly are you asking of me?"

Chandra studied him for a long moment, her pale eyes seeming to pierce into his very soul. "I sense you are a man with much pain, Danelor," she said softly. "Pain that limits you, that keeps you hidden away on this island."

"I'm not a man," Dane corrected. He buried his annoyance that she correctly perceived his weakness.

The dragon chuckled. "Fair enough—I sense that's true as well. But I'll keep it simple: I can help you. If you will aid me in ensuring the Dragon Who Isn't reaches the Forgotten Library, I will see to it that you are freed from your pain."

Dane blinked, caught off guard by her offer. Freed from his pain? The chronic agony that had plagued him for years, the ache that made even the simplest of tasks a trial?

"You can do that?" he asked, unable to keep the note of desperate hope from his voice.

Chandra inclined her head. "I can. And so much more, Danelor. All I ask is that you help me in this one task."

Dane shivered in anticipation. To be free of the pain that had haunted him for so long...it was a temptation he could scarcely resist. And if this task of hers truly could ensure the Dragon Who Isn't reached the Forgotten Library, then perhaps it was a worthy endeavor.

Dane took a deep breath, his gaze meeting Chandra's. "Yes," he said, a rush of hope filling him. "I'll help you."

Josephine

Jo's boots clicked against the polished marble floor as she and Gretchen strode into the lavish villa's reception area. She didn't want to be here—would much rather be on her airship, where she felt at home. But this visit was a necessary evil.

A burly man in a crisp suit stepped forward, hand raised to halt their progress. "This is as far as you go."

Jo squared her shoulders. "I'm Captain Josephine Prescott. Mr. Gibson requested this meeting."

The bruiser gave a curt nod. "I know. But I was referring to her." He jabbed a finger at Gretchen.

Gretchen bristled. "No way in the Abyss are you separating us. Where Jo goes, I go."

"Those are the rules," the man said, unmoved. "Mr. Gibson will see the Captain alone."

Anger flashed across Gretchen's face, and she opened her mouth, no doubt to unleash a blistering retort. Jo shot her a quelling look before she could speak.

"It's fine, Gretch. I won't be long." Jo's tone softened. "Wait for me here."

Gretchen held her gaze for a beat, then exhaled heavily. "You know I hate this cloak-and-dagger shit." Her eyes bored into the bruiser. "Just know if anything happens to her, you'll be spitting teeth for a month."

The man's expression didn't flicker, but there was a glint of amusement in his eyes. As if he doubted Gretchen's words. Clearly, he didn't know she was a Healer—and a Healer could do as much harm as help.

Grudgingly, Gretchen sank onto one of the plush couches, arms folded across her chest. Jo offered her a reassuring smile before turning to follow the bruiser into Gibson's inner sanctum.

"Captain Prescott." Across the room, Reginald Gibson rose from one of the armchairs, a welcoming smile on his face. He gestured to the empty seat across from him. "Please, have a seat."

Jo considered refusing the invitation, but knew that would only serve to antagonize the man. And he was not a person she dared anger. Gathering her courage, she crossed the room and lowered herself into the opulent chair, the fabric practically enveloping her.

"I trust you received my letter about the *Tempest*'s necessary repairs," she said, getting straight to the point.

Gibson studied her from head to toe. He took a sip of his

beverage before setting it down once more. "I did, along with the information regarding your request for a...change of vocation." He spoke the words with distaste. "I won't be covering the repairs. You can understand why, as the damage wasn't sustained during a dragon hunt."

Outrage rose in Jo's throat like bile. She swallowed it back. In her original missive, she hadn't dared explain anything about the Jade Court or talking dragons. She would have either been seen as a lunatic, a drunkard, or a liar. And none of those helped her plight in the slightest.

"But—"

Gibson waved a hand, batting away her protests. "You've reviewed your copy of our contract, I'm sure. I had my solicitor peruse it again." He smiled, a sly sickle of an expression. "I agreed to cover repairs for normal wear and tear and for damage sustained while on a hunt."

"We were shot full of holes by another airship!" Jo seethed.

The financier shrugged. "Understood, but again—not part of our contract. My hands are tied. I'm so sorry."

He wasn't, and it was infuriating. Jo huffed out a breath. "But without those funds, there's no way I can pay the current lease. I sank all I had into the repairs."

Gibson steepled his fingers, thoughtful. "That will be quite the problem, won't it?" He nodded. "You should reconsider the other portion of your letter. Hunting dragons...now, that's a task that gets coin flowing! And a task, may I remind you, the *Tempest* is well-suited for."

The idea of hunting dragons once more made a ripple of nausea course through her. Every time Jo considered it, her mind conjured the memory of Elazar on the deck, a harpoon piercing his shoulder as he shifted from dragon to man. All the blood on the *Tempest*'s deck...his blood. She had almost killed her nephew, the very person she had sworn to protect.

"No," she said firmly. "I won't be hunting dragons again. Not now, not ever."

Gibson regarded her, eyebrows raised. "Is that so?" He leaned back in his chair, head cocked. "May I ask why the change of heart, Captain? The *Tempest* was built for this very purpose."

Jo's fingers curled into fists at her sides. "I have my reasons, and they're my own." She refused to divulge the truth about Elazar. That knowledge was too dangerous to share, especially with a man as powerful as Gibson.

The financier studied her for a long, tense moment. "I see." He shrugged, a dismissive gesture. "Well, if you're unwilling to return to your original charter, then you're going to have a problem."

Jo's breath caught. The *Tempest* was her life, her home. The thought of being separated from her ship and her crew filled her with a sense of panic. "What are you saying?" she asked, unable to keep the edge from her voice.

Gibson leaned forward, his gaze unreadable. "Simply that if you're no longer willing to do the job you were contracted for, then I may have to reconsider our arrangement. The *Tempest* is, after all, my property."

Panic coursed through Jo. Without the *Tempest*, how would she ever find Elazar and rescue him from the Jade Empress? The ship was her only means of finding him.

"You can't do that," she said, hoping she didn't sound too desperate. "The *Tempest* is my crew's livelihood. Our home. We have nowhere else to go."

Gibson shrugged again, the motion infuriatingly casual. "Then perhaps it's time to consider your options, Captain Prescott. I'm a reasonable man, but I do have certain expectations."

Jo opened her mouth to argue, to plead, but the words

caught in her throat. She couldn't risk alienating Gibson, not when the fate of the *Tempest* and, by extension, Elazar hung in the balance.

Swallowing her pride, Jo forced herself to nod. "I...I understand. What do you suggest?"

Gibson grinned. "I have an option that you might find almost as thrilling as hunting dragons. Have you ever considered smuggling?"

Jo's heart sank as Gibson's words registered. The *Tempest*, a smuggling ship? It wasn't what her crew had signed on for. She had hoped to become a merchant vessel, something that she might be able to talk the crew into. It lacked the adventure and high revenue of dragon hunting, but it was honorable.

But the financier's veiled threat hung in the air, a silent warning that her refusal could cost her the *Tempest* and her crew's livelihoods. "Smuggling?" she repeated faintly.

Gibson's lips curled into a self-satisfied smile. "I think you'll find that smuggling can be quite lucrative, Captain. Certainly more so than your current arrangement."

Oh, Jo knew that first-hand. But it didn't mean it was a life she wished to return to. Jo's jaw tightened. "And what exactly would I be smuggling?"

"A little of this, a little of that." Gibson shrugged, dismissive. "The details can be worked out later."

Leaving the details for later was a dangerous prospect with someone like Gibson, but Jo saw that at the moment, she had little say in the matter. "And what about the repairs? You said you wouldn't cover them."

Gibson smiled. "Ah, yes. The repairs." He paused, as if considering his words carefully. "Well, if you agree to my...*alternative* proposal, I could be persuaded to lend a hand. Provided, of course, that our arrangement proves mutually beneficial."

"I'll need to discuss this with my crew," Jo said, her voice carefully neutral.

Gibson's smile widened. "Of course, of course. Take all the time you need. But do bear in mind that my offer won't remain on the table indefinitely."

Jo nodded stiffly, her mind racing. She couldn't bear the thought of turning the *Tempest* into a smuggling vessel, but if it was the only way to keep her ship and her crew afloat, she would have to swallow her pride.

As she rose from the chair, Gibson spoke again. "Oh, and Captain? Do try to keep an open mind. You may find that smuggling has its own...rewards."

Jo's stomach twisted, but she forced herself to nod. "I'll keep that in mind."

With a final nod, Jo turned and made her way back to the reception area, where Gretchen waited anxiously. The moment their eyes met, Gretchen's expression hardened, and Jo knew she would have some difficult conversations ahead.

Cailan

CAILAN STOOD ON THE *TEMPEST*'S DECK, MAX AT HIS SIDE. The rest of the crew—those who remained after the time the ship had been in port under repairs—stood in a line, eyes on Captain Prescott as she strode across the freshly swabbed deck.

The *Tempest*'s repairs had taken far longer than they'd hoped. Once the airship had limped to the nearest port, it became clear that bringing her back to optimal condition would take time. Precious time that it didn't feel like they had. Captain Jo's funds had dried up, going toward the ship's restoration. With an uncertain future and without the prospect of steady pay, several of the crew had already abandoned their posts.

Once the *Tempest* had been repaired, they'd set course for a port called Kingsden—Cailan wasn't familiar with it, though others in the crew seemed to know of it. According to Isaac the Navigator, their captain had a meeting with some bigwig.

Beneath Cailan's feet, the airship vibrated. Anyone else would think it just a normal aspect of the vessel. But Cailan knew differently. Somehow, in some impossible way, the airship was...alive. Sort of. Aware. Sapient. Cailan felt it every time he touched any part of the vessel with his bare skin.

The *Tempest* was as eager to leave port as her remaining crew. Now, they just needed to know the plan.

"I appreciate you all being timely," Captain Jo began, consulting her pocket watch. She snapped the lid closed, her gaze falling over her crew. Cailan noted the disappointed crinkle in the corners of her eyes, no doubt pained by the number of deserters. "I know everyone is eager to get back in the sky, and I promise we'll do so soon. But first, we much broach the topic of the *Tempest*'s new calling."

At that, everyone stilled, curiosity getting the better of them. This had been a point of discussion-slash-gossip for the last few weeks. Some suspected the *Tempest* would be relegated to a merchant cargo vessel. Others thought she should return to her calling as a dragoneering ship. But those crew members, Cailan knew, were delusional. Captain Jo wouldn't hunt another dragon, not after Elazar.

"So, what is it?" Ilyrana, the airship's blacksmith, asked.

Josephine wet her lips, her expression tightening. Cailan suspected that whatever she was about to say, many would dislike. "While on the surface, the *Tempest* will appear to be a simple cargo airship, we're going to specialize in smuggling."

Beside him, Max released a soft gasp of surprise. Cailan grinned. "This is close enough to my idea," he murmured to the Sky Warden.

"Not at all the same as piracy," Max shot back. But he knew by the tension in her shoulders that Max wasn't comfortable with the idea.

Cailan watched the crew's reactions closely, gauging their responses. As he'd expected, Ilyrana was the first to speak up, her lips pursed with distaste.

"Smuggling?" the Elven blacksmith scoffed, crossing her arms over her chest. "That's hardly the kind of work befitting the *Tempest* and her crew. We're an airship crew, not common criminals."

Claire, the cook, nodded in agreement. "I have to agree with Ilyrana. Smuggling is a dangerous game, one that's more likely to get us all killed than line our pockets." She cast a pointed look at the captain. "We're not trained for that kind of work."

It was Justice, the hulking Knossan Dragoneer, who voiced the concern Cailan knew they were all thinking. He stepped forward, his deep voice rumbling. "Captain, with respect, this doesn't feel right." Justice's dark gaze swept over the gathered crew, his long horns arcing with the movement. "We're meant to hunt and fight dragons, not engage in unlawful activities. Smuggling, no matter how you dress it up, is still a crime."

Josephine held up a hand, silencing the murmurs of agreement. "I understand your reservations," she said, her gaze steady. "Believe me, this isn't a decision I've made lightly. But the fact is, the *Tempest* can no longer function as a Dragoneering vessel. Not after what happened." Her voice nearly cracked at the end, the only loss of resolve she'd displayed so far.

More murmurs arose from the assembled crew.

"We need funds to keep the *Tempest* airborne, to continue our search." Josephine's voice took on a steely edge. "Smuggling, while not ideal, is the surest way to recoup our losses and keep this ship and crew afloat." She lifted her chin. "And I respect that some of you disagree with this plan. You are welcome to disembark and find work elsewhere."

There was a moment of absolute quiet, only punctuated by the calls of seagulls and the rustling of canvas balloon-sails. Then, one by one, crew members stepped out of line. First was Claire and her son, Oscar. She approached the captain and ducked her head in apology.

"I'm sorry, Cap." Claire's voice was regretful. "I've lasted as long as I could, but..." She shook her head.

"Say no more," Captain Josephine said, her tone neutral.

They were only the first of many. Cailan scowled, his irritation growing as one after the other, crew made their excuses and departed. Halafarin followed Claire, then Justice, Ilyrana, and Jolly. When all was said and done, only six remained: the captain herself, Gretchen, Cailan, Maxine, Isaac, and Galatea.

"Well, this will be a challenge," Captain Jo murmured, her stance relaxing. Defeat was evident in the way her shoulders drooped.

"Yeah, well, we're not used to things being easy." Cailan shrugged. "So, how do we do this?" He eyed their group. "Do we call dibs on what we want to do?"

A wry smile graced the captain's lips. "I don't think so, Airship Dragon." She exhaled softly, studying them. "I've already given some thought to the needs of the *Tempest* in the event we have slim pickings for the crew."

Inwardly, Cailan growled. She had suspected so many would leave? It had been a surprise to him.

Josephine studied them. "I'll take over from Halafarin, serving as both captain and pilot." She nodded to Isaac. "You'll remain Navigator, of course. Though now you'll also have command of the ship in my absence, as well as piloting."

Isaac gave a curt nod. Cailan had been surprised he'd stayed, after his earlier outburst. "Aye, just like old times."

Captain Jo flashed a brief smile, then turned to the rest of them. "Galatea, you'll continue with your work as engineer."

The Theilian's ears perked up at this, her posture rigid. Before the mutiny, she had simply been a deckhand. Galatea had taken it upon herself to learn more about the *Tempest's* engine room, but even Cailan knew that for her this was officially quite the promotion. "It will be my honor, Captain!"

A relieved smile touched the captain's face as she turned to Gretchen. "Since we won't need as much of your medical expertise, I hope, I'll need you to serve as bosun."

A tight-lipped smile crossed the Healer's face. "Like old times, indeed."

Before Cailan could wonder what Gretchen and Isaac meant by that, Josephine's focus was on him. "And for you, my Airship Dragon—I think you'll serve well as the marshal."

Cailan blinked, taking a moment to comprehend what she was saying. The marshal handled all of the ship's defenses— which might become even more necessary if they ran into any problems on a smuggling run. He wanted to question her assignment, but with a start, he realized he had come full circle. Cailan had served as a sentinel for Chandra. This was a task he had trained for.

"Sure, if you want a dragon in charge of something like that," he agreed with a lazy shrug. Wouldn't do to seem too satisfied by the position.

"I do," Josephine said, a glint in her eyes hinting that she saw right through him.

"And Maxine. Of course, you'll still serve as Sky Warden.

But now I'll also need you to serve as lookout and relay any important navigational information to Isaac," Captain Jo said.

Maxine nodded, her ebony curls waving with the movement. "I can do that."

Relief lit Josephine's eyes, which Cailan counted as a win. Hopefully she didn't think their outlook was as bleak now. Josephine took a step back. "You all have your new assignments. I'll give you the rest of the day to prepare, and tomorrow we'll head out on our first run."

2

DRAGON WINGS

Elazar

Sweat dripped into Elazar's eyes. He paused for a moment to wipe it away with the back of one grease-streaked hand, then heaved a long sigh

The metal skeleton for yet another set of mechanical wings stretched on the floor of the workshop before him. The frame had grown too long for the table he began his work on, and now he had to clamber around the wing as he set to work attaching the thin metal plates that served as the membrane.

The workshop was cramped, with little room to move around the growing wing. Tools and half-finished sections intended for the wing cluttered the workbench. Bits of metal and piles of gears covered every available surface. The air was thick with the scent of hot metal and machine oil.

This space, once a storage hold, was now Elazar's prison-slash-workshop. He supposed it could have been worse—they could have put him in an actual prison. Elazar knew from murmurs among the crew that this was the fate some of the Jade Empress' enemies faced.

Elazar sighed and bent back to his work, running a calloused hand over the delicate wing frame. As much as he loved this sort of work, it was hard to garner his usual enthusiasm in his current situation. But it was necessary—and he had to admit, it stroked his ego a bit when a formerly flightless dragon rejoiced that they could reclaim the sky.

The Jade Court had the sky, and all Elazar had was this workshop. He was the Dragon Who Isn't, a human—or dragon. *Drake?* He wasn't entirely sure anymore—with the ability to shapeshift. To them, he was an outsider. A curiosity at best and a threat at worst.

Running a hand over the plate of smooth metal he was preparing to attach to the strut, Elazar's mind wandered to his true home. The *Tempest*. His family and friends. By the winds, he missed Aunt Jo and Max. He shook his head, trying and failing to banish his errant thoughts.

He had entered this bargain with Belen for their sakes, though. To shield them from the wrath of the Jade Empress. But sometimes, like right now, Elazar couldn't help his own selfishness, wishing desperately that he'd never entered the bargain. That he'd stayed on the *Tempest* during that fateful moment when Aunt Jo and Max had begged him.

Elazar's thoughts kept drifting back to Max, try as he might to focus on the delicate work before him. He could still envision her in his mind's eye, the fury of the storm whipping around her. The gale carving her into something ethereal and fierce.

Elazar paused, setting down the tool in his hand as a realization dawned on him. The deep ache he felt whenever he thought of the *Tempest*, of his aunt and his friends—it was so much more than just missing them. His heart clenched at the thought of never seeing Max's smile again, of never hearing her laughter or feeling the playful shove of her shoulder against his.

He had always thought of her as a close friend, someone he could rely on and trust with his life. But now, with the distance between them, Elazar couldn't help but wonder if his feelings ran deeper than that. Could it be that he...loved her? Not in the way he loved his aunt, but in a way that went beyond the bounds of their friendship?

The idea was disconcerting. Elazar had never considered the possibility before. How could he, when he knew that was something Max herself didn't want? But now, with the threat of never seeing her again, the truth became painfully clear.

He *loved* her.

Elazar's hands trembled as he resumed his work, the metal plates clanging softly together. How could he have been so unaware? But maybe time away had made all the difference. What would he do if he ever saw her again?

The stark reality, though, was that he might *never* see her. He was a prisoner of the Jade Court. He swallowed hard, his throat tight with emotion. The Jade Empress had taken so much from him already—his freedom, his home, his sense of belonging. This was one more loss that he might never reclaim.

A screech tore his attention from his work and musings as the workshop door scraped open. He'd thought about oiling the hinges, but he preferred the advanced warning the door gave him.

A young woman with dark hair appeared in the doorway.

Tiberia, his keeper. So far, she hadn't been unkind to him, but Elazar didn't trust her. He didn't trust *anyone* belonging to the Jade Court.

"Good afternoon, Elazar. The Jade Empress requests to see you on deck." Tiberia smiled.

Elazar froze at her words, torn by mixed emotions. The deck. It meant he would see the sky again and breathe fresh air. Feel the breeze on his skin. But Belen...the prospect of being in the volatile Empress's presence was unnerving. Elazar feared displeasing her.

But this wasn't an invitation he could decline. He rose, picking up a rag to wipe the worst of the grease from his hands. "Do you know why?"

Tiberia shook her head, the motion causing her dark hair to sway. In the right light, Elazar had noticed it had a bluish sheen. "No, that's not something I'm privy to."

Elazar nodded. He paused long enough to check his reflection in a shiny piece of brass. He grimaced, grabbing a cloth to wipe another smear of grease from his face. Elazar used his fingers to comb his too-long hair back, then rubbed at the stubble peppering his face. He'd never had facial hair until recently, and unlike the hair on his scalp, it grew at a snail's pace. Nothing to be done for it at the moment.

As he followed Tiberia out of the cramped workshop, Elazar couldn't help but glance around, for a moment feeling as if he belonged on this airship. As if it was the home he missed.

But it wasn't. Elazar's gut clenched as he stepped out onto the deck. The familiar sights and sounds of the airship stirred conflicting emotions within him. The *Talisman* was a far cry from the *Tempest*, his true home. Gone were the comforting creaks of the wooden hull, the laughter and chatter of his crewmates. Instead, the air was thick with the metallic scent of the ship's engines and the occasional rumble of a dragon's voice.

Belen stood in the middle of the deck, the late afternoon sunlight glinting on her emerald scales. She was a beautiful and terrifying sight as far as dragons went, both regal and a threat to his life. But like the rest of her Court, her wings had withered away to nubs. Now a pair of steel wings sprang from her sides, crafted by Elazar.

And she wasn't alone. Five others stood nearby: three humans, a Knossan, and a Vangara. They stood tall, as if waiting for orders from the Empress. Elazar vaguely recognized them—the Knossan and one of the humans were part of the *Talisman* crew. The rest he didn't know, but suspected they heralded from other Jade Court airships.

Curious gazes fell on Elazar as he approached with Tiberia. Belen watched him, too, her emerald eyes fixed on his every move. The imposing dragon's gaze was downright predatory, but he forced himself to meet it with a neutral expression.

"Good afternoon, Empress," he said, inclining his head in a gesture of respect. Elazar knew he only drew breath because Belen needed him.

Belen's expression was unreadable. "I have a task for you."

He stood straighter, masking his apprehension. "What do you require of me?"

"I want you to train others in the art of creating mechanical wings for my Court," the Jade Empress stated, the words a command.

Dismay twisted in Elazar's chest. Training others meant sharing knowledge that made him invaluable. He feared it could lead to his own expendability. Worse yet, it risked revealing his Gearweaver magic—a secret that had remained hidden from Belen and her Court thus far.

"Train others?" he echoed, trying to buy time to collect his thoughts. "It's...intricate work."

"Do you doubt your ability to teach?" Belen's tone held an edge of challenge.

"No," he replied quickly, forcing calm into his voice. "I don't doubt my ability to teach. But these wings are complex. It will take time."

Belen's eyes gleamed with something that might have been satisfaction or amusement—Elazar couldn't tell. "Time is something you don't have, which is why you will train others to complete this work," she said.

Elazar blinked. "What?"

The Jade Empress huffed out a frustrated breath. "Crafting wings for my court was not your only promise, drake. Or have you forgotten?" Before Elazar could respond, Belen continued, "Begin with these individuals." She gestured with her claws toward the five standing nearby.

Elazar glanced at them again, trying to gauge their readiness for such an undertaking. His mind raced with the potential pitfalls—both practical and magical—of this new task. Regardless of his feelings, there was no easy way out of this.

"I understand," he said finally, bowing his head again.

"Good." Belen turned away, clearly dismissing him. "Begin immediately."

As Tiberia led Elazar and the new trainees back toward the workshop, Elazar's thoughts churned. He needed to find a way to train without revealing too much about his Gearweaving abilities. It would be a delicate balance—one that could determine not only his future but possibly the fate of those he held dear back on the *Tempest*.

For now, all he could do was focus on the immediate task at hand and hope for an opportunity to turn things in his favor.

3

BLOOD IS POWER

Josephine

"I didn't expect so many of them to abandon us." Josephine collapsed into the chair in the cabin she shared with Gretchen, head lolling back in exasperation.

"You have to remember, they didn't sign on for this," Gretchen said. She moved to sit on the bed opposite her partner. "And while they've weathered much..." The Healer shrugged. "Everyone has a personal line they won't cross."

"I knew the Elves would leave. And Justice," Josephine murmured. She lifted her head and sighed. The moral codes of Elves and Knossans were at odds with smuggling. "But the rest of them... I don't know how we're going to pull this off, Gretch. We barely have enough crew to get out of port for a ship this size."

"We've made it through tough times against the odds before," Gretchen said gently. "I know this isn't the path we wanted, but smuggling may yet lead us to new information. There could be leads on Elazar or the Forgotten Library among the cargo manifests and crew chatter at the ports we visit."

Josephine shook her head. "It's not just that. With the cost of the *Tempest*'s repairs after that last attack, I've fallen behind on my monthly payments. Even with Gibson helping to cover some of the repair cost." She grimaced, the name of the financier leaving a bitter taste in her mouth.

Gretchen's face darkened at the mention of Gibson. "How much do you owe the winds-cursed snake? Abyss take him! Now I know why I wasn't allowed in that meeting."

"Almost fifteen thousand regals," Josephine admitted. And yes, upon reflection, she was glad Gretchen hadn't been in the meeting. It was embarrassing enough to bring it to light now.

Gretchen whistled. "That's not an insignificant sum."

"No, it's not," Josephine agreed grimly. "Smuggling is our only chance of making that kind of money quickly. I just hope we can pull it off with our current crew."

She rose and began to pace, her boots clicking sharply on the wooden floor. Gretchen watched her, worrying at her lower lip. "We'll find a way. We always do."

Josephine paused in her pacing, meeting Gretchen's steady gaze. Some of the tension eased from her shoulders at the Healer's calm confidence. "You're right," she conceded. "One way or another, we'll make this work. We have to."

Gretchen patted the empty spot beside her on the bed, an invitation. "Come, sit with me."

Josephine crossed the cabin and lowered herself onto the

mattress. The springs creaked softly under her weight. The familiar scent of Gretchen's herbal remedies filled the air, calming Josephine's frayed nerves.

"So, what's our first smuggling run?" Gretchen asked, her voice full of curiosity. "Any of our old haunts?"

Josephine drummed her fingers on her thigh. "Gibson has a contact in Brinwald who needs a shipment of Spectralite crystals. Apparently, they're in high demand there."

"Brinwald?" Gretchen's brows flew up. "That's in the southern continent. Last I heard, they were in a no-holds-barred civil war."

"And that's why we're going," Jo said with a sigh. "Our decoy cargo will be standard medical supplies." She grimaced. "But yes, the Brinwaldian government has increased patrols to stem the flow of supplies to the rebels."

"And I suppose we're backing the rebels?" Gretchen quirked a brow.

"More money for getting the supplies to them," Jo confirmed. Her jaw tightened, a muscle working beneath the sharp line of her cheekbone. "But we need the money, and fast."

Gretchen's expression darkened at the reminder. She reached out and covered Josephine's restless hand with her own, stilling the nervous tapping. "We'll be careful. I'll make sure the crew is prepared for any trouble we might encounter."

Josephine nodded, some of the tension easing from her frame. "I know. I just..." She sighed heavily. "I hate putting them in danger like this. They deserve better than to be caught up in my debts."

"They're your crew, Jo. Your family." Gretchen's thumb traced soothing circles on the back of Josephine's hand. "They know the risks, and they're willing to take them. Because they trust you to lead them through it."

Josephine's lips quirked in a faint smile. "When did you get to be so wise, Gretch?"

"Oh, I've always been wise." Gretchen's eyes twinkled with amusement. "You're just finally starting to listen to me."

Cailan

THE RED MECHANICAL PARROT, SPROCKET, RESTED ON HER side atop the sturdy oak desk in Elazar's cabin. Well, it was Cailan's cabin at the moment. He'd claimed it when it was clear Elazar wouldn't return anytime soon.

He watched intently as Max, wearing protective goggles, worked on the intricate avian automaton. Her fingers moved with practiced ease, deftly handling the delicate gears and springs. Cailan stood by, prepared to hand her requested tools or parts from the jumbled assortment that lay scattered on the worn floorboards.

Around them, the cabin was bathed in the warm glow of mage-lights, their ethereal luminance casting dancing shadows across the walls and chasing away the deepening twilight that pressed against the small round windows.

Restoring Sprocket to her former operational glory had become a shared project for Cailan and Max during the *Tempest*'s repairs. Together, they'd made good progress in putting the cogwing back together again, and their work was nearly done.

The parrot had been a casualty of the battle with Belen's crew. Max's determination to revive the automaton was fierce, as if she thought that in doing so, she might restore Elazar to them, too.

And Cailan? He found himself surprisingly invested in the project, not just for the challenge it presented, but because it granted him more reasons to remain in Max's presence.

Not for romantic reasons, though. Gretchen, the ship's Healer, had suggested it, but Cailan and Max had both scoffed at the idea. Max had her own reasons, ones Cailan had become privy to and respected. And Cailan? The only thing Cailan currently felt attracted to was the possibility of extracting revenge on Belen.

But he did like the idea of having a friend. The only other time he'd felt so accepted in his life had been at the Vault of Fate, under Chandra's wing. But only Chandra had truly cared for him there. The other young dragons had despised him because they knew he was different. That didn't stop him from missing Chandra, from missing his life at the Vault of Fate, though.

But beyond the railings of the *Tempest*, his world was dead. Chandra was gone. The Vault of Fate, once a sanctuary, now stood as a mausoleum of murdered dragons and memories, echoing with the whispers of ghosts he wasn't ready to face.

The *Tempest*, with its motley crew, had offered him an unexpected refuge, a place where he could belong without the shadows of his past clinging to him.

Of course, that refuge was now facing its own uncertain future. With the *Tempest* embarking on a dangerous smuggling run to Brinwald, Cailan couldn't help but wonder if this newfound sense of belonging was in jeopardy. He knew Max was not thrilled with their new calling, even if it was necessary to keep the ship afloat.

"Hand me the arcane capacitor, will you?" Max's voice pulled him back to the present.

He blinked at the request. While Cailan had spent countless hours working on the *Tempest* and helped out in the arcane engine room when needed, he still didn't know what half of the parts were called, much less what they looked like. It was part of why his appointment as the marshal had been appealing. "Uh..." He hesitated, his gaze drifting uncertainly over the scattered array of metallic components.

Max gestured to the jumble of parts spread out before them. "It's to the left of the gyro stabilizer."

That particular part, the gyro stabilizer, Cailan could pick out from the rest, if only because of its unusual bulbous shape. He plucked the arcane capacitor from the array and handed it to Max. She accepted it with murmured thanks.

She carefully integrated other parts into the complex innards of the mechanical parrot. After a few more skillful adjustments, Max leaned back, scanning her work critically before nodding in satisfaction.

"I think we're done. Moment of truth." With a look of apprehension on her face, Max reached out and flipped the small switch beneath the bird's tail feathers to activate Sprocket. After a moment that stretched like an eternity, the parrot whirred to life. The sound of gears and cogs meshing filled the room, the chorus of a mechanical resurrection.

Sprocket's metal feathers, each painted vibrant colors to resemble a live parrot, rustled with a whispering shimmer. Her head turned from side to side, the movements mechanical and precise, though they lacked the lively motions she once possessed. The parrot's actions, though technically correct, felt devoid of the spontaneous energy that had once defined her.

A shadow of disappointment crossed Max's face, her eyes dimming. She reached out, tenderly tracing the contours of Sprocket's bronze beak, her touch gentle.

Well, damn. Cailan's expression darkened into a scowl as Sprocket stood motionless, her metallic form poised as if awaiting instructions. So very unlike the troublemaker that had nearly shorn Cailan's scalp during their first meeting.

"I really thought we could bring her back." Max's voice, tinged with defeat, cut through his thoughts. "I mean, all the way. Technically, Sprocket works now," she added, her words trailing off as she considered the parrot with professional pride and personal disappointment.

"Yeah," Cailan echoed her sentiment, his gaze lingering thoughtfully on the automaton. Despite the successful repair, Sprocket's essence—the spark that had given her a personality—seemed to have been lost in the process. But he had an idea of his own, one that had been ruminating in the back of his mind over the last few weeks.

Cailan drew a small knife from his belt. With a practiced movement, he pricked his finger. A bead of blood welled up to the surface. He held his finger over Sprocket, allowing a few precious drops of his dragon-imbued blood to fall onto the mechanical parrot's metallic feathers.

Max recoiled, her eyes widening in shock. "Cailan! What are you doing?"

"Just give it a second," Cailan murmured. He felt Max's annoyance warm on his skin. Cailan pulled out a handkerchief from a pocket, determined not to look like the feral creature he was in front of his friend.

Then, after a moment that seemed to stretch into eternity, the mechanical parrot quivered. A subtle, almost imperceptible tremor ran through her frame. Suddenly, as if sparked by some unseen force, Sprocket burst into a flurry of activity.

The parrot hopped energetically across the worktable, her movements imbued with new life. She began picking up nuts, bolts, and other small objects with her beak, tossing them around as if they were playthings. Sprocket's head tilted inquisitively, her eyes alight with a curious, almost sentient gleam. The cogwing turned towards Cailan and Max.

"Sprocket?" Max's word was a fervent whisper.

Then, in an unexpected display, Sprocket snatched up a discarded pencil and, with a burst of speed, took off into the air. She circled the room in graceful, swooping arcs, the pencil clutched in her beak like a proud trophy. The cogwing landed on the hammock and chortled merrily.

"By the storms," Max breathed, pressing a hand to her chest as she watched Sprocket play. Then she whirled to Cailan. "How did you do that?"

Cailan shifted uncomfortably under her intense gaze. "It's going to sound weird," he began slowly, "but ever since the battle with Belen a few months ago, I've felt like the *Tempest* has been...different." He hesitated before adding, "More alive."

Max's expression morphed into one of confusion, her brow furrowing as she tried to grasp his meaning. "What do you mean? It's an airship, not a living thing. And we were talking about *Sprocket*."

"I know, I know." Cailan's own frustration was evident as he ran a hand through his hair. The concept was difficult to articulate, even to himself. "But I promise it's related. And it's not like the ship talks or anything. It's just a feeling I get, like it's aware. Sentient."

The Stormcaller didn't look impressed by his fumbling explanation. "If anyone else told me this, I'd be questioning their mental state." She took a breath. "Okay, what does that have to do with Sprocket? How can...how can an airship and a cogwing become living things?"

Cailan decided it might not be a good idea to point out she had expressly *wanted* the cogwing to return to this state. The mechanical parrot was perched playfully on Elazar's hammock, hanging upside-down and chortling in a way that seemed almost boastful. It was so ridiculous that Cailan smiled before turning back to their conversation. "Blood is power."

Max nodded, her mind working to connect the dots. "Right. I know the arcane engine runs on dragon blood." Her lips pursed, thoughtful. "Wait, is that what did it? All of the dragon blood?"

Cailan shook his head. If that were the case, it would have happened long ago. And it would happen to other airships that used the same fuel for their arcane engines. But he suspected this was a recent change. "I have a theory. Elazar and I both bled all over the deck."

The Stormcaller's expression tightened at the reminder. Yeah, Cailan wasn't a big fan of that memory, either. Elazar had almost died to a harpoon fired by his crewmates, and Cailan had nearly bled out from Belen's talons. Neither made him feel all warm and fuzzy inside.

"You think that did something?" Max asked.

Cailan gave a noncommittal shrug, his thoughts still partly lost in the past. "I think Elazar's blood is what originally woke Sprocket." The idea that their blood might have mingled with the essence of the *Tempest* and sparked something extraordinary was a theory that seemed increasingly plausible. Strange, sure, but plausible. "Based on what happened with the ship, it made me think my blood might help Sprocket, too."

Max's eyes widened in realization as she absorbed the implications of Cailan's theory. She looked back and forth between Cailan and Sprocket. "Your blood brought Sprocket to life."

Cailan nodded, a grim set to his mouth. He wasn't sure how he felt about his blood animating mechanical creations. It was *weird*.

"Should we tell Captain Jo?" Max asked uncertainly.

Cailan paused, lips pursed with thought. The ramifications

of revealing this information were unpredictable, to say the least. If the knowledge that some dragon blood could imbue life into inanimate objects became widespread, it could spark a dangerous obsession among humans, potentially endangering his kind more than they already were. And Cailan wasn't exactly a dragon, not like Chandra and the others. Normal dragons didn't shapeshift.

Furthermore, there was the matter of Captain Jo's motivations. While Cailan respected her as a leader and trusted her to some extent, he couldn't entirely dismiss the possibility that she might be tempted to use this knowledge to her advantage. She was desperate for news of Elazar, and with the dangerous smuggling run to Brinwald looming, Cailan couldn't help but wonder if she might try to leverage this discovery for her own benefit.

"Maybe we should keep this between us for now," he said finally. "At least, until we understand it better. Besides, Captain Jo already has a lot on her mind."

Max appeared contemplative, her lips pressed in a pensive bite before she nodded. "You're right. This could be dangerous if the wrong people learned of it." There was a hint of reluctance in her agreement, a recognition of the potential significance of their discovery, but also an understanding of the danger it posed.

Their eyes met in silent agreement, a new secret forged between them. Cailan hoped he wasn't making a mistake, but his instincts said revealing this now would only lead to trouble.

For better or worse, it was their secret for the time being.

4

EXCUSES

Elazar

Elazar tightened the last bolt on the mechanical wing, stepping back to survey his work. The Jade Court engineers stood in a semi-circle around him, their expressions a mix of fascination and skepticism. He cleared his throat.

"This, uh, completes the framework," he began, trying to inject some enthusiasm into his voice but failing miserably. "The gears here—" He pointed. "—control the wing's movement."

One of the engineers, the Vangara, raised a scaly eyebrow. "Looks flimsy."

Elazar swallowed hard. "It may seem so, but the alloys used are both lightweight and strong." He had to watch every word, be mindful of everything he showed them. Elazar couldn't reveal that his Gearweaver magic made this much easier for him than for others. His magic told him on an instinctive level if something would work or not. Usually.

One of the human engineers, a man named Jarod, examined the intricate gearwork closely. "And how do the wings operate for the dragon they're attached to?"

Elazar ran a hand through his hair. That was another aspect his magic had simplified, but he'd come up with a slightly more difficult workaround. "These small mechanical sensors rest against the dragon's shoulders." He picked up one of the tiny sensors and held it out. "They detect changes in the muscle groups, which then trigger corresponding mechanical responses in the wings."

Jarod nodded but didn't look convinced. Elazar continued despite himself. "The key is synchronization between the gears in the wing and your sensor mechanisms. One wrong move and it won't fly straight."

He heard a scoff from behind him and turned to see the Vangara engineer smirking. "Bet you love showing off your tricks."

A flash of irritation crossed Elazar's face, but he suppressed it. "Just trying to ensure you understand."

Silence fell over the group as they took in his words, some scribbling notes while others whispered among themselves.

"Is there anything else?" The Vangara's voice cut through the quiet.

Elazar shook his head. "That's all for today." He motioned toward the workshop exit. "We'll continue tomorrow."

As they filed out one by one, exhaustion clung to him.

Every lesson drained him more than the last, not just physically, but emotionally.

Once alone, he leaned against the workbench and let out a heavy sigh. The memories of laughter-filled nights with Max on the *Tempest* contrasted sharply with his current reality. The gears and wires seemed less like a marvel and more like shackles chaining him to this fate.

"Keep it together," he muttered to himself.

He was so tired. But his nightly work, the secret project that consumed him, was far from finished. It had been days now, each night a stolen hour carved from sleep, fueled by a desperate need to enhance his wing augments. Elazar wasn't sure if Belen would consider his usefulness exhausted if these engineers took over his wing work, and this project was the only thing he'd been able to come up with as a saving grace.

Elazar fished the gold chain from beneath his linen shirt, the tiny arcane engine thumping against his chest with the motion. He pulled it over his head, then gently placed it on the workbench. The small device glowed faintly, a reminder of the magic that pulsed within it. He glanced at the door, then dragged heavy crates of scrap metal and parts into position, a makeshift barrier against any unwelcome intrusions. This part of his work was too risky to be seen by prying eyes.

He took a deep breath, pushing back his exhaustion, and focused on the wing augments before him. They were already an impressive piece of engineering, but they needed more. More strength, more versatility. If he was going to survive Belen, they had to do *more* than just help him fly.

Elazar reached for a thin sheet of zephyrium metal, a lightweight yet strong material that had been critical in his previous designs. The last few nights had been spent working with the metal to create small, interlocking pieces that could overlay his leathery scales, like plate mail but superior. He'd already created most of what he needed, tucked away in an innocuous crate beneath his workbench. The plates would need to fit seamlessly with the existing structure of the wing augments, allowing them to retract or expand as needed. Elazar envisioned how they would look—gleaming armor that could unfold at a moment's notice.

He worked for hours, soldering the plates into place and connecting them with a gentle touch of his inherent magic. The smell of heated metal filled the small workshop, mingling with his sweat. Elazar lost track of time as he immersed himself in the task, each successful modification fueling his determination.

When he almost couldn't keep his eyelids propped open any longer, Elazar took a step back to admire his progress. The wing augments now had an additional layer of protection—one that could extend over his dragon form like a second skin. He reached out and gently activated it. With a soft swoosh, the plates unfolded from their concealed positions along the wings. But seeing as they were unattached to a dragon at the moment, the armor ended up in a clattering jumble.

He allowed himself a small smile. This was something new, something powerful. Something that would afford him protection—well, if he were a dragon, at any rate. Elazar had considered making the armor dual-purpose so he could engage it over his human form, too, but had dismissed the idea. It seemed like it would make him more ungainly than anything else.

He returned the arcane engine pendant around his neck, feeling its comforting weight against his chest once more. As he cleaned up the remnants of his work from the bench, he couldn't help but think about Max—how she'd react to this innovation.

As he extinguished the workshop's lanterns and prepared to grab a few hours of rest, a sense of peace fell over Elazar.

THE GOLDEN MORNING LIGHT FILTERING THROUGH THE small portholes had awakened Elazar far too early. He had cleaned himself up as best he could to prepare for another day with the Jade Court engineers. Elazar knew that soon his meager breakfast would be delivered, before he began another long day of work.

A tap at the door drew his attention. It creaked open—he'd moved the crates blocking it before he'd fallen asleep the previous night. Tiberia strode in. She carried a tray laden with food and a bundle tucked under her arm.

"Good morning. You need to eat a hearty breakfast," Tiberia announced, placing the tray down beside his scattered schematics. The scent of warm bread and roasted meat filled the room, making Elazar's stomach twist with hunger.

"And what's that?" He nodded toward the bundle.

"Fresh clothing," Tiberia said, unfolding a crisp shirt and trousers. "Your current attire looks like it's seen better days."

Elazar frowned, his eyes narrowing. "Since when does Belen care about how I look?"

"She doesn't," Tiberia replied, her voice calm. "She's in a good mood because of your work with the engineers. But these —" She gestured to the food and clothes. "—are from me."

Suspicion flared hot in Elazar's chest. He crossed his arms, leaning back against the bench. "Why? What do you want?"

Tiberia met his gaze, unflinching. "You're valuable to her right now, and if you fall apart or starve yourself to death, it jeopardizes everything." She took a step closer, her gaze softening slightly. "But I decided you needed these things because...no one else will look out for you here."

Elazar's frown deepened as he searched her face for any

hint of deceit. "I don't buy it," he said finally. "People here do things for themselves or for Belen's favor. Not out of kindness."

She shrugged, a small smile playing at her lips. "Believe what you want. Eat something before it gets cold."

He watched her turn to leave but couldn't help himself. "Why are you different?" The question slipped out before he could stop it.

Tiberia paused at the doorway, glancing over her shoulder. Her midnight-blue hair cascaded around her face like a dark waterfall. "Because I've seen what happens when everyone stops caring. Not everyone in the Jade Court is cruel." With that, she left Elazar alone with his thoughts and newfound provisions.

Elazar stood for a moment longer before sighing and sitting down to eat. As he chewed on a mouthful of bread, he pondered Tiberia's words and actions, feeling more conflicted than ever about his place in Belen's twisted world.

He was flying.

The wind caressed the leading edges of his wings, the sun radiating warmth along the length of his back. Seagulls and a large brown pelican soared at his three o'clock, unbothered by the presence of the copper dragon in the sky.

Elazar reveled in the freedom of soaring through the endless azure expanse. The salty sea breeze buffeted his copper scales as he banked left, riding thermal currents. Below, clusters of lush emerald islands dotted the turquoise waters of the sea, their pristine beaches fringed by swaying palms.

Once, the mere thought of this dragon form would have filled him with dread and self-loathing. An unnatural abomination, neither fully human nor beast. But now? With each powerful downstroke of his leathery wings, he shed another layer of that ingrained insecurity. Up here, he was simply himself—unburdened, unconstrained.

Elazar spiraled higher, the scattered islands shrinking to mere specks against the cerulean canvas. He imagined streaking across that limitless sky, racing the clouds until the world fell away entirely. No more hiding, no more—

A distant clang shattered his tranquil reverie. His eyes snapped open to the dim confines of the *Talisman*'s workshop. The aroma of smoke and machine oil replaced sea salt and reminded him that his freedom was out of reach.

It had all been just a dream. A cruel illusion conjured by his subconscious to torture him. Elazar groaned, rubbing at his forehead with dismay.

A shaft of light from the corridor illuminated the workshop as the door opened. Rubbing sleep from his eyes, Elazar sat up, expecting to find Tiberia slipping inside. Instead, a jolt of fear and uncertainty shot through him when he recognized the gangly silhouette of Freyak, one of the Jade Empress's Vangara lieutenants.

"The Empress demands your presence," Freyak snapped, his yellow eyes seeming to glow in the darkness.

Elazar swallowed, glancing down at himself. Gone was the larger form of the copper dragon, a shape that would have stood a chance against the daunting Vangara. He threw back his thin blanket, swinging down from the hammock to the floor. Elazar shoved on his boots. "I'm ready."

The corridors of the *Talisman* were quiet, most of the dragon crew still slumbering. Elazar's footsteps echoed softly as he trailed behind the Vangara, who moved with a predatory grace that Elazar couldn't help but envy.

Passing the occasional crew member, Elazar caught glimpses of their wary expressions as they eyed Freyak. No doubt word of the Empress's summons had already spread. Elazar kept his gaze averted, unwilling to draw any undue attention.

Had he done something wrong? Said something to one of the engineers-in-training that he shouldn't have? Worry-inspired sweat beaded his forehead.

Finally, they emerged onto the main deck. The morning sun had just breached the horizon, casting a warm glow across the gleaming metal and lacquered wood of the airship.

"Move," Freyak growled, shoving Elazar forward.

Stumbling, Elazar quickened his pace, following the Vangara to the towering presence of the Jade Empress herself. Belen's emerald scales glinted in the sunlight, her wings of polished steel spread in a display that caught the golden rays.

The Jade Empress watched his approach. Elazar came to a stop before her, lowering his head deferentially. "Good morning, Empress."

Belen blew out a rumbling breath as Freyak moved aside, leaving Elazar alone before the large green dragon. "You have been with us for almost three months. What progress have you made on the location of the Forgotten Library?"

Elazar swallowed, eyes wide at the question. He had thought she would ask about his progress on the wings or the trainees, not this. His stomach soured. "Empress, I..." He trailed off, staring down at his feet. "My focus has been on the mechanical wing designs and training the new mechanics, as you commanded. I haven't had time to—"

A low, rumbling growl ripped from Belen's throat. "Excuses," she spat. "That is all I ever hear from you drakes."

Elazar flinched at the venom in her tone, his gaze flicking away from the Empress's imposing form. He opened his mouth to defend himself, but Belen cut him off with a savage swipe of her sharp talons.

The blow caught him on the right arm and his side, sending Elazar crashing across the deck. He landed hard on the wood, the breath knocked from his lungs for a moment. The fabric of his shirt was in ruins, splattered by the red of his welling blood. With a pained gasp, Elazar struggled up onto his left elbow, pain radiating along the right side of his body.

Hurt. He was injured, and in Elazar's experience, if he were badly enough off, he might shift into his dragon form...but was that something he wanted to risk, here and now?

"You are all the same—treacherous, deceitful *vermin!*" She reared up to her full height, her steel wings flaring menacingly. "Your kind betrayed my mate, leading the rest of my court to their doom. And now you dare to stand before me, wasting my time with your meaningless excuses?"

Elazar struggled to gather his thoughts. Agony clouded his mind. He knew he had to give her some sort of response, or she might kill him so quickly he never had a chance to shift. "Empress, I—"

"Silence!" Belen's jaws snapped shut mere inches from his face. The heat of her breath washed over him. "You will find the location of the Forgotten Library, or you will suffer the same fate as the other drakes who have crossed me."

Elazar's blood ran cold at the implied threat. "I..." He swallowed and tasted blood in his mouth. His vision blurred, going dark around the edges. "I will do as you command, Empress."

Belen's lips curled into a cruel smile, revealing sharp fangs. "See that you do." She turned, her steel wings casting a looming shadow over Elazar.

He must have blacked out. The next thing Elazar knew, Tiberia peered down at him, words coming from her mouth that he couldn't understand. She seemed to be asking him something, but Elazar had only a vague grasp of consciousness.

He shook his head, which sent the world spinning around him, so he shut his eyes.

The dragon was in there. He could feel it, lingering around the edges, just waiting to come out. If Elazar could shift, he knew that the magic might heal him. At least enough to think clearly, maybe.

"...need to get you to the workshop." Tiberia gently helped him upright, much stronger than she appeared.

Her words had finally penetrated the fog. Elazar hissed out an agonized breath. "Don't know if I can."

"We have to," Tiberia insisted. Her mouth was suddenly close to Elazar's ear. "It's bad enough you're a drake. If you keep showing weakness, it's over for you."

"She won't kill me. She needs me," Elazar murmured, though he wasn't as certain of those slightly slurred words as he wished.

"You don't know her like I do," Tiberia whispered. "Come on."

Elazar gritted his teeth as Tiberia helped him to his feet, his vision blurring once more with the effort. The pain in his arm and side was excruciating, blood dripping steadily down his torn shirt.

If he showed any sign of being unable to fulfill his duties, the Jade Empress would see it as a failure—and he didn't dare imagine the consequences. Steeling himself, he forced one foot in front of the other, leaning heavily on Tiberia.

The journey felt interminable, each breath a struggle. Finally, they reached the familiar confines of the workshop. Tiberia eased Elazar down onto the floor near the workbench, his vision swimming.

"Let me see," she said, gently peeling back the tattered fabric of his shirt. Elazar hissed as she examined the deep gashes on his arm and ribs. "It's not as bad as it looks. Nothing seems to be broken, at least."

Elazar let out a shaky breath. "Small mercies."

Tiberia moved with practiced efficiency, cleaning the wounds and applying a salve that sent a cooling relief through Elazar's battered body. As she wrapped the bandages, her brow furrowed in concentration.

"You'll probably have some scars," she murmured, her tone uncharacteristically soft. "The Empress doesn't pull her talons."

Elazar winced, both at the sting of the bandages and the reminder of the Empress's wrath. "I should have had a better answer for her."

Tiberia paused, her gaze meeting his. "You know as well as I do that the Empress accepts no excuses. She wanted results, and you couldn't give them to her."

Elazar looked away, guilt and shame warring within him. "I can't just magically produce the location of the Forgotten Library. I'm not—" He swallowed hard, the words catching in his throat. He wanted to say that he wasn't a drake, wasn't what Belen accused him of. But that wasn't fully true. "I'm not like the others."

Tiberia's hand stilled, her expression softening with an emotion Elazar couldn't quite place. "I know," she murmured. "But you need to find a way, Elazar. For all our sakes."

Elazar nodded, wincing as the motion sent a fresh jolt of pain through his side. "I'll try," he whispered.

As Tiberia finished tending to his wounds, Elazar couldn't help but wonder how long he could keep up this charade.

5

I Prefer Dragon

Maxine

The breeze on the weather deck caught Max's coiled curls, playfully tossing them back as she leaned against the railing. Sprocket perched nearby, the automaton whistling to herself. Max studied the sky ahead, an enchanted spyglass pressed to her eye. As they neared the airspace surrounding Brinwald, she'd taken to spending more time on deck. Working the *Tempest* as a smuggler was not what Max had signed up for, but she was determined to do her job and keep her crew safe.

Especially if it meant reclaiming Elazar.

Max rubbed at her eyes, fatigue weighing on her. But she

couldn't afford to let her guard down, not when they were entering such a precarious area. The airspace surrounding Brinwald was notoriously treacherous, even without the added danger of the ongoing civil war.

With a start, she spotted a small but swift airship on an intercept course. "Incoming vessel!"

Cailan appeared at her side in an instant. She hadn't even realized he was on deck. Max offered him the spyglass without a word. Cailan peered through the lens, his brow furrowing.

"I see people in uniforms. Military, maybe?" His tone was gruff as he handed the spyglass back to her. "I'm going to let the captain know." Without waiting for a response, Cailan spun and strode towards the bridge.

Max returned her focus to the approaching airship. Sure enough, she saw the uniformed crew Cailan had mentioned. They also appeared to be armed, which didn't come as a surprise, since Brinwald was in the middle of a brutal civil war. But it also meant that things might get prickly for the *Tempest*.

Sprocket edged closer to her, the mechanical parrot seeming to study the incoming vessel, too. "Don't get any ideas into that head of yours, Sprocket."

Cailan popped out of the bridge, heading their way. He moved with purpose, like a predator on the hunt. "Captain Jo says we have to let them board."

Max watched the approaching airship, struggling to swallow down her unease. She gripped the railing, mentally preparing herself to step in and try to smooth things over if necessary.

As the vessel drew closer, a voice boomed from a speaking horn. "We are the Marinport Port Authority. Your airship must be boarded and searched before you're allowed to dock."

"Marinport Port Authority. How redundant," Cailan

muttered under his breath. Sprocket chortled, as if she, too, found it funny.

Max shot him a pointed look, silently warning him to hold his tongue. The last thing they needed was for Cailan to antagonize the port officials. She took a deep breath, squaring her shoulders as the other airship pulled alongside the *Tempest*.

Max held out her arm. "Sprocket, to me." The cogwing angled her head, eyes glinting as if she might disobey. But a moment later, she obediently fluttered to Max's shoulder.

A group of five uniformed officials swiftly boarded the *Tempest*. The insignia on their uniforms marked them as the Marinport Port Authority. Max took a deep breath, pushing down her misgivings as she plastered on her most charming smile.

One of the officers, a stern-faced man with graying hair, approached Max and Cailan. "I'm Lieutenant Verin. We'll need to inspect your vessel and cargo before you're cleared to dock."

Cailan opened his mouth, but Max stepped forward and spoke before he had a chance. "Of course, Lieutenant. We understand the need for security, especially in these trying times. How can we assist you?"

Verin's gaze flicked between them. "Your crew will need to gather in one area while we search the ship. No one is to interfere with the inspection."

"Absolutely, Lieutenant. We will cooperate fully." Max inclined her head.

A young woman beside Verin held a clipboard. "Where is this airship registered?"

Max blinked. That wasn't something she was privy to. "Um..." She looked at Cailan, but he shook his head.

"Nera, Ganland," Captain Jo supplied, appearing from the bridge.

The woman jotted it down. Maxine relaxed, glad that she didn't have to provide all the answers.

Maxine watched as Josephine approached, her posture relaxed and expression warm. This was a side of the captain that Max rarely saw: a disarming charm that belied the steely determination that usually defined her. "Welcome aboard the *Tempest*," Josephine greeted the young woman with the clipboard. "I'm Captain Josephine Prescott. I hope our arrival hasn't caused any undue concern."

The woman blinked, seemingly caught off guard by Josephine's friendly demeanor. "Not at all, Captain. We're simply following standard protocol." She glanced down at her clipboard. "You said you're registered in Nera, Ganland?"

"That's right." Josephine nodded. "We're a merchant vessel, transporting much-needed medical supplies to the people of Brinwald." Her tone was bright, almost sugary. "The war has taken such a dreadful toll, you know. We couldn't stand by and do nothing."

Lieutenant Verin stepped forward, brows knitted. "Which side are you supporting in the conflict?"

Josephine's expression remained unruffled. "We're not taking sides, Lieutenant. We're simply trying to help those in need, as any good merchant vessel would do." She turned to Cailan. "Marshal Cailan, would you be so kind as to take these fine officers to the hold? I'm sure they'll be interested to see the supplies we've brought."

Cailan's gaze darted between Josephine and the Port Authority officers, but he nodded. "Of course, Captain." He gestured for the officers to follow him.

Maxine watched as the group disappeared below deck, admiring Josephine's deft handling of the situation. She hissed out a breath. "Should you really have sent them with Cailan?"

"It's his job," Captain Jo said, voice taut.

"You have an awful lot of trust that he won't get annoyed and do something rash," Max murmured.

A thin smile graced the captain's lips. "I believe that, when it counts, Cailan will come through."

Max strained to hear anything from below, but the only sound was the wind and the ever-present rumble of the *Tempest*. "That was some impressive work, Captain. I didn't know you had it in you to be so...disarming."

Josephine's lips quirked. "There's a lot you don't know about me, Max." Her gaze shifted to the hatch where the officers had disappeared. "But we'll need to keep up the act. Those officials are no fools, and they'll be looking for any sign of deception."

Max nodded, her own gaze settling in the direction the officials had gone. She sincerely hoped that Cailan was up to the task.

Cailan

Being the marshal, as it turned out, was a lot more stressful than Cailan had thought it would be. Sure, he knew he was charged with the ship's security, but he hadn't realized that smuggling might be more intense than hunting dragons.

At the very least, it was a lot more work for him.

When hunting dragons, at least you knew where you stood. There was going to be a fight, and it was kill or be killed. Smuggling, though? It required a lot more finesse and constant vigilance.

After appeasing the Port Authority, the *Tempest* had been allowed to Marinport's mooring terminal. It wasn't much of one, if Cailan was being honest. The port town had been ravaged by the civil war, which meant the mooring house was in disrepair. And Cailan hated that, since it meant trusting the stairs leading down wouldn't collapse as they disembarked.

Cailan trailed behind Josephine as they navigated the dilapidated streets of Marinport. His jaw clenched as he surveyed the crumbling buildings and the wary faces of the locals.

Josephine led him to a nondescript alleyway just past a fishmonger, where a hooded figure waited in the shadows. Cailan's hand instinctively went to the hilt of his cutlass. It was his best defense, aside from his dragon form—which he'd been ordered to keep hidden.

"Captain Prescott, so glad you could make it," the figure greeted, voice muffled by the hood. "I hope you're able to get some sight-seeing in on your trip to Brinwald."

Josephine nodded curtly. "We had to take our time, but the winds were on our side." She paused, slanting a look over her shoulder before adding, "And we had the fortune of admiring some beautiful sunsets."

Sight-seeing? Sunsets? Cailan narrowed his eyes. Why were they talking about scenic views?

The man pushed back his hood, revealing a smiling countenance. "The sun always shines on us, even in the darkest hour." He rolled his shoulders. "I'm Jacob. Since you're here, I assume you have the *medical supplies*?"

Captain Jo gave another sharp nod. "I trust you have the necessary arrangements in place?"

"Of course." Jacob gestured toward the alley. "I've brought along those I trust We'll unload everything quietly and without drawing attention."

"Excellent." Josephine's tone was clipped as she turned to Cailan. "Marshal Cailan will oversee the delivery."

What? Cailan blinked, annoyance prickling. He wanted to growl that he was no one's delivery boy, but he kept his mouth shut. This, he knew, was a dangerous task. One that Josephine had given him because she *trusted* him. The thought warmed him, made him want to succeed.

Jacob regarded him with a skeptical look but agreed. "Very well. My people have a wagon just outside the grounds. I'll have them bring it closer to the moorings."

"We're doing this in daylight?" Cailan asked, then belatedly realized he probably shouldn't have challenged their plan.

"Only the guilty hide their deeds under cover of darkness," Josephine said.

Yeah, and they probably get to live another day because they're smart. Cailan kept that to himself. She met his gaze with unrelenting intensity, letting him know very clearly that this was how it would be.

He huffed to himself. Then nodded. "Right. Whatever. Let's get this over with."

Somehow, Josephine hid the exasperation she no doubt felt. "I'll head back to the *Tempest*. We're overdue for a resupply, so I'll help the rest of the crew with that."

Cailan grimaced as he followed Jacob through the twisting alleys of Marinport. He didn't like this cloak-and-dagger business. Too many eyes watching them. Too many uniforms that he didn't recognize, soldiers that could belong to either side of this blasted civil war. Cailan knew they were watching the *Tempest* crew's every move. Watching *his* every move.

They reached a rickety wagon hitched to two scrawny horses on the edge of the mooring grounds. Cailan's lips curled in distaste. The rig didn't look like it could make it halfway across town, let alone out of the city. But he supposed that was rather the point. Who would suspect such an unassuming wagon to be smuggling valuable cargo?

Cailan maintained wary vigilance as they guided the wagon back to the *Tempest*'s mooring. His nerves only grew more frayed when they began loading the crates of medical supplies onto the wagon. Too exposed out here. Too many eyes on them.

Once the last crate was loaded, Jacob rifled through the contents with a dissatisfied frown. He turned to Cailan, voice low as he spoke. "Where are the crystals? You were supposed to provide us with a shipment of Spectralite crystals as well."

Cailan barked out a laugh. "You can't possibly think we'd store such valuable cargo in an obvious place like this." He leaned in close. "But I heard your family has a taste for eel guts. It's quite the delicacy around here, I'm told." He winked conspiratorially, then hauled over one of the crates. Nestled within each jar of stinking eel innards were the glinting Spectralite crystals, worth more than their weight in gold. Dangerous, illegal, and exactly what Josephine had promised to deliver. He pulled out one of the jars, glad that the murky contents hid the gleaming crystals.

Cailan kept his expression neutral. "I do hope you and your kin enjoy the treat. Eel guts never fail to put a smile on *my* face." He offered the jar to the man. Jacob's eyes widened in understanding. He nodded, then accepted the *delicacy*.

Cailan cursed under his breath as the jar slipped from Jacob's fingers, crashing to the ground. The greasy eel guts splattered across the cobblestones, but Cailan's attention was on the sparkling Spectralite crystals that tumbled free.

"No, no, no!" Jacob scrambled to scoop up the precious stones, but it was too late. The glittering shards had caught the light, drawing the attention of nearby soldiers.

"Halt! What's going on here?" one of the men shouted, hand going to the hilt of his sword.

Cailan growled. Their smuggling operation had been

blown wide open. "Damn it all to the Abyss!" He reached for his own blade.

Jacob and his men surged forward, desperate to recover the scattered crystals and escape before the authorities could confiscate them. Cailan found himself caught in the middle of the ensuing skirmish, parrying blows and dodging swinging fists as he tried to keep the soldiers at bay.

"The *Tempest*! Get to the *Tempest*!" he yelled, hoping his crewmates heard his frantic call.

From his vantage point, he caught a glimpse of Josephine, Isaac, and Galatea down by the docks, their heads snapping toward the commotion. He couldn't see their expressions, but he hoped they understood and made for the ship.

As he continued to clash alongside Jacob's fighters, Cailan clung to the hope that his crewmates would escape, even as the battle raged on around him.

Suddenly, a new voice rang out, cutting through the din. "There! That's the vessel we're after!" Cailan whirled to see a contingent of Port Authority officers marching toward the *Tempest*, their faces set with determination.

"Cut the lines!" Cailan roared, his voice hoarse with desperation. "Fly, damn you!"

Josephine, Isaac, and Galatea reached the *Tempest*'s gangplank, their faces etched with grim resolve. Cailan knew they had no choice—they had to escape before the authorities could seize the ship and crew.

As the *Tempest*'s engines rumbled to life, Cailan spared one last glance at the chaos unfolding around him. Jacob and his men were fighting a losing battle against the soldiers, their precious Spectralite crystals scattered and trampled underfoot.

Cailan gritted his teeth, then turned and found himself surrounded. Port Authority guards with pistols and armed soldiers hemmed him in.

"You're coming with us," a soldier with rows of gleaming medals pinned to his chest declared. "Drop your weapon."

Cailan heard the patter of boots rushing up the mooring tower in a vain attempt to halt the airship. They would be too late, but the odds were still good that one of the patrol airships would go after the *Tempest*. And with her arcane engine bereft of its normal fuel source, the former dragoneering vessel was no faster than any other steam airship. He had to get up there!

And there was only one way to do that.

He shoved his cutlass into his baldric, unwilling to abandon the blade. It was better to have it out of his way, at any rate. Cailan held up his hands. "What's the big deal? Haven't you guys ever seen eel guts before?"

"You know that there was more than eel guts in those jars," one of the soldiers said, stepping closer.

"Really? I'm as shocked as you are." Cailan glanced overhead at the *Tempest*. She had cleared the mooring tower and— what was that?

A colorful blur arrowed down at the soldiers.

Cailan watched in dismay as Sprocket swooped down, her multicolored feathers flashing.

"Sprocket, no!" he cursed under his breath, certain the crazy bird was going to get herself broken again.

Sure enough, a soldier raised his pistol and took aim at the mechanical avian. Cailan winced, but the shot went wide, missing Sprocket entirely. "Blast that infernal machine!" the soldier growled, turning his attention back to Cailan.

Cailan braced himself as the soldiers closed in, their weapons trained on him. He couldn't help but feel a flash of pride at Sprocket's valiant, if misguided, attempt to distract the enemy. Maybe the little automaton was trying to make up for almost taking off his head the first time they met.

"You're coming with us, smuggler rat," one of the soldiers

sneered, leveling his pistol at Cailan's chest. "Looks like your ship's leaving without you."

Cailan arched an eyebrow, his expression infuriatingly nonchalant. "Rat? I'm offended. I prefer *dragon*."

Before the soldier could react, Cailan's form began to shift and expand. His body elongated, scales erupting across his skin as he transformed in a flash of silver.

The soldiers stumbled back in shock, their weapons wavering. But they recovered just as quickly, and in his larger form, Cailan didn't have much room to maneuver.

He whirled, lashing out with his tail—low enough to sweep the nearest in the ring of soldiers off their feet, sending them staggering backwards into their mates. Cailan had learned much in the way of tactics to fight humans during his time at the Breakwater Isle Brawl, though never against such a large number. Still, humans were humans.

The soldiers on his other side rallied even as the others fell, some taking aim with pistols and others brandishing swords or knives. Cailan didn't have the benefit of armor like a hardscale dragon. If those weapons connected, he'd have problems.

He reared up on his hind legs, buffeting the incoming combatants with the largest gust of wind he could manage— which wasn't as much as he'd like. But Cailan followed it up with a roar that sent the scrawny cart horses into a panic. The wagon veered wildly, spilling the rest of its contents in a beautiful display of chaos that granted Cailan the precious seconds he needed.

Cailan crouched, gathering his muscles, and leaped into the air. His wings snapped out then beat frantically as he struggled to gain altitude. Taking flight from a standstill wasn't difficult, but he had to navigate the tall trees, the nearby buildings, and the mooring tower. Fouling his wings on any of those would ground him.

He heard more gunshots in his wake, but none that threatened him. Sprocket caught up, flying alongside him with a triumphant squawk.

"That was really stupid, you ornery tin can," Cailan called to the cogwing.

Sprocket chortled.

"Whatever," Cailan muttered. "Let's get back to the *Tempest*."

Then, he'd have a date with the arcane engine. He needed to fuel it with dragon blood—and fast.

6

OUTCAST ISLAND

Belen

"Empress, you have received a missive from Outcast Island," Freyak announced, striding onto the sun deck where Belen had been soaking in the late afternoon warmth.

She lifted her head, studying the Vangara. Freyak normally knew better than to interrupt her at this time, which meant this missive had importance. And Outcast Island...that was where she had sent Danelor for migration season.

Others in the Court saw Danelor and his peers as defective, creatures who were better off dead. Aberrations that would only further sully the already-damaged Jade Court. Belen understood these arguments, but as hard as her heart had become...she refused to destroy the surviving chimeras. Belen knew other dragons saw this as a weakness, which meant she had to present herself as more dominating, more ruthless. It was exhausting, when all she wanted was to right old wrongs and avenge her mate.

"Open it so that I may read it." Belen nodded to Freyak, who moved to comply. The paper the missive came on was too small and fragile for her claws.

The Jade Empress craned her neck, scanning the page. A surge of white-hot anger coursed through Belen's veins as she read the name *Chandra*. Her treacherous sister, the one who had turned her back on the Jade Court at the moment they needed her most. The memory of their last encounter on Outcast Island flooded back—Chandra's defiant roar, the satisfying crunch of bone as Belen's jaws clamped down...

She had been certain Chandra was dead. To learn that the Seer still drew breath was an insult, claws in the face of Belen's power and authority. Her tail lashed, scales scraping against the wood beneath her. How dare that wretched dragon show her face again after such betrayal?

Freyak took an instinctive step back, his eyes downcast as he sensed the Empress's fury radiating off her in waves. Belen forced herself to take a deep breath, calming the raging inferno within. She could not allow her anger to cloud her judgment, not when the stakes were so high.

Continuing to read, Belen's brow furrowed as she absorbed Danelor's words. Chandra claimed she could aid in Belen's goals...if only the Jade Empress brought the Dragon Who Isn't to Outcast Island.

How convenient that the very creature Chandra sought was already within her grasp.

The drake whelp, Elazar—he was the key to everything. Even if he insisted otherwise. Belen found him irritating, his only redeeming quality his clever mind that allowed him to craft new wings for her Court. He claimed to know nothing of the Forgotten Library.

Chandra, however, was certain he did.

"Freyak," Belen rumbled, "summon Tiberia. I must update her on her current responsibilities. And tell the bosun we'll need a dinghy prepared when we arrive at Jadefire Island."

"A dinghy?" Freyak repeated, head tilted.

Belen gave him a toothy smile. "Yes. We have cargo to ferry to Outcast Island."

If Chandra believed she could manipulate events to her own ends, she would soon learn the folly of crossing the Jade Empress. Belen would bring the Dragon Who Isn't as requested—and in doing so, she would be her traitorous sister's end.

Elazar

It was fortunate that the five Jade Court engineers were far enough along in their training to begin work in earnest on their own mechanical wings. Slowed by the still-healing gashes on his arm, Elazar could do little but oversee their work and offer tips.

He may have fallen behind on his own wing production, but convalescence meant that he now had time to devote to the Forgotten Library. Privately, Elazar wondered if that had been Belen's plan all along. Was she manipulative enough to know that if he were injured, he couldn't work on the wings? Or just cruel?

Elazar leaned back in his chair, the draconian tome open before him, but his eyes unfocused. He had been poring over the text for hours, searching for any scrap of information that might give him a clue about the Forgotten Library. But the dense archaic language eluded him. With a frustrated sigh, he closed the book, wincing as the movement jarred his injuries.

Tiberia's kindness had been a rare bright spot in his confinement, but Elazar remained wary. The Jade Empress's attendant could just as easily turn on him if it suited her purposes.

Elazar's gaze drifted to his shirt. Tiberia had brought him a new one, and the linen hid his chain and arcane engine. Would things have gone differently if he'd crafted the armor to protect his human form, too? It was something to consider.

Wincing, he moved over to the workbench where he had a fresh sheet of paper. Integrating that into the augments would take time, but he had some ideas on how—

The workshop door slid open with a creak, admitting a familiar figure.

"Tiberia." Elazar greeted her cautiously, setting aside the paper and pencil.

She held a plate of food, moving to place it on the desk not far from the closed book. "I brought your meal. How are your wounds healing?"

Elazar struggled to rein in his resentment. It wasn't Tiberia's fault the Empress had lashed out at him. But she was a part of the Jade Court, and he couldn't help the way he felt. He shrugged, only using his left shoulder—moving the right in such a way still tweaked his healing arm. "The same."

Tiberia studied him, then nodded. "I see." She took a step

backward, as if she were about to leave, then paused. "I also came to tell you that migration is at an end."

Elazar cocked his head, wondering what that meant for him. He had missed observing the Jade Court's summer migration to the continent, spending most of his time belowdecks in the workshop. Initially, he had been curious, hoping to see how the dragons went about feasting on ore and gems. But quickly, the scope of his captivity drained any such curiosity.

Tiberia stood near the door, unmoving, as if she hoped he would ask. When he didn't, she finally said, "I suspect the Jade Empress wants you to make progress on the Forgotten Library because of how close we are to the end of migration."

"I don't know why that matters." Elazar shook his head.

"Because she believes the Forgotten Library is somewhere in the Dragon Latitudes," Tiberia explained.

At that, Elazar frowned. Hadn't the Dragon Latitudes been mapped extensively? He glanced at a map pinned to the wall. Then a thought occurred to him: just because maps existed didn't mean they were *accurate.* Or that anyone knew what was on a particular island. Take the dragon nesting islands, for instance. Aboard the *Tempest,* Elazar could point out the islands labelled as the nesting islands belonging to dragons, but he couldn't have told anyone which Court called which home. And he still couldn't, actually. Not for lack of trying, but due to the secrecy and danger involved in getting that information from the dragons.

Gingerly, he crossed his arms. "That may be so. But I still don't know how to find it."

Tiberia sighed, then took a step closer again. "I think you can, with enough time."

Time. Elazar scoffed at the idea. "The Jade Empress doesn't come across as the patient sort."

"She may not, but she is." Tiberia was quiet for a moment before adding, "She's been searching for twenty-five years."

A quarter of a century seemed like a small amount of time for a dragon. They could live hundreds of years—unless a dragoneering crew or their own kind slaughtered them first. "On the deck, when I was hurt...you said I didn't know the Empress like you did. What did you mean by that?"

At his question, Tiberia winced. Elazar half expected her to insist she'd never said such a thing, that he'd hallucinated it due to his pain. But she surprised him. "Because I've been around her for a very long time."

Elazar quirked an eyebrow. "Unless I'm a terrible judge of age—which is entirely possible—you don't look much older than I am."

"I'm twenty-six," Tiberia said with a shrug. "But I've been a part of the Jade Court all my life."

Elazar frowned, his mind racing with a variety of thoughts. "When did these dragons start with airships?"

Tiberia's lips pursed, and Elazar really thought she wouldn't tell him. But she said, "From what I know, about twenty-five years ago."

Right around the time commercial dragon-hunting began. That was...odd. Elazar and the other dragon hunters had never heard of an airship fleet crewed by dragons, though he supposed it was possible they worked hard to keep that a secret, too. And the skies were endless. If a library could be forgotten, how easy would it be to miss a vessel?

"If I find this Forgotten Library...do you know why the Jade Empress wants it?" Elazar asked.

Tiberia swallowed. "I'm sorry, that's not a topic I can speak on."

Elazar nodded. Just as he suspected. At least she had been

forthcoming with other information. "I understand. Thanks for stopping by with the food and checking on me."

A smile crossed her face. "You're welcome." Tiberia turned for the door once more, then glanced over her shoulder. "Two more days in the air."

Two more days.

ELAZAR'S FIRST CLUE THAT THEY'D REACHED THE END OF migration came from the calls of the crew and the constant sound of movement overhead—both humanoid and dragon. Were they at Jadefire Island? Was it possible he'd recognize the island? He peered out the small porthole, but he was on the starboard side and only had a view of sky above and sea below.

But he had felt the telltale descent of the airship as the *Talisman* moved from airborne to settling with her hull in the water. Elazar assumed it was to allow for easier removal of cargo and passengers. It was a common enough practice in areas that didn't boast a proper mooring, and he assumed that was the case here. Other vessels would have noticed a dragon island with moorings.

Elazar expected that he, too, would disembark—but hours passed, and no one came for him. Had they forgotten about him? A small part of Elazar almost wished that was the case. But Belen was determined, and he doubted she had forgotten about her prisoner.

His answer came late in the afternoon, when the workshop door creaked open and a Vangara stared at him. "You are coming with me, Dragon Who Isn't. Pack whatever you need. You will not be returning."

Elazar wasn't sure where they were taking him, but he

knew he should be prepared. Moving to a storage trunk in the corner, he pulled out a worn canvas bag.

First, Elazar packed a set of clothes—a linen shirt, wool trousers, and a vest. He then carefully placed the draconian book he had been studying into the bag, along with the broken pocket watch he still carried from the *Tempest*.

Reaching for his leather tool belt, Elazar packed his engineering tools. But the Vangara clicked his tongue in annoyance.

"You won't be needing any tools where you're going," he said gruffly.

Elazar paused, tools still in hand. "Where am I going?" he asked, looking over at the lumbering dragonkin.

The Vangara scowled. "You'll find out. Now, hurry up."

Frustration welled up in Elazar's chest. Here he was, being led blindly to some unknown destination, with no explanation or answers being provided. He wanted to argue, to demand more information, but he knew it would be futile. The Vangara clearly wasn't going to tell him anything.

Jaw clenched, Elazar put his tools back down with more force than necessary. The sound echoed through the workshop. He took a deep breath, trying to rein in his rising irritation. Arguing now would only make his situation worse.

"I'm ready," Elazar said tersely, swinging the bag over his left shoulder. He met the Vangara's glare with a steely look of his own. Wherever they were taking him, he would face it with his dignity intact.

The Vangara grunted in reply and motioned for Elazar to follow. Elazar took one last look around the small room that had been his prison for months. Then, shoulders squared, he stepped out into the unknown.

Elazar followed the Vangara out of the workshop and onto the *Talisman's* main deck. His earlier suspicions were confirmed as the gentle rocking of the ship and the lack of the familiar hum of the airship's engines told him they had indeed landed on the water.

A sturdy gangplank stretched from the *Talisman's* hull to the shore of a lush tropical island. Was this Jadefire Island? Were they taking him to the home of the Jade Court?

But instead of leading him down the gangplank, the Vangara steered Elazar towards a smaller dinghy airship moored nearby. Elazar eyed it warily, tightening his grip on the duffle bag's strap. "I thought we were going to the island," he said, his voice edged with trepidation.

The Vangara let out a rough laugh. "The Empress has other plans for you, Dragon Who Isn't." He reached into a pouch and produced a thick, dark cloth. "I'm going to tie this over your eyes."

Elazar recoiled instinctively as the Vangara moved to blindfold him. "Wait, why? Where are you taking me?"

"Enough questions," the Vangara snapped. "Do as you're told."

Elazar hated this feeling of helplessness. With a resigned sigh, he allowed the Vangara to tie the blindfold tightly around his head, plunging him into darkness.

"I don't understand," Elazar said, his voice barely above a whisper. "Why the secrecy? Where are you taking me?"

The Vangara's only response was a firm hand on Elazar's shoulder, guiding him forward. Elazar had no choice but to comply, as he stepped carefully onto the small dinghy. The air was thick with the scent of saltwater and the distant cries of seabirds.

As the dinghy lurched into motion, unease washed over Elazar. Trapped in the darkness, he had no idea where they were headed or what the Jade Empress had in store for him. All he knew was that he was at the mercy of his captors, and the future looked increasingly bleak.

Elazar lost track of how long he was a passenger on the dinghy. He tried to peek glimpses beneath the blindfold, but with dusk approaching, the few times he caught sight of anything, it was only the never-ending dark of the sea below. By the time they reached their destination, it was full night and the Vangara guided him off the dinghy and into...

The blindfold fell away from Elazar's eyes.

A tunnel. They were in a tunnel system of some sort. Elazar's dismay grew as the Vangara hustled him into the cool clammy depths. The tunnels were lit intermittently by hurricane lanterns. Elazar tried his best to memorize the route, but quickly realized it was a losing proposition.

"A prisoner for you, Blightwalker!" the Vangara called, raspy voice echoing against the stone.

Blightwalker? Elazar expected to hear the scrape of talons against stone, but a moment later he instead caught the uneven cadence of boots. A man appeared, framed by the nearest hurricane lantern. The man paused when he saw Elazar. "Who is this, Rakesh?"

"Meet the Dragon Who Isn't." Rakesh the Vangara gave an ironic half-bow, then pushed Elazar closer to the man called Blightwalker. "He will be here with you until he reveals the location of the Forgotten Library. You may use whatever methods to encourage him."

The man's eyes widened, then he gestured for Elazar to follow. "Come along, then. I have this in hand, Rakesh."

"You do not command me," the Vangara hissed, glaring at the man. But then, without other options, the dragonkin turned and plodded away.

Blightwalker waited until he heard the echo of Rakesh's footsteps fade away, then turned to Elazar. "This way," he said simply, beckoning Elazar to follow.

Elazar fell into step behind the man, wincing as he noticed

his uneven gait. Blightwalker's limp was pronounced, a hitch in his stride that spoke of some old injury or other issue.

"Where are we?" Elazar asked, glancing around the tunnel. The air was cool and damp, the stone walls glistening with condensation.

Blightwalker didn't answer right away, leading Elazar deeper down the winding passage. "A dead volcanic island," he finally said. "Outcast Island. That's all you need to know for now."

Elazar frowned, not satisfied with the vague response, but he kept his questions to himself for now. *Outcast Island?* That wasn't a name he'd seen on any maritime charts.

After what felt like an eternity of walking, Blightwalker paused in front of a yawning cave entrance. "This will be your new home, Dragon Who Isn't," he said, gesturing inside.

Elazar bristled at the moniker. "That's not my name. I'm Elazar."

Blightwalker chuckled, his stern mask dropping with the sound. "Is that so? Well, Blightwalker isn't my name either. My name is Danelor."

"Why are you here?" Elazar asked, unable to hide his curiosity. Maybe the *why* would answer more of his questions.

Danelor stilled, his gaze dropping. "I'll stop by with something for an evening meal in an hour or so, along with fresh water. You'll find a cot and blankets inside the cave. We may be in the tropics, but this cave can grow surprisingly cold."

Elazar blinked, his mouth firming when he realized the other man wasn't going to answer. Danelor turned and hobbled away, leaving Elazar alone in the dark cave entrance. Elazar sighed, adjusting the strap of his duffle bag on his shoulder, and stepped into the cave.

The interior was spacious, with a high arched ceiling that cast deep shadows. A flickering lantern provided meager illumination, casting an orange glow over the rough-hewn walls. Elazar scanned the space, noting the promised cot and blankets.

Why did the Jade Court have this island, this cave system? And who was Danelor in the grand scheme of the court?

Elazar set the bag down and sank on the cot. He'd have plenty of time to ponder that, it seemed.

7

HIGHER LEARNING

Josephine

"**W**hat in the winds was *that*, Marshal?" Josephine snapped when Cailan stalked onto the bridge.

As soon as the words tumbled out, Josephine wished she could recall them. Not because of the way he growled deep in his chest, but because Jo knew that, in Marinport, Cailan had been bereft of options. He was in human form, but Jo wouldn't have been surprised if he shifted and roared at her. As it was, Cailan's golden brown eyes narrowed.

"What did you expect me to do, *Captain?*" Cailan spat, the honorific dripping with sarcasm. "That operation was doomed from the start. I knew it, but you insisted we go through with it." He ran a hand through his short, pale hair, frustration evident in his sharp movements. "I'm not even *human*, in case you've forgotten. I did the best I could. But that idiot Jacob had to go and botch the whole thing." Jo opened her mouth to defend herself, but Cailan barreled on. "So, tell me, Captain, how is this *my* fault?"

The words hung in the eerie silence of the bridge. Jo took a deep breath, steeling herself. "You're right," she said quietly, meeting his gaze. "It wasn't your fault." Surprise flitted across Cailan's face, his brow furrowing. "I shouldn't have put you in that position. I owe you an apology."

It was the least she could do. Jo couldn't tell him she feared their failed mission had doomed her with Gibson. She watched as he processed her words, the tension slowly bleeding from his shoulders.

"I..." Cailan started, then paused, seemingly at a loss for words. "I appreciate that, Captain. I'm *almost* sorry I growled at you."

Almost sorry. That was Cailan in a nutshell. But this was also why she knew he was their best option as Marshal—he didn't back down. Wasn't afraid to tell someone exactly what he thought.

"If this is what we're stuck doing," Cailan began, "then maybe we can find some easier smuggling jobs. At least until we get better at it. And maybe get more crew."

Josephine let out a heavy sigh, shaking her head. "I'm afraid there's nothing easy about smuggling, no matter the job. It's always going to be risky business."

Cailan's eyes flashed with frustration. "There's got to be some jobs that aren't complete suicide missions. What about smuggling silk or spices? Winds, even booze would be better than this."

Despite the gravity of their situation, Jo couldn't help the small chuckle that escaped her lips. "Booze? You want us to become rum runners now?"

Cailan folded his arms across his chest. "I'm just saying we need something lower profile. Jobs that won't end with us fighting off a battalion of soldiers." He paused. "Or rather, *me* fighting off a battalion of soldiers. Bad enough they saw my true form." The marshal huffed out an unhappy breath.

Jo's brief moment of amusement faded. "I'm afraid that's not an option," she said. "We're going to have to take the highest paying jobs we can get."

Cailan's expression clouded over. "Why? Is this because of the repairs on the *Tempest*? I know the damages were extensive, but—"

"It's not the repairs," Jo cut him off abruptly. She hesitated, reluctant to reveal the true reason they desperately needed an influx of cash. Jo scrambled for some reasonable excuse. "It's just that...with less crew, we have less shares to go around. I need to make sure everyone is fairly compensated for the risks they're taking. That's all."

She held her breath, hoping her thin explanation would satisfy him. Jo noted the doubt lingering in Cailan's eyes, but he simply gave a curt nod. "Fine. I suppose that makes sense."

His words were terse, and Jo wanted to be done with this conversation. "Thank you for the blood for the arcane engine, by the way." She nodded toward the telltale bandage wrapped around his arm.

"Couldn't let us fly off at a leisurely pace." Cailan shrugged. "Needed some speed, and I could provide it." They both knew that even with the gift of Cailan's dragon blood, escape had been a narrow thing.

"All the same, we couldn't have done it without you." Josephine offered him a smile. Without Cailan, how would that doomed run have ended? With her and the rest of the crew imprisoned, the *Tempest* impounded? It was too terrible to think about for long. "You've earned yourself a break. Our next port is Kingsden. You should have some shore leave."

The Marshal's eyes narrowed. "Kingsden?"

"It's where we'll receive our next mission," Jo said with a nod, though she saw Cailan was suspicious of her true intent. "Kingsden is the port we're working out of, for now." She hoped that explanation would soothe his ruffled feathers—scales?

Cailan angled his head, considering, then nodded. "Shore leave might not be the worst idea." He slipped out of the bridge.

A WEEK LATER, AT THE MOORING IN KINGSDEN, JO STOOD on the deck of the *Tempest*, overseeing the organized chaos unfolding before her. The crew moved with well-practiced efficiency, unloading crates and hoisting supplies with pulleys.

She might have a skeleton crew, but everyone knew how to pull their weight. Galatea worked with Isaac to bring aboard barrels of fresh water. The balloon-sails had been temporarily deflated, allowing Cailan and Max the chance to patch any worn sections. Sprocket perched atop a barrel, the restored cogwing squawking as if she were directing the crew.

The midday sun glinted off Jo's silver-streaked black hair, pulled back into a tight bun. Aviator goggles rested atop her forehead like a makeshift crown. Jo's attire was a blend of form and function: high-waisted, dark brown leather trousers tucked into worn knee-high boots; a crisp white blouse visible beneath a tailored waistcoat adorned with brass buttons; and an earth-toned, mid-length leather jacket that fluttered ever so slightly in the breeze. In truth, the outfit was almost too warm for the tropical port, but Jo needed to exude authority for what was to come.

She wasn't looking forward to her meeting with Gibson.

"Get it together, Jo," she whispered to herself, steeling her resolve.

"There you are," a familiar and welcome voice called. Jo turned, relaxing at Gretchen's approach. Her partner's usual easygoing demeanor was replaced by a furrowed brow and eyes lined with worry. "I was looking for you."

"This is where I usually am on port days," Jo said, adding a lilt of playfulness to her words.

Gretchen scoffed at Jo's attempt at levity. "I don't like this one bit and you know it."

Jo exhaled slowly, her shoulders drooping ever so slightly under the invisible weight of responsibility. "I don't have a choice, Gretch," she replied, her voice steady despite the storm brewing inside. "I have to meet with him. We're already doing as he asked. There should be no issues."

Gretchen studied Jo for a heartbeat, the hard lines of her face softening momentarily. With a curt nod of acceptance, she murmured, "Just be safe." Before Jo could respond, Gretchen pulled her into a fierce kiss. It was a kiss that spoke volumes, charged with worry and blooming with love. Gretchen's lips moved against Jo's with a desperate intensity, conveying every ounce of her feelings in the brief, blistering contact. Their breaths mingled, hearts raced, and for a fleeting moment, the world around them stilled, suspended in the space of their embrace.

As they reluctantly broke apart, Jo managed a small, grateful smile. "I'll be back before you know it," she said, the reassurance meant as much for herself as for Gretchen. With a final squeeze of her hand, Jo strode toward the skyway that would lead her off the *Tempest* and to the docks below.

The scent of saltwater and sound of distant bells greeted Jo as she stepped onto the bustling port. Wooden piers groaned under the weight of cargo and passengers, while exotic aromas wafted from the stalls of local merchants. Jo wove through the vibrant crowd, focused on her destination.

She found a hackney cab pulled by a mechanical horse. The creation brought Elazar to mind, but she pushed away all thoughts of her nephew for later.

"Where to, Miss?" the driver asked.

"The Gibson villa, please," Jo replied.

The ride to Gibson's villa was a jarring, uncomfortable affair. Jo gripped the edge of the rickety seat as the mechanical hackney lurched and bounced along the uneven cobblestones. The rhythmic chugging of the pistons that powered the metal horse's legs grated on her nerves, a poor substitute for the smooth glide of a well-maintained airship.

When the hackney finally drew to a stop, Jo let out a small sigh of relief. She stepped out onto the drive and made her way toward the house.

As she approached the entry doors, one of the villa's guards stepped forward, recognition dawning on his face. "Captain Prescott," he said, inclining his head respectfully. "Mr. Gibson has been expecting you." With a curt nod, the guard pulled open the door, ushering Jo inside. "This way, please." He led her down a grand hallway.

Jo followed him to the same room as before—drawing room, office, or library, she wasn't sure. They were all the same, as far as she was concerned. All that mattered was that Reginald Gibson reclined in the same chair as before, like a king holding court. A thick cigar balanced between his fingers, a plume of fragrant smoke curling around him.

"Ah, Captain Prescott," Gibson greeted, his tone holding a

pleasantness that didn't extend to his eyes. "I'm so pleased you could join me once more."

Josephine swallowed, refusing to allow the financier's cool demeanor to rattle her. "Mr. Gibson," she replied, inclining her head in a terse acknowledgment.

Gibson's lips curled into a faint smile as he gestured at a chair across from him. "Please, have a seat. We have much to discuss."

Josephine reluctantly took the offered seat, perching on the edge as if ready to spring into action at a moment's notice. Her gaze remained steady as Gibson took a slow drag from his cigar.

"I must say, your work has been quite...subpar," Gibson mused, his eyes glinting with a hint of amusement. "The *Tempest*'s first smuggling mission was quite the debacle, wouldn't you agree?"

Heat rose to Josephine's cheeks, embarrassment coursing through her. The Brinwald mission had been a colossal failure, one that had nearly cost them dearly.

"The crew has been...adaptable," Josephine replied carefully, her voice betraying none of the turmoil she felt. "We've learned from our mistakes."

Gibson's gaze narrowed, and Josephine could practically feel him probing for any sign of weakness. "Indeed," he murmured, taking another long drag from his cigar. "Well, I'm pleased to see that you're not shying away from our new business arrangement."

Josephine's jaw tightened, but she refused to rise to the bait. "The *Tempest* and her crew will only improve," she said, her tone clipped.

Gibson nodded, eyes on his cigar for a moment. "You know, Captain Prescott, I heard some interesting things from the eyes and ears I have in Marinport."

Jo's breath hitched. She was momentarily surprised to find

he had contacts there—but of course, he did. How else had the original job been arranged? Jo lifted her chin. "Really? Such as how the contact botched everything?"

Gibson chuckled. "Among other things." His gaze snapped to her, intense. "I heard there was a dragon. One that seemed to be on your *crew*."

Shock jolted through her. Suddenly, Jo's throat was dry, and she desperately wished for a drink. Gods, she was going to have to bluff her way out of this. "A dragon?" Jo asked, feigning confusion. "The *Tempest* is a former *dragoneering* vessel. Why would a dragon be aboard?" She paused, allowing incredulity to leak into her voice. "And furthermore, *how?* I'm well-versed in the sizes of dragons, and while one might sit aboard the deck, they'd make for a poor crew member." Jo finished with a laugh, deciding the best course of action was to make this a joke.

Gibson studied her, then nodded. "I agree. I believed it an outlandish rumor when I heard it." He shrugged, then took a puff of his cigar. "The idea of a dragon aboard an airship is... well, I suppose it *is* entertaining." He chuckled.

Jo wished she could join in his laughter, but she had seen the Jade Court and their airships. *Entertaining* wasn't the word she'd use. But she nodded silent agreement.

She cleared her throat. "So, is this all we have to discuss? To clarify this...strange rumor?"

Gibson waved a hand, dismissive. "No, no, the dragon rumor is not why I've called you here," he said, his lips curling into a thin smile. "It's time to discuss your next assignment. But I'm not sure you and your crew are up to it." He took a drag of his cigar before continuing, "Which is unfortunate, with how behind you are on the lease payments. I'm very much considering ending your lease. There are so few vessels with arcane engines. I have several buyers lined up already."

Josephine knew he was baiting her. "What is it? My crew

and I fought *dragons*. We can handle whatever you have for us." Never mind that she was at less than half of the crew the *Tempest* really needed.

Gibson smiled. "I like your spirit. I have another job in mind for you. One that could be...quite lucrative, if handled properly."

Josephine felt a knot of dread form in the pit of her stomach. "I'm listening," she said, bracing herself for what she was sure to be a trap. But what else could Jo do?

Gibson leaned back, savoring the moment. "I have a certain client," he began, "who has expressed a keen interest in...let's call it *higher learning*." He lifted his eyebrows. "And I have it on good authority you're searching for the Forgotten Library."

The color drained from Jo's face, and she fought to maintain her composure. Gibson knew more about her activities than she'd realized. Though she should have assumed that nothing was safe, considering his network of spies.

The silence between them grew heavy. Jo met Gibson's gaze unwaveringly, despite the riot of emotions within. She was about to cross a line, she just knew it. But what choice did she have? The *Tempest* was in jeopardy.

"So far, it seems more a thing of legend than truth," Jo said, keeping her tone neutral.

"But I think even legends exist because of a grain of truth," Gibson shot back, the words far too reasonable. She hated that it made sense. "I doubt an intelligent woman like you is off chasing shadows. Wouldn't you agree?"

Jo pursed her lips. "Yes."

Gibson smiled, reminding Jo of a cat cornering a mouse. "Then I'd like you to find this library. And then, once found, liberate as many books and relics as you can and return them to me." He made a sweeping gesture with one hand. "And then consider your debts...caught up."

Caught up? She bristled. "If you expect that much of me, the ship may as well be paid off! I should be clear!" As soon as the words left her lips, a sense of foreboding filled her chest. Gibson's face was unreadable, but she felt the dangerous shift in the air. She may have just signed her own death warrant with her insistence.

He regarded her with his icy gaze, silent for ten seconds. Twenty. Thirty. Far too long. Then, "Do you know what happens to those who demand things from me, Captain?" Gibson smiled, and it was anything but friendly.

"I'm not making demands," Jo said quickly. "But even you *must* admit that what you ask is...monumental. I could sell those items on the black market and net enough to pay off the ship tenfold."

That was another mistake. Gibson pursed his lips, glancing at a guard who stood in the shadowy corner of the room. "Jonah, I think it's time we show the Captain here what happens to those who try to cut me out of the loop."

Jonah straightened, then nodded. "Of course, Mr. Gibson."

Gibson smiled. "Cut off the good captain's pinky finger. You can let her pick which hand."

Jo's eyes widened, and she took a tentative step backward, clutching both hands under her armpits. The guard approached, pulling out a dagger. She had to think fast.

Just as the guard reached for her, the door burst open with a crash. Cailan charged in, cutlass raised, followed by a crowd of Gibson's other guards.

"Captain Jo!" he yelled, before launching himself at Jonah.

Cailan whirled and slashed, but was quickly surrounded by Gibson's men. After a few clashes of steel, he retreated to a corner, cutlass still held ready. Cailan breathed hard, bleeding from a few shallow cuts but otherwise unharmed.

Gibson watched with amusement. "My, my," he drawled,

his voice dripping with mockery, "is this the nephew I've heard about? He certainly knows how to make an entrance." Gibson's amusement faded, his eyes growing cold as he regarded Cailan. With a flick of his hand, he motioned for his guards to stand down. "The boy has provided enough entertainment for the day."

"I'm not a *boy*," Cailan growled. Despite being cornered, he didn't look ready to give in.

Gibson turned his piercing gaze to Jo. "Consider this a gift, Josephine. But gifts come with a price."

Jo's shoulders tensed, bracing herself.

"You have two months to either pay a substantial sum towards your debt or plunder this library and return the items to me," Gibson stated. "Fail to deliver, and I will seize your ship *and* your life as compensation. Do you understand?"

"Perfectly," Jo grated.

His words hung heavy in the air, an ominous ultimatum. A muscle in Jo's cheek ticked, but she held Gibson's ruthless stare. There was no bargaining with a man like him. All she could do was accept his ruthless terms, for now.

"Very good," the financier murmured. "Then I trust you'll be under way soon. You might want to stop at the port town called Alder. You know of it?"

Jo nodded. It was small and not one she and the *Tempest* had frequented, but she'd seen it on the charts. "Yes."

"Might be a worthwhile place to seek out information," Gibson suggested with a wink.

"We won't let you down," Jo murmured

"See that you don't." Gibson's words were clipped. "The buyer is quite eager. I hope you'll provide prompt service."

Outside, Jo strode quickly from the building, the confrontation with Gibson weighing heavily on her mind. With Cailan at her side like an irritated shadow, they made their way back toward the airship moorings.

"What was that about?" Cailan demanded once they were a reasonable distance from Gibson's headquarters. "He wants the *Tempest*? And he wants you *dead*?" His voice lowered to a growl.

Jo shook her head. She didn't want to think about that right now. "You could have been killed, Cailan. What were you thinking, barging in like that?"

Her stern tone made Cailan bristle. "I had a feeling you might be in over your head," he snapped. "And it looks like I was right. What was I supposed to do? Leave our captain to those goons? You'd come back short a finger."

Jo stopped and turned to face him. Her expression softened. Cailan was rash, but in some ways, he reminded her of Elazar. "Thank you," she said quietly. "But Gibson...he's not someone to trifle with."

Cailan's eyes glinted with defiance. "Yeah, I get that. But neither am I." His steps were heavy, as if his dragon form bore down with each footfall.

They continued walking. The bustling port faded into background noise as Jo's thoughts turned inward. How was she going to untangle this mess? It was going to be impossible to appease Gibson at this rate. Especially with only two months to locate a library that might be more myth than truth. At least this ultimatum aligned with her hunt for Elazar.

"What does that snake even want with you?" Cailan asked, breaking the silence. "How can he make those demands?"

Jo took a deep breath, keeping her gaze fixed ahead. "Gibson holds the title to the *Tempest*. I owe him a significant debt, and time is running out to repay it."

Cailan rubbed his chin as he processed the information. "So, that's what this is all about? The ship?"

Jo nodded, her voice cracking slightly. "Yes. And if I default on the loan, we lose her." And Jo would die.

A heavy silence fell between them. The only sounds were the distant cries of seagulls and the comforting clamor of the surrounding port. Cailan slowed as he pondered their predicament.

Finally, he stopped and turned to face Jo, his eyes blazing with determination. "Then we'll just have to make sure that doesn't happen. Sounds like we either need to come into a lot of money or make better headway on the library."

Jo met his gaze, taken aback by the fierceness in his expression. In that moment, her doubts began to recede. With her crew at her side, perhaps they could find a way through this after all.

"You're right," she said. "Gibson wants to back me into a corner, but we still have moves left to play." She placed a hand on Cailan's shoulder. "Thank you. Having you here...it reminds me I'm not alone in this fight."

Cailan looked away, embarrassed. "Yeah, well, what are airship dragons for?" he mumbled. But Jo saw his faint smile at her words.

With renewed resolve, they continued onward. The coming days would be difficult, but if anyone could outmaneuver Gibson, it was the crew of the *Tempest*. Jo squared her shoulders, her stride growing more purposeful. They would find a way.

"How far are we from Alder?" Jo asked as she strode onto the bridge, a mug of coffee in one hand. A week had passed since her meeting with Gibson, and time wasn't a luxury she could afford.

"Morning, Cap." Isaac, who had been pulling the night shift, eyed the coffee with outright jealousy, rubbing at his forehead. But he was due to sleep, and they both knew coffee was the last thing he needed at the moment. "And as for an answer to that...depends on the *Tempest*, at this point."

Jo took another sip of coffee, hoping it might add clarity to the coming conversation. "What do you mean by that? It always depends on the *Tempest*."

"Aye, but this is different." Isaac gestured to the pilot's seat, and then the navigation panel. "I'm not sure what's going on, but the *Tempest* isn't responding to my heading. Every time I try to steer her on course, she drifts back to her original trajectory."

Jo frowned, her gaze sweeping over the controls. "Have you checked the engines?"

"Gally's on it," Isaac assured her. "I wanted to look into all possible answers before disturbing you. But this isn't normal behavior for the *Tempest*."

Nodding, Jo moved to stand beside him, her eyes narrowing as she watched the airship stubbornly maintain her own course. Something was off, that much was clear. The *Tempest* was a well-oiled machine, responsive to the slightest touch of the helm. For her to defy the controls...

"Can I ask you to remain here for a few more minutes?" Jo asked, though she wished she could send Isaac to find his bed. "I want to see what Gally's found."

"I'll manage a little longer," he agreed with a yawn.

Jo hurried down to the engine room. As she walked, she brushed her fingers against the *Tempest's* bulkhead. Was it her imagination, or did the airship feel...different? Almost as if there was a vibration that hadn't been there before.

Their inability to keep to a course was worrisome. How else were they to reach Alder and find out information about the

Forgotten Library? They needed to diagnose the problem and then get back on course.

Josephine strode into the engine room, her gaze immediately landing on Galatea, the Theilian woman bent over the *Tempest*'s schematics.

"Gally," Jo called out. "Anything new?"

Galatea straightened. "I've been going over the ship's systems, but I can't find anything wrong."

Jo frowned. "Nothing?"

Galatea nodded, her clawed fingers tracing the intricate diagrams. "That's the strange part. Everything appears to be functioning properly. The engines, the core, the flaps—all in working order." She paused, her expression shadowed by a hint of uncertainty. "I'm still learning the nuances of the arcane systems, Captain. It's possible I'm overlooking something."

Josephine studied the Theilian for a moment, hearing the unspoken worry in her words. Galatea had been with the *Tempest* for years, ever since Jo had taken her in as a young, wary stowaway.

Jo placed a reassuring hand on the engineer's shoulder. "I trust your judgment." She gestured to the schematics. "If you can't find the problem, then it's not a mechanical one."

Galatea's posture relaxed slightly, some of the tension leaving her frame. "Thank you, Captain. I'll keep digging, but..." She hesitated. "There's something...off about the *Tempest*'s energy. I can't quite put my finger on it."

"Off, how?" Jo asked.

"I'm not sure." Galatea shook her head. "It's subtle, but I can sense a shift in the way the power flows through the ship. I worry that it's a symptom of weaning her from the dragon's blood fuel."

At that possibility, Jo pursed her lips. They both knew that they'd never use dragon blood as callously as they had previously. But what if Gally was right, and that was the source? The *Tempest* was designed to function with or without it—she just couldn't reach her top speed without the specialized fuel.

"It's not that," a new voice announced. Cailan appeared at the bottom of the stairs that led to engineering.

Josephine regarded Cailan with a measured gaze, her lips pressed into a thin line. "If it's not the fuel or a mechanical issue, then what is it, Cailan?"

Cailan's mouth quirked into the hint of a smirk. "You're not going to believe me," he said, shaking his head.

"Try me," Josephine replied evenly. "I've seen some pretty unbelievable things in my time."

Cailan studied her for a moment, as if weighing the wisdom of sharing his suspicion. Finally, he spoke. "I think the *Tempest* is alive. And I think she's searching for Elazar."

Josephine blinked, caught off guard by the sheer audacity of Cailan's claim. "Alive?" she echoed. "How is that even possible?"

Cailan shrugged, a faint smile playing on his lips. "Sprocket's alive, isn't she?" He hiked a thumb toward the cogwing, who had apparently decided to listen to the conversation. "You know as well as I do that Elazar's blood has been spilled on this deck more times than I can count. And mine, too." He tapped a finger against the bulkhead, as if emphasizing his point. "Blood is power. And we all know my blood alone is enough to give this airship some *oomph*. Maybe the *Tempest* has absorbed that power, that magic, and now she's..." He trailed off, his gaze drifting towards the glowing arcane engine, the airship's beating heart.

Josephine's mind raced, processing Cailan's words. It was true that Sprocket was no ordinary automaton, and Elazar's abilities as a Gearweaver were likely the source of the cogwing's sentience. Never in a thousand years would Josephine have considered that Elazar could bring an entire *airship* to life, though. Nausea rose as she recalled his blood seeping into the deck when he'd been harpooned as a dragon. She shook her head to banish the awful memory, the one that kept her up at night.

"So, you really think the *Tempest* is...what, sentient?" Josephine asked, her voice tinged with skepticism. "And that she's searching for Elazar?"

Cailan nodded, his expression earnest. "Yeah. Think about it—why else would the *Tempest* refuse to follow Isaac's heading?"

"Because mechanical issues happen, even to airships powered by dragon's blood," Jo said, though she wasn't sure why she was arguing. Maybe because the thought of the airship being alive was a frightening concept. Living things were often illogical, whereas mechanicals were not. They behaved in expected ways, even when they failed.

"Maybe for normal airships," Cailan agreed. "But at this point, we've flown *way* past normal and into the meridians of weirdness."

Josephine considered his words, her mind whirling with the implications. If Cailan was right, and the *Tempest* was indeed a living, sentient being, then everything they thought they knew about the airship would need to be reevaluated. And the idea that the ship could be actively searching for Elazar...

Josephine regarded Cailan with a thoughtful gaze, weighing his words. As outlandish as the notion seemed, she had to admit that the marshal's theory held some merit.

"All right, Cailan," Josephine said finally. "Let's say you're right, and the *Tempest* is searching for Elazar. Where exactly is she taking us?"

Cailan shrugged. "It's not as if I'm privy to the will of an airship. My guess is she's following some kind of...instinct. We know he was taken by the Jade Court. I'd bet good regals that's where the *Tempest* is headed."

Josephine nodded slowly, considering their options. They could continue trying to force the *Tempest* back on course, but that would likely be an exercise in futility.

"Then it seems we have a choice to make," Josephine mused. "We can fight the *Tempest*'s will, or we can work with her." She met Cailan's golden-brown gaze. "What do you think we should do?"

Cailan grinned. "I think we should let the *Tempest* lead for now. If she's really after Elazar, then that's what we want, right? We'll get to him faster that way."

Josephine couldn't argue with that logic. Finding Elazar had been her driving purpose since the moment he was taken. If the *Tempest* could guide them to him, it was an opportunity she couldn't pass up.

"We'll give it a shot," Josephine agreed, straightening her shoulders. She turned her gaze upwards, addressing the *Tempest* itself. "I don't know if you can understand me, old girl. But if you can lead us to Elazar, we'll follow wherever you take us."

A low hum reverberated through the ship in response, almost an affirmation. Working with a potentially sentient airship would take some getting used to.

"I'm going to the bridge," Josephine said decisively. "It seems I have a new navigator to work with."

She turned and strode from the engine room, Cailan on her heels. The future was unclear, but she felt a glimmer of hope. With the *Tempest* on their side, perhaps they stood a chance of succeeding after all.

8
The Path Ahead

Elazar

A fitful night's sleep gave way to the surprising sight of a bowl of cold porridge. Elazar hadn't expected Danelor to provide anything beyond the meager rations he'd offered the night before, but here it was, a gesture he couldn't quite understand. Elazar set the now-empty bowl and spoon aside, surveying his new surroundings. The space was roomier than his workshop on the *Talisman*.

Kneeling beside the cot, Elazar unbuckled the worn canvas bag that held his meager possessions. He carefully extracted a spare shirt and pair of trousers, running his fingers over the clean fabric. Elazar discarded the idea of changing into them so soon, returning them to the bag. Best to save the clothing as long as he could, since there were no assurances of replacements.

Beneath the clothing, he found the draconian book he had salvaged from the *Tempest*'s library. Elazar hesitated, then set the book atop the cot.

His hand paused over the broken pocket watch that lay at the bottom of the bag. Elazar studied the age-hazed face, not for the first time wondering why he'd been compelled to keep it. Like the book, it had been one of the few mementos from his parents. With a sigh, he returned the watch to the duffle, tucking it safely beneath the cot.

Settling onto the thin mattress, Elazar opened the book, its pages yellowed with age. He ran his fingers over the illustrations, his mind racing with questions about the Forgotten Library and his own role in unfolding events.

The sound of a bark echoed down the tunnel and into the cave. Elazar's head shot up in momentary alarm.

"A dog?" Elazar cocked his head, rising. He carefully closed the book and placed it on the cot. Cautiously, he approached the entrance to the cavern.

There were no doors to keep him inside, like on the *Talisman*. Elazar sucked in a breath, thinking. Was he free to roam? Did he dare?

He hated this feeling of uncertainty, of vulnerability. The fear of the unknown. Elazar had never been bold like the *Tempest*'s Dragoneers, but he'd never been a coward, either—no matter what his bullies had thought. But his time as Belen's indentured servant had robbed him of his former confidence.

"I can do this. What's the worst that could happen?" Elazar absently rubbed his right arm, just above one of the still-healing slashes delivered by Belen. A reminder of exactly *what* could happen.

The small arcane engine was warm against his chest, hanging from the golden chain. *Too bad that new armor won't work as a human.* His fingers drifted to it, stroking the fabric of the shirt concealing the engine. He had been a dragon once. Maybe he still was a dragon, even if he didn't wear the form. Elazar couldn't hide in this cave for the rest of his days.

Decision made, he stepped into the tunnel. Elazar paused when he heard the telltale click of claws against stone. He fought the impulse to retreat as a fresh wave of fear swept over him.

A fuzzy pale form rounded a corner. A canine, tail wagging. No, *not* a dog, Elazar corrected himself. An aralez. The creature gave a soft woof and approached, head cocked to one side.

Elazar stared at the aralez. He had a memory of this canine, though it was admittedly hazy. His traumatic transformations had affected his memory. "I know you," Elazar said, a memory itching to the surface of his mind. "At least, I think I do."

The workshop on the Dauntless, *Belen's flagship. Max sitting atop a crate as the door opened. A Vangara ushered Cailan inside, though he was a dragon, accompanied by a fluffy, winged dog.*

The memory was fleeting. Elazar shook it away, unable to recall much beyond that. The aralez turned in a tight circle and then bowed on his forelegs, peering up at Elazar with an almost beseeching look. Then he rose and bounded away a few steps, peering over his wings at Elazar.

"Follow you?" Elazar asked, suddenly nervous. "I don't know if it's safe." But even as he said the words, he felt a rising irritation with himself. He had to get past this fear he felt somehow. Swallowing, he followed the aralez.

The aralez loped ahead, his fluffy tail swishing as he led

Elazar down the dimly lit tunnel. Elazar followed cautiously, the underground chill seeping through his thin shirt.

After a few twists and turns, the tunnel opened into a broad cavern. In the center lay a large blue dragon.

Elazar's breath caught in his throat as he took in her slumbering form. Even at rest, she exuded an aura of power. But as his gaze traveled lower, he saw the ragged state of her wings. The membranes had been torn to ribbons, leaving her grounded. Reminiscent of the Jade Court dragons he'd helped, but different. As if someone had shredded her wings on purpose. A pang of sympathy tugged at his heart. He knew what it was like to be caged, deprived of the freedom to soar.

The aralez bounded over to the dragon, sniffing her flank before nudging her with his snout, letting out a soft woof.

The dragon stirred, her eyelids fluttering open to reveal too-pale irises. She blinked slowly, taking in the aralez before her gaze shifted to Elazar. A low rumble emanated from her throat, a warning that vibrated through the cavern.

The aralez barked in response, putting a huge paw on the dragon's much larger front claws. The canine's tail wagged back and forth, though not in a way that telegraphed joy. Something was off. The formerly cheerful aralez turned toward Elazar, then lifted his lips in a snarl—aimed at the blue dragon.

"Oh, peace, Vesper," the dragon said with a gusty sigh. "I'm sure our visitor means no harm."

Elazar frowned, certain that the aralez hadn't been snarling at *him*. He watched as Vesper danced away from the dragon, still presenting a curious mix of aggression and uncertainty. The aralez moved to sit nearby, eyes never leaving the dragon.

Elazar swallowed. "Hello? You're right, I won't hurt you."

"I know." With effort, the dragon moved into a sitting position. Her speech wasn't Island Common, but draconian. Elazar understood her, regardless. "It appears I have a visit from the Dragon Who Isn't himself."

Elazar rubbed his forehead. "I really hate that name. I don't understand it. You can just call me Elazar, please."

The azure dragon nodded. "And you may call me Chandra."

Chandra. Elazar's eyes widened. While his memories were hazy, he remembered that name. "You're Cailan's mentor. The Seer."

She inclined her head with a touch of sadness. "Yes. Though my gift has done little more than sow the seeds of sorrow." Chandra shook her head. "I often wonder if the cost is worth it, in the end."

Elazar frowned. "The cost of what?"

Chandra glanced away. "The cost to keep the world safe. To do so, I've had to cause great harm to those I care about." The aralez growled again, eliciting a soft sigh from Chandra once more. "*Really,* Vesper. All is well, for the moment."

Elazar glanced between Vesper and Chandra. "Why are you here? Why did Belen imprison you?"

"Many reasons," Chandra said, pain in her tone. "But mostly because she believes I cost her everything."

Elazar watched Chandra with growing uneasiness. She spoke of great harm and sorrow, and he couldn't help but wonder how he was connected to it. He didn't *want* to be connected to it. He was about to speak, but a new sound echoed down the tunnel: the shuffle of footsteps.

Elazar stiffened, his gaze snapping towards the entrance. A tall, broad-shouldered figure emerged from the shadows, and Elazar froze. It was Danelor. Was Elazar going to be in trouble for speaking with Chandra?

Chandra seemed entirely at ease. "Ah, Danelor. Good morning."

Danelor approached, moving slowly as if he were trying to conceal his limp. His gaze shifted from Chandra to Elazar. "What's going on here?"

"I was merely visiting with our new guest," Chandra said, her tone light, but Elazar detected a subtle undercurrent of wryness.

Elazar couldn't hold his tongue. "Am I allowed outside of my cavern, then?" he challenged, glaring at Danelor.

Danelor's expression remained impassive. "You are, for as long as it takes you to figure out where the Forgotten Library is."

Elazar blinked, taken aback by the man's matter-of-fact response. He had expected more resistance, more threats. That was the Jade Court way...wasn't it?

"And what if I can't find it?" Elazar asked, his voice colored with trepidation.

Danelor shrugged. "Then you'll remain here, I guess."

Chandra spoke up, her voice soothing. "There's no need to worry, Elazar. We'll help you. You're safe here, for now."

Elazar's gaze snapped to the azure dragon. "*Safe?*" he echoed. "How can I be safe when I'm a prisoner?"

Chandra met his gaze steadily. "You are *not* a prisoner here, Elazar. You are a guest, and you are free to explore this island as you see fit." Her pale eyes held a depth of understanding that caught Elazar off guard.

Danelor cleared his throat, drawing Elazar's attention back to him. "The Seer speaks the truth. You are not a prisoner, but a guest. However, you *do* need to focus your efforts on uncovering the location of the Forgotten Library. That is why you are here, after all."

A surge of renewed frustration swept through Elazar. "And what if I don't *want* to help the Jade Court anymore?"

Danelor's expression remained impassive. "Then you'll

remain here, regardless. Whether or not you help us is your choice."

AT FIRST, ELAZAR HAD BEEN HESITANT TO REVISIT Chandra's cavern. Partially because he still felt like too much of a prisoner, but also because he wasn't sure what to make of her. She was the Seer, the one who had told Belen of the Dragon Who Isn't.

About *him*.

And his life had turned upside down because of it.

He couldn't help the rush of resentment he felt. But on the third day, he sought her out again to stave off his loneliness. Danelor dropped food by regularly, but Elazar didn't want to talk to him. He didn't trust anyone who worked with the Jade Court.

Elazar ducked his head as he stepped into the cavern. Chandra lay curled in its middle, Vesper resting off to her right. To his surprise, Danelor sat nearby.

Elazar tensed, not wanting to intrude on their conversation, but Vesper's soft whine of recognition gave him away. The large aralez lifted his head, ears perked, and Chandra turned her gaze to Elazar.

"Ah, there you are," she said, her voice warm with welcome. "Come, join us. It's time we had a talk, the three of us."

Elazar hesitated, glancing uncertainly at Danelor, who remained silent, though he, too, was watching Elazar. Swallowing, Elazar approached and found a place to sit, keeping a respectful distance.

"I...I'm not sure I understand," he admitted. "Why am I included in this?" Elazar hadn't expected any sort of welcome, despite Danelor's insistence that he wasn't a prisoner.

Chandra regarded him steadily. "Because, Elazar, to understand the path ahead, you must have a map of the trail that led you here."

He pursed his lips. "I already have a pretty good idea about that." The words were more cutting than intended, but Elazar felt they were warranted.

Chandra sighed, her tattered wings shifting with the exhalation. "It is a long and difficult tale, Elazar. One that is forged of pain and heartbreak." She paused, her expression grave. "But you must understand—the future hangs in the balance, and we cannot afford to keep you in the dark any longer."

"The dark?" he repeated, gaze shifting to Danelor. The other man simply shrugged. "Are you sure this is something we should talk about in front of..." He winced, stalling out.

"Go on, say it," Danelor prodded, his tone almost amused. "I've been called many things in my life. Whatever you're about to say is probably one of the kinder names."

Elazar gritted his teeth. Not that he'd been around him much, but he couldn't figure Danelor out. "The enemy."

Chandra shook her head. "That's the first thing we must clear up. The two of you are more allies than enemies."

That seemed unlikely. Elazar crossed his arms. But...it was possible that whatever information Chandra had, it might help with his search for the Forgotten Library. After a moment, he rose and found a place to sit on Chandra's other side, closer to her. Vesper trotted over and plopped down beside him, dark eyes never leaving Elazar, ears pricked. Tentatively, Elazar reached out and scratched the aralez behind the ears and deep into his furry ruff. Vesper arched into it with a contented sigh.

"I don't know how we can be allies in this situation," Elazar said.

"That is part of my tale," Chandra explained. "You—and others—are bound by the threads of what I'm about to tell you.

Long ago, before she ascended to the title of Jade Empress, Belen was a dragon with a kind heart. And she was fiercely loyal to those she loved—a trait I've always found admirable, though admittedly it is now twisted."

Belen, *kind?* Elazar found that difficult to believe. "What changed?"

The azure dragon flexed one of her foreclaws. "That part of the story will come in time. But you both must know that when Belen first joined the Jade Court, she was full of joy and ideas for improving life there. For all the denizens, including the drakes who served the dragons."

Elazar frowned. He noticed that when Chandra spoke the word *drake*, Danelor stiffened. "Wait, hang on. What exactly *is* a drake?" Elazar had been called that before, and maybe he'd finally get some answers.

"*You're* a drake," Danelor said, unable to hide the surprise in his voice.

Elazar shook his head. "I don't know what that means, though." He gestured to himself. "As far as I know, for the first twenty-five years of my life, I was a human. I certainly looked like one."

Seeing his confusion, Chandra explained, "Drakes are a subspecies of dragon, like the Vangara. Generally smaller, with softer scales. Able to channel magic. Each can shift into a single other form."

"You *really* didn't know what you are?" Danelor's brows were raised, baffled.

"No," Elazar admitted. "I had no idea." So, he wasn't a dragon, not exactly. Did this mean Cailan was a drake, too? Probably. "I've heard none of this before."

Chandra nodded. "Yes, drakes are secretive. And from what I've seen, humans aren't aware of the difference."

Elazar had a thousand questions. If he was a drake, did

Chandra know who his parents were? Were his parents alive somewhere out there? And if so...why had they abandoned him? He tamped the questions down as the Seer continued.

"The drakes felt mistreated by the dragons. Eventually, they rebelled against the Jade Court. They allied themselves with humans, and there were heavy losses on both sides." She arched her neck, shaking her head. "Including Belen's mate."

Elazar's eyebrows shot up. He hadn't realized Belen was widowed. No wonder the green dragon had become bitter. Across from him, Danelor studied the floor as if it had suddenly become extremely interesting, his expression unreadable.

"But that was not the end," Chandra went on heavily. "A pair of drakes made it back to the island. The Jade Court dragons didn't understand why. It was only later they realized the drakes had used their magic to tamper with the dragonfruit trees."

Elazar frowned. How did one tamper with trees?

Chandra's expression was grim. "By the time the dragons figured it out, it was too late. The mature dragons' wings had already begun withering away to nothing."

Elazar's mouth fell open as the pieces dropped into place. This was how the dragons had lost their wings. But...Jadefire Island was a nesting island. There were more than mature dragons there. "And the young dragons? What happened to them?"

"*I'm* what happened to them," Danelor said.

Elazar blinked in surprise, trying to process what he meant. "I'm sorry, *what?*"

"I was a whelp. We grew sick. Some of us died." Danelor's lips drew into a taut line. "And those of us who didn't die *changed.*" He waved a hand to encompass his body.

Wait, what? Elazar shook his head. "You're a *dragon?*"

"No, I'm clearly *not,*" Danelor muttered with the same

stubbornness Elazar had once used to insist that he wasn't a dragon, either.

"It takes a very long time for whelps to grow and mature, and the tainted dragon fruit twisted the young in unexpected ways," Chandra explained. "The magic changed the whelps at their core, making them something other than dragons. *Chimeras.*"

"Can you shift?" Elazar asked, suddenly curious.

"No." The single word was as neutral as possible, but Elazar still detected a note of sourness in Danelor's voice.

Elazar understood that feeling. He nodded. "I can't, either. I mean, not on purpose." Not without almost dying. He wasn't about to admit that aloud.

Chandra offered them a fanged smile. "You see? The two of you are allies more than enemies, with more in common than you knew." But there was an edge of brittle pain in her voice, as if the memories had opened an old wound.

"I didn't know," Elazar murmured. He shot an apologetic look at Danelor.

"The Jade Empress does not like to speak of it," Chandra said. The azure dragon's tail twitched, restless. "You understand now why Belen struggles to trust you. Why she behaves as she does."

Elazar nodded slowly. "Because she sees me as an enemy who hurt her in the past."

It didn't matter that he *wasn't* the drake who had killed her mate, ruined her wings, or corrupted the whelps. Elazar had seen it often enough among dragon hunters. If a dragon killed a loved one, the survivors wanted *all* dragons to pay. It was seen as a sort of righteous vengeance, but at the core, it wasn't. And before he'd known the truth of himself, Elazar had felt the same.

"Yes." Chandra lowered her head until they were on a

level. "And now you have the power that comes with knowledge."

Elazar glanced at Danelor, a man who was supposed to be a dragon, sitting across from the Dragon Who Isn't. *Ironic.* "You told Cailan I'm not supposed to find the Forgotten Library." He paused. "So why tell me these things? If I'm such a threat, why not strike me down?" Beside him, Vesper whined, as if disliking the notion that his current ear-scratcher might die.

Chandra shifted, slowly moving from her sprawl into a proper sitting position. "I tell you, because the path of fate has changed. In this moment, we stand at a crossroads, and even I cannot tell which fork in the road leads to ruin."

Elazar rubbed the back of his neck with his free hand. "I'd settle for the road that gets me back to the people I care about."

The dragon laughed. "Wouldn't we all? But that's the hard part. And it's up to you to make the choice."

"What choice?" Elazar asked.

Chandra craned her head lower, squinting at him. *Oh.* She had vision problems, Elazar realized. "Will you find the Forgotten Library and try to mend the rifts of the past, or will you let it remain lost to potentially protect our world from something much worse?"

Elazar swallowed. "No pressure, huh?" Beside him, Vesper whimpered, nudging Elazar with his nose. Elazar glanced at Danelor, the man who had known from a young age what he was meant to be, but wasn't. Elazar thought of the dragons he had constructed wings for, considering the awful way their once proud wings had withered away. And then his mind turned to Belen, a dragon Chandra claimed had once been kind, her heart shattered and her love twisted by the death of her mate.

Each was a small thing, something that, in the grander scheme of the world, hardly mattered. Tiny tragedies in a greater tapestry. But to the ones affected, it mattered. It was their life, their entire world. The more Elazar thought about it, the more he saw the ripples these small traumas had created. How hate and mistrust festered and infected others. Hadn't he experienced it firsthand, during his imprisonment on the *Talisman*?

"I'm going to find the Forgotten Library," Elazar whispered. Not because Belen demanded it, but because it was the right thing to do.

Chandra smiled. "I knew you would."

DANELOR BECAME SOMETHING OF A TENTATIVE ALLY ONCE Elazar made his declaration. Every afternoon, Elazar found himself in Chandra's lair with Danelor as they went through the draconian book.

"I didn't know a book such as this existed outside of drake or dragon custody," Chandra murmured when Elazar first showed her the tome. "Where did it come from?"

Thoughtful, Elazar sought an answer beyond *it's been in my sea chest for years*. He racked his memory until he settled on something that he thought was the truth. "I think it was on the island where my aunt found me."

That caught Chandra's attention. "Tell me what you remember of this island."

Elazar chewed his lower lip. "I don't remember *anything*. Aunt Jo found me when I was a toddler. She thinks I was a year-and-a-half, two years old at most." He paused. "Why? Do you think I was born on the island where the Forgotten Library is?"

"No," Chandra said, voice soft. "I simply thought you might confirm a suspicion I had." Before Elazar could ask more, she gestured to the surrounding cavern. Stacks of books lined its perimeter. "Perhaps if we combine your book with these from the Vault of Fate, we'll uncover something."

Elazar watched as Danelor carefully flipped through a book from the Vault of Fate, his lips pursed in concentration. The chimera paused on a page, tracing a line of text with his finger.

Elazar turned to Chandra, his draconian book open in his lap. "This passage mentions a *Wellspring*," he said, tapping the page. "Do you know what that refers to?"

Chandra's pale eyes studied the text, her expression thoughtful. "It's an old term, one I'm not entirely familiar with." She shook her head slowly. "My apologies, Elazar, but I cannot say for certain what it means in this context."

Danelor rose from his seat, placing the book back on the stack. As he did so, his gaze fell upon Elazar's book, and his eyes widened.

"That illustration," he said, gesturing to the page Elazar was reading. "It looks a lot like your pocket watch."

Elazar frowned, glancing down at the image. Indeed, the intricate design on the page *did* bear a striking resemblance to the broken timepiece. "How do you know about my pocket watch?" he asked, annoyance creeping into his tone.

Danelor shrugged nonchalantly. "You had it out the other day. I couldn't help but notice."

Elazar couldn't recall leaving the watch out, but the illustration was an exact match. He turned to Chandra, holding up the book. "Do you know what this means?"

The azure dragon considered the image. "I'm afraid I don't recognize it," she admitted. "But it seems to be of some significance, given its inclusion in this text."

Elazar nodded, his mind racing. "I'll go get my watch." He rose from his seat. "Maybe there's a connection we're missing."

Moments later, he returned, the pocket watch in his hand.

Carefully, he compared the casing to the illustration, tracing the delicately engraved patterns with his fingertips. Danelor leaned in, his expression one of keen interest.

"You're right," Elazar murmured, "they're identical." He paused. "But this book is old. Far older than the pocket watch."

"I believe," Chandra said, squinting at the watch's silver case, "the book was exposed to the elements for a time." Her gaze settled on Elazar meaningfully. "It was kept from direct damage, but time still took a toll. I don't think this book is more than a century old."

Danelor gave an amused snort. "The book is still *old*."

"You think the pocket watch could predate the book?" Elazar asked, uncertain. He opened it, peering at the hazed clock face. "It's never worked."

"I don't know that it's actually a watch," Chandra mused. She tilted her head. "Drakes are clever. Some crafters would create items that looked like one thing, but were truly another."

"Really?" Personally, Elazar wasn't feeling very clever at the moment. Then he blinked, realizing he had done something similar when he'd enchanted his wing augments to retract into his golden chain. "Oh."

"If it's not a watch, then what is it?" Danelor frowned at the possibly-not-a-pocket watch in question.

"Perhaps the book will explain." Chandra gestured with a talon.

Elazar nodded and set to reading.

He pored over the pages of the draconian book, face scrunched in concentration. The language was archaic and difficult to parse, the words unfamiliar when he murmured them. Still, he pressed on, determined to uncover the secrets hidden within.

As he read, Chandra studied the book over his shoulder. When Elazar turned a page, the dragon's breath hitched.

"What?" Elazar asked, glancing back at her.

Chandra gestured to the open book. "The design on the watch's face matches that illustration. See? It seems to be a sigil, or a mark of some significance." She leaned closer, squinting at the page. "I'm not entirely certain, but I believe it may be connected to the Forgotten Library."

Elazar's heart raced. "The Forgotten Library? But how?"

"May I?" the Seer asked, tapping a talon against the book.

Elazar surrendered it without protest, glad that someone had finally found something potentially helpful. Chandra, squinting as if nearsighted, vacillated between the book and the pocket watch, turning it over to study it from every angle.

At last, Chandra made a satisfied rumble. "It took a bit for me to untangle some words, but this phrase here matches the writing on the bottom of the pocket watch." She turned it over to reveal an engraving that Elazar had never studied closely, assuming it to be a maker's mark. "If I understand correctly, it says something to the effect of *tap the heart of magic to find your way home.*"

Elazar frowned. "What does that even mean?" *Home.* The *Tempest* was home. His heart squeezed at the memory. That couldn't be what this meant.

Chandra gestured to the stack of books from the Vault of Fate. "Some books mention storms could blow a traveler off course. Drake, dragon, human, or mystic...we're all the same. I suspect this device could be used to navigate."

"But it's a—" Elazar cut himself off. "Right. Might not be what it looks like." He cocked his head. "So, it's like a homing beacon or a compass? How do I make it work?"

"Do you have magic?" Chandra asked, her question laden with curiosity.

Elazar glanced between Danelor and Chandra. They both

knew he was a drake, which meant he had magic. Slowly, he nodded. "Yes."

The dragon smiled. "Then do as the engraving suggests. Hold the watch in your hand and tap your magic. Try to apply it to the device."

Elazar held the worn pocket watch in his palm. He focused, drawing on the familiar sensation of his Gearweaving magic—the ability to blend engineering and arcane energies. But as he tapped into that well of power, nothing happened. The watch remained stubbornly inert.

Disappointed, Elazar looked up at Chandra. "It's not working. I don't understand."

The azure dragon regarded him calmly. "Don't be discouraged. The magic of this device may simply require a more delicate touch." She gestured to the book. "The text suggests the *heart of magic* must be found. Perhaps the solution is not as straightforward as we had hoped."

Elazar nodded, turning the watch over in his hands. The engraved words stared back at him, tantalizing in their mystery. "So, what now? I can't just sit here while the Jade Empress demands I find the Forgotten Library."

Chandra let out a soft rumble. "Be patient, Elazar. The answers you seek will reveal themselves in time. For now, focus on understanding the magic within you. It may be the key to unlocking the watch's secrets."

Vesper padded over, nuzzling against Elazar's leg. The aralez whined softly, as if sensing his frustration.

Elazar reached down to scratch behind Vesper's ears, drawing comfort from the gesture. "I just want to find this library. And then I want to go home."

9

UNEXPECTED REUNION

Josephine

Josephine sat in the pilot's seat, her hands resting lightly on the *Tempest*'s controls, more out of habit than anything else. The airship had long since taken to dismissing any attempts she or Isaac made to pilot her. Never had Jo imagined the vessel would turn into a headstrong mechanical, but here she was.

"I certainly hope you know what you're doing," Josephine murmured to the airship, running a hand along the smooth contour of the instrument panel.

It was late, with the stars bright overhead. Gretchen, she knew, would be in their bed, fast asleep. Weariness tugged at

Jo, but with the *Tempest*'s new nature, they couldn't moor the ship to allow more of the skeleton crew to rest at the same time.

She rubbed at her eyes, failing to stifle a yawn. By the winds, this was exhausting. Josephine wished she could trust the airship, but that just seemed...outlandish. She was still coming to terms with the *Tempest* having sapience and its desire to seek out Elazar.

Josephine's eyes grew heavy as the gentle hum of the *Tempest*'s engines lulled her into a light doze. She jolted awake, mentally chiding herself for letting her guard down.

The *Tempest* had slowed considerably, its progress almost cautious. Josephine frowned, peering out the bridge windows as the first rays of dawn painted the horizon in hues of orange and pink.

Something had captured the airship's attention. Jo rose from the pilot's seat and made her way to the deck, the wooden planks creaking beneath her boots. The *Tempest* had oriented herself towards a rugged, volcanic-looking island in the distance, its rocky cliffs rising sharply from the dark sea.

Josephine squinted against the growing light. There was something about this place that drew the *Tempest*, a strange sense of urgency emanating from the sentient airship. Jo took a steadying breath, her gaze sweeping across the landscape. But she saw nothing unusual, so retreated to the bridge.

"What are you sensing, old girl?" She rested a hand against the *Tempest*'s controls. "Is Elazar out there?"

Josephine's thoughts were interrupted by a sudden commotion. Sprocket swooped into the bridge, squawking. She flapped around as if malfunctioning, knocking over a stack of charts, and sent Jo's mug of cold tea clattering to the floor.

"Sprocket!" Josephine snapped, stepping forward to grab the errant bird before she could get into more trouble. "What in the name of the four winds are you doing?"

Sprocket darted just out of reach, her mechanical eyes gleaming. She let out a series of rapid clicks and whistles, the sounds urgent.

Jo sighed in exasperation, waving her hands to shoo the bird away. "Go on, get out of here. You're causing a mess."

Ignoring her, Sprocket fluttered around the bridge once more before zipping out the door. Josephine watched through the bridge's windows in disbelief as the cogwing headed straight for the distant volcanic island.

"Blast it," she muttered under her breath. Sprocket could be a nuisance at times, but the cogwing was one of the few things she had left of Elazar. Jo had been glad Max and Cailan had taken pains to repair the automaton. And now, they might lose her.

Cailan emerged from belowdecks, his blond hair tousled from sleep but his eyes alert. "I'll go after her," he announced, stifling a yawn. "The flying tin can will take me seriously. Probably."

"Cailan—" Jo started to protest, but he had already shifted into his dragon form with graceful ease. He glanced down at her, as if daring for an argument. And really, she didn't want to argue. She wanted Sprocket back. "Be careful."

He chuckled, the sound a low rumble. "I'm looking forward to a good coffee after this." Cailan took to the air with powerful beats of his wings, following Sprocket through the sky. Jo watched him go, worry and relief warring within her.

The volcanic island loomed ahead. Waiting.

Chandra

CHANDRA'S SLEEP WAS RESTLESS, PLAGUED BY WORRIES she couldn't quite put her talon on. A strange darkness loomed in the corners of her mind, a wrongness that clung to her like oil. Something that could not be easily shed.

With a sigh, she rose into a sitting position. She didn't need more rest—she slept too much these days. The bright spots in her day were the visits from Danelor and Elazar.

Nearby, Vesper stirred, his huge white head lifting. He gave a soft, inquiring woof, rising to his feet. The aralez was still cooler toward Chandra than she liked, but he remained by her side. Now, he stared at the entrance.

"Is something there?" she murmured. But Vesper had shifted his focus back to her with an intensity that was almost eerie.

And then the vision took her, a prickling sensation crawling down Chandra's spine.

At first, it seemed like an innocent scene—the facade of a magnificent building, one she innately knew had been constructed by magic.

But something was wrong. Terribly, horribly *wrong*.

The building's facade fractured, a strangely luminous darkness gleaming through the cracks. Chandra watched, transfixed, as the exterior crumbled, shards of stone raining down like jagged tears. And beneath the rubble, something stirred—a dark presence that made the dragon's heart pound in dread.

Yes, this is what will be. What must be.

Chandra tried to look away, to will the vision to stop, but it was as if an unseen force held her gaze captive. The darkness grew, tendrils of shadow lashing out and consuming everything in its path. The Forgotten Library—for that was what Chandra was certain she saw—was devoured, reduced to nothing.

A shudder ran through Chandra's massive frame, and she let out a low, rumbling growl of alarm. This was no mere vision of destruction—it was a harbinger of something far more sinister. Something she had never encountered, even in her darkest premonitions.

"I can't allow that," she whispered. Vesper woofed agreement, the first time he'd shown genuine support for her in days. Chandra glanced at him, surprised.

Then, something else clamped down over Chandra. No, she had been wrong. The vision...that was what *must* be. It was the Seer's job to ensure it came to pass. If she didn't, the world would be in terrible danger.

Chandra shook her head, trying to win free of the confusion. Her mind swam with the possibilities, locking her into a momentary state where she didn't know which way to go. The Forgotten Library...it needed to remain hidden. She couldn't allow—

No, the Library had to see the light of day once more. Had to become a part of the world.

Chandra sucked in a steadying breath. Her mind reeled, grappling with the growing horror as realization struck her.

But before she could contemplate her newfound knowledge, a new vision gripped her. This one was more immediate. She saw the outline of a familiar form—Cailan, soaring over the rugged landscape of the volcanic island.

Chandra's pale eyes opened, still clouded with the remnants of the vision. She glanced at Vesper, who stood alert, his ears pricked and tail wagging in anticipation.

"Cailan," she whispered, her voice barely audible. "I saw Cailan."

Vesper responded with an excited bark, which echoed through the cavern. His wings fluffed out, and he bounced on his paws, ready for action.

"Calm yourself, Vesper," Chandra murmured, though she

couldn't suppress a small smile at his enthusiasm. "Yes, Cailan is coming."

Vesper's barking grew louder and more insistent. Chandra knew he was as eager as she was to see the opal dragon again. The aralez's noise soon roused Danelor from his nearby quarters.

Danelor appeared at the entrance to the cavern, his figure silhouetted against the dim light. He rubbed his eyes, his movements careful. "What's going on? Is everything alright?"

Chandra turned her gaze toward him, her expression serene despite the turmoil within. "Prepare for a visitor."

Danelor's brow knit in confusion. "A visitor? Who—?"

"There is no time," Chandra interjected gently but firmly. "He is almost here. Then, you will see." With a groan, she rose. "Let's go meet him."

"It would at least be helpful to know what I'm walking into," Danelor commented as they made their way down the tunnel.

"Our visitor is a drake," Chandra explained, continuing onward.

"Drake?" Danelor tensed, but walked alongside her as quickly as he could. He had a pair of daggers sheathed at his sides, and Chandra knew he was proficient with them. He had to be, to have survived this long. For now, those daggers were as close as the chimeras came to talons of their own.

"Yes," Chandra confirmed, blinking as they exited the cave and into the brightness of the breaking dawn.

Cailan

"Get back here before I use your tail feathers to pick my teeth!" Cailan called after the fleeing cogwing as he shot after her.

The wind buffeted his wings and chest, a welcoming embrace. As much as he liked his work on the *Tempest*, it required his human form more often than not. There was freedom in his primary form, a wild ferocity that Cailan relished.

Cailan pushed himself harder, his wings slicing through the crisp morning air. The stubborn little mechanical avian was *fast* when she wanted to be. Below him, the vast expanse of the ocean shimmered under the light of a rising sun. The tropical hues of dawn painted the sky in a riot of colors—deep oranges, soft pinks, and a hint of violet that bled into the lingering night.

Sprocket darted ahead, her mechanical feathers catching the sunlight and scattering it like tiny prisms. Her course was set, headed towards the volcanic island that now loomed ever closer.

The island grew closer with every wingbeat. Lush greenery covered its lower slopes, gradually giving way to barren rock and inactive vents as altitude increased. Then he glimpsed a familiar rocky outcropping, one that had once been used to moor small airships.

He knew this island.

This was the island where Belen had imprisoned Chandra.

The island where Belen had *killed* Chandra.

He trembled with growing anger as the realization swept over him. Cailan's muscles tensed, claws curling into incarnations of fury, tail lashing the air.

Ahead, Sprocket veered lower, skimming just above the treetops before diving toward the black sand beach at the base of the dormant volcano. Cailan's attention snapped back to Sprocket, and he followed her descent without hesitation.

The cogwing landed on a large rock, the tide playing against its base. Sprocket preened her metal feathers and gave Cailan a knowing look as he landed nearby, his wings sending up a spray of sand.

"Do you know what this place is?" Cailan demanded of the automaton, unable to hide the hot fury in his voice. The memory of Chandra's sacrifice was still seared into his mind. The image of her clashing with Belen in a desperate and doomed battle haunted him.

Sprocket had the audacity to just *look* at him, head tilted at a coy angle.

Cailan stared back at the cogwing, hating the unwelcome flood of emotions. If it wouldn't require more repair, he'd like to whack the flying annoyance with his tail, right into the sea.

He sucked in a breath. Had to get himself under control. Cailan had found Sprocket, so that much was done. They could fly back to the *Tempest* and put this awful island behind them.

"Come on, let's get back," Cailan grumbled to Sprocket, opening his wings.

Sprocket stared at something over Cailan's shoulder. Then he caught the crunch of boots against stone and sand. The opal dragon whirled, his entire body tensing. He was prepared to take on whatever threat the Jade Court had left behind.

A man hobbled out of the mouth of a cave that opened onto the beach. He had dark hair that held a glint of purple, no doubt a trick of the morning sun.

"Seems the Jade Court's standard for guards has gone downhill," Cailan said, loud enough that he knew the man heard.

Then, a voice he'd never thought he'd hear again called out. "Cailan!"

There, just behind the strange man and framed by the dark

opening, stood Chandra, her eyes narrowed against the too-bright morning sun.

"Chandra?" Cailan breathed. All the fight left him as he stared at the dragon he had mourned. Surely, this was some cruel illusion, a figment of his imagination. Cailan's mind reeled. The battle between his mentor and Belen had been to the death—and only Belen had emerged. Chandra was dead, wasn't she? And yet, here she stood, alive and whole.

"Cailan," Chandra repeated, her voice tinged with wonder. She took a tentative step forward, Vesper at her side. The aralez wagged his tail and barked a single, ringing woof.

Cailan was transfixed, unable to move, to speak. He could only stare, drinking in the sight of his mentor, the dragon who had raised him. A thousand questions swirled in his mind, but they all paled in comparison to the overwhelming relief that flooded him.

"It's really you," Chandra murmured.

Cailan opened his mouth, but no words came. He felt as if the world had shifted beneath his feet, leaving him unbalanced and adrift. Chandra was alive, against all odds, and he couldn't fathom how or why.

"I...you..." Cailan sputtered at last, shaking his head. His gaze swung from Chandra to the human. "I thought Belen *killed* you!"

Chandra laughed. "As did I. But it seems fate had other plans." At her side, the canine whined. Was it Cailan's imagination, or did the aralez seem...uneasy?

Cailan swallowed, his pulse thundering so hard that he couldn't think. He had come here for a reason, and that had long since derailed. But his mind was so scattered that he couldn't pull himself back to the task at hand.

The dark-haired man stepped closer to Chandra, a pair of daggers sheathed at his sides. Cailan snarled a warning.

"Peace, Cailan," Chandra chided, then turned to the man. "Yes, Danelor?"

The man, Danelor, frowned at Cailan, then pointed into the distance. "There's a dragoneering vessel. It's not safe out here."

Dragoneering vessel. Oh, right. Cailan glanced over his shoulder to verify that the one the man pointed out was the *Tempest,* and not another airship that had come onto the scene. "It looks like a dragoneering ship, but it's not really," Cailan said with a wave of a claw. And now he remembered why he had come. He twisted to eye the pesky cogwing. Sprocket shrieked and leaped into the air as Cailan spoke. "I'm here for—"

"Me. You're here for me." Elazar stood in the cave mouth, his hair lit a fiery red-gold by the early morning sun.

The Dragon Who Isn't, in human form.

Josephine

Everything was chaos, and Jo didn't care.

As soon as she'd sighted Elazar with the enchanted spyglass and yelled as much, the *Tempest* had powered up and soared toward the island on her own. From there, it had only been a matter of disembarking.

Josephine pulled Elazar into a hug so fierce, she thought she might never let him go. Drawing back a little, Josephine cupped Elazar's chin, searching his face. There was relief there, but also lingering fear and uncertainty. Josephine's expression softened, and she brushed a stray lock of hair from his forehead. It had grown longer in his time away from human civilization.

"I'm so glad you're safe." She sighed.

"But I don't know if *you're* safe now," Elazar said, his voice almost ragged.

She huffed out a breath, memories of what had led to their separation rearing up. "Don't you ever *dare* do that again," Jo whispered, unable to hide her feelings on the matter. "Flying off like that? Leaving us behind to worry?"

He was a few inches taller than she, but despite that, he flinched like a chastened child. "It was the only way I could think of to..." Elazar's gaze swept from Josephine up to the *Tempest*. "I thought it would work. And then, when it didn't, I bargained the only thing I knew would keep you and the *Tempest* safe."

Himself. Josephine shook her head. In what world did he think that was a reasonable trade? Did he *not* understand that she would fight a thousand dragons for his sake? Tears stung her eyes, but she didn't let them fall.

"I stand by what I said. Don't you *ever* do that again." Josephine gave him a stern look. "Come with us. We'll fly away from here."

Elazar managed a small half-smile. Then he pulled back, freeing himself from her embrace. "I can't. Not yet, anyway. I have to find the Forgotten Library. I made a promise."

Josephine couldn't fathom why Elazar wouldn't simply return with them. The *Tempest* was his home, his family—how could he possibly think of staying behind? She searched his face, trying to understand, but his expression had shifted, the brief relief and joy now clouded by something else.

"Why?" she pressed. "What's so important about this Forgotten Library that you'd risk staying here?" Jo gestured to the volcanic island surrounding them. "It's not safe. Come back with us, Elazar. That's where you belong."

Elazar's gaze dropped, and for a moment, Josephine saw a

glimpse of the boy she'd raised—uncertain, afraid. But then he straightened his shoulders, meeting her eyes with a newfound resolve.

"It's a long story," he whispered. "But I promise, I'll tell you everything soon." His eyes flicked to the man standing beside the blue dragon. "Danelor, will there be any trouble with them staying here for a while?"

Danelor's expression brightened at the question. "No trouble at all. As long as everyone keeps the peace, you're more than welcome."

The Jade Court man was...not what she expected. Regardless, Josephine's jaw tightened, her protective instincts warring with her desire to respect Elazar's choices. She wanted to drag him back to the *Tempest*, to safety, but she knew that would only push him further away. With a reluctant sigh, she nodded. "All right," she conceded. "We'll stay. But the moment things go south, we're leaving. Understood?"

Elazar's expression eased, and he reached out to briefly squeeze her arm. "Understood. Thank you, Aunt Jo."

Josephine watched as he turned and headed back towards the blue dragon and the man called Danelor, her heart heavy. She couldn't shake the feeling that something was terribly wrong, that Elazar was in more danger than he was letting on. Possibly more danger than even he knew. But for now, she would have to trust that he knew what he was doing.

10

FAMILY FOUND

Elazar

The *Tempest*'s arrival caused a whirlwind of confusion on the island. The first hour, once Aunt Jo had released Elazar from her embrace, had been more tense than he'd liked. It mostly involved Cailan yelling, Aunt Jo making demands, and Chandra and Gretchen trying to talk both of them down while simultaneously not starting an incident with the Jade Court. A hint of amusement played on Danelor's face the entire time. Maybe he preferred bickering humans to bickering dragons.

Once everyone was mostly calm, they moved inside to Chandra's lair, which had the most room. Moving inside only further riled Cailan, which confused Elazar until much later, when Gretchen explained how Cailan had almost died in that very cave.

"I have to find the Forgotten Library," Elazar said, not for the first time. Mostly because people kept talking over one another—over *him*—and he had fallen into a loop of repeating himself.

"No, you really *don't*," Cailan snapped, turning toward Chandra. He had remained in his dragon form, and judging by the constant twitch of his tail, he was annoyed. "Tell him."

The blue dragon sighed. "The ripples of fate have changed since we last spoke, Cailan."

The opal dragon wasn't going to let his mentor's words sway him. He slammed his foreclaws against the stone floor. "We can't allow the Jade Empress to find the Library or..." Cailan faltered, clearly trying to hide whatever emotion he was feeling and utterly failing. "Everything we've suffered has been for *nothing!*"

Chandra gave him a sad smile. "Never make the mistake of believing that your past has done nothing to create who you are today."

"That's not what I mean, and you know it," Cailan shot back, shaking his head. He scanned the cave, searching for allies. Finding none, he stormed out, wings clamped tightly against his sides.

Elazar watched Cailan's retreating form with a pang of guilt. He understood the opal dragon's anger and pain, but the path forward was not as clear-cut as Cailan believed.

"Elazar," Aunt Jo said, placing a hand on his shoulder. Her voice was gentle, but he could hear the underlying concern. "What's going on? Why do you feel you must find this library?"

Elazar took a deep breath, gathering his thoughts. "The Jade Court has suffered at the hands...er, claws of the drakes," he began, his tone somber. "Years ago, a group of drakes rebelled against the Jade Court dragons, and in the conflict, the mature dragons lost their ability to fly." He paused, his eyes meeting Aunt Jo's. "And they lost more than that. The young dragons were afflicted, too. The Jade Empress is desperate to restore her court. She believes the Forgotten Library may hold the answers." Elazar glanced toward Danelor, who gave a small nod of confirmation.

Josephine's mouth was set in a grim line as she listened.

"I…I made a deal with Belen." Elazar's voice wavered. "If I help her find the Forgotten Library, she'll leave you and the *Tempest* alone."

Josephine's expression shifted, her eyes narrowing. "Yes, your siren friend told us as much. That was a bargain you never should have struck."

Elazar flinched at the hurt in her tone. "I had to, Aunt Jo. I couldn't let her come after you. Not after everything you've done for me."

"You've put yourself in danger. And for what? To protect us?" Josephine ran a hand through her hair, the gesture uncharacteristically frazzled. "Dammit, Elazar. We're your family. We could have figured something out together."

Elazar opened his mouth to respond, but the words caught in his throat. He hated seeing the anguish on his aunt's face, knowing he caused it. All he'd wanted was to keep his loved ones safe.

"What's done is done." Gretchen cut into the conversation as she often did. She swept an arm around her partner. "And you already knew all this, even if you didn't wish to believe it."

Elazar studied his aunt and realized Gretchen was right. But Aunt Jo hadn't wanted to believe it. And then, with a pang, Elazar realized why: dragons had already taken family members from her. He'd never thought of it from that angle, but by the same token, Elazar wouldn't have changed anything. There had been no other way.

"Elazar is right, you know." Elazar turned to see Danelor striding into the cavern, attempting to mask his limp. "The only way for him to leave this island is if he seeks the Forgotten Library," Danelor continued, his tone firm. "The Jade Empress will never let him go otherwise, not now that she knows what he is."

Josephine huffed out an unhappy breath, but to Elazar's surprise, she didn't argue. Instead, she let out a weary sigh and nodded.

"I was afraid of that," she admitted. "The *Tempest* and her crew will assist you. I won't send you off to face this alone." Elazar opened his mouth, ready to protest, but Aunt Jo raised a hand, silencing him. "Don't even think about it. If you think you're searching for this Forgotten Library without us, you've got another thing coming."

Despite the gravity of the situation, Elazar felt the corners of his mouth twitch upward in a small smile. Of course, Aunt Jo wouldn't let him go off on some perilous quest without her. That was simply not how things worked on the *Tempest*. She pulled Elazar into another fierce embrace.

Elazar returned the hug, feeling the tension in his shoulders ease. As they parted, Elazar met Danelor's inscrutable gaze. "Then let's get started."

Maxine

MAX LONGED TO SPEAK TO ELAZAR ALONE, BUT THAT didn't seem to be on the cards—at least, not anytime soon.

Her first order of business, though, had been to go after Cailan before he did something stupid. The mercurial opal had gone back out to the volcanic beach, staring out at the lapping tide as if it was the source of his frustration.

"Want to talk about it?" Max asked, approaching from the side where he could see her.

Cailan's shoulders hunched, the tip of his tail twitching. "No."

Max sighed. She stepped closer, resting a hand on the warm scales just below where his wings met shoulder. "It's okay to feel hurt, you know. You thought she was dead. And now you feel like there was no point to any of what you've gone through."

"Because there *wasn't*," he growled, though Cailan didn't edge away from her. "If we just...find the Forgotten Library like Belen wants, then what was any of this for? All those aspirants who died on the Vault of Fate? Everything we've been through?"

Max was momentarily surprised that Cailan was thinking beyond himself. He often seemed selfish, and it was difficult to reconcile that with him in this moment.

But she didn't have an answer. Max shook her head. "People—and I'm including dragons here—can change. Change their minds on things. Circumstances force reconsideration." She gave him what she hoped was a reassuring pat. "You should understand that. You went from hating Elazar to liking him."

Cailan snorted. "You severely overestimate how I feel about that copper dragon."

Liar. Max smiled. "Okay, fine. But focus on the fact that Chandra is *alive*." She peered up at him. "Isn't that worth something?"

Reluctantly, Cailan tilted his head to meet her gaze. "Well, yeah."

"So, isn't that worth being *happy* about?" Max prodded.

"I can be happy and pissed off at the same time." Cailan snorted. "It's one of my many talents."

Max laughed. "And your charms." Then she sobered. "But come on. How do you think Chandra feels with you stomping out like that?"

Maxine watched as Cailan's expression shifted, the hardness in his gaze softening. She knew she had struck a chord.

"You're probably right," he admitted gruffly. "Chandra's been through enough without me making it worse."

Maxine smiled, giving his wing a gentle nudge. "Then let's go back and see her. I'm sure she'll be happy to have you."

Cailan hesitated, his eyes darting back towards the *Tempest*, the airship settled on the waters nearby. "I don't know, Max. I've got a bad feeling about this."

"Hey." Maxine stepped in front of him, placing a hand on his chest. "Chandra's alive, Elazar's safe—for now, at least. And we're all here together. That's what matters, right?"

Cailan's golden gaze met hers, and Maxine saw the conflict warring within him. Finally, he sighed, his shoulders slumping in resignation. "All right, fine. Let's go."

Maxine grinned, heading towards the cave entrance. Cailan followed, his talons ticking against the dark rock.

The air was thick with tension as they approached the cavern where Chandra and the others were waiting. Maxine felt Cailan's agitation, his muscles coiled like a spring, ready to react at the slightest provocation.

As they entered the chamber, Chandra turned to face them. For a moment, the world seemed to hold its breath. Then Chandra inclined her head, a small, understanding smile playing at the corners of her mouth. "Cailan. I'm glad you've returned."

Cailan shifted, his claws flexing, but the edge of hostility in his posture relaxed. "Chandra," he acknowledged with a rumble. "I, uh..." He cleared his throat, glancing away. "I'm sorry. For earlier."

Chandra dipped her head in acceptance. "There is no need for apologies. I know this has been a difficult time for you. To be reunited with both your mentor and your brother at the same moment can take a toll."

Wait, what? Beside her, Cailan went still, as if he, too, were replaying those last words. *Brother?* Max's brow furrowed. What did she mean by...?

Oh *gods.* Now, so much made sense. Why Cailan and Elazar antagonized each other. Some inborn instinct, latent and waiting for the other. Max had experienced it often enough with her own siblings.

"What in the winds do you mean?" Cailan snapped, either not making the connection or simply rejecting it.

Elazar wet his lips nervously. He glanced around, as if Chandra might mean someone else. Danelor, clearly wanting no part of this, merely shook his head and crossed his arms.

"*Brothers?*" Captain Jo repeated, her gaze sweeping from Elazar (who was very much human) to Cailan (who was still very much dragon). "But when I found Elazar, he was alone!"

Chandra nodded. "Because I had already taken Cailan's egg. I couldn't carry both, nor was I ever meant to. You were *always* destined to find Elazar."

Max watched many emotions cross Elazar's face at this: utter confusion, sadness, relief, and short-lived anger. Max knew her friend, knew in her heart that this was too much for him right now. Gods, and she didn't even know what had happened to him since she'd seen him fly away with the Jade Empress on his tail!

"I...I need time to think," Elazar said, the words a rush as he beat a hasty retreat.

"Elazar!" Captain Josephine called after him.

Gretchen caught her arm before she could chase him down. "Give him a little time, love. He's not flying off again. Elazar has been reunited with people he loves under hard conditions and just received information he never expected."

"You need to work on your timing, dragon," Captain Prescott said to Chandra.

To her credit, the Seer only chuckled. "There was no other time for this."

Cailan seemed to have made a small recovery. He glanced from Captain Jo to Chandra. "After all this time, you *finally* throw me one of the scraps I've been asking for. Will you tell me what I am now, too?"

"We know what you are," Danelor said before Chandra could. "You're a drake. And like your brother, you have a legacy of harm against the Jade Court."

Unlike Elazar, there was no sympathy in Cailan's golden-brown eyes. He met Danelor's gaze, unflinching, and said, "Good. It's only fitting with the harm the Jade Court has done to me."

Max sighed. So much for her hard work improving Cailan's mood.

11

DRAKE MAGIC

Elazar

Brother.

Elazar stared at the dark cave floor, in the moment feeling as if it were the only safe place where he could turn and not feel utterly overwhelmed.

A distant part of him felt a strange satisfaction at the knowledge he had a brother. That he had blood kin. Ever since the revelation that he wasn't human, Elazar had felt adrift, despite knowing that Aunt Jo counted him as family, no matter what.

He didn't know how long he sat there brooding, but a short time later, he heard the sound of boots on stone.

"I want to be alone," Elazar called.

"Yeah, well, since when have I ever listened to you?" Cailan said, stalking into the cave, now in his human form. "I'm not about to start now."

There was something annoyingly comforting in Cailan's snark. Elazar studied him. "Did you know?"

"Of course not." Cailan moved to sit on Elazar's cot, clearly deciding to claim the most comfortable part of the cave. "If I'd known, I would have needled you about that, too."

That was certainly true. Elazar pulled the pocket watch out, turning it over in his hands as he thought. "Do you think it's true?"

"I don't think it's information Chandra would drop like that if it weren't. And it's Chandra, so of *course* it's true." Cailan sounded reluctant to admit it. "I'd rather have found out in a different manner."

Elazar nodded. The Seer had likely mentioned it since they hadn't figured it out on their own.

"But on the other claw," Cailan said, giving Elazar an appraising look, "turns out you were right all along. You're not a dragon."

Elazar shrugged. "We're drakes. From what I've learned, they're still a sort of dragon." He glanced at Cailan. "And I guess that was news to you, too. What do you think?"

Cailan snorted. "I think I'm still a dragon. Once a dragon, always a dragon." Though something in his tone told Elazar that Cailan wasn't quite happy with dragons right now, either.

"I'm beginning to understand why Cailan could so nonchalantly throw you overboard from the *Tempest*," Max commented, striding in to join them. She paused, glancing between them. "Sorry. Hope you don't mind me coming in. I decided to keep an eye on that one." The Stormcaller pointed at Cailan.

To the contrary, relief washed over Elazar at the sight of

her. "No, glad to have you. Now it's almost like old times, except I'm not big and scaly."

"Not for the moment, anyway," Cailan pointed out.

Elazar frowned. "I haven't shifted in months." Then he shook his head. "But that's not something to argue about right now. Maybe you can help me figure out how to find the Forgotten Library."

Elazar watched as Cailan's expression shifted, his jaw tightening. "Actually, I'd rather *not* find the Forgotten Library," Cailan muttered, crossing his arms.

Max let out an exasperated sigh. "That's not really an option at this point, is it? Elazar's been tasked with finding it, and the Jade Empress isn't going to just let it go."

Elazar felt a pang of guilt. He knew the situation had become increasingly dire, with so many people's fates tied to his actions. "Max is right," he said quietly. "I have to do this—it's the right thing to do. And Chandra agrees." Turning his attention to the pocket watch in his hands, Elazar ran his thumb over the intricate design. "This watch...it might be the key. Chandra thinks it's connected to the Forgotten Library, but I can't seem to activate it."

Max leaned in, her expression filled with curiosity. "What do you mean, *activate* it? Is it more than just a timepiece?"

Elazar nodded. "Chandra told me the drakes sometimes made devices that looked like one thing but were actually another. Like this." He flipped the watch open. "We think it's actually a compass."

"Shitty compass without the cardinal directions on it," Cailan pointed out, though his voice was ripe with jealousy. Was he annoyed that Chandra had spent time with Elazar, or was something else eating at him?

Whatever it was, Elazar ignored it. "That's because it's not activated yet. Chandra thinks I need to tap into my magic to unlock its secrets."

Cailan cocked his head, skeptical. He narrowed his eyes, and a moment later, he cursed softly. "Winds, it *is* magic."

Elazar raised his brows. He had forgotten that Cailan was sensitive to magic. His excitement grew. "Can you tell how to activate it?" Elazar held it out toward his brother. (And wow, how strange was it to think of Cailan as a *brother*?)

Cailan accepted it, though there was reluctance in his every move. He pursed his lips, turning it over in his hands. "My magic doesn't work like that. I can see that it's magical, sure. But to tell you how to—wait." The contrary man's eyes widened, and he exchanged a look with Max. "The *Tempest*."

The Stormcaller nodded, her eyes bright. "That's right! Maybe that's how."

Elazar didn't have the faintest clue what they were talking about. "The *Tempest?* Is she okay?" He hadn't been able to come aboard the airship, not yet, though it was something he was looking forward to.

Cailan snorted, waving a hand dismissively. "Okay? The *Tempest* is more than *okay*. She's *alive*."

Elazar blinked, his brow furrowing in confusion. "Alive? What do you mean?" The *Tempest* was an airship, a machine. How could she be alive?

Cailan jerked his chin toward Sprocket, who perched atop a stone ledge, preening her metallic feathers. "Like her. The *Tempest*, she's...sentient, in her own way."

Elazar's eyes widened as understanding dawned. The way the airship had seemed to respond to his presence, as if she were watching him... He remembered the curious, almost protective feeling he'd sensed, though he'd dismissed it at the time.

"You're saying the *Tempest* is self-aware?" Elazar asked, his mind racing. If that was true, then perhaps the airship's unique nature could somehow be the key to unlocking the secrets of his pocket watch.

Cailan nodded. "Yeah, and as stubborn as the day is long. The *Tempest* has been leading us here." He paused, his expression darkening. "To *you*."

Elazar felt a pang of guilt. He knew his absence had worried the *Tempest*'s crew, especially Aunt Jo. But the thought of the airship herself searching for him was both unsettling and strangely comforting.

"So, you think the *Tempest*'s...sapience might help me activate the watch?" Elazar asked, turning the device over in his hands once more. "Chandra said I need to tap into my magic, but maybe the *Tempest* can help me do that."

Cailan shook his head. "No, that's not what we mean." He glanced at Max. "You tell him."

Max blinked, clearly not expecting to be put on the spot. "Me?" When Cailan merely grinned at her, she gave him a dirty look and then pasted on a smile as she turned to Elazar. Max walked over to sit beside him. "This is going to sound awful, but...bear with me a moment. You bled out on the *Tempest*'s deck."

Elazar made a face. "Not something I want to think about right now but, go on." He had struggled to forget it, but now that it was out there, his mind kept cycling back to the sensation of a harpoon piercing his shoulder. To staring at Aunt Jo when he thought he was dying, wishing for one last whisper of comfort.

The Stormcaller gave his hand a brief squeeze, as if she sensed his unpleasant memories. "We already know there's magic in your blood. It fuels your arcane engine. And you used it to write your magical scripts against the skirates in Rotgut Bay."

Elazar stared at the timepiece as Max's words sank in. His gaze shifted to Cailan, whose expression held a hint of triumph, as if he'd cracked some great mystery. "Wait, you think my blood is what will activate this?"

Cailan leaned back, a smug grin spreading across his face. "Took you long enough."

Elazar shot his newfound brother a frustrated look, but before he could respond, Max let out a soft laugh, drawing their attention.

"Brothers," she murmured, shaking her head in amusement.

"So, what, I just prick my finger and drip it onto the watch?" Elazar asked, trying to steer the conversation back to the matter at hand.

Cailan shrugged. "Worth a try. Can't hurt, at least."

Elazar glanced down at the pocket watch. The thought of using his own blood to activate it made his stomach churn, but if it was the key to unlocking the secrets of the Forgotten Library, he knew he had to try.

"Wait." Max touched Elazar's arm. "If you're supposed to activate it with your magic, do it the exact way you would if it were anything else."

Her suggestion confused him, but only for a moment. "So, you don't think I feed it like an arcane engine?"

She shook her head. "I mean, I could be wrong, but that's *passive*. I suspect you need to take action."

It made sense, and Elazar felt an odd rightness with the idea. Even when he crafted the wings for the Jade Court, he had written a script to make the parts work together as a whole. He glanced at Max and Cailan. "Either of you have a knife?"

"Just Fang," Cailan said, pulling the cutlass from the baldric at his back.

Max rolled her eyes. "I do." She pulled a small knife from her boot, handing it hilt-first to Elazar.

Elazar stared down at the timepiece cradled in his palm. With a steadying breath, he drew the tip of the small knife across his fingertip, wincing at the sharp sting. A single bead of crimson welled up, and he carefully traced a rune onto the watch's surface.

As he watched, the etched lines glowed, a faint shimmer of magic sparking to life. Elazar's eyes widened, but the glow quickly faded, and the watch remained stubbornly still.

Disappointment filled him, and he let out a frustrated sigh. "It didn't work."

Cailan leaned in, his brow furrowed. "What did you write?"

"*Arunaktiva*," Elazar replied, turning the watch so his brother could see the now-faded runes. "A rune that means to activate or awaken."

Beside him, Max hummed thoughtfully. "Maybe you need to try a different word? Something more specific to what you're trying to unlock."

Elazar nodded, considering her suggestion. He knew Chandra had said he needed to tap into his own innate magic to make the watch reveal its secrets, but he was still learning to control and understand that part of himself. Choosing the right word, the right combination of power, could be the key.

Steeling himself, Elazar milked another drop of blood from his fingertip. This time, he traced the rune for *Arunapo*—to awaken and set in motion—onto the watch's surface.

The moment the crimson lines touched the metal, a surge of energy thrummed through Elazar's veins. He felt a stirring deep within, a dormant power sparking to life. The watch glowed, the runes shimmering brighter and brighter until Elazar had to squint against the light.

Suddenly, the watch snapped open, and a beam of golden light shot forth, projecting an ethereal map into the air above them. Elazar's breath caught in his throat as he recognized the familiar landmasses and archipelagos—this was a map of the Dragon Latitudes, but unlike any he had seen before.

"The Forgotten Library," Elazar breathed, his eyes wide with wonder as he took in the intricate details of the projection. Tiny glyphs hovered over a specific island, and a thrum of magic radiated from the map.

Cailan leaned in, his eyes narrowed as he studied the arcane image. "So, that's where we need to go."

Elazar nodded. "It would seem so." He glanced up at Max, who was staring at the map with awe.

"Then what are we waiting for?" she said, meeting Elazar's gaze with a smile. "Let's go find the Forgotten Library."

12

⧼Threads of Fate⧽

Cailan

The hour was late, but the tunnels were lit with lamps that allowed Cailan to traverse the short way to Chandra's lair. Captain Jo, Gretchen, and Max had returned to the *Tempest* for the night, albeit reluctantly. None of them had wanted to leave Elazar behind, but for now, they had to.

As for Cailan, he wanted answers.

Vesper lifted his head, ears pricked with interest as Cailan entered. His tail thumped against the floor. Chandra had been resting, maybe asleep, but one of her eyes opened.

"Danelor? Oh...no, it's you." The Seer rose stiffly.

Cailan tensed at the other man's name, jealousy roiling through him. Chandra was *his* mentor. He shook away the thought, walking closer with arms crossed. Cailan had decided to remain human, for now. He wasn't happy with his dragon heritage at the moment.

"You've known about me, all along," Cailan said, unable to mask the bitterness in his voice. "And you only tell me any of this today. In front of everyone."

Chandra sighed. "I couldn't—"

"I don't want to hear about prophecies or fate right now!" Cailan snapped, hands fisted at his sides. "You knew I had a *brother!* That I'm not really a *dragon!*" Waves of frustration twisted with the grief that swept through him, and it took Cailan a moment to realize he was trembling.

Vesper whined softly and rose, padding over to give Cailan's hand a gentle lick. Cailan ignored the aralez, staring at Chandra—daring her to say something, *anything*, to make this right.

And she knew it, too. Chandra lowered her head, resting her chin atop her crossed foreclaws. "The things you want me to say are placations. They'll sound good in the moment, soothe your anger. But they won't grant you the healing you desire. Only time will do that."

Cailan shook his head. "Maybe so. But...you could have at least told me you'd live. That I'd see you again." He hated the remembered swell of grief filling him when he'd thought the only person in this world who'd given a damn about him had died.

"Just because I'm a Seer doesn't mean I foresee *all* things," Chandra said. Then, voice softer, she added, "I was supposed to die. Or so I thought."

Her words were chilling and brought Cailan up short. "Was it a prophecy?"

Chandra hesitated before shaking her head. "No." She sighed. "I believe I was saved by Vesper, unwilling to let me go, even though it was my time."

Cailan glanced at the canine. The aralez stared up at Cailan, as if trying to impart something important. His tail wagged back and forth, then he turned toward Chandra and whined. Vesper's gaze snapped back to Cailan, full of an intensity Cailan didn't understand.

"You were good to save her," Cailan murmured, stroking Vesper's ears and earning a frustrated whimper. "Okay. So, why are you here? You should go back to the Vault of Fate." Cailan pointed to the tunnel. "That man claimed you're not a prisoner, so leave!"

Chandra gave him an almost amused look, then fanned out her tattered wings. "How would I leave? I can't fly. And if I swim, well..." The azure dragon shivered. "I wouldn't want to."

Cailan's jaw tightened, disliking that she was right. Chandra had never wanted the aspirants to swim around the Vault of Fate, either. Not since the time an orca had taken a single young dragon. Even dragons could fall prey to creatures of the deep.

"Fine. Then Elazar can make you wings, and you can leave that way." Cailan knew he sounded petulant but didn't care.

Chandra gave him a fond look, then shook her head again. "What do I have to go back to? I know what happened to my aspirants. I don't know if I can bear to return."

Cailan wanted to argue, but he had been to the Vault of Fate after the slaughter. He recalled the horrors there and couldn't fault Chandra's reluctance. He bowed his head. "You're staying here, then?"

The look Chandra gave him was downright coy. "Not exactly."

Cailan pursed his lips. "So, where are you going?"

"With you, of course." Chandra's pale eyes bored into his. "The threads of fate are tangling, Cailan. I must do what I can to correct matters."

Elazar

Elazar had thought the previous day was complicated, with the unexpected arrival of the *Tempest*, but the next day became another hurdle when Tiberia arrived aboard the same type of small airship that had brought Elazar to the island.

And she wasn't alone. A pair of Vangara accompanied her, including Freyak, who Cailan seemed to know and dislike. The feeling was clearly mutual, based on the dragonkin's sneer.

Elazar rubbed the bridge of his nose. Once again, he felt like he was explaining the same thing over and over, and no one was listening. Mostly because arguments had broken out among the various groups. Finally, he pulled out the former pocket watch-turned-compass, flicking the cover open. The golden-edged image of the Dragon Latitudes swarmed to life, the sudden glow catching everyone's eye.

"I know how to find the Forgotten Library," Elazar declared, holding the compass up so the light reflected against the ceiling. He tightened his grip on the glowing compass. All eyes were now fixed on him, the sudden attention making his skin prickle.

Freyak stepped forward, his clawed hand outstretched. "The Empress needs that compass. Hand it over, drake."

Elazar backed away, shaking his head. "No, I can't. I need to be the one to find the Forgotten Library."

"He speaks the truth," Chandra said, earning a glare of mistrust from the Vangara.

Tiberia moved between Elazar and Freyak, her expression resolute. "Perhaps we can come to an arrangement. I'm sure it would satisfy the Empress if Danelor and I accompanied you on your journey to the Forgotten Library."

Elazar hesitated, glancing uncertainly at Danelor. The chimera had been surprisingly kind, but Elazar wasn't sure he could trust the man completely. Still, Tiberia's offer was tempting—it might allow him to fulfill his promise to the Jade Empress while still keeping the compass in his possession. He could right these wrongs and then be free of this burden forever.

"I..." Elazar started, his gaze flickering between the three of them. "I need time to think about this."

Freyak let out a frustrated growl, his tail lashing. "The Empress doesn't have time for your hesitation, drake. Either hand over that compass or—"

"Enough, Freyak." Danelor's voice was quiet but firm, cutting off the Vangara's threat. "Tiberia's suggestion is reasonable and you know it. Let the drake consider it."

A flicker of relief washed through Elazar at Danelor's intervention, but the tension in the air remained thick. He knew he had to tread carefully, lest he provoke the Vangara's anger.

"I'll do it," Elazar said, his voice steadier than he felt. "I'll take Tiberia and Danelor with me to the Forgotten Library. But the compass stays with me."

Elazar watched warily as Freyak glared at him. The Vangara's narrowed eyes radiated barely contained aggression. The hulking dragonkin took a step forward, his clawed hand flexing.

"This better not be some *drake treachery*," Freyak growled, his gravelly voice full of menace. "You'd do well to remember that the Empress demands results, not excuses." Elazar swallowed hard, fighting the urge to shrink back. Freyak turned his attention to Tiberia and Danelor, his lips curling into a sneer. "And you two," he rumbled. "You know what will happen if you disappoint the Jade Empress."

Tiberia met Freyak's gaze unflinchingly. "We understand," she replied evenly.

Danelor nodded in agreement, his features betraying no hint of emotion. Elazar found it interesting that Danelor's normally sunny disposition cooled around the other members of the Jade Court. Though, perhaps it shouldn't be that surprising.

With a final pointed glare in Elazar's direction, Freyak turned and stalked out of the cavern, his heavy footsteps echoing off the stone walls.

Elazar released a shaky breath, his shoulders sagging with relief. He glanced at Tiberia and Danelor, uncertain of what to say. "I appreciate your willingness to accompany me," he began hesitantly.

"But we'd rather you didn't," Cailan added before Elazar could say more. "Seeing as how you hate drakes and all."

Elazar leveled a scowl at Cailan. "That's not what I was going to say."

"We don't *hate* drakes, but we have reason for caution," Tiberia said, clearly trying to patch things.

"Yeah, well, I could say the same about you." Cailan crossed his arms. He seemed to be in one of his moods.

"Marshal." Aunt Jo's voice cut through the tension, the word brooking no argument. Though Elazar knew she wasn't happy with the situation, she had accepted it. Cailan blew out a frustrated breath, then took a step backward, though nothing else in his demeanor shifted.

Elazar was thankful for the breather. He took the opportunity, turning to Danelor and Tiberia. "If you'll allow it, the *Tempest* is available for us to find the Forgotten Library."

Tiberia nodded, though uncertainty crossed Danelor's face at the offer. "I'm sure we'll need something more substantial than an airskiff, and the Jade Court airships are likely too large." Tiberia pursed her lips. "But can we trust all of you? Former dragon hunters that you are." Tiberia's gaze roved to Elazar's aunt.

"Elazar made a promise, and we'll make good on it," Aunt Jo said.

Anticipation swept over Elazar at the prospect of returning to the *Tempest*. "How soon can we leave?" he asked, unable to hide his eagerness.

Aunt Jo smiled at him, no doubt understanding his excitement. "We can be off as soon as you're ready," she said. "But we'll need to stop at a port to gather supplies for the journey. I'll need to check if the *Tempest* is amenable to that detour."

Elazar nodded, understanding the practicalities. He glanced at Tiberia and Danelor, hoping they would be agreeable to the plan.

Tiberia spoke up, her cool gaze meeting Elazar's. "That's acceptable. In fact, the Jade Court can provide the supplies you need, though it may delay our departure by a day or two."

Elazar's heart sank at the prospect of the extra delay, but he knew it was a small price to pay for the resources they would need. "A day or two is fine," he said, trying to keep the impatience from his voice. "I'm just grateful to be heading back to the *Tempest*."

Aunt Jo nodded, a hint of a smile tugging at the corners of her mouth. "I'll make the arrangements. We'll gather a list of supplies needed from the Jade Court."

Tiberia inclined her head. "And once you do, we'll gather it shortly." She turned to Danelor. "We have duties of our own to attend to."

"You may need additional preparations," Chandra interrupted, rising slowly. "I'll travel with you as well."

Elazar blinked, startled by this addition. The Seer's wings were still in ruins. If Elazar had time and materials, he could make her new wings...but both were currently in short supply.

His aunt took it in stride, though. She nodded. "It's irregular, but...you're not as large as some of the other dragons we've encountered. I think we can find room for you on the deck. I'm sorry to say we won't have a way to keep you out of the weather, though."

The Seer lifted a foreclaw, waving away the concern. "I've been inside so long, time in the sun and wind will do much good for me, I think. And I don't mind storms, either." She glanced at the aralez. "Vesper will need a place to stay indoors if the weather is foul, however."

"Easily arranged." Aunt Jo smiled at the winged canine. She ticked off on her fingers. "We'll plan for Tiberia, Danelor, you, and your aralez."

As Tiberia and Danelor departed, Elazar felt a surge of relief. He was one step closer to returning to the *Tempest*, to his family, and to the chance of unlocking the secrets of the Forgotten Library.

Elazar turned to Aunt Jo. "Thank you," he said, his voice sincere. "For everything."

Aunt Jo reached out, tugging him into another hug. "You're my family, Elazar. Whatever happens, that will never change."

Elazar nodded, understanding the unspoken emotions. They had learned so many things about him lately: he was a drake; he had a brother. What other secrets were out there?

And what would they mean for his life with the people he loved?

13

REMORAS

Elazar

Three days later, Elazar crossed the gangway to the *Tempest*, emotions tangling within that he couldn't even name. He placed his hand on the *Tempest's* railing, and the moment his skin touched the weathered wood, the ship almost seemed to sing. It was as if the *Tempest* had a heartbeat of her own, like a living entity.

Cailan's words echoed in Elazar's mind: the way he had described the *Tempest* as more than just a vessel, as if she were a sentient being. Elazar had suspected something had changed about the *Tempest* months ago—a strangeness that had developed. But he hadn't expected it to be this. It was like connecting with a primordial force—something vast and unknowable, yet familiar, like the awe one might feel in the presence of a whale breaching the ocean's surface.

The *Tempest* had always been a constant in his life, a home that had sheltered him. But now, it was as if he were seeing her through fresh eyes. A sense of concern and then joy washed over him. The *Tempest* welcomed him back. Elazar swallowed, overcome by the rush of sensations. He swayed on his feet despite gripping the rail.

"Hey, are you okay?" Max asked from his side, worry in her voice.

Elazar hissed out a breath. "Yeah. I just wasn't...quite expecting that." Even though he'd known. The *Tempest's* awareness had grown since he'd last felt it.

Elazar steadied himself, glancing up to see Galatea and Isaac approaching. Galatea's amber eyes regarded him with relief, while a grin cracked Isaac's weathered face.

"Welcome back, lad," Isaac said, his deep voice rough but not unkind.

"Thanks, Isaac. Happy to be back." Elazar nodded to Galatea. "Gally, glad to see you."

The Theilian gave him a fanged grin. "We're so glad to have you back. I—" Galatea halted when new footsteps announced the arrival of others.

Glancing back, Elazar spotted Tiberia and Danelor. Each carried a knapsack of items for the trip. The chimeras halted as they stepped onto the deck, uncertain of their next move. The *Tempest* crew stared at them.

Aunt Jo followed them onto the ship and the crew's attention snapped to her. "Crew, I'd like you to meet our guests. This is Tiberia, an attendant to the Jade Empress, and Danelor." Before anyone could react, she continued, "They're going to accompany us to the Forgotten Library. And they will do their part around the ship."

Elazar smiled, proud of his aunt. She was giving Tiberia and Danelor a chance, despite her lingering distrust. And while he couldn't fault her for the distrust—winds knew, he felt the same—they needed the chimeras along for this to work.

As the crew dispersed—including Max, to Elazar's dismay—he caught Tiberia's gaze. She offered him a small, tentative smile, and Elazar felt a ghost of hope.

Elazar watched as Tiberia stepped forward. "Thank you, Captain Prescott," she said, inclining her head. "We appreciate the opportunity."

Josephine's gaze swept over Tiberia and Danelor, her expression unreadable. "Don't mistake this for charity," she said bluntly. "You'll be expected to pull your weight. We're running a skeleton crew, and we can't afford any dead weight."

Danelor inclined his head. "Understood, Captain. We'll do whatever is needed to help."

Tiberia nodded. "I have experience on airships, though I may need some guidance on specific tasks." She gestured to Danelor. "My brother, unfortunately, has never worked on an airship. And he has certain...needs."

Brother? Elazar stared at the pair in surprise, then glanced between them. Tiberia and Danelor *did* share a similar bone structure, especially in their faces. And they both had the same dark hair, though Tiberia's tresses had a midnight-blue cast in the sunlight, while Danelor's had hints of deep purple. *Chimeras.* Did their hair color hint at potential dragon color? Elazar ran a hand through his own copper-colored hair.

Aunt Jo nodded. "That's fine. We can work with someone willing to learn. What sort of needs must we account for?"

Was it Elazar's imagination, or did Danelor's cheeks redden? "I couldn't tolerate the Jade Court airships during migration. Too much noise. And my eyes are sensitive to light, sometimes."

Aunt Jo's brow knit as she no doubt struggled with solutions. Elazar lifted a hand. "I might be able to do something about that."

Everyone's attention fell on him. Aunt Jo snapped her fingers. "Of course. What do you propose?"

"I could..." Elazar hesitated, then cleared his throat. He didn't want to reveal his magic to the chimeras, though his aunt already knew some of his capabilities. "I could make some adjustments to soundproof whichever cabin Danelor is staying in. It'll be easier if it's away from the arcane engine and galley." Elazar paused as he thought it through. "As far as the light, since the ship needs to be crewed at all times, maybe Danelor could work at night primarily?"

As he outlined the plan, Aunt Jo nodded along. "That sounds reasonable to me."

Danelor glanced at his sister, then focused on Elazar. "You could do that?"

"Sure," Elazar agreed, pleased at the relief clear on both chimeras' faces. While he hadn't known Tiberia had a brother —much less that it was Danelor—it was clear she cared for his well-being. "I can take care of it after I stop by navigation."

"Do that. We'll find a suitable cabin in the meantime," Aunt Jo said, waving him off.

Sprocket, who had been perched on a mast, swooped down, fluttering in front of Elazar, as if leading the way to the bridge. He chuckled. "I didn't forget my way around, you know."

The cogwing chortled, looping around to settle on Elazar's shoulder. Metal talons dug into his skin.

"Ouch," he grumbled, though Elazar couldn't help but give Sprocket a fond look. "Take it easy."

Isaac had been making preparations on the bridge, and

looked up at Elazar's approach. "I've been told you're the one with information on our heading."

"In a way," Elazar agreed. "What I have is a map unlike anything you've seen before." He retrieved the timepiece-turned-compass from his pocket.

Isaac narrowed his eyes. "That's the old pocket watch Jo picked up on Dead Man's Dare, back when we found you!"

"I thought it was a broken pocket watch for years, too," Elazar admitted. He flicked open the timepiece and the golden spectral image emerged.

Isaac's eyes widened, a low whistle escaping his lips. "By the gods..." He leaned in, studying the swirling projection with rapt attention. "Is this...magic?"

Elazar nodded, a small smile playing on his lips. "Drake magic, to be precise." He traced a finger along the ghostly contours of the map. "It's a compass. Or a map. It's confusing."

The navigator chuckled. "Some compass," Isaac whispered, then followed it up with a whistle of appreciation. "*Drake magic*. I always knew you were more than just a human lad, Elazar." He shook his head, a hint of a smile on his lips. "Even if much of the old crew didn't care for you. I knew differently."

A rush of pride warmed Elazar. The navigator had always been a grounding presence on the ship—someone Elazar respected and admired over the years. To have that respect returned, and to see the wonder in Isaac's eyes, filled Elazar with a comfort he hadn't known he needed.

Isaac leaned back, stroking the short beard on his chin thoughtfully. "So, where does this map say the Forgotten Library is hiding?"

Elazar opened his mouth to reply, but before he could speak, Sprocket launched from Elazar's shoulder. She snatched the compass from his palm. Elazar cried out in surprise, reaching for the precious artifact. "Sprocket, no! Bring that back!"

But the cogwing had already alighted on the *Tempest's* navigation console. She dropped the compass onto it with a *thud* and then preened.

Elazar hurried to the console, Isaac beside him. Gently, he tried to pick up the compass, but to his dismay, it refused to budge. It was as if the compass had been welded to the ship. "What in the...?" Elazar murmured, his frustration mounting.

Isaac watched, eyebrows raised high. "It seems our mechanical friend has decided for us," he observed, a hint of amusement in his gravelly voice.

Elazar shot the navigator a desperate look. "But I need that compass! It's the key to finding the Forgotten Library."

Isaac cocked his head, considering the situation. "I understand. But it also appears that the *Tempest* has other plans." He gestured to the glowing map that still shimmered above the console.

"The *Tempest*..." Elazar breathed, realization dawning on him. "She's going to use the compass to navigate to the Forgotten Library?"

Isaac nodded. "I suspect so. The *Tempest* has gotten headstrong, putting me out of a job. It seems she's taken a liking to that compass of yours."

Elazar stared at the compass. The *Tempest* had just claimed a part of Elazar's heritage as her own. Or maybe it had always been hers, too, since his blood had awakened her.

Sprocket let out a series of shrill squawks and whistles, her feathers gleaming in the glow of the spectral map. Elazar ran a hand through his hair. "Well, I suppose we'll trust the *Tempest*, then."

Maxine

As the *Tempest* soared away from the volcanic island, Max was certain this journey was going to be unlike any other. She had learned from an amused Isaac that Sprocket and the *Tempest* had appropriated Elazar's compass. Cailan, ever unpredictable, stomped around the airship deck. Max assumed he was upset with Chandra, given his pointed avoidance of the deck area where the Seer resided.

Maxine leaned against the aft railing, tracing the weathered wood as she gazed out at a distant storm. The clouds churned, ominous, as she assessed the power of the winds and the way the lightning charged the air. As a Stormcaller, Max was finely attuned to the shifts and moods of the skies. She knew this storm, despite its fierce appearance, posed no threat to the *Tempest*.

The sound of someone clearing their throat drew her attention, and Max turned to see Elazar making his way toward her. She'd been hoping for a chance to speak with him alone, or as close to alone as one could get on the bustling airship.

"Hey," she greeted him. Max wanted to throw her arms around him and pull him into an exuberant hug, but she didn't know if that would make things awkward. "How's it feel to be back aboard?" Max knew the past few days had been a whirlwind for Elazar, with the revelation of his true nature as a drake and the discovery of his familial connection to Cailan. She couldn't imagine how overwhelming it must feel to have so many long-held secrets and mysteries unraveled at once.

He settled beside her at the railing, the wind tousling his hair. It was longer than she'd ever seen it, a sign of his months away. The last time he'd had a trim had likely been before he'd first turned into a dragon. Elazar wore it loose, and Max found it flattered him. Stubble dotted his cheeks, a marked departure from his formerly smooth skin. He'd never had even a hint of stubble before. A thought occurred to her: perhaps drakes matured differently than normal humans. Cailan, too, had only recently shown any signs of stubble.

"It's good to be back. *Really* good." A tentative smile crossed his face. Then Elazar rubbed his forehead. "But it's also difficult. Most days, I wish I could go back in time. Just be the keeper of accounts again." He stared over the side of the airship at the sea far below.

"You were never *just* the keeper of accounts," Max reminded him, her voice soft. The golden chain attached to the small arcane engine peeked out from beneath the collar of his shirt. "You were always a Gearweaver."

He must have expected her to say *drake*. Elazar's shoulders relaxed at her words. "Well, yeah. But you know what I mean." He sank against the railing until his chin rested against it, and the simple shift in posture spoke volumes. Just like old times, Elazar was completely comfortable around her. Willing to show his vulnerabilities. "I never asked for this."

Maxine nodded in understanding. "I can only imagine." She edged closer until her hip bumped his. "But you don't have to go through it alone."

He turned to look at her, a small, grateful smile brightening his face. "Thanks, Max. I...I should probably get some rest." Elazar pushed himself upright, the weariness clear in his movements.

"About that," Maxine said, glancing over her shoulder. "While you were gone, Cailan kind of...claimed your cabin." She watched Elazar's expression shift, the beginnings of a grumble forming on his lips.

"Of *course*, he did," Elazar muttered, shaking his head. "Typical Cailan." Despite the exasperation in his tone, Maxine saw fondness lurking beneath the surface.

Maxine reached out, touching Elazar's arm and drawing his attention. "You can always bunk with me if you need a place to rest," she offered, then regretted the words as soon as she spoke. But she couldn't call them back without adding further embarrassment. Elazar's eyes widened at the suggestion. She cleared her throat. "I mean, with our current crew numbers, there's plenty of room. And you're my best friend, so you're always welcome."

Elazar's expression shifted into one Max couldn't quite decipher. "I might just take you up on that if I can't deal with Cailan," he said.

She smiled, hoping he didn't think her a fool. "Anytime, Elazar."

As Elazar turned to make his way below deck, Maxine blew out a breath, her gaze once more falling to the storm on the horizon. Wrangling a hurricane felt like a simpler thing than figuring out how to tell Elazar her feelings. That was a storm she hoped she had the grit to face another day.

Cailan

CAILAN STRODE INTO THE CABIN. EVEN DURING HIS absence, the space had kept Elazar's lingering scent—a mix of machine oil and faint spice. The scent was stronger now, reinforced by the copper dragon's return. Cailan's golden eyes narrowed as he surveyed the tidy quarters, his jaw tightening.

"So, the prodigal dragon returns," he drawled, leaning

against the bulkhead. "And you just waltz back into this cabin like you never left."

Elazar had been going through supplies at his desk. He stood his ground, meeting Cailan's gaze levelly. "This is *my* cabin, Cailan. You know that. I'd appreciate if you'd give me time to settle in."

Cailan scoffed, crossing his arms over his chest. "Oh, I'm sure you would. But in case you forgot, a lot's changed since you abandoned us and flew off to cavort with the Jade Court." Even as he spoke, Cailan knew he was being unfair with his accusations. But the unsettled frustration deep inside him wouldn't ease, and Cailan didn't know what else to do. He gestured around the cabin. "This space is mine now."

Elazar's lips pursed, eyes narrowing. "You were on the *Tempest* long enough with me to know these are *my* quarters. I'm open to sharing, though, if that's what you want."

"It's *not* what I want," Cailan shot back, though a treacherous part of him disagreed—that was *exactly* what he wanted. "Find some other place to bunk. I'm the marshal, and this is mine."

Elazar refused to be cowed. "I don't care about your rank, Cailan. This is my cabin." He paused, his expression softening. "What's your problem, anyway? I thought you'd be happy to see your mentor, at least."

Cailan flexed his fingers, dreading the thought of explaining his turmoil to Elazar, of all people. He was deeply upset that Chandra had withheld such important information from him for so long. Worse still, it seemed Chandra now favored others over him.

"*You're* my problem," Cailan growled, though it wasn't true. He jabbed a finger into Elazar's chest. "You can have this cabin. See if I care!" At the moment, Cailan just wanted to escape and not confront any of his conflicted emotions.

Cailan spun on his heel, stalking out the door. Elazar called his name, but Cailan ignored it. He wanted to be angry right now, wanted others around him to feel the hurt he felt. Briefly, he considered paying a visit to Chandra, since she was the source of his pain. He dismissed the idea, though.

The stars were bright overhead, lighting up the night sky like thousands of sparks. The gentle hum of the *Tempest*'s engines lulled Cailan, soothing the irrational rage that swarmed his mind. He shook away the growing calm. "I want to be mad right now, you stupid ship."

Cailan considered shifting—maybe the exertion of flight would burn off some of his unhappiness. But right now, shifting only served as a reminder that Chandra had hidden his heritage from him for years.

As he paced, Cailan spotted a familiar silhouette near the aft railing—Danelor, the so-called chimera. A surge of resentment welled up inside him. Danelor, a lackey of the Jade Court, was the perfect target for Cailan's anger.

Cailan approached, his footsteps deliberately heavy. Danelor turned, cocking his head as he took in Cailan's tense posture.

"Well, if it isn't one of the Jade Court remoras," Cailan sneered, his voice dripping with disdain.

"Chimera," Danelor corrected, his tone annoyingly pleasant. "You're thinking of the sucker fishes that eat parasites on sharks."

"Oh, I said *exactly* what I meant." Cailan narrowed his eyes. "And I think you're doing the same thing here."

Danelor cocked his head, a hesitant smile on his face. "I'm here at the Captain's invitation." His gaze fell to Cailan's clenched fists. "Is something wrong?"

Everything is wrong. Cailan wanted to scream, to roar at the heavens. Instead, he assessed the chimera's moonlit form.

This man had hobbled around the cavern, and every instinct buried within Cailan declared he would be easy prey. "You helped keep Chandra prisoner, didn't you?"

Danelor's expression hardened. "When I arrived, she was no prisoner. I helped see to her needs, though."

"*Liar,*" Cailan growled, taking a step closer to the other man.

The chimera froze, as if he understood the danger he was in. One of his hands drifted to his waist, but he must have left his daggers back in his cabin. Without any sort of defense, Danelor edged to face Cailan and meet his gaze. "I understand your anger, but I'm not your enemy. Perhaps we got off on the wrong foot, but—"

"Save it." Cailan cut him off. "I don't care about your excuses."

Cailan surged forward, his fist lashing out toward Danelor's face. But to his surprise, the chimera caught his strike with ease, his grip like iron. He was faster than he looked.

"I don't want to fight you," Danelor said, his voice a low rumble.

"Well, that's too bad," Cailan hissed, his other fist swinging in a powerful arc. Danelor deflected the blow with a quick twist of his arm. Wasn't this the same man Cailan had seen walking with an obvious limp back on the island? Cailan's frustration mounted as Danelor continued to evade his attacks, the chimera's calm demeanor only fueling his rage.

"Enough of this!" Cailan's rage surged to the surface. Silvery magic rippled over him, wings bursting from his back, fingers elongating into wicked talons. Towering over Danelor, Cailan bared his fangs in a menacing snarl.

With a swift motion, he pinned the chimera to the deck, his claws pressed against Danelor's chest. The man's rapid heartbeat pounded just beneath Cailan's scaly palm, and it only fueled his ire.

"You think you can just fly onto my ship and expect me to welcome you with open arms?" Cailan demanded. "You and your court are the reason Chandra suffered. The reason I—" He cut himself off, the words catching in his throat. Cailan hated the vulnerability that seeped into his tone, the pain and confusion he felt. Before he could continue his tirade, a familiar voice cut through the tension.

"*Cailan!* What in the blazes are you doing?"

Cailan froze, his grip on Danelor loosening as he turned to face the furious visage of Captain Josephine. Her eyes were narrowed, lips pressed into a thin line.

"Captain," Cailan acknowledged, his tone edged with a hint of defiance. "I'm dealing with a security threat."

Josephine's brow arched, her expression unimpressed. "That's not how I see it, *Marshal*." Cailan felt a growing pang of guilt with each word. "Stand down. Now."

Cailan hesitated, his talons flexing against Danelor's chest. But to keep his place on the airship, he had to obey the command. Slowly, reluctantly, he retracted his transformation, his scales receding until he stood before her, fully human once more.

Josephine sighed, her disappointment clear. "I expected better from you, Cailan. You're the marshal—you're supposed to set an example, not start fights with our guests. *Protect* our guests, in fact."

Cailan opened his mouth to protest, but the words died on his tongue. He knew Josephine was right. As the ship's marshal, he was supposed to maintain order and serve as a protector, not give in to his own personal grudges.

"I'm sorry, Captain," he murmured, his gaze dropping to the deck. "It won't happen again."

"My quarters. *Now*." Josephine hooked a thumb in that direction, just in case he'd forgotten the way.

Cailan felt a twinge of shame, realizing how far he had misstepped. How much he'd let his temper take the reins and gain control. As the *Tempest*'s marshal, he was supposed to be better than that.

He cast a singular glance back at Danelor, who seemed none the worse for the confrontation. The chimera watched him warily, as if Cailan were a wild beast about to snap. Which hadn't been far from the truth. With a sigh, Cailan turned and followed the captain.

Josephine

SHE HAD HALF-EXPECTED THE UNRULY MARSHAL WOULD refuse her orders, which would lead to further complications. Josephine was relieved when Cailan stalked after her, his arms crossed.

But as he entered her quarters, Josephine studied him, noting that now his attitude was all an act. There was something in his eyes that belied his true feelings.

"What was that out there?" Josephine asked. She remained standing.

A muscle quivered in Cailan's jaw. "I was angry."

She had thought as much. Josephine began a leisurely pace of the room. "When I appointed you as marshal, I expected better of you. I thought you could overcome this temper of yours. Was I wrong?"

He bowed his head. "No."

"Then what happened?" Josephine asked. "If you have

proof that the chimeras are a danger, that's one thing. But to attack someone unprovoked is another."

Josephine watched as Cailan swallowed and nodded, his expression shifting from defiance to something more pensive. It was clear the young man felt chastened, but there was a reluctance in him to express what was truly wrong.

"Well?" Josephine prompted, her tone softening slightly. "Out with it."

Cailan let out a heavy sigh, his gaze dropping to the floor. "I...I thought Chandra was dead," he admitted quietly. "And now she's not, and I don't know how to feel about that."

Josephine paused in her pacing, considering his words. "Happy, perhaps?" she suggested.

Cailan shook his head. "It's not that simple." He looked up, his expression troubled. "Something doesn't feel right about all of this. Chandra kept so much from me—from all of us. How can I just accept her return, when there's clearly more going on that she's not telling us?"

Josephine studied him, seeing the turmoil behind his guarded expression. As much as Cailan tried to project an air of bravado, he was still young, still grappling with the complexities of the world and his place in it. This revelation about his mentor had clearly shaken him more than he wanted to admit.

"I understand your hesitation," Josephine said, her voice gentle. "Betrayal can be a bitter pill to swallow, especially from those we thought we could trust." She moved closer, placing a hand on his shoulder. "But Chandra is alive, and from what I've seen, she seems to have your best interests at heart. Perhaps it's worth giving her time to earn your trust once more."

Cailan met her gaze, his expression torn. "I just..." He paused, searching for the right words. "I thought I knew where I stood, you know? And now everything feels...different."

Josephine nodded slowly. "Change is never easy, especially

when it challenges what we thought we knew. But sometimes, the most important discoveries come from embracing the unknown." She gave his shoulder a reassuring squeeze. "Take some time to process this, Cailan. But don't take it out on anyone else on the ship—especially our guests."

Cailan seemed to consider her words, the tension in his frame gradually easing. Josephine saw the metaphorical gears turning in his mind, weighing the options before him. Finally, he nodded, some of the hardness on his face softening.

"All right," Cailan murmured. "I'll...I'll try." He turned for the door.

"Cailan?" Jo's crisp voice made him turn back toward her. "I expect you not only to apologize to Danelor, but help him learn his way around the airship." Her hard gaze and down-turned lips left no room for argument.

Regardless, Cailan's hackles rose. "*What?* That's the last thing I want to do!"

"I know." Josephine crossed her arms. "That's why it's an order."

With a frustrated growl, Cailan whirled and stalked out the door. Josephine rubbed her temples and hoped she hadn't made things worse.

14

Take it or Leave It

Danelor

Dane hated feeling useless. And so far, on this airship, that's exactly how he felt. But he wouldn't let it show.

Tiberia had found a multitude of ways to assist, everything from helping with meal preparation to swabbing the deck. They were tasks she could handle with ease, since *her* body hadn't betrayed her.

Dane sat on an overturned barrel, working through a tangled mess of ropes. The lines twisted and knotted in ways that felt like they mirrored his own entangled life. Despite the frustration of the task, he found solace in the minor victory of untangling each knot. It was nice to see some progress, at least.

Whatever Elazar had done to soundproof the cabin Dane was using had worked like a charm. When the sounds of the airship became too much for him, he had a safe place to retreat to.

As he worked, Dane noticed movement out of the corner of his eye. Cailan, in human form, approached with his usual confident stride. Despite his deep-seated wariness, Dane found himself subtly drawn to Cailan. His light blond hair gleamed in the sunlight, nearly white in its brilliance, and his golden-brown eyes carried an intensity that was captivating, despite the danger he posed.

"You look like you're having fun," Cailan remarked, stopping a few feet away.

Had the marshal returned to antagonize Dane again? In some ways, Cailan's behavior the previous night had been remarkably like that of some of the Jade Court dragons he apparently disdained. But Dane was certain he'd glimpsed pain in the depths of Cailan's eyes. Not a physical pain like Dane's, but a deeply emotional one.

Dane glanced up from the ropes, continuing with his work. "Yeah, it's like a puzzle. Just takes a bit of patience." Dane wasn't sure what to make of Cailan's presence, and he didn't want to get into any more fights with the volatile drake.

Cailan crossed his arms, his eyes narrowing slightly. "Look, about what happened last night..." he started, then trailed off as if he wasn't sure what came next.

Dane glanced up, raising an eyebrow but saying nothing, his smile never faltering. A smile, he had learned, could disarm humans. Dane just wasn't sure it would work with Cailan.

Cailan shifted his weight from one foot to the other, clearly uncomfortable. "I shouldn't have attacked you like that. It was...unnecessary."

Dane chuckled softly. "Was that an apology?"

Cailan's jaw tightened, but he didn't back down. "Yeah, well, it's the best you're getting right now. Take it or leave it."

Dane sighed, shaking his head. "Fine. Consider it taken." He continued working on the tangled ropes, determined to not let Cailan get under his skin.

There was a moment of silence between them, the creaking of the ship and the brisk snap of the balloon-sails filling the void. Cailan broke the silence first. "Seriously, don't you ever get tired of smiling?"

Dane paused in his work, eyebrows raised. "It's not that hard. You should try it sometime." His legs were aching again—a reminder that pain didn't care about time or place. Dane lifted the ropes. "But these won't untangle themselves. I'd better get back to it." He hoped Cailan hadn't caught the shadow of pain across his face. The other man might see it as a weakness.

Cailan ran a hand through his short blond hair, looking almost sheepish. "I know my first attempt at an apology sucked. I'm not great with...people stuff." He took a breath. "I'm sorry for attacking you. It was wrong, and I was out of line."

Dane felt the sincerity this time. The walls Cailan had put up lowered just enough to let a bit of truth slip through. Dane nodded slowly, feeling the tension between them ease slightly. "That makes sense, as you're not exactly human. Apology accepted," Dane said quietly, the ready smile slipping back onto his lips. "Life's too short to hold grudges."

Cailan looked as if he wanted to argue with that nugget of wisdom. But after a beat, he blew out a breath. "Good. Now that we've got that out of the way, I'm supposed to show you how to do some tasks."

Dane raised an eyebrow. "Tasks? Like what?"

"Everything from securing cargo to basic maintenance," Cailan replied.

Even though Dane wanted to contribute, he hesitated. He flexed his legs, feeling the familiar ache. "Sure, show me the ropes—literally and figuratively," he said with a chuckle. "But not these. I've had enough of these." Dane let his current project coil onto the deck at his feet.

Cailan's shoulders relaxed. "Yeah, you might appreciate a change of scenery. Come on."

Cailan

CAILAN DIDN'T *WANT* TO ENJOY ACQUAINTING DANELOR with the various tasks on the *Tempest*—he clung to the stubborn desire to dislike the chimera. The problem was, Danelor was far too likable for his own good.

There was something wrong with Danelor, something that went beyond the whole chimera problem and his *much too optimistic for his own good* demeanor. Cailan saw it in his cautious movements, the masked winces that made Danelor grit his teeth. He was trying to hide something, or at least didn't want others asking about it.

And that, Cailan could understand. And respect. So he didn't ask.

Cailan dipped the brush into the thick, dark varnish and dragged it along the grain of the wood. "You have to get an even coat," he instructed, his voice clipped. "No gaps."

Danelor nodded. "Got it," he said, his deep brown eyes

focused on Cailan's demonstration. Cailan hated how those eyes made him feel—like the chimera saw right through him.

Cailan handed over the brush, his irritation at himself rising when Danelor's fingers grazed his own during the exchange. Because something deep inside Cailan had sought that connection. He eased away as soon as he could, trying to mask the retreat with airy casualness.

Danelor took the brush and applied the varnish with careful strokes. His movements were slower and more deliberate than Cailan's own hurried efficiency. Cailan watched the way Danelor's hands moved, their grace belying the pain he knew was there.

"You're doing fine," Cailan muttered, more to distract himself than to offer encouragement. "Just don't take all day."

A soft laugh escaped Danelor. His mouth quirked into one of his constant smiles. "I'll try not to."

Why did that laugh bother Cailan so much? Why did everything about this chimera bother him? The way his long, dark hair, tinged with a subtle purplish hue, caught the light, or how his smile seemed genuine even when everything else was falling apart?

Cailan's gaze dropped to the deck, focusing on a knot in the wood as if it held all the answers. It wasn't supposed to be like this. He was supposed to be annoyed with Danelor for being too optimistic for his own good.

"You seem distracted," Danelor noted quietly.

"I'm fine," Cailan snapped a bit too quickly, then sighed. "Just...focus on the varnish."

But as he watched Danelor work, those infuriatingly soft eyes concentrating on each stroke of the brush, Cailan couldn't deny what he felt any longer. There was an attraction there, a pull he couldn't ignore or explain away. It frustrated him deeply. He didn't want this complication. He didn't want to care about someone who could so easily see through his defenses.

"Cailan?" Danelor's voice broke through his thoughts.

"What?"

"You've gone quiet."

"Just thinking," Cailan grumbled. Then he came up with the *perfect* conversational topic. "You know, I have some experience with helping dragons stuck in human form."

Cailan caught the hint of interest in Danelor's eyes as he continued his work. Danelor's focus shifted momentarily from the task at hand, and Cailan knew he had his attention.

"Do you mean with shifting?" Danelor asked, keeping his voice casual but not quite hiding the curiosity beneath.

Cailan leaned against the railing, arms crossed over his chest. "Yeah."

Danelor paused, turning toward Cailan. "So, what did you do? Is there some kind of magic involved?"

"Magic?" Cailan let out a humorless chuckle. "Not exactly. More like gravity."

The chimera's eyebrows drew together. "Gravity?" He dabbed the brush into the varnish and set back to work.

"Elazar didn't believe he was a dragon," Cailan said, a vindictive satisfaction warming his voice. "So, I had to show him in a way he couldn't ignore."

Danelor's brush paused mid-stroke. "What did you do?"

Cailan smirked, enjoying the memory despite its brutality. "I threw him over the side of the *Tempest*."

The shock on Danelor's face was almost comical. "You *what*?"

"You heard me." Cailan's tone was flat, devoid of remorse. "It was...necessary. To help him understand he was more than human." He'd convinced himself, of course, that it was the only way.

"And it worked?" Danelor asked, resuming his varnishing but with noticeably more care in his movements.

Cailan shrugged, though he couldn't quite suppress the pang of guilt that rose within him. "Yeah, it worked. Forced him to shift...or shatter every bone in his body when he hit the water."

Danelor nodded slowly, absorbing this information. "Why do I suspect you'd enjoy throwing me overboard, too?" Amusement colored his tone.

Cailan's smirk widened at Danelor's jest. "You've got that right," he replied, though his thoughts wandered down a different path entirely. Throwing Danelor overboard was the last thing he wanted to do. Other ideas had been creeping into his mind. There were other things he'd enjoy doing with Danelor, things that had nothing to do with varnishing decks or shifting forms. He'd never admit it to the chimera, of course. He wasn't sure if he even wanted to admit it to himself.

As he watched Danelor's hands move gracefully along the wood, Cailan caught himself briefly imagining those same hands in different, more personal tasks. The thought made him uneasy, and he glanced away, chastising himself for letting his guard down, even in his own thoughts.

"So," Danelor said, pulling Cailan out of his confusing thoughts, "how did Elazar react after that?"

Cailan shrugged, trying to seem nonchalant. "He was pissed, of course. But he got over it. Eventually."

Danelor laughed softly. "I can imagine. You don't seem like the type to handle things delicately."

"*Delicately* isn't my style," Cailan agreed, forcing himself to focus on the conversation. "I get things done."

Danelor nodded thoughtfully. "I suppose there's a place for that approach."

"There is," Cailan said firmly, though part of him

wondered if there was room for a softer touch in his life—one that didn't involve throwing people off airships.

He glanced at Danelor again, noticing the way the light caught in his hair, turning it almost amethyst in hue. He wanted to reach out, run his fingers through those dark strands and see if they felt as soft as they looked.

"Why are you staring at me?" Danelor asked suddenly, snapping Cailan out of his thoughts once more.

"I'm not staring," Cailan growled too quickly. He turned away abruptly, cursing himself for being so obvious.

"Right," Danelor said with a knowing smile, but thankfully didn't press the matter further.

Cailan busied himself with another section of the deck, trying to shake off the uncomfortable mix of attraction and irritation gnawing at him. The last thing he needed was to get tangled up in feelings for *anyone*. He was already wounded by Chandra and didn't need any other complications in his life.

15

STORM AHEAD

Elazar

Elazar rummaged through the supply crates in the *Tempest*'s hold, searching for a specific gasket he needed for a minor repair. As he shifted a heavy box, a flash of movement caught his eye.

Tiberia walked into the hold, peering around as if searching for something. Elazar rose out of his crouch. "Good morning, Tiberia. Need a hand?"

The chimera flinched at his voice, but calmed when she saw it was him. "Oh, hello. I was told there was a crate of oranges down here. We need them in the galley."

Elazar had already come across them on his hunt for parts.

"See the crate over there with the blue stripe?" He pointed to Tiberia's left. "You'll find what you're looking for inside."

Pleased, Tiberia followed his directions and located the oranges. "Thank you."

Elazar nodded, curiosity getting the better of him. "How are you and Danelor adjusting to life on the *Tempest*? It must be quite a change from the Jade Court."

Tiberia's expression remained neutral, but Elazar detected a hint of uncertainty in her voice. "It's...an adjustment. The crew is not what I expected. They're..."

"Rough around the edges?" Elazar offered with a small smile.

"*Kind*," Tiberia finished, the corner of her mouth twitching slightly. "You forget the airships I'm familiar with are run by dragons."

He shook his head. "I won't forget that soon." Had Tiberia faced mistreatment within the Jade Court? Elazar knew Danelor had issues. But on the *Talisman*, Tiberia had seemed so...together. As if she had found her place in the world. Had it all been an act? He wanted to ask but didn't know how to frame the question in a way that didn't seem outright rude. "And how is Danelor doing?" That seemed like a safer topic.

Tiberia smiled, though there was something tentative in her expression. "The adjustments you made have helped him greatly. And he's able to do his part around the airship."

Elazar nodded. He'd discovered that Cailan, of all people, had been assigned to show Danelor how to complete certain tasks around the *Tempest*. Elazar wondered if there was a story behind that he wasn't privy to. Tiberia didn't bring it up, so it was possible she didn't know, either.

"I'm glad to hear it," Elazar said.

"Elazar, please report to the bridge." Isaac's tinny voice rang through the *Tempest*'s paging system. The Navigator was currently in command of the airship, with Aunt Jo taking a rest period.

"Sounds like you had better go," Tiberia gestured upward.

"Yeah," he agreed. "But I'll look forward to whatever's being made with those oranges!" Elazar nodded to Tiberia and hurried up the narrow steps to the deck.

He found Isaac just outside the bridge, studying a growing bank of threatening clouds. Clouds the *Tempest* seemed headed toward. Max stood with the Navigator, glancing from him to the storm.

"What's going on?" Elazar asked as he approached.

Isaac gestured toward the storm. "We have a problem. The *Tempest* won't change course to go around that mess, and Max says that storm is staying put."

Elazar raised his brows at that. Max's secret had gotten out to the remaining crew. He noted she didn't seem worried that Isaac knew, so Elazar decided to not focus on that. "Okay. So, what do you think I can do about that?"

Isaac sighed. "I was hoping you might talk sense into this vessel."

Talk sense into...? Elazar swallowed. It made sense, but a part of him was still coming to terms with the *Tempest*'s sentience. But he talked to Sprocket all the time, didn't he? This was the same, but on a grander level.

"Well, let's give it a try." Elazar nodded toward the bridge and slipped inside.

Sprocket perched atop the back of the pilot's seat, as if the cogwing had decided it was meant for her. Elazar plopped into the seat, ignoring Sprocket's ruffle of metal feathers. He rested his hands on the controls, surprised by the thrum of vibrance he felt. Then he hissed out a breath, almost feeling as if the *Tempest*'s vivacity tickled the dragon within him.

He studied the instrument panel. All the levels looked as

they should, and nothing felt amiss to his Gearweaver magic. After all the wings he'd created for the Jade Court, he'd become practiced at sensing areas that would cause problems or failures.

"Okay, *Tempest*," Elazar murmured. "That's a hefty storm ahead. And you know we usually go around them." He paused. "Unless you're planning to set down in the water while it passes over?" Elazar wasn't fond of that solution, but they'd weathered storms similarly before.

He felt a sensation of disagreement. This would be a lot easier if the *Tempest* could actually communicate. "Max can't move it, either. If you fly into that storm, you could be destroyed." And her crew along with her.

Now there was a sense of...was that *smugness?* The compass flashed open on the navigation panel, displaying the map once more. But this time, it had updated to show the brewing storm. Something pinged within the clouds, and it took Elazar a moment to realize it was their destination.

"You *can't* be serious," Elazar groaned.

"What?" Isaac asked, walking over.

Elazar turned to the Navigator. "The Forgotten Library is *inside* that hurricane."

Max's eyes widened as she stepped over to peer at the spectral image. "That makes sense—it must be a *magical* storm. That's why no one's been able to find the library before."

Isaac frowned, his brow furrowing. "But a storm that size will tear apart any ship that tries to enter it. Even the *Tempest* won't be able to withstand those winds and lightning."

Elazar's gaze drifted back to the compass, watching as the blip within the storm pulsed, almost beckoning them forward. "The *Tempest* is gambling that won't be the case."

Isaac's eyes narrowed. "How is that possible?"

Elazar took a deep breath, his cheeks warming. "Because of me."

The Navigator was clearly dubious. He frowned. "What do you mean? How can *you* stand a chance against that behemoth?"

Elazar rubbed his forehead, turning in the pilot's seat. "Because before I knew what I was, I was already using my magic to strengthen the *Tempest*'s aurora."

Isaac blinked. "No wonder her warding's lasted so long. The protections you overlaid must have eroded first."

Elazar nodded. That was certainly the case—the warding he'd placed what felt like ages ago had eroded through time, the elements, and use. "I designed protections to safeguard against dragons. A storm won't be too different." Probably. He hoped.

Isaac glanced at the navigation panel. "You don't have much time, unless this headstrong ship slows to give you a chance."

"And we should probably have everyone awake and ready," Elazar agreed, gently patting the controls. "*Tempest*, can you slow? I need time to work on the aurora."

In answer to his request, Elazar felt a noticeable slowing of the airship—and the readouts on the panels showed he was right. He sighed with relief.

"Never thought I'd see the day we had to talk sense into a vessel," Isaac said with a sigh.

Elazar chuckled. "Never a dull moment. I need to get some supplies and then get to work."

He rose, offering the pilot's chair to Isaac, for all the good it would do them. Elazar slipped out of the bridge, Max at his side.

"Looks like you get to do this for real," she said.

Elazar blew out a breath. "It felt different when I was

putting up protections just because I could instead of..." He glanced at the looming storm. "Instead of hoping I can make something to withstand that." He swallowed. "You sure you can't tame it? Convince the storm to let us through?"

Max shook her head. "When Isaac called it a *behemoth*, he wasn't wrong. You don't want me trying anything with a storm like that. I'd be more likely to make it worse."

Well, it had been worth asking. Elazar nodded as they headed for his cabin together.

"You're not worried, are you?" Max asked.

"Of course, I'm worried. That storm looks like it could turn the *Tempest* into toothpicks." Elazar sighed.

He pushed the door open quietly. After all of his stomping around and general bad mood, Cailan had come back asking to share the cabin with him. Cailan was supposed to be sleeping now, and with how agitated he'd been, Elazar was loath to wake him. But when the door cracked open, the room was aglow with a lantern and Cailan was shoving boots onto his feet. He blinked at them, clearly still waking up.

"Oh, I didn't think you'd be awake," Elazar said.

"Yeah, well, the ship had other plans." Cailan yawned. "I felt us slow, so thought I'd better see what's going on."

"I'll fill you in while Elazar gathers supplies," Max volunteered.

Grateful, Elazar headed to the desk, pulling out the chair and plopping down. After his return to the *Tempest*, he'd taken time to gather some of the specific supplies he used with his Gearweaving aboard the airship. Mostly paper and pens— which had been a part of his former assignment as the keeper of accounts.

Elazar stared down at a blank sheet of paper, his mind racing. He knew the *Tempest* was counting on him to protect them from the looming storm, but the enormity of the task was terrifying.

"What to do first?" he murmured to himself. Lightning was dangerous, especially around airships. Dragoneering vessels like the Tempest had warding in place to divert lightning, but in a storm like the one ahead, they were sure to be struck no matter what. And that was an exceedingly dangerous threat, considering the gases in the *Tempest*'s balloon-sails and the very flammable wood of the ship. It was safest to assume they would be struck and needed to absorb the blast somehow.

"*Fulgarisca* it is, then." Taking a deep breath, he sketched out the matching rune, hoping it wasn't a mistake.

Next, Elazar sketched a rune to reinforce the *Tempest*'s structural integrity, *Fortiari*. He imagined the airship's frame becoming as unyielding as steel, able to withstand the battering winds. Elazar hoped that adding intent to the rune would further strengthen it.

Wiping sweat from his brow, Elazar sat back to assess his work so far. He wet his lips, then dove back into his work. He moved on to a more general rune, one that would brace the airship's existing aurora against the storm's onslaught.

Elazar paused, his pen hovering over the paper. What if his precise, technical approach wasn't enough? The storm was a force of nature, unpredictable. Elazar tapped the pen against the paper, then wrote once more. This time, he left his rune purposely vague. Elazar hoped it might serve as a catch-all, allowing his magic the creative latitude to fill the gap. It wasn't something he practiced often, but he hoped it might help, in this case.

"Done." He set the pen down and held up the stack of paper.

"Great. You wrote a book. Now what?" Cailan asked.

"Now I have to apply the spells." Elazar rose from his chair.

Cailan frowned. "Didn't you just do that?"

Oh. Elazar realized that outside of the battle at Rotgut Bay, Cailan had never seen his usual way of working magic. "I did the first step. But there's still more I have to do." He hesitated as he headed for the door, recalling Cailan's aptitude for seeing magic. "You can help. Let me show you."

Elazar exited his cabin, Cailan and Max trailing behind him. The wind whipped at his hair as he stepped out onto the *Tempest's* deck. The storm clouds loomed ever closer. He scanned the area, searching for a spot shielded from the gusting wind.

There. The area beside one of the *Tempest's* emergency dinghies would be perfect. Elazar hurried over, the others close on his heels. He crouched and placed one spell he'd prepared flat against the deck.

Cailan peered over his shoulder. "Now what?"

"I have to invoke the spells I wrote," Elazar explained. He ran his fingers over the intricate runes, feeling the power contained within. "This is where I use my magic."

Max leaned in. "Maybe you should add your blood to the equation? Seems like that would help anchor the magic, you know?"

Elazar grimaced. He'd never been fond of the idea of using his own blood in spellcasting, but he had to admit that after his success with the compass, Max had a point. "You might be right." He glanced up at her. "Pass me a knife, would you?"

With a nod, Max produced a small blade and handed it to him. Elazar took a deep breath, then nicked the tip of his left index finger.

"All right. Here goes." Elazar pressed his bleeding finger to the paper and murmured, *"Fortiari."* Immediately, the page erupted in a brief, magical flame, causing Cailan to take a step back in surprise. The fire consumed the paper, leaving nothing but a faint shimmer in its wake.

"Whoa," Cailan breathed, his eyes wide. "That's some serious magic."

Elazar allowed himself a small smile. He clambered to his feet, placing a hand on the railing. He felt the *Tempest's* answering vibration, coupled with the unmistakable ripple of magic sweeping across the aurora. "Do you see it?" He glanced back at Cailan.

"What?" Cailan asked, blinking. Then he narrowed his eyes, nodding. "Yeah. There's a glow around the ship now."

Elazar grinned, deciding it was time to make further use of his brother. "Can you see if there are any weak areas around the aurora that need extra support?"

"I...yeah." Cailan seemed surprised that he was being included. "You mean, like, fly around and see?"

Elazar chuckled. "How else would you do it?"

"Just don't blame me if I get struck by lightning or blown into the sea." Cailan took a few steps backward to give himself room. Elazar watched as Cailan shifted into his opal dragon form, his brother's lean frame lengthening into glittering scales and leathery wings. He shook out his wings, glancing at the monstrous storm. With a powerful downward sweep of his wings, the opal dragon launched himself into the air, quickly gaining altitude.

"Be careful up there!" Max called after him. "Those gusts will get nasty the higher you go."

Cailan didn't respond, but Elazar noticed his flight path become more cautious as he circled the *Tempest*, scanning the shimmering aurora intently. Trusting Cailan to alert him to any weak points, Elazar turned his focus back to his own task.

Crouching low again to escape the worst of the wind, he

smoothed out another page of runes and pressed his bloody fingertip to the paper to activate the magic. This was *Fulgarisca*, the protection against lightning. The page ignited, searing its power into the *Tempest*'s deck and leaving only dying embers in its wake. Elazar rose and made his way stern-ward, seeking his next casting spot. He had several more spells to invoke before they reached the outskirts of the dangerous storm.

Elazar pressed on, making his way past the raised quarter-deck toward the *Tempest*'s aftcastle. Overhead, he caught glimpses of Cailan's draconic form through the scudding clouds, opal scales flashing when the sunlight struck them.

"There's some weakness above the mizzenmast and a patch on the starboard side of the hull," Cailan reported, swooping over Elazar and Max. A gust of wind snagged his wings, sending the opal well past them before he fought his way back. With care, he landed on the deck, quickly shifting to his human form. He was windblown, chest heaving from exertion. "You got that?"

"I did, thanks." Elazar had two pages left, the perfect amount. He glanced at Max. "Can you tell Isaac we should be ready in a half-hour? That will give him time to rouse everyone."

Max nodded. "Will do." She hurried off.

Elazar headed toward the mizzenmast, surprised when Cailan trailed behind. "Thanks for checking the aurora. That was a big help."

Cailan hesitated, then nodded. "Sure. It seemed in my best interest to make sure we don't get torn apart."

"Always so selfless," Elazar murmured as he crouched down with the next spell. He rubbed the bridge of his nose, beginning to feel the fatigue that accompanied using too much magic too quickly.

"One of us has to be practical," Cailan shot back, though there was no venom in his tone, only mild amusement. Whatever had him out of sorts seemed to have receded, leaving them with the surly Cailan they were used to.

Elazar could work with that.

16

CRADLE OF STORMS

Josephine

"Jo, you need to get up."

Gretchen's insistent prodding was unwelcome. As it was, Jo—and everyone, really—was getting far too little sleep. And Jo wanted to cling to every shred she could.

"What is it, Gretch?" she asked, her voice thick with drowsiness.

Gretchen's expression was somber, her lips pressed into a thin line. "Jo, you need to get up. Isaac reports we're nearing the Forgotten Library, but..." She hesitated, her gaze shifting.

Alarm shot through Jo, chasing away the fog of slumber. She sat up abruptly, all senses on high alert. "But what?"

"But we have to pass through a monstrous storm to reach it," Gretchen finished, her tone grave.

Jo's brow furrowed. "Then we'll just go around, like we always do." She dismissed the concern with a wave of her hand.

Gretchen shrugged, her expression unreadable. "That's what I said, but Isaac and Maxine insist the library is in the *middle* of the storm."

If Isaac and Max were this insistent, it likely meant trouble. Those two knew what they were talking about. She swung her legs over the side of the bed, reaching for her boots.

"Then I suppose we have no choice." Jo laced up her boots. Passing through such a storm would be treacherous, but if the Forgotten Library truly lay on the other side... Jo couldn't ignore the opportunity, not when it could hold the key to saving her nephew, her crew, and the very airship they called home. She snatched up her coat and pulled it on, then met Gretchen's gaze with a determined nod. "Let's go see what we're up against."

They strode up the narrow stairs to the deck together. Jo found that she and Gretchen were the last to arrive—even the chimeras had shown up to the muster.

And true to the report, a huge storm boiled ahead of them. Jagged shards of lightning illuminated dark streams of heavy rain. The reverberation of thunder rattled the airship, rattled their very bones. Jo cursed under her breath.

This was the sort of storm one avoided at all costs.

"What's this madness I hear that we have to go into that mess?" Josephine barked.

"I'll show you." Isaac nodded toward the bridge. She followed him inside, watching as the compass's ephemeral map misted into existence. Sure enough, their destination appeared to be in the middle of those angry thunderheads. "You see, we really have no choice. According to Maxine, the storm is staying put."

"That's not..." Josephine shook her head. Surely, she was still waking and had misheard. "That's not normal."

"No, it's magical," Maxine confirmed, coming in after them. "I promise it's *not* moving." Her own gaze fell on the roiling clouds shown by the map. "I think we may be in the area known as the Cradle of Storms."

Josephine raised her eyebrows. Like most captains, she knew of the Cradle of Storms—an area of exceptionally warm seawater said to spawn hurricanes that plagued the oceans. But never had she heard *magic* might play a role.

"If that were so, then wouldn't it move? Eventually dissipate?" Josephine asked.

Max shrugged. "If it were mundane, maybe. But...it's not." Her expression sobered. "We have to go *through* it."

"We'll be torn apart," Jo whispered. Even as she said the words, she felt the *Tempest* lurch forward, as if the airship was heedless of the danger before them.

"No, we won't." Elazar leaned heavily against the door, his face pale. "At least, I hope not."

Magic. He had done something with his magic, and it frightened Jo that she didn't know what. She schooled her features to hide her fears from him. There was no turning back from whatever he had done. "You look as if you spent yourself! What did you do?"

Elazar winced. "Added protections to the aurora and the ship. Didn't think it would cost me as much as it did."

"Sit." Jo pointed to the pilot's chair. Elazar looked on the verge of collapse.

"But—" Elazar's eyes widened.

"It's either that or go to your quarters to rest," she shot back. "And I'd rather have eyes on you right now."

Josephine watched as Elazar gingerly lowered himself into the pilot's chair. Her nephew's face was ashen, his movements clumsy, and she could practically feel the strain of his magic pulsing through the air.

"It's your seat, Aunt Jo," Elazar murmured, his voice weak.

Josephine waved a dismissive hand. "Right now, the *Tempest* pilots herself." She glanced out the bridge windows, where the monstrous storm loomed ever closer. "So, it matters little. You've done your part. Now let the rest of us work."

Elazar looked ready to protest, but before he could get a word out, she turned on her heel and strode onto the deck.

Gripping the smooth metal of the railing, Josephine watched as they approached the storm's edge. Thick roiling clouds blotted out the horizon, flashes of lightning dancing across the sky in a dazzling, dangerous display. The air grew stifling, charged with electricity, and Josephine tasted the tang of ozone on her tongue.

"Should we be out here?" Tiberia asked, her tone uneasy.

"You're welcome to return to your cabins, now that you're aware of what's in store for us," Jo called over her shoulder. Though the young woman had experience on airships, it was doubtful the Jade Court would have ever attempted to fly through such a storm, either. She didn't fault Tiberia's caution. "But there are protections in place, thanks to Elazar. And if those fail, there's no safe place on this ship."

"That's not as comforting as you think, love," Gretchen commented with a wry smile. The wind whipped her greying locks into her face.

"I'm not here to provide comfort," Jo shot back, her tone harder than she liked. But it was the truth.

"We already secured everything on deck that we could.

Chandra is belted down tight," Danelor said. "And Tiberia and I moved anything else to the hold already."

"Excellent," Jo said with an approving nod. "In that case, go to your cabins." She glanced at Gretchen. "You should, too."

Gretchen gave her a combative look. "Don't think you can get rid of me so easily."

"I'm not. We'll ring the bell if we need you," Jo said, hating that her tone was so curt. But the fewer on deck for this, the better. Tiberia and Danelor hurried off, and after a moment, Gretchen followed suit.

The *Tempest* plunged onward, her reinforced hull cutting through the clouds. The aurora held, protecting them from the rain that raced down its translucent surface in rivers. Josephine braced herself as the airship shuddered, buffeted by the howling winds. Overhead, the balloon-sails strained, the fabric billowing and snapping as it fought to keep them aloft.

What if Elazar's shields failed? Jo glanced back the way they'd come. It would be hard to turn the airship—especially if the *Tempest* fought them—but what if it was necessary to survive?

A violent gust of wind rocked the *Tempest*, and Josephine stumbled, clutching the railing to stay upright. Chin down, she made her way across the deck to where the blue dragon was huddled on the deck. Her claws dug into the wood, and enchanted ropes crossed her back, effectively belting her in position.

"Seer, do we make it through this?" Jo demanded, the storm almost snatching the words from her tongue.

Chandra's eyes were closed tightly, but she gave a shallow nod. "We must reach the Forgotten Library. The Dragon Who Isn't will see us through."

Josephine's jaw tightened. All this couldn't fall onto Elazar's shoulders. He was only one person, and this... She swallowed. This was nature at its worst. Jo hurried back toward the bridge and found the Skywarden staring into the maw of the hurricane.

"Max, can you do anything to ease this cursed storm?"

Maxine's gaze flicked to Josephine, her expression grim. "No. It's too much. I've never felt a power like this before."

"This is madness." Cailan stalked past them. The rain had breached sections of the aurora, slicking his hair and making his skin glisten in the lightning. "It's actively *trying* to keep us out."

"What are you doing?" Max called after him. Cailan headed for the bow.

"If it wants to keep us out, there may be a way in, and I'm going to try to find it," the marshal yelled back.

Jo hoped he knew what he was doing.

Cailan

IT WAS NEARLY IMPOSSIBLE TO SEE ANYTHING IN THE storm's fury. The bands of rain were so thick, the world seemed to be nothing but darkness punctuated by slashes of lightning. Even to Cailan's magical senses, the storm appeared sooty black, though he knew in his bones that magic had spawned it.

Cailan wasn't totally soaked through, thanks to Elazar's work on the airship's protections, but now that the aurora was failing, he had serious concerns. "Come on, come on," Cailan murmured, shielding his eyes with one hand. He searched for any break in the oppressive darkness. The roaring winds and lashing rain slashed the visibility to mere inches beyond the tip of his snout, but then he spotted something: a faint glimmer of light ahead.

"There!" he shouted, voice barely audible over the howling wind. "I see a way through!"

He received no response from the crew, but he had expected none. His words had been for the *Tempest* alone. Cailan wrapped his hands around the railing as tightly as he could, searching for some sense that the airship had heard and understood.

The vessel shuddered—no, that was a definite pause. Then slowly, battling the gale, she shifted course. Cailan's eyes were mere slits against the battering wind. Elazar's protections, the airship's aurora, were being torn away with each passing second. Fat raindrops pelted his face, and he shook his head in a futile attempt to clear his vision.

Come on. You can do it. He silently willed the *Tempest* onward. But what if the airship *couldn't* do it? If Elazar's exhausting work hadn't been enough? There was no escape at this point. Even Cailan's dragon form would be shattered by the ferocity of this storm.

Cailan squeezed his eyes shut. Rain hammered against the deck, its cold, stinging droplets seeping into every crevice, saturating the air with a chilling mist.

Just as Cailan feared they might falter, the *Tempest* burst through the veil of darkness. Cailan's eyes flew open. He lifted a hand to mop away some of the water from his face, though it did little good. The howling gale fell silent, and the relentless downpour ceased. He blinked, disoriented, as he gazed up at the clear blue sky overhead.

"We did it," Cailan whispered, sinking against the railing. He released a shaky breath, his tense muscles beginning to relax. He scanned the deck, checking on the rest of the crew. Only Max had remained on deck through the worst of the storm—which made sense, given her magic.

Captain Jo emerged from the bridge, her face pale and eyes

lined with stern worry. "We're through. How did the *Tempest* fare?"

Cailan pulled a face, wondering if he needed to remind the captain that he didn't speak airship. But she had a point—he likely would have sensed something wrong from the ship by now. "She's fine. Made it through the worst of it."

Josephine's expression softened ever so slightly, the lines of worry smoothing from her face. "Good. I'm glad to hear it," she murmured. Then, her eyes widened. "Wait. Is that...?"

Cailan turned, leaning over the railing to follow her gaze. Below, nestled among the sapphire waves, an island emerged with steep cliffs jutting defiantly from the sea.

But this was no ordinary island. Carved into the mountain that dominated its landscape stood a colossal structure. Atop it, a palatial dome sparkled in the sunlight, surrounded by towering spires that promised views extending in all cardinal directions. The sheer scale of the edifice was staggering—next to it, the *Tempest* would seem merely a child's plaything.

"I'm thinking yes," Cailan said, excitement threading through him.

"I'm going to the bridge so we can decide how to moor," Captain Jo said.

Cailan nodded, though the awe-inspiring structure before them distracted him. The Forgotten Library stood in all its glory, a beacon in the sparkling waters. He could scarcely believe they had reached their destination after everything they'd been through.

Then, a glimpse of movement at the periphery of his vision caught his attention. Cailan narrowed his eyes, scrutinizing the cliffs that cradled the building. His breath caught as massive stone figures emerged from the cliffs, larger than the *Tempest*. Colossal golems, their bodies carved from the very stone of the island, splashed through the churning tide, drawing inexorably closer to the airship.

"Captain!" Cailan shouted, his voice carrying across the deck. "We've got company!"

Josephine whirled, hurrying back to join Cailan by the railing. Her expression hardened as she spotted the golems. "All hands, battle stations!" she barked.

The rush of footsteps met Cailan's ears, even as he was in the midst of shifting into his dragon form. His transformation was quick, and he was pleased to see that the *Tempest* crew was just as alert. Max, Isaac, and Galatea rushed to his location. Tiberia and Danelor emerged from their cabin belowdecks, too.

"How do we fight *that?*" Isaac asked, throwing up his hands. "It's bad enough we just got through the storm!"

"Normal weapons won't do much against them." Max studied the golems, thoughtful. "Magic?"

Elazar staggered out of the bridge, still far too pale. He leaned heavily against the doorway.

"Not you. Go sit down," Cailan growled.

Elazar shook his head. "I have to—"

"*Not you*," Cailan shot back, tail twitching. "You're nothing but a distraction if you collapse on deck."

Elazar gave him a chagrined look, the frustration in his eyes apparent. "Fine. What are you going to do, then?"

That was a *really* good question. Max was right, weapons wouldn't work on the golems. The obvious answer was for the *Tempest* to stay out of reach of the constructs, but that wouldn't exactly help with accessing the island.

"They're golems," Max commented. "Not elementals. Someone's commanding them."

She had a point. Cailan nodded. "Then I'm going to go say hello." He crouched, preparing to leap into the air.

"Take Sprocket," Elazar suggested.

What? Cailan wanted to argue that he didn't need the contrary tin can with wings, but he knew that would only prolong things. "Fine."

With a chortle, Sprocket fluttered out of the bridge to join him. Cailan stalked back to the bow. The golems were closing in, though at her current altitude, they weren't a danger to the *Tempest.*

Time to find out who's controlling them. Cailan launched skyward.

17

PARLEY

Cailan

Sprocket shot toward the stone golems, eyes glinting with curiosity. Cailan cursed. "Don't get yourself squashed!" he called after the cogwing. Sprocket ignored him, of course.

The *Tempest* had drawn to an uneasy aerial halt. Cailan backwinged to hover below the bow and loosed a roar. The golems slowed, saltwater sloshing around their gangly legs. Behind them, he glimpsed a flash of movement.

"And here comes the warm welcome," Cailan muttered.

Winged forms, flying quickly in their direction. His gaze shifted from the golems to the newcomers, and then back again.

The approaching creatures had the definite silhouette of dragonkin.

He was right. Moments later, three dragons—no, *drakes*, Cailan corrected himself—swooped around the golems. A white drake with pearlescent scales alighted on the shoulder of one golem, glaring at Cailan. A black drake hovered to one side of the golems, and a coral-colored drake on the other.

"Who dares breach the Eye of the Storm?" the white drake demanded, his voice ringing out in challenge.

Distantly, Cailan recalled Selene's words, long ago at Ship's End. She had insisted the Forgotten Library was the home of drakes—but Cailan hadn't really believed it. He had thought they'd stumble upon ruins. Not this.

"My name is Captain Josephine Prescott of the airship *Tempest*." Above him, Captain Jo stood at the bow, a speaking horn in hand. "We're not here for a fight."

"How did you survive the storm?" the coral drake asked, curiosity ripening her voice. "You should have been torn apart!"

"Yeah, we're quite aware of that, *thanks*," Cailan grumbled, lashing his tail. "We've been searching for the Forgotten Library."

The white drake's eyes narrowed, his lips pulling back in a sneer. "You've found it. That much is true. But the odds of you leaving alive have just been reduced."

The stone golems cracked their knuckles in a menacing display, and Cailan bristled in response.

The coral-colored drake spoke, her voice holding a cautious note. "This is the first time in known history that a ship of any kind has breached the Eye of the Storm. We should tread carefully."

The black drake nodded in agreement, his gaze sweeping over the *Tempest* and her crew. "I detect six dragonkin among you, but I only see one. Where are the others?"

Cailan glanced up at the captain, aware that the situation was rapidly escalating. He knew they had come too far to turn back now, but he also didn't want a confrontation that could endanger his family.

"We'll be happy to make introductions under parley conditions," Josephine answered.

"*Parley,*" the white drake spat. "You're trespassers and should be dealt with as such!"

"Come now, Asher," the coral drake chided. "We should at least hear them out. It's not every day unfamiliar drakes arrive on our shores."

The white drake, Asher, gave them a contemptuous look. Then, his gaze fell on Sprocket, who still hovered near Cailan's side. "Whose golem is that? Is it yours?"

Cailan blinked, then shook his head. "What? No. She's not a golem. But she *is* annoying."

Asher stared at Sprocket. "It's animated. Most *certainly* a golem." His gaze swung back to Cailan and then over the *Tempest*, something changing in his demeanor. "We'll speak on this later."

"Sure, whatever floats your airship." Cailan watched as the white drake whirled in the air, flapping back toward the shores of the island.

The stone golems turned and lumbered back the way they'd come, crashing through the surf. Cailan had hoped they would simply return to the cliffs, but instead they loomed on the beach, blocking any path to the Forgotten Library.

The coral-colored drake cleared her throat, drawing Cailan's attention. "Please, come join us on the beach. We should parley, as your captain suggested."

Cailan glanced up at Josephine, receiving a curt nod in return. With a resigned sigh, he folded his wings and descended, Sprocket following close behind. As he landed and his claws sank into the sand, the other two drakes touched down with equal grace, their keen gazes locked on him.

The *Tempest* maneuvered slowly, taking more time than Cailan would have liked to move into position for Captain Josephine's disembarkation. He noted she was the only one to come ashore, a clear sign she didn't trust the situation and wanted the crew ready to make a quick escape if necessary.

She strode over to stand beside him. "Thank you for agreeing to parley. As I said, I'm Captain Josephine Prescott."

"I am Asher, Guardian of the Forgotten Library," declared the white drake, his voice tinged with disdain. "And these—" He gestured towards the coral and black drakes. "—are my companions, Oriana and Zark." The drakes gave Cailan an expectant look.

So much for being the captain's nameless protector. Cailan shifted uncomfortably, aware of the golems looming behind the drakes. "Cailan. I'm the ship's marshal."

Asher's eyes narrowed. "You are only *one* of the dragonkin we sensed with the airship. Where are the others?"

Cailan hesitated, unsure of how much to reveal. "My...crewmates are aboard the *Tempest*. We're not here to cause trouble. We just need to get into the Forgotten Library."

Oriana, the coral drake, spoke up. "The library has never been open to outsiders. Why do you seek it?"

Josephine stepped forward. "We're searching for information that may help to right an old wrong. My—I mean, our...shipmate, Elazar, believes the answers lie within the Forgotten Library."

Cailan pursed his lips, not missing her careful phrasing. She purposely concealed her relationship to Elazar. But why? Because he was a drake and she wasn't? It made sense, in a way.

Asher's gaze flicked to Josephine, then back to Cailan. "And is this Elazar drake or *other*?"

Cailan winced. He didn't want to reveal too much, but he also didn't want to risk angering the drakes further. "Elazar is...one of us."

Asher's lip curled. "I see. So, you expect us to let you romp into the Forgotten Library, when you can't even be honest about the members of your party?"

"I'm a drake." Elazar's voice rang out, magnified by the speaking horn, which he'd apparently claimed. He clung to the *Tempest's* railing, peering down at them.

Zark, the black drake, flapped up to peer at Elazar. "You are only one, though." He studied the others on deck, then aimed a claw at someone Cailan couldn't see from his vantage point. "There. Two more stand there. But where are the others?"

The chimeras strode into Cailan's line of sight. But who else did she mean? *Oh.*

Beside him, Captain Jo released a soft breath of realization. "Oh, no."

Before anyone else could speak, Chandra appeared at the bow, looming over the others. "I am the fifth, and as for the sixth..." She gestured with a claw to the airship. "It's the *Tempest.*"

Elazar

Elazar wasn't sure if things could get any stranger, but at least they had safely navigated through the hurricane, and now he could finally rest.

Following a tense parley on the beach, the drakes of the Forgotten Library had agreed to host the crew of the *Tempest.* The airship herself was securely moored against one of the cliffs, providing straightforward access for disembarking and allowing the crew to perform checks.

The Forgotten Library was a sight unlike any Elazar had encountered before. Years ago, he had dreamed of visiting the Archives, the renowned library in Ravance. He remembered the sketches of the Archives well, but they paled in comparison to this marvel.

The library's structure, seamlessly forged from the island's stone, was clearly not crafted by any conventional method—it was too perfect, not shaped by human hands. Elazar recognized that such flawless construction must involve magic, and not just any magic, but a powerful, ancient magic that he had not known to exist in their world.

The three drakes who had greeted them were not the only occupants. The island seemed to support a healthy population of fellow drakes who peered at them—especially Chandra—curiously as they made their way through the grand facade.

They shared a tense but delicious meal in the Celestial Hall, which Elazar presumed was the great hall of the library. The huge room boasted rows upon rows of tables, some equipped with benches, others left without, accommodating both bipedal guests and those in drake form. Above them, the ceiling was enchanted to display a mesmerizing night sky. It shone with stars even by day, casting a magical illumination over the entire hall.

At the end of the meal, Oriana rose. She nodded toward their guests. "Now that we've eaten, we'll be happy to have further conversations with you, Captain Prescott and Seer Chandra. While we do so, one of our drakes will show your crew to their accommodations."

Elazar stiffened. He didn't like the idea of being separated from his aunt—it seemed dangerous. Cailan must have had the same thought, because he pushed away from the table (in his drake form), drawing attention. "Hang on, don't you think some of us *drakes* should also be in attendance?"

"We have separate plans for you," Zark replied, his tone less than reassuring.

"Yeah, that's not how this is going to work." Cailan shook his head. Elazar wanted to tell him he was pressing his luck, but knew Cailan would just ignore him. "You talk to us together, or not at all."

"*I'm* strongly considering not at all," Asher commented.

Elazar's anxiety spiked at Cailan's frustration. He knew his brother was only looking out for them, but the drakes' distrust was clear. Elazar didn't want to jeopardize their chances. Too much was on the line.

Oriana studied Cailan, her golden eyes narrowing. "Very well. *Elazar* will join our group." She gestured to another of the drakes. "Escort the rest of the crew to their accommodations."

Cailan's mouth dropped open, first in surprise, and then to prepare for what would be an angry retort, but Elazar quickly placed a hand on his scaled shoulder. "Thank you," he said, meeting Oriana's gaze. "We appreciate your hospitality."

With a curt nod, Oriana turned and led the way out of the Celestial Hall. Elazar fell into step beside her, acutely aware of Cailan's disgruntled presence in his wake.

The corridors of the library were awe-inspiring, the walls etched with beautiful carvings and glowing runes. He tried to glimpse the spells imbued in the runes but was moving too quickly to make them out. Elazar tried to take it all in, but his mind raced with questions. Why had the drakes included him and not Cailan? Was it because of Cailan's attitude? And what did they have planned for the others?

Oriana ushered them into a room that looked like a grand study, filled with towering bookshelves. "This is the Ember Chamber. Please, have a seat." She gestured with her tail to the empty chairs. For Chandra, she nodded toward a large rug that had been laid out. "Apologies, Seer. It's the best we could do on short notice."

"It will serve me well." Chandra eased down onto the rug, Vesper settling at her side.

Elazar exchanged a look with his aunt, then they each claimed a chair. Oriana, Asher, and Zark moved to sit upon huge pillows that served as drake seating. As Elazar took his place on an uncushioned oak chair, he couldn't help but think that the drakes' seating looked far more comfortable.

"Every room within the library has a name and a purpose," Oriana explained. "Just as every inhabitant of this island has a purpose. The Ember Chamber symbolizes the spark that brings warmth and unity to the drakes of the Forgotten Library." She turned a scrutinizing gaze on Elazar and the others. "What is *your* purpose for seeking the Forgotten Library?"

Aunt Jo nodded to Elazar. "It's better if he tells you."

Elazar drew a shaky breath, aware that the moment of truth had come. "We're here because of the Jade Empress," he began. A momentary ripple of disquiet passed through the gathering. "She thought because of my unique...condition, I could find the Forgotten Library."

Asher's gaze sharpened, like talons aiming for the heart. "*Unique condition?* What do you mean by that?"

The question hung in the air, an uncompromising demand for truth. Elazar swallowed. "She believes I'm connected to the prophecy of the Dragon Who Isn't."

"Don't lie to us," Asher cautioned, his voice a growl, taking Elazar aback with the intensity of his warning. "Lies have a way to revealing themselves, and you won't like the result."

Elazar's cheeks warmed. "There's no lie. Belen thinks I'm the Dragon Who Isn't."

"His words are true." Chandra's voice was a soft rumble

that drew everyone's attention. "I apologize for speaking out of turn. I know my welcome here is...tentative."

The trio of drakes exchanged glances. Then Oriana shook her head. "No apologies needed, Seer. We know that you're unlike most dragons."

Chandra offered a toothy smile. "More than you know."

"This prophecy...it was one of yours?" Asher asked, almost hesitant.

The Seer shrugged the remnants of her wings. "It's one that predates my time as Seer, as most do." She cocked her head, thoughtful. "Regardless, you can believe the veracity of the Dragon Who Isn't."

Oriana's attention snapped back to Elazar. "Now, tell us about this Dragon Who Isn't. Are you...not a drake when you shift?"

"Show us your natural form," Asher suggested, his tone chill.

Oh, winds. Not that. A prickle of embarrassment ran down Elazar's spine. Would they think he'd lied about being a drake since he couldn't shift on demand?

His aunt touched his arm. "There's no shame. Just tell them."

Easy for her to say. Elazar bowed his head. "I can't shift. At least, not when I want to."

The drakes were quiet for a moment. Elazar didn't hazard a look at them, too mortified by his own lack of ability. Then, Zark said, "But you wear a nexus chain. And you clearly have magic. Are you under a curse of some sort?"

A curse. Elazar almost wanted to laugh, recalling a time when he was sure he'd been cursed into dragon form. "A curse? No. I just...*can't.* I don't know how."

"In his defense, we were both certain he was a human for the first twenty-five years of his life," Aunt Jo added.

The Forgotten Library drakes exchanged looks. Asher studied Elazar with an intensity that was disconcerting. "Explain what you mean by that," the pearly-white drake said, his words clipped. His gaze darted to Chandra, but the Seer remained silent.

Aunt Jo cleared her throat. Elazar nodded to her. The drakes would find out their relationship eventually—it was better to put it out in the open now. "Many years ago, I found a little boy abandoned on an island." She gestured toward him. "Elazar. I raised him as if he were my own, believing that he was the child of my deceased sister." Her voice shook with remembered emotion.

"Which island?" Asher demanded.

"Asher, this isn't relevant to—" Zark began, but a glare from the Guardian cut him off.

"It's called Dead Man's Dare," Josephine said.

Asher stared at Elazar. Then he shimmered with magic, his form diminishing until he was a man—a tall man, but a man nonetheless. He had long pale hair that was almost white, and strikingly handsome features. Elazar swallowed, feeling as if he were staring at an older, more mature version of Cailan.

Asher stalked over to Elazar, reaching out to grasp his chin. Elazar wanted to flinch away, but every move Asher made registered as a predator, even as a human. Confusion gripped Elazar, and he didn't dare move in the unpredictable drake's clutches. "I should have realized it sooner. You have Macawi's build. It's been so long..." His voice had grown soft, reflective, but there was still a fierceness in his eyes. Then, he released Elazar and whirled to face Chandra. "Seer, how can this be? Why did you not tell us sooner?"

"We'd appreciate knowing what *any* of this means," Aunt Jo said, somehow keeping her tone neutral, though her fists were clenched and she had a protective tilt to her chin.

"You're not the only one," Oriana agreed.

"Now is the time," Chandra murmured, her words only adding to the confusion. "Your conclusions are correct, Asher."

Asher took a step backward. "One of my lost whelps. The young I was forced to abandon." He gave Elazar another intense look. "I am your sire."

Elazar stared. He felt as if, for a moment, time had stopped while he registered the word. "I... What?"

"You are my son," Asher clarified, his words crisp. "One of the whelps I thought lost to me forever." Then, he frowned. "And this woman raised you as a *human*."

Elazar frowned, affronted that this drake would insult his aunt. "There's nothing wrong with that."

"No, of course not," Oriana said, drawing their attention once more. "And while later we most *certainly* will need to have a celebration for this most unlikely of reunions, we should remain on task."

"I want to know how my whelp ended up with humans," Asher said, utterly ignoring the coral drake. He stared at Aunt Jo in an aggressive manner that Elazar didn't like.

"I'd like to know how you could abandon your child and then take offense to the woman who raised him," Aunt Jo said coolly. "If I hadn't come along, who knows if Elazar would even be here today?"

Elazar felt much the same. The sting of abandonment warred with a strange sort of satisfaction. Elazar had uncovered more of his roots, but the knowledge left him deeply unsettled. He wasn't sure he liked what he'd found. "You shouldn't be upset with my aunt. And she has a valid question."

Asher's jaw clenched, a muscle ticking. Then, he nodded. "You were *not* abandoned by choice." He paused, for a moment so still that he almost resembled a marble statue. "Your mother, Macawi, and I wanted nothing more than to raise our whelps somewhere safe. Somewhere free of dragon tyranny." Asher lifted his chin. "But we fought the Jade Court and lost."

Elazar's gut twisted as new certainty settled over him. "Are you the drake who crippled the Jade Court's ability to fly?"

Asher snorted. "If only. I have command of stone, the power to animate it." He sighed, as if recalling an old memory. "No, your mother is the one who ultimately clipped the wings of the Jade Court."

Elazar swallowed. If his mother—his *mother!*—had been the one to wreak such disaster upon the dragons, then might she be the one to fix it? He was torn between the horror that his true parents could do such a thing, and the fervent hope that it could be corrected easily. And soon.

"Could she...could she undo it?" Elazar asked.

At the question, Asher went rigid again, shaking his head. "No. I'm done here." He turned and stalked from the Ember Chamber, leaving them behind in startled silence.

Elazar blinked, befuddled by all that had just transpired, his hope sinking. He looked at the remaining Forgotten Library drakes. "Do you know why?"

Chandra was the one who answered, however. "Because his mate...your mother...is dead. Killed by the Jade Court."

18

Family Resemblance

Cailan

"Seems like you've been getting on well with Danelor," Max commented as she stood beside Cailan in a corridor.

Frustrated by his lack of inclusion, Cailan refused to be shown to their guest accommodations. Max remained behind, ostensibly so he wasn't alone. Cailan suspected Max's aim was to keep him from causing trouble.

He narrowed his eyes at her assessment. "I was ordered to show him the ropes."

At that, Max's expression brightened. "That's adorable. Exactly how you and Elazar became friends!"

"Friends?" Cailan couldn't help but laugh. "You think we were ever *friends?*" He crossed his arms.

The mage rolled her eyes. "You think you're not?" She nudged him with an elbow. "The chimera seems nice, though."

Cailan snorted. "Too nice for his own good. It's uncanny. That chimera isn't right."

Max raised a brow. "Only *you* would consider someone too nice and equate it to being a bad thing."

The sound of a door opening and then closing with a *thud* spared Cailan from further conversation related to Danelor. "Looks like things are going well," Cailan murmured to Max, head cocked with interest at the sight of a man with white-blond hair storming up the hallway from the direction Captain Jo and Elazar had gone.

Max studied the stranger, narrowing her eyes as her gaze slid from the man and back to Cailan. "No way," she whispered.

"What?" Cailan asked, frowning.

The Stormcaller hissed out a breath. "It's just..." She hesitated. "Maybe I didn't get the best look at him."

"You can't leave me hanging. What did you see?"

Max swallowed, glancing away. "Okay, I only had a quick glimpse of him. But...he looked a lot like you."

Cailan blinked. "What?"

"You heard what I said," she whispered. "But don't tie your tail in a knot. I could be wrong. And what if it's common for drakes to look similar in their shifted form?"

Cailan pursed his lips. As men, he and Elazar looked nothing alike. At least, *he* didn't think so. He and Max stood in silence, pondering the mystery of the angry man, as they waited for Captain Jo, Chandra, and Elazar.

A quarter-hour later, they emerged, flanked by the drakes

Oriana and Zark. Oriana frowned when she saw Cailan and Max, clearly not expecting that they'd refuse the hospitality.

"I suppose we'll show *all* of you to your accommodations, then," Oriana said, her tone artificially bright.

"Sure," Cailan muttered, though his focus was fully on the captain, Chandra, and Elazar.

His brother looked as if he were barely holding it together. Oh, anyone else might think Elazar was fine, but he definitely *wasn't.* His face had a pinched expression, his shoulders tense. Captain Jo, meanwhile, maintained a neutral look, though there was a glint in her eye that spoke of slumbering frustration.

"Seer, allow me to show you to accommodations that will be more suitable for you," Zark suggested, showing the blue dragon and her aralez elsewhere.

Max fell into step beside Elazar, and he seemed to relax fractionally. Cailan moved alongside the captain, and together, they allowed the drakes to usher them to a wing of the structure that seemed to be used as quarters.

"You should find that the rest of your companions already have rooms here," Oriana said, nodding to the corridor before them. "Are any of you mated pairs that we should know about?"

"I should be with Gretchen, the ship's Healer," Captain Jo said.

"We'll make certain that's so." Oriana nodded, serene.

Cailan followed Oriana down the corridor, trying to ignore the sting of unease that had settled between his shoulder blades. Beside him, Elazar walked with an uncharacteristic distance in his eyes. Whatever had been discussed, it clearly weighed heavily on him, leaving Cailan to simmer with curiosity.

Oriana led them into a spacious common area, bathed in a warm, golden glow. Plush seating arrangements, upholstered in rich velvets and brocades, were scattered throughout. Cailan couldn't help but be impressed by the grandeur.

"Consider this your sanctuary for the time being," Oriana said. "Relax. Gather your thoughts. If you need anything at all, simply press that button." She gestured to a nearby wall, where a curious, jewel-toned button awaited. "Now, while we are delighted to host you," Oriana continued, her tone turning regretful, "we insist that you remain within either your rooms or this common area. The Forgotten Library is immense and... certain areas are off-limits to guests."

Irritation flared within Cailan at the drake's warning, but he forced himself to nod in acknowledgment. He had to play nice, for now.

"We understand," Josephine spoke up, her tone diplomatic. "Thank you for your hospitality."

Oriana inclined her head. "Sleep well. We will speak more in the morning." With that, she turned and left, the heavy doors swinging shut behind her.

As soon as the drake was out of earshot, Cailan whirled on Elazar and Captain Jo. "What happened?"

"I'm also curious," Gretchen agreed as she moved to join them, her tone droll. "But you should watch your tone, Marshal."

"Don't care." Cailan's gaze was on Elazar.

Captain Jo nodded, moving to sit on one of the couches. "The short version is that we told them why we've come. They're not pleased that we've come at the behest of a dragon court, and Elazar didn't get to fully explain our reasoning before the discussion went off course."

"Went off course how?" Max asked before Cailan could.

Elazar swallowed, lifting his gaze to Cailan. "Asher is our father. Chandra confirmed it."

What? Of all the things Elazar could have said, Cailan had not expected that—no matter what Max had suggested. The Stormcaller clapped a hand over her mouth, her eyes wide. Cailan felt as if he had just been swept into the magical storm once more.

For years, his questions about his parentage had been met with silence. And now, in a span of days, he'd discovered not only a brother, but a living father? Cailan shook his head, disbelief warring with a rising tide of emotion. "*What?*"

"He and our mother are the ones who led the drake uprising against the Jade Court," Elazar whispered. "They're the reason for...*everything.*"

The reason for everything. Elazar's soft, heartbreaking words felt as if they had kicked Cailan in the teeth. He stared at his brother and then spun, stalking toward the door that led out of the common area, away from their evening accommodations.

"Cailan! What are you doing?" Max called after him in alarm.

"Marshal, stand down!" Captain Jo snapped.

Cailan called forth his dragon form, motes of magic dancing along his skin until, an instant later, he was on four legs and glancing at them over a wing. "It's time for answers."

No one was going to stop him—not right now. He stormed into the corridor, talons ticking against the stone floor. Ahead, the sinuous neck of a curious drake peered around a corner at him, eyes widening when they no doubt realized he was a free-range guest.

The tap of hurried footsteps announced someone had followed him. "Cailan!" Elazar's voice.

"Don't try and stop me," Cailan snarled, deciding it was a suitable warning for both Elazar and any of the Library drakes.

"I'm not trying to stop you. I'm coming with you." Elazar had broken into a run to catch up.

Coming along? That surprised Cailan, and he slowed for a

beat, shifting his weight from one clawed foot to the other. "Broke out of your stupor, did you?"

"You weren't there." Elazar shook his head. "It wasn't easy."

"I wasn't invited. And it's never easy." Cailan turned a corner, coming upon a knot of three drakes. They stared at him, shocked. "We want to talk to Asher."

Cailan bristled as the three drakes stared at him and Elazar. The one in the middle, a female with shimmering yellow scales, lifted a claw in a placating gesture.

"I'll see what I can do," she said. Without another word, she turned and hurried down the corridor.

Cailan shifted his weight, his tail lashing behind him. Beside him, Elazar fidgeted, as if he were uncomfortable in his own skin. Cailan glanced at his brother, his brow furrowing. An uncharacteristic twinge of sympathy stirred. "At least you're not alone," Cailan said, voice soft.

Surprise flashed in Elazar's eyes, and a small smile touched his face. "I'm glad for that."

After what felt like an eternity, the yellow-scaled drake returned, gesturing for them to follow. "This way."

The brothers followed, winding through the grand hall-ways of the Forgotten Library. Moments later, she showed them to a private living area.

And there, standing by the window, was Asher in his scaly form. The drake turned, his golden-brown eyes narrowing as he regarded them. His expression was one of obvious frustration and upset.

Cailan's hackles rose, a low rumble building in his chest. This was the drake who had abandoned them, the one respon-sible for the upheaval that had shaped both of their lives. He wanted answers, and he wanted them *now*.

Beside him, Elazar shifted nervously, his gaze darting

between Cailan and Asher. Their drake escort slipped past them, closing the doors and leaving the three of them alone.

Asher blinked, sucking in a breath, his emotions receding in the face of obvious surprise. "There are *two* of you."

Cailan took a step forward, his talons rasping against the polished floor. "Yeah, there are," he growled, his voice rough with emotion. "Time for some answers."

Asher's gaze was momentarily vacant, as if he were staring into the distance. "You both survived...just as she said you would."

"She who?" Cailan snapped.

"The Seer," Asher said.

Winds, *Chandra*? Did he really mean...? A roaring filled Cailan's ears, the world shrinking around him until all that remained was the echoing truth. He finally understood Elazar's reaction, the way his brother had looked as if the very foundation of his world had crumbled. Because it had.

"I don't understand." Elazar's voice was barely a whisper.

Asher moved away from the window, closer to them. "I should probably start from the beginning, then." He gestured to the nearby seats. Cailan considered staying in his current form out of spite, but relented and shifted to human, sinking down onto a cushion beside Elazar. Asher shifted as well, then sat opposite them. "Many years ago, your mother and I were drakes of the Jade Court."

Cailan frowned. He wanted to interrupt, to say that he hadn't even known what a drake *was* until recently, much less that the Jade Court had been a home to them, but he stayed quiet.

"You were their slaves," Elazar hazarded.

"We weren't called that, but yes." Asher nodded.

Cailan listened intently, head tilted, as Asher spoke. He was still adjusting to this revelation that he and Elazar were the sons of drakes. "You're saying the dragons didn't call you slaves," Cailan prompted, leaning forward, "but there was little difference?"

Asher nodded solemnly. "That's right. We drakes were vital to the functioning of the Jade Court, but we had no autonomy, no say in our own lives. We were at the mercy of the dragons."

A sudden chill prickled through Cailan. "What did the drakes do, exactly?"

"Everything," Asher replied, his voice bitter. "We were the ones who made the small improvements, the innovations that made life easier for the dragons. But it came at a great cost to us."

The information twisted uncomfortably inside Cailan. He listened, fingers tapping against his leg, unable to find a resting place for his hand, let alone the unsettling truth Asher laid bare.

"So, you and...our mother," Cailan asked, sparing a glance for Elazar, who sat silently beside him, "you decided to stage a rebellion?"

A shadow fell over Asher's face. "We couldn't stand the injustice any longer. Not once we had our first clutch to think of." His gaze shifted between Cailan and Elazar, a deep sorrow welling in his eyes. "We couldn't bear the thought of our children suffering the same fate. We wanted you to be free."

"Oh, that part worked out just great," Cailan said, unable to mask his bitterness.

Asher's jaw tightened. "How was I to know you'd both end up at the mercy of the Jade Court again?" He shook his head, drawing in a steadying breath. "We worked with other drakes, found a nearby settlement of humans who'd also felt the dragons' wrath. An accord was struck. We launched an attack on the Jade Court, crippled their forces enough to buy the fleeing drakes time."

"And how did that turn out for *you?*" Cailan drawled, unable to resist needling the other drake, despite the warning pressure of Elazar's hand on his shoulder.

Asher's eyes flashed. "Not as well as we'd hoped. There were still too many dragons. Some drakes fled to far corners of the world. A few came here." He gestured around them at the grand library. "But Macawi and I, we feared the Jade Court wouldn't rest. So, we hatched a plan to corrupt the dragonfruit harvest, a blight that would wither their wings."

"What?" Cailan blinked, his breath hitching. The plan was both impressive and horrifying in its cruelty. "Well, that sure did the trick."

Asher shot him a venomous look. "At a terrible cost. And too late. The Jade Court had already found our island. A group of apex and leviathans..." He shook his head, hands fisted in his lap, knuckles white. "They slaughtered everyone. Macawi... She was among them. I thought you were dead, too. Still in your shell."

Belen may not have killed Chandra, but her court killed my mother. Cailan's own hands curled into fists. "You didn't come back. Didn't even try to find us."

Each word Asher spoke seemed carved from stone. "I thought everyone I ever cared about was gone. I was lost, without hope. You can't imagine the depths of despair I felt, the way I craved oblivion." He swallowed, the apple of his throat bobbing. "But then...I found this place. And with it, a reason to live. Something to believe in."

"Great, so a bunch of musty books were more important than your own sons," Cailan spat, not caring how childish he sounded. He was pissed. And beneath the anger, a deep, aching hurt throbbed.

"I refuse to drown in grief," Asher said, crossing his arms. "Would you have acted differently?"

"No," Elazar answered quietly. "You didn't know. Just like..." He scrubbed a hand through his hair. "For the longest time, I thought I was human. I hated dragons. Believed my parents had died in a dragon attack."

"Turns out you were half-right," Cailan muttered.

Elazar ignored him. "So, I understand why you didn't look for us."

But something Asher had said snagged in Cailan's mind. "I don't believe you."

"What?" Elazar frowned.

"Not you." Cailan turned his attention to Asher. "*You*. You said Chandra told you we would survive. *You knew*."

"Hearing a Seer's prophecy and believing it are two entirely different things," Asher shot back. "And how could I believe her? She's the one who told me to have Macawi corrupt the dragonfruit. She set us on this path to ruin."

Cailan blinked. "If Chandra told you to do it, there was a reason."

"I highly doubt that now," Asher grumbled. "And how would you know anything about it?"

"Because she raised me," Cailan retorted.

Asher swore, a harsh sound—some dialect of draconic that Cailan wasn't familiar with. "The Seer...*raised* you?"

"Yes." Cailan sank back against the cushions, crossing his arms.

Their father frowned, a crease deepening between his brows. "This changes things." He rubbed his forehead, his gaze distant. "We should all rest. The hour is late." Asher paused, glancing at Elazar. "And perhaps tomorrow we'll see what we can do about your...shifting problem."

Elazar's eyes widened. "You can do that?"

Asher offered a wry smile. "You're at the Forgotten Library. Many things are possible here. But for now, rest." He rose to his feet, fixing Cailan with a pointed look. "Return to your assigned chambers and don't wander. I can't guarantee your safety."

A low growl rumbled in Cailan's chest. "I'm not scared of whatever monsters you're hiding here."

Asher's smile sharpened, turning almost feral. "You should be."

19

HIGH PRICE

Maxine

Max caught the sound of approaching footsteps—the solid thud of boots against the polished floor—and peeked out of her room. Elazar and Cailan were heading her way, their voices strained. She slipped into the hallway. "Hey, are you okay?"

The brothers stopped, their conversation abruptly cut off. Irritation pulled at Cailan's features, while Elazar just looked... drained.

"No ravenous library beasts ate us, if that's what you mean," Cailan said.

"Well, that's in our favor," Max replied. "Was it...helpful?"

"Frustrating more than anything." Cailan shook his head. "I'm gonna sleep." He stalked to the door of his assigned room and shoved it open with his shoulder, leaving Elazar with Max.

"You haven't said much," Max observed, taking a step closer to him.

Elazar rubbed the bridge of his nose. "It's more like...I don't even know where to start. What to think."

"Do you want to talk about it?" Max offered. "Sometimes it helps to get things out in the open."

He let out a long breath. "I..." His gaze flicked towards his room, then back to her. "Maybe. I don't know. All I know is sleep is the last thing on my mind right now."

She could see it in the tension around his eyes, the way he held himself. His mind was a tangled knot of thoughts. Max gripped his arm lightly, giving him a gentle tug. "Come on."

"What?" He blinked at her.

"Just come on." Max grinned, a mischievous glint in her eye. She pulled him along with her into her room, which was small but surprisingly luxurious. The Forgotten Library clearly had style. Max gestured toward the bedside table, where a deck of cards lay beside a crystal water carafe. "Found these in the nightstand drawer. Let's play."

"Play...cards?" Elazar slowly came out of his daze. "Oh." He picked up the deck, frowning. "These aren't normal playing cards."

"Nope. And they're old," Max agreed. "But definitely meant for a game. See that card? The rules are written on it." She pointed, and he easily spotted the indicated card beside the carved box.

A slow smile spread across Elazar's face, chasing away some of the tension that had gathered there. "You're right. It sounds...fun. And a distraction is exactly what I need."

Maxine watched him as he picked up the old deck of cards,

his brow creased in concentration as he shuffled them. She settled onto the plush bed beside him, drawing her legs up to sit cross-legged. The velvety fabric whispered softly beneath her.

"All right, let's see what we're dealing with here." Elazar dealt the cards, his movements as precise as meshing gears.

He laid the first card face-up between them, and Maxine noticed how the muscles in his shoulders remained tense, even as he tried to relax. "So," she began, keeping her voice gentle, "what exactly happened back there with Asher? You seem a little...shaken."

Elazar hesitated, his fingers hovering over the next card in the deck. "It's...a lot to process." He sighed, his gaze fixed on the designs of the cards.

"Is he really your father?" Max asked cautiously, hoping she wasn't overstepping.

"He and Chandra both seem to think so." Elazar's voice was barely audible. "I don't know what to believe." He shook his head. Then, voice cracking, he told her all he knew. How his mother had corrupted the dragonfruit with magic. How the dragons killed her.

Maxine's heart ached for him. No wonder Elazar was reeling. To learn of his mother's death, the knowledge of his parents' rebellion—it was a crushing truth to uncover. "And Asher just left you?" she asked softly.

"He thought Cailan and I had died with our mother." Elazar's voice was heavy with sorrow. "He's been hiding here in the Forgotten Library ever since."

Maxine reached out and gently squeezed his hand. "It's a lot to take in all at once. It's no wonder you're struggling."

Her words seemed to offer him a small measure of comfort. Elazar nodded, some of the tension easing from his shoulders. He smiled, a lighter note entering his voice as he said, "Now, how about we try this out?" He released her hand and picked up the deck. "Ready for a proper game?"

"Bring it on." Maxine grinned back, her earlier concerns momentarily forgotten.

As they played, she couldn't help but steal glances at him, her gaze tracing the line of his jaw, the tiny crow's feet that appeared around his eyes when he concentrated, or the flash of triumph when he made a clever play. How had she never noticed her attraction to him before?

Finally, Elazar laid down his last card, a triumphant grin spreading across his face. "I believe victory is mine."

Maxine laughed, shaking her head in amusement. "Good game. You're a natural at this."

Elazar picked up the cards, shuffling them once more. "This was a good idea you had. I really needed something like this. Something normal."

She watched the blur of cards in his hands. "I thought you needed it. You know I'm always here for you, right?"

Elazar smiled, the expression genuine. "I really missed you while I was..." The apple in his throat bobbed, and he shook his head. "Anyway, I missed you."

Max wanted to ask about his time with the Jade Court—not for her own curiosity, but for Elazar's welfare. How had they treated him? She glimpsed a few new scars on his arms, but those could have come from airship mishaps as easily as from a dragon. Max would have to wait until he was ready to talk about it.

So instead, she reached over to smooth a flyaway hair behind his ear. "I missed you, too. I wasn't expecting to see you again like this."

He raised his brows. "What, you mean with longer hair?"

Max laughed. "No, without scales and wings. The last time I saw you—before you disappeared—you were a dragon."

Elazar chuckled, too. "Oh." He ran a hand through his hair, thoughtful. "When all this is over with, I'm getting a proper haircut."

She raised her eyebrows at that. "Are you sure you want to do that?"

Confusion crossed Elazar's face. "What do you mean?" He paused. "Wait, are you saying you like it?"

Max cocked her head, giving him a broad smile. "Maybe I am."

He glanced down at a lock of hair he'd captured with his fingers. "Then I'll think about keeping it."

Josephine

"Rough night?" Gretchen murmured, pressing a steaming mug into Jo's hands. The aroma of coffee laced with something warm and subtly sweet wafted up to tempt her.

Jo scrubbed a hand over her tired eyes. Even though exhaustion clung to her like a shroud, sleep had been a fickle companion, riddled with fitful dreams that left her more weary than before. And naturally, she'd only drifted off into a truly restful slumber an hour before she was meant to wake.

"What is this, exactly?" She lifted the mug, taking a cautious sip. It tasted like coffee, but smoother, richer, with a delicate hint of vanilla. Definitely not the bitter brew she was used to.

"Local specialty," Gretchen said with a wry smile. "They take their coffee seriously here."

Jo hummed in approval, taking another longer sip. The warm liquid chased away the fog in her mind. "Between this and everything we learned last night, it's a wonder any of us slept at all."

Gretchen's smile faded. "You're worried about Elazar." It wasn't a question.

Jo let out a sigh, dropping her gaze to her knotted hands. "What if he...what if he forms a bond with this drake, this *stranger*, who only decided Elazar was worth acknowledging yesterday?" It felt selfish, even petty, to begrudge Elazar this reunion with his family. But the gods knew she loved him like a son—and she had for years. The thought of losing him, of him choosing a life that might not include her...it was almost unbearable.

"He's a grown man, Jo. You know he'll..." Gretchen coughed, amending her words. "Well, I was going to say *fly the nest*, but given the circumstances, that might be a poor choice of words."

A small chuckle escaped Jo's lips at the absurdity of it all. "I know. He has every right." How could she explain the fear that clung to her? The fear of being forgotten, cast aside, replaced? It all sounded so childish, so ridiculously unfair to Elazar. And she knew it. She heaved a weary sigh.

"Love, you're entitled to your feelings." Gretchen put an arm around her. "Just best if you don't wear them outside of this room."

The last thing Jo wanted was to make this about her own insecurities. "I won't. I just need a moment to mope." She took another fortifying gulp of the fragrant coffee. She needed a clear head. With a determined breath, Jo set the mug down and pushed herself up from the bed.

Gretchen watched, her gaze intent, as Jo moved toward the wardrobe, pulling out her familiar captain's attire—the supple leather, the feel of the worn fabric against her skin, all a comfort in the face of uncertainty. "What does the day hold, love?" Gretchen asked.

"More talks with the drakes," Jo said, slipping into her trousers. "I need to understand where Elazar fits into all of this, what they might offer in the way of assistance for the Jade Court." As she reached for her shirt, Gibson's voice echoed in her mind. She rubbed her temples at the burgeoning headache.

"A long day, then," Gretchen murmured, coming up behind her. Jo felt the brush of Gretchen's fingers against her nape as the other woman helped her with the buttons of her shirt.

"I could have managed that," Jo said, a slight flush warming her cheeks.

"Of course, you could." Gretchen's voice dropped to a murmur, close to her ear. "But I fear I'll need to seize every opportunity to be near you while we're here. Your schedule seems...demanding." She chased her words with a mischievous wink.

"Probably," Jo conceded. "But the sooner we get some answers, the sooner we can get back on course." She offered Gretchen a wry smile. "And perhaps then, I'll be able to steal a moment or two for less official engagements."

Gretchen nodded. She paused, giving Jo's hand a gentle squeeze. "We'll figure this out. Elazar isn't going anywhere, I'm sure of it."

Jo returned the squeeze, silently hoping Gretchen was right. With a final nod, she pulled on her boots and the two made their way out to the common area.

The rest of the *Tempest*'s crew was already gathered, a mouth-watering spread of food laid out on a long table. Tiberia and Danelor occupied a table by themselves, speaking in hushed tones. Elazar, Cailan, and Max were seated at a larger rectangular table with plenty of space for Jo and Gretchen to join them. Gally and Isaac were conspicuously absent—no doubt taking advantage of the opportunity to catch up on some much-needed sleep.

"Good morning. I trust everyone slept well?" Jo cast a glance around the table, noting the shadows under a few eyes. Even Cailan, his usual sullenness amplified this morning, managed a curt nod of acknowledgment. The others murmured greetings. Jo noticed they, too, were nursing mugs of fragrant, steaming coffee.

Just as they were finishing their breakfast, a silver drake appeared in the arched doorway. "Captain Prescott?" His gaze swept over the assembled group. "The Conclave requests your presence. Yours as well, drakes."

Conclave? Jo met Gretchen's gaze across the table, a silent question passing between them. She rose to her feet. "Lead the way." Elazar and Cailan stood as well, their movements echoing hers.

"*All* of the drakes," their escort clarified, tilting his head. "I was informed there are four, not including the Seer and the... ah, the airship."

Josephine blinked, turning to Elazar for clarification. He must have understood, because his gaze shifted to where Tiberia and Danelor sat, separate but still a part of their strange assembled family. Outsiders, but not.

"They mean you two, I think," Elazar said.

Josephine watched, uncertain, as Tiberia and Danelor rose to join them, their expressions unreadable. The five of them followed the silver drake deeper into the labyrinthine heart of the Forgotten Library.

Josephine's mind spun, struggling to make sense of everything that had transpired. The revelation of Elazar and Cailan's father, the existence of this Conclave that apparently governed this hidden place... She had questions, a veritable storm of them, but she forced herself to remain present, to project an air of calm she didn't quite feel.

The silver drake led them into the Ember Chamber, the same room as the previous night. Now, sunlight streamed through a circular opening in the ceiling to bathe the space in a warm glow. Three other drakes waited for them, their scales gleaming like fired metals in the light. Josephine recognized Asher, Oriana, and Zark from their previous encounter. Each inclined their heads in a gesture of greeting.

"Welcome, Captain Prescott, and...others." Zark's gaze swept over their group, lingering on Tiberia and Danelor before returning to Josephine. "Let us begin with introductions, as is only proper, given that not all parties are acquainted."

It seemed a reasonable enough request, and the introductions proceeded smoothly enough until it was Tiberia and Danelor's turn. As the chimeras offered their names, Josephine noticed the way the three drakes studied them, their gazes intense.

"Tiberia and Danelor," Asher murmured, his attention darting between the chimeras and Elazar and Cailan before settling back on the newcomers. "And where, precisely, do you hail from?"

A beat of silence. The siblings exchanged a loaded look, before Tiberia inclined her head. "We are from the Jade Court."

The air in the room seemed to crackle with tension. Asher's eyes narrowed, while Oriana and Zark leaned forward, their interest piqued. Before any of the drakes could comment, Josephine approached. Elazar and Cailan flanked her, their presence a clear show of support. "Thank you for receiving us." She addressed the assembled drakes, her tone measured. "I must confess, this is the first I've heard of a Conclave governing the Forgotten Library."

Zark inclined his head in acknowledgment. "As you can see, Captain, this island harbors a significant population of drakes. It is our duty, as the Conclave, to ensure the well-being of all its inhabitants. We are, in essence, the caretakers and protectors of this place." His eyes narrowed. "Which is precisely why we are intrigued by your sudden interest in it."

Oriana fixed them with a steady gaze. "The Conclave seeks to understand your motivations. Tell us, Captain—what purpose brings you to the Forgotten Library? We were unable to delve too deeply into the matter last night." She aimed an annoyed look at Asher, who ignored her.

Josephine's gaze flicked between Elazar and Cailan, then back to the assembled drakes. She shifted uneasily, her stomach twisting as Gibson's command echoed in her mind. She couldn't speak, not with *that* truth hanging over her.

Luckily, Elazar stepped forward, as if sensing her hesitation. He drew himself up, meeting the drakes' gazes head-on. "I already told you that the Jade Empress sent me. However, I was...unable to fully explain the circumstances." He glanced at Tiberia and Danelor, a silent acknowledgment of their plight. "I'm not here just for her self-serving needs, though. I want to correct a terrible wrong that was done."

At his words, Asher's eyes narrowed to slits, his nostrils flaring. Jo braced herself, expecting an outburst, but the drake seemed to catch himself. He exhaled heavily, clamping his jaw shut, though his displeasure was clear. Oriana gestured for Elazar to continue.

"Drakes attacked the Jade Court." Elazar's voice didn't waver. "And I'm not condoning the conditions that led to the uprising, but..." He shook his head, his expression pained. "The price the dragons paid was...excessive."

"No more excessive than the loss of our freedom," Asher shot back, his voice tight.

"I understand all about losing freedom." A chilling edge, one Jo had never heard before, crept into Elazar's voice. She still hadn't spoken with him at length after his capture by the Jade Court—an oversight she hoped to remedy soon. "I bartered mine away trying to atone for that attack. I have spent *months* crafting wings for maimed dragons. Dragons forced to rely on airships, their birthright stolen from them."

Asher went still as stone, his eyes blazing with anger. "They lost their wings as a lesson. A warning to never again cross our kind."

"I don't care about lessons." Elazar's voice was unyielding. In that moment, Jo felt a surge of pride for the young man standing before them, unrelenting in the face of Asher's fury. "It was wrong. They have suffered for it. For decades. As have their whelps."

Asher drew in a sharp breath, but Oriana stopped him from speaking with a raised claw. "Their *whelps?*"

"Yes." Elazar gestured to Tiberia and Danelor, his expression somber. He opened his mouth, as if to speak on their behalf, then seemed to think better of it. "Tell them, Tiberia. Tell them what you told me."

The young woman swallowed, her gaze darting between the assembled drakes before settling on a point somewhere past them. A small nod was all the confirmation she offered.

"The blight, the corruption from the dragonfruit...it did more than cripple the wings of the mature dragons. Many of the whelps...the young ones..." Tiberia paused, swallowing hard, her throat working. "More than half...they didn't survive."

A hush fell over the chamber. Josephine watched as the expressions of the Conclave members shifted. Their initial, guarded neutrality gave way to something akin to horror. Asher's eyes were wide with disbelief, his lips parting in a silent gasp.

"That's...that's *impossible*," he whispered, his voice rough. "Macawi would never knowingly harm a hatchling! How could so many have perished?"

Zark, who had remained silent until now, let out a low rumble, a sound that seemed to resonate within Josephine's very bones. "Not impossible, Asher. Tragic, yes, but not impossible." His gaze shifted to Tiberia. "The corruption you speak of...it must have been potent indeed to claim so many young lives."

Tiberia lifted her chin, a spark of defiance in her eyes. "It did not claim all. Some of us...we were transformed. Reshaped into these forms you see before you." She gestured to herself and Danelor.

Oriana's shock was clear, her coral scales seeming to pale. "And those who survived...they *changed*? Into...human form?" She shook her head slowly, as if trying to grasp what she was hearing.

"Though we *are* dragons at our core," Danelor added, "we have learned to thrive in these human forms, imperfections and all."

Elazar stepped forward again, spine rigid as he addressed the Conclave. Jo could almost see the dragon within him. "The Jade Empress—Belen—she is desperate. She believes that the Forgotten Library holds the key to restoring the Jade Court to its former glory. To restoring their wings...and their whelps." He paused, his gaze hardening as he continued. "That is why she's enlisted my...*assistance*." Another beat of silence, then: "I don't want to see more innocents suffer. I want to find a way to undo the damage that was done."

"Belen will never be permitted within the bounds of the Forgotten Library." Asher's voice was low, dangerous.

"Then at least offer some other form of aid." Elazar's gaze

locked with Asher's. "With all the power this place is said to hold, surely there's *something* you can do."

Josephine watched the exchange unfold, lips pursed. Asher's initial reaction to Tiberia's revelation had been visceral, his expression betraying a depth of pain that Josephine couldn't fathom. This ran deeper than a simple political dispute.

"We will *never* help the Jade Court!" Asher roared, his voice echoing through the chamber as his claws slammed against the stone floor. "Not after what they did to our kind! To our *children!*"

Oriana moved forward, positioning herself between Asher and the others. "Asher, you cannot be so quick to dismiss their plight. If what Tiberia says is true, then the Jade Court has suffered a tragedy of unimaginable proportions."

"*Tragedy?*" Asher spat the word back as if it were poison. "They brought this upon themselves with their arrogance! Their cruelty!"

The air crackled with tension, thick with old hurts and simmering resentments. Josephine snuck a glance at Elazar, wishing there was something, anything, she could do to help, but this was a storm she couldn't navigate for him.

Zark lifted a claw, silencing the escalating argument with a gesture. "Enough. This requires careful deliberation." His gaze swept over the assembled group, his expression unreadable. "The Forgotten Library may indeed hold the answers you seek, but unraveling the threads of this situation will take time."

Asher's jaw tightened, his displeasure clear in the set of his wings, the way his tail twitched, but he held his tongue.

"In the meantime," Zark continued, his voice smooth as polished stone, "we must determine the wisest course of action. The Jade Court's plight, tragic though it may be, cannot be our only consideration. We must also consider the ramifications of any actions we might take."

Josephine watched as the Conclave members exchanged weighted glances, a silent conversation passing between them. She could practically feel Asher's resistance radiating off him like heat from a forge.

"Very well," Asher conceded at last, his voice tight. "We will discuss this matter further amongst ourselves." He turned his gaze on Josephine and the others, his eyes hard as obsidian. "But do not mistake our willingness to deliberate for acceptance. The Jade Court will never be welcomed here. Their crimes are not so easily forgotten...or forgiven."

As the Conclave members murmured amongst themselves, Josephine edged closer to Elazar. She placed a comforting hand on his arm, offering him a reassuring squeeze.

"We'll find a way, Elazar," Jo said. "The Forgotten Library holds answers, I can feel it. And the Conclave...they're willing to at least consider helping. Even if it's not going to be easy."

"I hope you're right." His gaze drifted towards the huddled drakes, coming to rest on Asher. "But something tells me this is far from over."

20

DRAKE CULTURE

Elazar

"Come with me."

Elazar hadn't expected Asher—his *father*, a thought that still felt strange—to snag his arm as they exited the chamber, the tension of the meeting clinging to them like cobwebs. In fact, after Elazar had declared his intention to help the Jade Court, he'd assumed Asher would want nothing more than to wash his claws of him. And, perhaps, Cailan.

"Where exactly do you want to take my brother?" Cailan's voice held a warning edge as he moved closer, placing himself protectively between Elazar and Asher—who, Elazar now realized, had shifted to his human form. He hadn't even registered the change before.

Asher's jaw was a tight line, his annoyance clear, but he ignored Cailan, his focus solely on Elazar. "You mentioned having difficulty shifting. Do you want help with that or not?"

Elazar hesitated, weighing his options. He desperately wanted to master his shifting, but the idea of leaving the others, especially Aunt Jo, made him uneasy.

"I don't know..." Elazar glanced over his shoulder, torn.

Asher let out a frustrated sigh. "Look, I know we have a... complicated past. But I can help you with this." His voice softened, just a fraction. "Your friends can manage without you for a little while."

Elazar chewed on his lip, his gaze seeking Aunt Jo's. She offered him a reassuring smile and a small, encouraging nod. "Go on, Elazar. We'll be right here when you get back."

Elazar drew a breath, steeling himself. "All right. I'll go with you."

A ghost of something akin to approval crossed Asher's face. "Good. Follow me."

Elazar walked beside his father, his gaze drawn to the grandeur of the Forgotten Library. Towering, arched corridors of gilded stone, intricate carvings, and colorful mosaics depicting powerful figures and mythical creatures unfolded around him. His fingers trailed along the cool stone, tracing the lines of a striking bas-relief. Asher's brisk pace offered little opportunity to dawdle, which was unfortunate.

"I know I have a long way to go to make amends. For the... perceived abandonment," Asher said, his voice echoing softly as they walked. "I hope that by helping you master your shifting, it can be a small step towards rebuilding trust between us."

Elazar considered this, his expression carefully neutral. He couldn't deny the allure of Asher's offer. The chance to finally understand his dragon nature...it was something he'd craved ever since he'd woken up with scales and wings. But the wounds of the past ran deep, and trusting this virtual stranger didn't come easily.

"Perceived or not, it felt like abandonment." The words left his mouth before he could stop them, sharpened with the sting of hurt.

Asher drew in a sharp breath. "If I had known...if I'd thought there was even a chance..." He shook his head, his jaw tight. "You didn't see what the dragons did, Elazar. The destruction. You didn't see your mother...surrounded, *overwhelmed*...by dragons ten times her size."

Elazar shivered. He'd fought enough dragons aboard the *Tempest* to know how formidable—how utterly lethal—they could be. A single drake, caught off guard, wouldn't stand a chance. "I'm sorry," he murmured. "About your mate. About my mother."

Asher nodded. "I am, too." His features relaxed, a touch of wistfulness in his gaze. "She was...the best part of me." Then, squaring his shoulders, he gestured for Elazar to follow. "Come."

Asher ushered Elazar into a spacious chamber that had been set up as a sort of workshop, though not the same as those Elazar was accustomed to. In the center of the room, a Theilian woman sat hunched over a workbench, working with a set of tiny, gleaming tools. She glanced up at their entrance, her dark eyes alight with curiosity.

"Rasmira, this is my son, Elazar." Asher gestured between the Theilian woman and Elazar. "Rasmira is a drake, like us. She's our resident jeweler."

Elazar frowned. He'd always assumed that all drakes shifted into a human form, just as he and Cailan did. But this

Theilian woman...she was undeniably a drake, if Asher was to be believed.

As if sensing his confusion, Rasmira offered him a warm smile. "Drakes are capable of taking on a variety of secondary forms, Elazar, not just human," she explained patiently. "My lineage, for example, has always favored the Theilian visage. We find it...agreeable."

Elazar nodded, feeling a blush creep up his neck at his own naiveté. "I see. I'm still learning about all of...this."

Rasmira chuckled softly. "Well, you've certainly come to the right place for learning." Her gaze swept over him, assessing. "Asher tells me you've been having some difficulty with your transformations. Hmm, yes, I see you already have a nexus chain. That's often the root of such difficulties—the lack of a nexus chain, that is."

"I...what?" Elazar's brow knit, his confusion deepening.

"This." Asher reached beneath the collar of his own linen shirt, pulling free a gleaming gold chain that hung heavy in his hand. "Somehow, you already have one."

"Oh." Elazar's cheeks burned, but his own hand flew up to touch the chain at his neck. He only had one by sheer luck—he was certain Cailan didn't know exactly what it was, either.

"May I?" Rasmira asked, her palm open.

He nodded, carefully pulling the chain over his head. The tiny arcane engine suddenly felt heavy in his grasp, its blue light pulsing steadily.

"What...is *that*?" Asher asked, his voice carefully neutral, though Elazar sensed a current of aloofness humming beneath the surface.

Elazar carefully placed the chain and arcane engine into Rasmira's outstretched hand. "It's an arcane engine. I made it." He hesitated, then added, "I have this...ability. Gearweaving. It lets me combine engineering and magic."

Asher remained silent as he, too, examined the device. Elazar shifted uncomfortably under his father's scrutiny.

Rasmira, however, didn't seem to notice the tension. She let out a soft gasp, her eyes widening. "Gearweaving, you say?" She reached for a pair of strange goggles resting on her work-bench—each lens a different color and shape, crafted from what looked like polished gemstones—and slipped them on. Leaning closer, she peered at the engine through the multifaceted lenses. "Fascinating. I'd heard whispers of such a gift, but I never dreamed I'd encounter it myself." Her voice held a note of genuine awe. "Truly remarkable!" Gently, she set the chain and engine down on a square of soft, dark blue velvet, her dextrous fingers tracing the metalwork with rever-ence. "This is a marvel of craftsmanship, young drake. Rest assured, it will be treated with the utmost care while it is in my custody."

Elazar watched, a ball of anxiety forming in his stomach, as Rasmira continued her examination. Her expression shifted from curiosity to a thoughtful frown. What secrets was she uncovering with each passing second?

After what felt like an eternity, she let out a soft hum, her fingers never straying from the chain. "Interesting. It appears the magical matrix within your nexus chain has sustained some internal damage. Nothing irreparable, mind you. A few strategic adjustments should do the trick." She glanced up at Elazar. "May I?"

Relief surged through Elazar. "Of course." He hesitated, then asked the question that had been nagging at him. "How... how does the nexus chain actually help with shifting?"

Asher, who had remained silent throughout Rasmira's examination, finally spoke. "The nexus chain acts as a focus for a drake's shifting ability." He paused, then added, "As well as an amplifier for our magic. It streamlines the transformation, makes it smoother, more stable. Though most drakes can shift without one."

"Indeed." Rasmira nodded in agreement, though her focus remained on the nexus chain. "It helps to channel and direct the drake's innate magic, you see, allowing for a greater degree of control." She paused, glancing up at Elazar. "Have you experienced any...involuntary shifting episodes, Elazar?"

Elazar felt heat creep up his neck, staining his cheeks. "Well, yes. But only under...extreme circumstances." His gaze dropped to the floor.

"What sort of circumstances?" Asher's voice was sharp.

Elazar winced. "Every time it's happened...it's only ever been when I was...well, about to die."

Asher's hands curled into fists. "You should be able to shift at will. *Effortlessly.*"

"But I don't know how." Frustration welled up inside Elazar.

Rasmira set the nexus chain down on the velvet cloth, her expression softening with understanding. "It's not uncommon. Some young drakes...they experience developmental delays, difficulties mastering their magic, their flight, their shifting."

Asher crossed his arms over his chest. "It's the consequence of being raised as a human for so long. Your body...it never had the chance to acclimate to its true nature."

Elazar's stomach dropped. He thought of his own struggles with flight, the awkwardness he still felt whenever he took to the skies, the reliance on his augments. "So, I'm...broken, in a way?"

Rasmira quickly shook her head. "Don't mistake me, Elazar. You are not broken. Simply...different." She offered him a reassuring smile. "With proper guidance and training, I have no doubt that you can overcome these hurdles."

"Rasmira is right." Asher nodded curtly, some of the

tension easing from his shoulders. "Your situation is...less than ideal, but it is not irreparable either. That is why I brought you here."

"Why are you *really* doing this?" Elazar asked, his focus on Asher.

Asher's face clouded, a shadow of regret darkening his eyes. "I know I have much to answer for, Elazar. Debts that can never truly be repaid. But you are my son, and I will not fail you again. I want to help you. In whatever way I can."

Elazar searched his father's face, trying to gauge the truth behind his words. Could he bring himself to believe them? To trust this drake, this stranger, with his heart as well as his magic?

As if sensing his hesitation, Rasmira held up the nexus chain. It gleamed in the warm light, the polished metal drawing his attention. "Your skepticism is understandable, Elazar," she said gently. "But I assure you, Asher's heart is true. We only wish to help you uncover the depths of your own power."

Elazar pursed his lips, weighing his options. Maybe...maybe accepting Asher's offer, tentative though it was, would smooth the path ahead. Build a bridge, however fragile, between them. And if it ultimately aided his goal of helping the Jade Court, the chimeras...wouldn't that make the risk worthwhile? A sudden thought struck him then, sending a jolt of excitement through him. What if the chimeras, born of drake magic, could benefit from the same techniques? The corrupted dragonfruit had passed on Macawi's ability to shift into a human form...perhaps her legacy extended further than any of them had realized.

That thought, the hope it ignited, was the push he needed. "All right," Elazar said, straightening his shoulders. "I'm ready."

Elazar took the chain back, running his hands over the metal. Nothing about it felt different. He slipped it back over his head, the arcane engine settling against his chest. Elazar tucked it beneath his shirt, the metal warm against his skin.

"The adjustments I made will smooth the process, make your transformations more intuitive," Rasmira explained, gesturing to the chain. "Now then, let's see what you can do."

Elazar took a deep breath, his nerves humming with anticipation. Closing his eyes, he turned his focus inward, seeking that elusive spark within. The nexus chain thrummed against his chest, a steady pulse of energy that spread outwards, warming his skin, tingling through his veins. It was unlike anything he'd ever experienced. Focusing his will, he pictured the transformation, the way his body had contorted, reshaped itself in those moments of desperate survival. He imagined scales rippling across his skin, claws extending, his human form falling away...

He wasn't sure what to expect. Every previous shift had been a blur of pain and terror, his body overcome by instinct, driven by a primal need to survive. This...this was different. Controlled. Or so he hoped.

A gasp escaped his lips as his fingers elongated, nails thickening, sharpening into wickedly curved talons. Muscles spasmed, his body rebelling against the unfamiliar sensations as a searing heat built beneath his skin. The transformation seemed to stretch on forever. He felt the wings unfurl behind him, seeming to tear through flesh—

"You did it!" Rasmira's triumphant cry cut through the haze.

Elazar opened his eyes, but the world was a dizzying kaleidoscope of colors and blurred shapes. He tried to glance over his shoulder, to glimpse his transformed self in the reflection of a polished copper panel on the far wall, but the movement sent nausea surging through him. He caught flashes—gleaming copper scales, the blurred edges of powerful wings—but it wasn't enough to ground him.

"How was it?" Asher's voice seemed to come from a great distance.

Elazar swallowed, struggling to find his equilibrium. "Dizzy...everything's spinning." This wasn't right. Cailan never mentioned this, never spoke of feeling...unbalanced.

Rasmira's face fell. "Vertigo? That's...that's not how it's supposed to work. The modifications should have made the transition seamless." She exhaled sharply. "I don't understand."

Elazar concentrated on slowing his breathing, on finding a center in the whirl of chaos that had become his world. The vertigo gradually subsided, replaced by nausea and a disorientation that clung to him like a shroud. He forced himself to raise his head, though the world still swayed around him. "Do you think it's my arcane engine?" he asked, his voice hoarse. The thought of relinquishing it, of losing the freedom his augments provided...it was almost unbearable. But if it meant mastering his shifting, if it meant bridging the gulf between who he was and who he was meant to be...well, what choice did he truly have?

Rasmira shook her head, her brow still creased with concern. "No, no. The integration...it's flawless, really." She paused, studying him with renewed intensity. "Perhaps it's simply a matter of practice? Like exercising a muscle that's been dormant for too long. With time, the transitions may become smoother, less disorienting."

Hadn't Cailan suggested something similar when Elazar had first struggled with flight? He vaguely recalled those early attempts, the frustration, the exhaustion that had clung to him like a second skin. Practice hadn't helped then. Only the augments had given him the help he needed. And he couldn't exactly engineer a solution for magical vertigo...could he?

"It's worth a try, at least." He couldn't quite hide the disappointment that colored his words. "At least I can shift now. If I need to."

"Yes, but it should be as effortless as breathing." Asher sounded almost as disheartened as Elazar felt.

"I'm going to try again." Elazar drew himself up, pushing past the disappointment, the echo of fear that whispered in the back of his mind. What if he couldn't control it? What if he became trapped, his human form lost to him forever? "Maybe it was just...a fluke."

But finding his way back to his human form proved more difficult than he'd expected. He concentrated, picturing his reflection in the captain's cabin mirror, the familiar lines of his face, the feel of his own body, his humanity... For a heart-stopping moment, panic seized him. The magic sputtered and died, leaving him adrift. Then, with a rush of heat and a bone-jarring lurch, he shrank, collapsing in on himself, the world tilting once more as his senses overloaded.

He stumbled, crashing to his knees, his hands bracing against the cool stone floor just in time to prevent a face-first meeting. Sweet relief washed over him as he realized he was back. Human. Whole. Then a different, far more awkward realization dawned.

He was naked.

"Winds above..." Elazar muttered, scrambling to cover himself with his hands, acutely aware of Rasmira and Asher's stunned silence. "At least I'm not dizzy anymore?"

Rasmira, bless her, had the presence of mind to avert her gaze, snatching up a heavy, emerald-green robe from a nearby hook and tossing it to him. "The vertigo...perhaps it was a side effect of acclimating to a larger form?" she offered, though he could hear the uncertainty in her voice. "As for your current... predicament, it seems we still have some work to do."

Asher sighed, running a hand over his face. "We'll get there. In the meantime, I believe it's time we had a talk about pocket dimensions."

Cailan

"So, what's it take to wrangle a tour around here?" Cailan drawled, deliberately letting his gaze linger on the arched doorway through which Elazar and Asher—his *father*, winds, the word still felt strange in his mind—had disappeared. He wasn't jealous. Not exactly. A touch put-out that he hadn't been invited along? Yes.

Oriana and Zark exchanged wary looks. "The Forgotten Library isn't some...tourist attraction, drake," Zark said, his tone clipped.

"See, now that's the thing." Cailan grinned, all sharp teeth and feigned innocence. "Tell me I can't go somewhere, and it becomes infinitely more appealing. So really, I'm asking for a tour for everyone's benefit. Save yourselves the trouble of having to chase me down later."

Beside him, Max shifted, her gaze curious, no doubt wondering if he was simply bored or if something more calculated lay beneath his words. The truth, as always, lay somewhere in between.

The two Conclave members hesitated, clearly weighing their options. Oriana let out a long-suffering sigh. "Honestly, such impertinence should see you tossed out on your tail, but..."

"But that would be incredibly rude," Cailan interjected, savoring the irony, "and we wouldn't want that, would we? Besides, I'm one of you now, right? Don't I deserve a grand tour of my ancestral home? What if I decide I want to stay?" He paused, considering. "Would that even be allowed?"

"All drakes are welcome to call the Forgotten Library home, so long as they will abide by our laws, respect our traditions, and dedicate themselves to the preservation of this place." Frustration colored Zark's words, though whether it was directed at Cailan's persistent questioning or the audacity of his request, he couldn't be sure. "Though, perhaps we can attribute your profound lack of manners to your extended separation from drake culture."

"So, educate me." Cailan gestured around them. He didn't bother pointing out that he was perfectly capable of being a disruptive force regardless of his upbringing. It was simply too much fun to resist. And besides, keeping one's opponents off-balance was often the quickest way to gain an advantage.

"Perhaps it's not the worst idea." Oriana's agreement was tentative. "Unfortunately, neither Zark nor I have the time to spare for such educational pursuits." She glanced over her shoulder, summoning a nearby drake attendant with a flick of her tail. "Please send for Iaxis. I'm sure the archivist would be delighted to assist." The attendant dipped his head respectfully and hurried off.

A few moments later, a lithe Elf with long sapphire-blue hair braided down his back approached them. He paused a few paces away, eyeing them with open curiosity. "Ah, the newcomers, I presume?"

Cailan frowned, his brow furrowing. "You're an Elf." He stated it as a fact, not an accusation, though there was an edge to his voice.

"In this form, yes," the Elf agreed easily. He lifted a hand, spreading long, slender fingers as if testing their flexibility. "I find this visage more conducive to the precision my work demands."

So, this Iaxis was a drake. Huh. Interesting. Not everyone ended up looking human. Cailan filed that nugget of information away for later. "Right. Well, I'm Cailan, and I'd like to have a look around."

"I'm coming, too," Max announced, her expression daring him to even think about objecting.

"As are we," Tiberia said, joining them before Cailan could come up with a suitable retort. Danelor trailed in her wake, his usual cheer undimmed, though he moved more slowly than his sister.

Cailan shot Danelor a withering look, but the other man simply grinned back, seemingly oblivious to the intended sting.

"Oh, come on," Danelor chided, his tone light. "Surely, we're allowed to have a bit of adventure now and then?" He winked, and Cailan couldn't help but roll his eyes. Trust Danelor to find a silver lining, no matter the storm.

This unexpected turn of events gave Iaxis pause. He frowned, his gaze flitting between them, taking in their mismatched little group. "I see," he murmured, more to himself than anyone else. "A human mage—not a drop of drake blood in you, I sense—and..." He squinted at Tiberia and Danelor, his expression perplexed, as though they were a particularly confounding sentence he was attempting to translate. "Now, you two are fascinating. Wait...are you the *chimeras* I've heard whispers of?"

"We are," Tiberia confirmed with a curt nod.

Iaxis studied Tiberia and Danelor, his fascination growing with each passing moment. The Elf's lips moving silently as if testing out different theories. "*Most intriguing,*" Iaxis said at last, tapping a finger against his chin thoughtfully. "I must confess, I've only encountered mention of your kind in ancient texts."

Texts. The single word drew Cailan's attention like a moth to a flame. He wasn't the only one. Hope bloomed on Danelor's face, transforming his features. "Texts?" he breathed, his excitement clear. "You mean there's mention of creatures like us?"

Tiberia, ever cautious, inclined her head, acknowledging Iaxis's words but keeping her own counsel. "Then perhaps this is an opportunity for you to expand your knowledge as well, Archivist," she said, her tone cool.

"Indeed," Iaxis agreed, his eyebrows lifting high on his forehead, a touch of irony in his tone. He then swept their little group with a stern look. "A word of caution, however. The Forgotten Library is not a place for the careless or the curious. The knowledge contained within these walls can be dangerous in the wrong hands. I must insist that you refrain from touching anything without express permission."

"Or what?" Cailan asked, unable to keep the note of challenge from his voice.

Iaxis sighed, his shoulders slumping slightly. "Three years ago," he began, his voice taking on a distant, haunted quality, "a young drake apprentice of mine was tasked with dusting a collection of magical relics. He had a terrible fear of spiders, and in a moment of panic, he stumbled back, jostling a vase. It shattered against the stone floor, and the poor drake...he simply vanished. Never seen again."

"Right. No touching freaky vases." Cailan resisted the urge to glance over his shoulder, half-expecting to see a shadowy figure lurking behind the towering bookshelves.

Iaxis nodded, apparently satisfied with Cailan's subdued response. "Excellent. Now then, if you'll follow me..." He turned, his blue braid trailing behind him like a tail, and strode off down one of the corridors.

Cailan fell into step beside Max, giving her a sideways glance. "Why the sudden interest in musty old books?" he asked, unable to keep the amusement from his voice.

Max, however, was clearly more focused on matching the Elf's surprisingly long strides. "Someone has to keep you out of trouble," she said breathlessly, her gaze fixed on Iaxis's retreating back.

Cailan clutched a hand to his chest, feigning offense. "I'm wounded. To even *think* such a thing of me." Max snorted, but her eyes crinkled at the corners with mirth.

Behind them, Danelor kept pace only due to his stature. A grimace touched his handsome face, but he was clearly determined not to be left behind.

"These books," Iaxis announced as they entered what Cailan thought must be the main library area, because of its vast size, "are older than any living drake. Most predate the construction of the library itself."

"So, they're just gathering dust?" Cailan couldn't help but ask, unable to grasp the point of preserving something no one could even read.

Iaxis shot him a look that could have curdled milk. "The knowledge contained within these pages is invaluable. It is our sacred duty to protect them. To ensure that it endures, for generations to come."

Danelor was unusually quiet, his gaze wide with wonder as he took in the endless rows of books. "Where did they all come from?"

Iaxis hesitated, his fingers trailing lightly along the spine of a particularly worn volume. "The Forgotten Library has served as a sanctuary for knowledge for centuries," he explained, his voice low. "Many of these tomes were brought here by those who sought to protect their contents from those who would... misuse them."

"Misuse, huh?" Cailan arched a brow, a slow grin spreading across his face. "Sounds like you've got some pretty dangerous stuff hidden away in this place."

The Elf turned somber. "The knowledge contained within these walls is not to be treated lightly. It has the power to reshape the world. For good or for ill." He turned to face them. "Do any of you know the true purpose of the Forgotten Library? The reason it was created?"

Cailan shrugged, leaning back against a nearby bookshelf, unable to suppress his amusement at the Elf's earnestness. "Well, it *is* called the Forgotten Library. If we knew its purpose, it wouldn't be very forgotten, would it?"

Iaxis sighed, a hint of something that might have been disappointment momentarily marring his features. "The Forgotten Library was built in the aftermath of the Forgotten War, the great struggle between sorcerers."

Max's eyes widened at the word *sorcerer*, as though Iaxis had uttered a profanity. Cailan frowned. Chandra, for all her quirks, had ensured he received a thorough education, and yet this war was something he'd never encountered. "What's that?" he asked, tilting his head. Judging by the blank expressions on the chimeras' faces, he and Max weren't the only ones who found the term unfamiliar.

"The Forgotten War," Iaxis explained, his voice taking on the patient tone of a scholar addressing a classroom of particularly slow students, "was a series of devastating conflicts waged by powerful magic wielders. They sought to control everything. Power consolidates, you see. And absolute power..." He shook his head, his expression turning grim. "It was a dark time. A catastrophe that indelibly scarred the world. The names of those involved have been lost to time, a deliberate omission intended to dissuade others from following in their footsteps."

"Wait." Max held up a hand, interrupting Iaxis's lecture. "Is this...are you talking about the *Manifestation?*"

Genuine amusement crossed Iaxis's face. "I believe that is what some called it, yes. Particularly in those regions where the true cause of the...upheaval, shall we say, remained shrouded in mystery."

Max's lips pursed as she considered this. "The Manifestation was what ignited magic in the world. Sparked the creation of mages. And other mystic races."

Iaxis nodded. "Indeed. The sorcerers, in their arrogance, manipulated the very fabric of existence, twisting it to their will. Creating entire species to serve as their soldiers. Krakens, dragons, Theilians, Knossans, and so forth."

The Elf crooked a finger at them, then set off once more at his brisk pace. Thankfully, instead of plunging deeper into the labyrinthine corridors, he remained on the ground floor of the chamber, his path circling them closer to the soaring walls. He stopped before a magnificent stained-glass window, its surface shimmering with an array of vibrant colors. It depicted a scene of chaotic battle: figures locked in a desperate struggle, their features twisted with fury. With a flick of Iaxis's wrist and a murmured word in a language Cailan didn't recognize, the stained glass came alive.

"Whoa," Max breathed, her eyes widening as the scene above them bloomed into motion. Danelor let out a soft exclamation of surprise, echoed by Tiberia's sharp intake of breath.

The stained-glass figures moved with a grace that belied the violence of their actions. Their forms shifted seamlessly from flesh and blood to something altogether more monstrous. They wielded sword and magic with equal skill, unleashing torrents of fire and ice, calling down bolts of lightning that crackled across the impossibly vibrant sky. Some shapeshifted, their bodies contorting, growing, twisting into monstrous behemoths unlike anything Cailan had ever witnessed, even in the volumes of Chandra's collection. Villages burned, towns crumbled into dust, and entire civilizations were wiped from existence, trampled beneath the feet of these...*sorcerers*. Races

Cailan had never even imagined were swept aside, erased from history with a casual brutality that turned his stomach.

"What...what are we witnessing?" Tiberia whispered, her voice trembling.

"The legacy of the Forgotten War," Iaxis replied, his voice somber. "A history best not forgotten, lest it repeat itself."

Cailan tore his gaze from the horrifying spectacle unfolding above, his mind reeling. "There's a whole heap of irony in that statement that I'd love to unpack later," he commented. "I'm starting to think *Forgotten Library* was an understatement. More like *We Buried This Trauma Deep For A Reason Library*."

"That name would be way too long," Danelor murmured, subdued. "But I think you're on to something."

"What happened?" Max asked, voice soft. "How did it end?" She paused. "It *did* end, right?"

Cailan wasn't entirely sure what she meant by that—wouldn't they know if such a war still brewed?—but Iaxis nodded, his gaze fixed on the stained glass tableau above. The scenes of destruction continued. Entire continents were rendered into desolate wastelands, the brilliant hues of the glass somehow making the devastation even more horrifying.

"But what stopped them?" Tiberia pressed, her voice tight. "If those sorcerers were anything like dragons, even the threat of mutual annihilation might not have been enough to deter them."

"Faedra," Iaxis said, the name uttered as a prayer. At that moment, a blinding flash of gold and silver light erupted across the stained glass, momentarily obscuring the carnage beneath.

Max blinked, shielding her eyes from the sudden glare. "Faedra? The goddess of magic?"

"The very same." Iaxis's lips pursed thoughtfully. "Now, it's important to note that the surviving accounts of this era are contradictory, at best. Depending on which texts you consult, Faedra either intervened, single-handedly defeating the sorcerers, or..." He hesitated. "Some claim the sorcerers united their might, turning on the goddess, either slaying her or banishing her from this realm. The truth remains shrouded in mystery." He shrugged. "Regardless of which version holds true, the result was the same. The sorcerers' combined power, their very essence, was harnessed to create the Forgotten Library."

"That doesn't make sense." Cailan shook his head, baffled. He'd devoured every book in the Vault of Fate—twice. And Chandra's personal library was nothing to scoff at. How could something of this magnitude—a war that had nearly unraveled the very fabric of reality—simply vanish from history? "Wouldn't there be traces? Whispers? Wouldn't it be common knowledge?"

"The *Forgotten* Library," Iaxis reminded him patiently. "Born from the ashes of the *Forgotten* War." He waved a dismissive hand. "And then, of course, there's the matter of persuasion. I suspect those who orchestrated this *forgetting* made quite liberal use of their magic to ensure its efficacy."

Forget. They had forgotten entire civilizations. Forgotten a war that had nearly shattered their world. Gooseflesh pebbled Cailan's arms. "Those histories...they deserve to be remembered," he said, his voice tight with a sudden, unexpected anger. "The people who died...they should never have been forgotten. That's how tragedies repeat themselves. That's how monsters are born." He thought of Chandra's pronouncements, the weight of her prophecies. She'd always stressed the cyclical nature of time, the echoes of the past resonating into the present.

"If the world knew the truth...they would come for this place," Iaxis said, his voice dropping to a low murmur. "And who can say what havoc they might wreak?"

"But how...how did drakes come to be a part of all of this?" Danelor asked, tilting his head, his brow creased.

"It is said," Iaxis began, his voice taking on the tone of someone reciting a familiar tale, "that magic changed the dragons who served during the Forgotten War. *Transformed* them. They became the first drakes, infused with magic, bound to this place, to its purpose." He paused, his gaze meeting Cailan's. "They were made to be the guardians of the Forgotten Library, charged with protecting its secrets from those who might seek to exploit them."

"So...you've been guarding this place ever since?" Cailan asked, the pieces of the puzzle clicking into place, forming a picture that was both awe-inspiring and terrifying.

Iaxis nodded. "For centuries, the drakes have served as the caretakers of the Forgotten Library," he confirmed. "Ensuring that its knowledge and its artifacts remain hidden."

"Well, that explains why you didn't exactly roll out the welcome mat," Cailan muttered, a wry grin tugging at his lips.

The archivist chuckled, the sound surprisingly warm. "Indeed. Context is essential. Now, perhaps you can better understand our caution with outsiders. There's far more at stake here than a few dog-eared pages."

Cailan listened, the implications of the Forgotten Library's history settling heavy in his gut. It wasn't just the knowledge itself that posed a threat, but the very power that resided within these walls. "So, if it's not just the books themselves we need to worry about...what else is lurking in this place?" he asked, his gaze sweeping over the endless rows of books, his imagination conjuring up all manner of terrifying possibilities.

Iaxis's expression turned grave. "Ah, yes. The relics. That is where the *true* danger lies." He strode across the chamber, his steps measured, coming to a halt before a glass case filled with what, at first glance, looked like a jumble of dusty trinkets and tarnished ornaments—the sort of odds and ends one might find in a back-alley pawnshop. "The books may hold powerful knowledge, yes, but they are not the only treasures entrusted to our care." He gazed at the seemingly mundane objects, then moved to a separate pedestal where a single massive gemstone pulsed with an inner light. "The Forgotten Library is home to countless artifacts. Objects of *immense* power. You have witnessed the scope of the Eye of the Storm." He flicked a meaningful glance at the hurricane that churned just beyond the Library's island.

"The stone...it's powering the storm," Max whispered, her gaze fixed on the mesmerizing gem, as if drawn to its depths.

The archivist nodded. "The Eye of the Storm was but one of many weapons wielded during the war, though now we have repurposed it. Bent its power to a more benevolent purpose." His gaze returned to the glass case. "But not all artifacts can be so easily tamed. So, we guard them. Protect the world from their potential for destruction."

Cailan snorted, affecting a dismissive air, hoping to prod the Elf into revealing more. "Hard to believe a bunch of trinkets could be so dangerous." But even as he spoke, he discreetly channeled his magic. Iaxis wasn't exaggerating. Powerful energies pulsed within that seemingly innocuous collection.

The archivist, bless his naïve heart, took the bait. His eyes widened, a hint of indignation in his expression. "You have no idea, young drake. Perhaps another time, I shall show you more. But for now, I believe we have seen enough." He gave Cailan a long, considering look. "You know, I find myself in need of a capable apprentice. One with such a keen interest in the past..."

Cailan rolled his eyes. "I'm *done* with mentors," he said, his voice flat. The last thing he wanted was another authority figure to disappoint him.

Iaxis looked momentarily dismayed, but he nodded in

acceptance. "As you wish. Then, allow me to escort you back to your quarters."

As they followed the archivist back through the labyrinthine stacks, Cailan exchanged a worried glance with Max. She looked as uneasy as he felt. Cailan couldn't shake the feeling that they had stumbled into something far more dangerous than they'd initially realized. The Forgotten Library might hold the answers they sought, but it also harbored secrets that could very well consume them.

21

Strong Feelings

Blending into the shadows, becoming invisible...it was second nature to Tiberia. Years of navigating the treacherous currents of the Jade Court had taught her and the other chimeras to blend into the background. Anomalies at best, prey at worst, they'd learned to survive in a world that saw them as expendable. Outright killings were rare now, thanks to Belen's fleeting but furious wrath, but *accidents* still befell those who strayed too close to a dragon's claws.

So, when Tiberia murmured that she needed to take a walk to clear her head, Danelor didn't question her. He understood.

They both did. Navigating a world where being *seen* could mean becoming a *target* required a certain...resourcefulness.

Crouched beneath a heavy table in the Ember Chamber, hidden by the tasseled brocade tablecloth, Tiberia waited. She could have endured the agonizing suspense until the drakes deigned to share their decision, but her patience had worn thin. She had come too far, waited too long, to be a passive observer now. She *had* to know.

Time crawled by. She dozed fitfully, her muscles aching in the cramped space, but her senses remained on high alert.

Finally, the heavy oak doors creaked open, and Tiberia held her breath as the Conclave filed in. She noticed that Iaxis, the archivist, was among their number.

Shaking off her sleepiness, Tiberia focused, her senses sharpening as the drakes settled onto their cushions. The meeting began with the usual banalities—polite, meaningless phrases that seemed universal among dragons, drakes, and humans alike. But soon the conversation shifted to the matter that had brought them all here: the fate of the Jade Court.

"You can't be serious that we'll aid those *dragons*," Asher spat.

"We are all aware of your *strong* feelings on the matter, Asher," Zark observed wryly, his tail twitching in amusement. "Though, I must confess, I find it rather ironic, given your own whelp's determination to assist them."

The mention of Elazar brought a ghost of a smile to Tiberia's lips. All her life, she had been told of the cruelty of drakes. Elazar had proven those assumptions false. Perhaps it was because he hadn't been raised among his kind, hadn't learned their prejudices, or perhaps his inherent nature was simply...kinder. Whatever the reason, she admired his dedication to helping those in need. Even those who might not deserve it.

Asher scoffed. "He's naive. He doesn't understand the depths of the Jade Court's depravity, not like *I* do."

"On that point, we are in agreement." Iaxis leaned forward, his expression thoughtful. "Aiding those so-called chimeras...it's a dangerous proposition, fraught with unforeseen consequences. In fact," he added, his gaze hardening, "I believe that assisting any of them is fundamentally against the interests of the Library. We should be rid of them. All of them."

Asher growled deep in his chest. "You are not suggesting we kill them, are you? My long-lost whelps are in their number, and I don't see them being very...*appreciative* of harming their companions."

Tiberia's eyes widened.

"There are alternatives," Zark hazarded, his tone carefully neutral. "Ways to change their perception."

"You're suggesting *Eletheria's Blessing*." Asher's lips curled back, revealing his fangs. "One of the most potent relics from the Forgotten War."

"It's practical." Zark shrugged. "But think, Asher. It's clear your whelps don't trust you. They feel you abandoned them." At the black drake's words, Asher visibly deflated. "Eletheria's Blessing could change that. With a single use, you could erase the past they remember and replace it with one in which you are united as a family."

Tiberia froze, her breath catching in her throat. The Jade Court was capable of terrible acts, yes, but *this*? This was cruelty of an entirely different order. A cruelty cloaked in compassion, making it all the more insidious, all the more dangerous.

She saw a war raging within Asher—the longing for connection battling with the terrible betrayal. "I will...consider it," Asher conceded at last, his voice strained. Then, as if eager to shift the conversation away from such treacherous ground, he asked, "And what of the Seer?"

"Her talents could prove useful," Oriana suggested thoughtfully, her gaze distant.

Iaxis, however, seemed less certain. He tapped a claw against his chin. "I spoke with her briefly," he said, "after I concluded my tour with the others. There is something about Chandra...something..." He trailed off, his scaled brow furrowing as he searched for the right words.

Before the archivist could elaborate, a sharp knock sounded at the chamber door. "Enter," Zark called.

Tiberia, like the others, assumed it would be one of the library attendants. But instead, the doors swung open to reveal Chandra, her white aralez padding silently beside her. A shiver ran down Tiberia's spine. The timing was...uncanny. Too perfect to be mere coincidence.

"What is the meaning of this intrusion?" Asher demanded.

Oriana, ever the diplomat, glanced at Asher and then said, "Seer! We were not expecting you. To what do we owe the honor?"

Chandra smiled, but the warmth didn't reach her pale eyes, which glittered with a cold, unsettling light. The aralez beside her whimpered, his ears flattening against his skull as he pressed closer to his mistress. Tiberia scarcely dared to breathe.

Tendrils of dark power, like inky smoke, unfurled from Chandra, coiling around each of the drakes with a terrifying, sinuous grace. They gasped, their eyes widening in surprise, but made no move to resist the magical assault. Tiberia watched in horror as the darkness seeped into their scales, their struggles ceasing as their gazes turned vacant, glassy.

"Good," Chandra's voice was a silken whisper that held an undercurrent of something cold. "Your proximity to the potent magic of this place...it makes this almost too easy." The

Conclave drakes sat immobile, their bodies slack, their minds seemingly enthralled. Chandra studied them, one by one, then nodded, a satisfied smile curving her lips. "You will continue with your deliberations, but you will do me no harm. The non-drakes...eliminate them. But spare the chimeras. They will serve a different purpose."

Tiberia gasped, her hand flying to her mouth to stifle the sound. It was a mistake. A potentially fatal one.

Chandra's head snapped towards her hiding place, her eyes narrowing. "Well, well. What do we have here?" She strode towards the table, her movements predatory. Lowering her head, she peered into the shadows, her pale eyes boring into Tiberia's. Gone was the vague, unfocused gaze Tiberia had come to associate with the Seer. These eyes were sharp, alert, filled with a chilling awareness. "You thought you were so clever, didn't you, little one?"

Tiberia stared back, fear a cold boulder in her stomach. This wasn't the Chandra she'd known on the *Tempest*. This was...someone else. Someone colder, crueler. Vesper whined, his distress confirming Tiberia's own growing terror. "Dane told me...you promised to help," she stammered.

"I promised to free *him* from his pain," Chandra corrected, her voice devoid of warmth, "and I *will*. But you were never part of the bargain."

Tiberia swallowed, fear a bitter taste in her mouth, her mind racing. Bolting from beneath the table, was tempting, relying on her agility to outmaneuver the older dragon. But the chamber offered little in the way of cover, and the memory of that dark, coiling magic chilled her to the bone.

Flight alone wouldn't work. Tiberia chose to fight.

She sprang from her hiding place, in the same motion grabbing the tassels of the tablecloth and yanking it off. Goblets clattered and plates shattered, sending shards of porcelain skittering across the stone floor. She didn't care. The clatter only added to the chaos, a distraction she intended to exploit. Swinging the tablecloth like a weapon, she hurled it at Chandra, aiming for the dragon's face. The tassels sparkled in the light as the fabric struck the azure dragon's eyes.

Chandra roared, a sound of surprised fury, her claws lashing out blindly. Tiberia didn't hesitate. She bolted for the chamber doors.

But she wasn't fast enough. A tendril of that same dark power snagged her ankle, wrapping around her like a living shadow. Tiberia froze, a whimper escaping her lips as her legs buckled beneath her.

"You're resourceful, I'll grant you that, niece," Chandra said as she moved closer, the tablecloth discarded to the floor. The azure dragon tapped a claw against the floor. "One of you, make yourself useful. Find a suitable place to keep this chimera contained. Until she is needed."

"Of course, Seer." Oriana bustled forward, her eagerness to please sending a fresh wave of despair through Tiberia.

Tiberia tried to fight off the magic, but whatever had claimed her was too strong. She couldn't move of her own volition. She twisted, sending a beseeching look at the other drakes as her feet followed Oriana.

Asher's eyes met hers, but the look in his golden gaze wasn't one of rescue. It reflected her own dawning horror.

Maxine

"So, how did things go with your father?" Max asked that evening, catching Elazar alone after dinner. They had retreated to an area the drakes called the Brew Nook, where a machine that seemed magical created coffee or tea on demand. Naturally, Elazar found it fascinating. Max considered it miraculous and didn't care how it worked, so long as it provided the requested brew.

He offered her a tired smile, the usual spark in his eyes dimmed. He sipped a coffee with a faint spicy scent from the mug in his hand, but it seemed to do little for his exhaustion. "I can shift now. On command, I mean. No need for a near-death experience to trigger it." He raked a hand through his long hair. "But..."

"But?" Maxine tilted her head, setting her coffee down on the nearby table.

His face contorted, a grimace of remembered discomfort. "It...makes me dizzy. *Really* dizzy. And I haven't quite figured out how to..." He paused, clearing his throat, a faint blush creeping up his neck. "How to, uh, manage the whole *clothing* situation."

Maxine studied him, taking in the rumpled state of his shirt. She might have teased him about his *wardrobe malfunction*, but the underlying discomfort in his voice was impossible to ignore. "Shifting makes you dizzy?"

Elazar nodded miserably. "The actual transformation...it doesn't take long. I think. But when I complete it, the world just spins. It's like being caught in a whirlpool. I can't focus on anything." His frustration was plaintive. "Why can't this be simple? Easy?"

"You're so focused on what's wrong that you're forgetting the amazing thing you're doing," Max said, offering him a warm smile. "You're transforming into a *dragon!* It's not like you're slipping on a new pair of boots and falling on your face. Give yourself a break."

He blinked, then chuckled. "You're probably right. It just makes me feel...lacking." Elazar pursed his lips.

There it was. He disliked being bad at anything—though Elazar usually knew his limits. After all the years of secretive bullying Elazar endured on the *Tempest*, he wanted to be seen as competent, especially now.

Max reached out and patted his shoulder. "Let's see if you're better at turning into a dragon than I am." She paused, focusing on her magic. It rose to her call, and Max allowed a gentle breeze to tousle Elazar's coppery locks. "Nope. That little gust didn't help me turn into a dragon. You're definitely better at shapeshifting."

Elazar laughed. "I don't think that was a fair contest."

He said something else, but Max didn't hear it. Something called to her, to her power. It had been a mistake to use her magic at all. The dark, seductive energy of the Eye of the Storm drifted around her, tempting her with promises of power.

"Max, are you okay?" Elazar's voice pierced her thoughts.

He'd moved closer, searching her face. Max blinked, startled. She had to do something to settle herself, to distract her mind from the summons of the relic. And Elazar was there, so very close.

Without thinking, she closed the distance between them, leaning in to press her lips against his.

The kiss was soft, tentative, a brush of warmth that surprised them both. Max's pulse raced as the realization of what she'd done slammed into her. She shouldn't have been so reckless. Had she just ruined her relationship with her best friend? What if he didn't feel the same? Max drew back, swallowing.

Elazar stared at her, his eyes wide, his lips parted in surprise. "Did you...I mean, did you *mean* to do that?"

Max's cheeks burned, her entire body flushing with heat.

All thoughts of the Eye of the Storm, of sorcerers and ancient relics, disappeared, banished by the sheer force of her own impulsiveness. "I...yes," she admitted, the words tumbling out in a rush. "I've been wanting to do that for a while now."

There. She'd said it. No more hiding, no more pretending. Max held her breath, her gaze fixed on Elazar, bracing for his reaction.

To her immense relief, his expression relaxed. The initial confusion melted away, replaced by a look of quiet understanding. He reached for her hand, his calloused fingers gently intertwining with hers. "I didn't know," he said, his voice rough with emotion. "I mean, you never seemed interested in anyone."

"That changed," she murmured, her gaze dropping to their joined hands. "When I thought I'd lost you, it made me realize..." She paused, searching for the words to express the jumble of emotions that had taken root within her. "It made me realize how much I care about you. "

A slow smile curved Elazar's lips. The tension that had knotted his shoulders eased. She'd been so terrified of ruining their friendship, of pushing him away. But it seemed her feelings weren't as one-sided as she'd feared.

"I missed you so much while I was gone," Elazar confessed. "Being trapped, I had a lot of time to think. And I realized..." He paused, his gaze meeting hers. "I realized there was more to how I felt about you, too."

Maxine's breath caught at his words. "Oh?"

A touch of vulnerability softened his expression. "Remember how angry you were that I left you behind on the airship? I did it because I couldn't bear the thought of anything happening to someone I loved."

The memory sparked a mote of anger, the old hurt flaring briefly. He'd dared to leave her, as if she were incapable of protecting herself, of fighting alongside him. But then she recalled his parting words, the raw emotion in his voice as he'd told her and Captain Jo that he loved them.

"Never leave someone you love behind again," she whispered, leaning closer. Then, unable to resist, she swatted him playfully on the arm.

"Ouch," Elazar protested, but he laughed. "Okay, okay. Lesson learned." Then he cleared his throat, and a shadow of uncertainty returned to his features. "You...you know I'm not entirely human, right? This whole...drake thing." He made a vague gesture with one hand.

Max rolled her eyes. "I've known ever since a certain annoying opal dragon enlightened me. Trust me, I know what I'm getting into." She reached up, her fingers brushing a stray lock of hair from his forehead. "And we can take things slow, Elazar. I know you've got a lot on your plate right now."

"Can we?" Elazar asked, relief in his voice. "Because everything else has happened so fast. I could use something slow."

Max nodded, offering him a reassuring smile. "To be honest, I was hesitant to bring this up now, too, but..." She shrugged. "I didn't want to wait any longer." And, she admitted silently, she desperately needed something, *someone*, to distract her from the allure of the Eye of the Storm.

"I wish you had told me sooner," Elazar said, his voice a low murmur.

"*You* could have said something first," Max countered, raising an eyebrow.

He sighed, a rueful smile touching his lips. "Believe me, I thought about it. But I didn't want you to feel...obligated. Or pressured."

His words warmed her, a comforting glow spreading through her chest. Elazar was so different from the man she'd been forced to marry all those years ago—kind, considerate, genuine. "And that's how I know you really *do* care."

"So..." He hesitated as he studied her. "Where do we go from here?"

Maxine considered his question, acutely aware that they were navigating uncharted territory, both literally and figuratively. "One day at a time, I think," she said, choosing her words carefully. "See where things lead us. No need to rush into anything. We can just...enjoy being together, without pressure or expectations."

Elazar nodded, a thoughtful expression on his face as he absorbed her words. "That sounds perfect." He reached out, gently tucking a stray curl behind her ear, his fingers lingering against her cheek.

Danelor

TIBERIA DIDN'T RETURN TO THEIR SHARED ROOM THAT night.

Dane paced, torn between worry for his sister and the knowledge that she was more than capable of taking care of herself. They'd beaten the odds, survived the whims of fate and the cruel indifference of dragons to become the resourceful, resilient chimeras they were today.

Still, he couldn't help but wonder where she'd gone, what she was planning. They'd spoken briefly before dinner, and she'd been adamant—the drakes wouldn't help them. And while Dane preferred to err on the side of optimism, he had to admit, she was probably right.

Life as a chimera had taught him a simple truth: you could either embrace pessimism, brace yourself for the worst at every turn, or you could choose to believe in something better. The dragons had expected them to cower, to exist in a perpetual state of fear and despair. Dane, however, had refused to give them that satisfaction. There was a certain power in choosing hope, in clinging to the possibility of a brighter future. Sure, it led to occasional disappointments, but it also made life...well, worth living.

And then Chandra had appeared in his life with promises of ending his constant pain. The drakes were a part of that promise, weren't they?

But what if they weren't? Chandra had never said the drakes were the key...only that the Dragon Who Isn't must reach the Forgotten Library. And Elazar had.

Dane stared at the far wall of the room as if it held all the answers. He drummed his fingers against his upper arm, ignoring the familiar twinge of pain in his right shoulder. It was always worse at night.

"Sometimes you have to forge your own path," he murmured, the words a mantra he'd clung to in the darkest of times.

He could sit here, stewing in uncertainty, waiting for Tiberia to return, for the drakes to decide their fate, or he could take matters into his own hands.

Taking a deep breath, Dane pushed off the bed, wincing as his joints protested the sudden movement. Pain flared in his shoulder, radiating down his arm. He ignored it.

He crept to the door, pressing his ear against the cool wood, listening for any sounds of movement in the hallway beyond. Silence. Slowly, carefully, he turned the handle, easing the door open just enough to slip through.

Magical orbs spaced along the walls bathed the hallway in a soft ethereal glow. Dane blinked, his eyes adjusting to the dimness as he padded down the corridor, away from the rooms assigned to the *Tempest's* crew. At an intersection, he hesitated.

Left or right? He chose left, reasoning that it seemed to lead deeper into the library's heart.

Dane moved as quietly as he could, each step calculated to minimize the sound of his footfalls. The magical lights cast strange shadows that danced and shifted as he passed.

He knew he was taking a risk, but the need to find answers propelled him forward. Every few steps, he glanced over his shoulder, half-expecting to see a stern-faced drake rounding the corner, ready to reprimand him for his transgression.

Then a faint sound snagged his attention.

Footsteps. Soft, deliberate, coming from somewhere ahead.

Dane froze, his breath catching in his throat. He pressed himself against the nearest bookshelf hoping to remain unseen. The footsteps drew closer, accompanied by the rustle of fabric.

Panic rose in his chest. Had he been discovered? Would he be thrown out of the library?

The footsteps stopped. Dane held his breath, willing his heart to quiet its frantic tattoo against his ribs. He could sense a presence nearby, just around the corner. The silence stretched.

Then, a silhouette emerged from the shadows, the faint glow of the magical orbs illuminating the sharp angles of a man's face, his golden-brown eyes almost luminescent.

22

DEALING WITH DRAGONS

Cailan couldn't shake the feeling of restlessness that chased him. Sure, he was a little jealous that Asher had taken such a vested interest in helping Elazar overcome his...challenges. But this tumultuous sensation that something wasn't quite right ran deeper than petty envy.

Determined to shake off the feeling, he delved into the library, ignoring Iaxis's warnings about unauthorized exploration. The few dusty tomes he pulled from the shelves and flipped through were written in languages that swam before his eyes, indecipherable, though they pulsed with a faint magical glow when he discreetly channeled his own power. Not that this was particularly surprising. The entire library hummed with a latent energy, magic woven into its very foundations. He wouldn't be surprised if it seeped into the water they drank and the air they breathed.

Cailan's boots echoed against the polished marble floors as he rounded a corner and stopped short, his breath catching in his throat. There, a few paces ahead, stood Danelor, frozen as a deer caught in a predator's gaze.

Memories flooded Cailan's mind—their confrontation on the deck of the *Tempest*, the frustratingly pleasant hours he'd spent showing the other man the ropes, the sheer unyielding sunshine that seemed to radiate from Danelor's very being. He wanted to be irritated, but...he wasn't. And that, in itself, was infuriating.

"Didn't take you for a rule-breaker, feather-brain," Cailan said, allowing a hint of amusement to color his voice as he stalked toward the chimera.

Danelor visibly relaxed as he recognized Cailan. "There's a lot you don't know about me," he replied, a playful lilt in his voice.

Cailan swallowed, the unexpected warmth in Danelor's gaze sending a strange thrill through him. Despite his better judgment, Cailan felt himself drawn to Danelor. There was something about the chimera's open, unguarded demeanor, his easy smile, that intrigued him.

"What are you doing skulking around down here?" Cailan asked, keeping his voice carefully neutral.

Danelor's gaze swept over him, resting for a heartbeat on Cailan's lips before returning to meet his eyes. "Tiberia and I don't think the drakes intend to help us."

Cailan couldn't fault their pessimism. From what he'd overheard, Asher's hatred for the Jade Court ran deep. And honestly, who could blame him? "So, you're...what? Searching for a cure yourself?"

"Exactly," Danelor whispered, his gaze darting to the nearest bookshelf, as if afraid of being overheard.

Cailan hadn't expected to be right. It was a ridiculous notion. The library was a sprawling labyrinth, crammed with countless artifacts and mountains of texts. It could take a lifetime to sift through it all, to find anything remotely useful, and this feather-brained chimera thought he could stumble across something in a single night? Laughable.

"And how's that working out for you?" He couldn't resist the barb, the needling tone that came so easily.

Hurt flickered in Danelor's eyes, quickly masked by another easy smile. "I haven't been at it long," he said, his voice even. "I'm well aware this might take some time."

But did they have time? Cailan's mind raced. What would happen when the drakes officially rejected the Jade Court's pleas? Would they be cast out, forced to return to a world where dragons ruled the skies and chimeras lived in the shadows?

"Why are *you* sneaking around?" Danelor asked, his question breaking through Cailan's spiral of thoughts.

"I'm not *sneaking*," Cailan muttered, a defensive heat rising in his chest. "I'm...exploring."

A knowing smile curved Danelor's lips. "Right. Well, I'll let you get back to your explorations, then." He turned, his attention seemingly drawn to the nearest bookshelf.

Cailan huffed out a breath, unable to let it go. "You're going about this all wrong, you know."

Danelor's brow rose in surprise, and he glanced back at Cailan, curiosity in his eyes. "What do you mean?"

Cailan ran a hand through his hair, exasperated. "Look, a place like this...it has to have some kind of system, right? An organizational method. These books, these artifacts...they're not just haphazardly tossed onto shelves. There has to be a logic to it." He ran his fingers along the spines of several books, noting the subtle differences in their bindings and the strange symbols etched into some of them. "See these markings? They're probably part of the organization system."

Danelor moved closer, his shoulder brushing against Cailan's as he leaned in for a closer look. "I hadn't even noticed those," he admitted. "That's impressive, Cailan."

The unexpected praise caught Cailan off guard, and he felt heat creep up his neck. He shrugged, trying to downplay his own skills. "Yeah, well, I picked up a few things here and there."

"From where?" Danelor asked, genuine curiosity in his voice.

Cailan hesitated, memories of long hours spent in Chandra's company flooding back. "Chandra," he muttered finally. "She taught me a lot."

Danelor's expression shifted, understanding dawning in his eyes. "That must have been quite an education."

"It was." Cailan surprised himself with the lack of bitterness that tinged the words. Perhaps time and distance really *did* dull the sharp edges of old wounds. "Anyway," he continued, turning back to the bookshelves, "if we can crack this organizational system, we might actually stand a chance of finding something useful." He paused, a new thought striking him. "Though that assumes what we're looking for is even in a book. Could be an artifact, a relic...something a little more...hands-on."

The chimera nodded, a thoughtful frown creasing his brow. "Given what Iaxis said about those relics, you're probably right."

The tension that had lined Cailan's shoulders since their

arrival at the Forgotten Library eased for the first time. This, at least, was something he understood. A puzzle to solve. A mystery to unravel.

"You know," he said, tapping a finger against the worn spine of a nearby volume, his mind already racing ahead, "the drakes must have some kind of system for cataloging the artifacts, too. We just need to find it."

Danelor's eyes lit up. "That makes sense. And Iaxis, as the archivist...he'd have access to something like that, wouldn't he?"

A slow grin spread across Cailan's face. "Oh, he definitely *would*. But we both know we can't exactly stroll up and ask him for a peek, can we?"

"Definitely not," Danelor agreed with a chuckle as he considered the problem.

"Maybe I should have taken him up on that apprenticeship offer after all," Cailan suggested, though they both knew it was a jest. Then, a spark of inspiration ignited in his mind. "What if we found Iaxis's work area? He's got to have a study or a secret lair. Somewhere he keeps his records."

Danelor's eyes widened at the idea. "That could work. But it's risky, Cailan. If we're caught..."

"We won't be," Cailan said, injecting more confidence into his voice than he felt. "We just need to be smart about it." He glanced around. "Come on, let's see if we can track down Iaxis's lair. That's our best bet for finding some kind of artifact catalog."

Cailan set off, his senses on high alert, scanning the endless rows of bookshelves for any sign of watchful drakes or other lurking inhabitants. Danelor kept pace beside him, his footsteps nearly silent on the polished stone floor.

After what felt like an eternity of searching, they stumbled upon a secluded alcove tucked away in the far recesses of the main floor. Nothing about it stood out in any way, but Cailan didn't think the archivist was the sort to have an ostentatious workspace.

"This looks promising," he murmured to Danelor, who nodded in agreement, his eyes gleaming with anticipation.

Cailan tested the handle, half expecting to find it locked, but it turned easily in his grasp. He exchanged a surprised glance with Danelor before pushing the door open, slipping inside, and quietly closing it behind them.

The room was clearly a study, a haven for a scholar. A large desk dominated the center of the room, its surface cluttered with scrolls, quills, and open books. More bookshelves lined the walls, these filled with volumes bound in rich leather and secured with silver clasps. Cailan's gaze was drawn to a stack of letters resting on the corner of the desk, the topmost one addressed to Iaxis in an elegant, flowing script.

"Winner, winner, dragon dinner," Cailan said, a grin spreading across his face.

They began their search, careful not to disturb anything more than necessary. Cailan rifled through drawers, skimming over parchments and maps, while Danelor methodically examined the shelves. At the moment, there were no signs of the pain Cailan knew plagued the chimera.

"Cailan! Over here!" Danelor's hushed voice echoed from the far corner of the room. Cailan crossed the study, finding the chimera standing before a heavy oak cabinet, its doors thrown open. Stacks of thick leather-bound ledgers filled the shelves. "Look at this. This has to be it. Why isn't any of this locked up?"

"They probably don't need to," Cailan said absently, his attention already drawn to the tantalizing volumes. Why would they? Until the *Tempest's* arrival, visitors to the Forgotten Library were practically unheard of. The very notion of security must seem almost ludicrous in a place no one visited. He moved closer, peering over Danelor's shoulder as the chimera lifted one of the ledgers, carefully opening it.

Page after page of meticulous records greeted them, decades of careful documentation. Each entry contained a detailed description of an artifact or book, along with its precise location within the library.

"We did it!" Danelor breathed, his eyes alight with triumph.

Cailan nodded, a thrill of excitement coursing through him. "Now all we have to do is figure out what we're looking for."

"Look here." Danelor's finger traced a line of spidery script on the yellowed page. "Eletheria's Blessing. It says it has the power to alter memories."

Cailan frowned. "That sounds dangerous. But possibly useful." He glanced at Danelor, noticing the determined set of his jaw. "But it's not exactly what we're looking for, is it? Let's see what else is tucked away in this treasure trove."

They spent the next hour poring over the detailed records, their hushed whispers the only sound in the study's stillness. Cailan jotted down notes on scraps of parchment he'd found. As the night deepened, he found himself increasingly aware of Danelor's presence beside him—the warmth of his body, the soft rasp of his breath.

Finally, Danelor stifled a yawn, his hand briefly covering his mouth. "We should probably call it a night," he said. "Don't want to risk getting caught. And we both need to be somewhat coherent in the morning, wouldn't you say?"

Cailan agreed, though reluctantly. He was enjoying this easy camaraderie that had sprung up between them. He closed the ledger, carefully placing it back in its designated spot, ensuring everything was returned to its original state. As they slipped out of Iaxis's study, excitement and apprehension coiled in Cailan's gut.

"Same time tomorrow night?" Danelor asked, a hopeful smile playing on his lips.

"Wouldn't miss it," Cailan replied, surprised by the sincerity that resonated in his own voice.

They stood there for a moment, neither quite ready to break the fragile connection that had formed between them. Cailan found himself studying Danelor's face, taking in the way the light cast shadows along his jawline, the way his eyes seemed lit with a hidden depth.

Cailan stiffened as Danelor leaned in, his breath warm against Cailan's cheek. He braced himself for a whispered secret, maybe a conspiratorial revelation about their search. Instead, Danelor's lips brushed against Cailan's, a sudden, feather-light touch that sent a jolt of surprise—and something else, something warmer and more unsettling—straight through him. For a heartbeat, Cailan's mind went blank. The kiss was fleeting, but it left him breathless, frozen in place, caught completely off guard by the sheer audacity of it.

Danelor pulled back, his gaze searching Cailan's face, a question in the depths of his rich brown eyes. The unguarded hopefulness in his expression was disarming, and Cailan found himself speechless.

"What...what did you just do?" he stammered, his voice barely a whisper.

A warm smile touched Danelor's lips. "Something I should have done sooner."

Cailan's mind reeled. This wasn't what he'd expected. Not from Danelor, not from *anyone*. A tangle of emotions surged through him—anger, confusion, a spark of fear, and something else. "Why?" he demanded, his voice rough with the conflicting emotions warring within him. "Why did you do that?"

Danelor's smile faltered slightly, replaced by a look of quiet determination. "Because I wanted to," he said simply. "And because I thought...maybe you needed it."

He wasn't wrong. The realization twisted the knot in Cailan's gut even tighter. His first instinct was to lash out, to push Danelor away, to retreat behind the familiar walls of sarcasm and indifference. But...he couldn't. Not when a deeper, more primal part of him craved the sweetness of that unexpected kiss.

"You don't know what you're getting into," he warned, taking a step back, putting space between them. Cailan needed to breathe. He needed time to make sense of this.

"I'm accustomed to dealing with dragons," Danelor replied, offering him another of those too-kind smiles. He turned to leave, his footsteps echoing softly in the stillness, but his uneven stride had returned. "Goodnight, Cailan."

Cailan swallowed, watching as Danelor disappeared around a bend in the corridor. He couldn't shake the warmth of that kiss, the ghost of Danelor's touch, the tangle of emotions that had taken root within him.

Elazar

"Try again," Asher said, his tone even as Elazar shifted to his human form once more—naked, as had become the frustrating norm. "Reach into yourself, into your pocket dimension, and bring out the clothing with your shift."

"Reach into *myself*," Elazar muttered, his patience wearing thin. Despite their daily practice sessions, each transformation into his drake form brought another round of nausea and disorientation. Having to factor clothing into the equation only added to the complexity. "What if there isn't a pocket? What if my clothes have just...*vanished*?"

Rasmira, who was nearby working on what appeared to be a complicated metal armature, glanced up. "Matter doesn't simply disappear. It exists *somewhere*."

Elazar frowned. "How can that be the case? I gain several hundred pounds along with wings and a tail when I shift." He gestured to his currently bare form. "There's no *scientific* explanation for that. It defies the laws of physics. The conservation of mass, for one."

Asher and Rasmira exchanged amused looks. "Science and magic are two very different disciplines. Though they do, occasionally, share certain fundamental laws." She held up a clawed finger, forestalling his next argument. "Mass and energy cannot be created or destroyed, merely transformed. A fundamental principle of both realms."

"Hence the shift," Asher added, a touch of wry amusement in his tone.

Elazar pursed his lips. "I still don't understand."

"Because you're thinking about it too much," Asher said after a moment, thoughtful. "This is *not* one of those things you overthink."

Rasmira nodded. "Yes. This is more of a subconscious skill. When you shift now, are you thinking about your wings, tail, claws, scales, and so forth?"

"Well, no," Elazar murmured. "I'm too busy thinking about the shift. And the vertigo."

"Hmm." Asher tapped a claw thoughtfully against the stone floor. "Perhaps that's the root of the problem, then. The vertigo. Until you overcome that obstacle, accessing your pocket dimension is likely to remain a challenge."

Elazar sighed with dismay. He imagined his pocket dimension—wherever it was—overflowing with discarded clothing, a chaotic jumble of shirts and trousers he couldn't retrieve. Cailan had mentioned that these pocket dimensions had a limited capacity, and the thought of reaching his limit, of being unable to shift without shedding his clothes, was worrisome. "And the dizziness...it's not getting any better."

Asher sighed. "Then perhaps, for now, it's best to only shift when absolutely necessary."

Elazar frowned, disliking that option, too. Why couldn't this be simple? Easy? But his father was right. Limiting his transformations, frustrating as it was, might be the wisest course of action. The problem was, now that he knew he *could* shift, that he could tap into this hidden part of himself, the thought of being restricted felt like a cage.

"I suppose that's the most logical option," he conceded, "but I don't want to be caught out in the open without clothes every time." He shook his head. Taking a deep breath, he straightened his shoulders. "Let's try again."

He closed his eyes, focusing his will, reaching for that welcome surge of power. It responded instantly, coursing through his veins, a tingling warmth that twisted into a searing heat. Muscles spasmed, bones shifted, and the world around him dissolved into a dizzying blur of colors and disjointed sensations. The familiar nausea rose, a wave of vertigo that threatened to pull him under. He gritted his teeth, fighting against the urge to vomit, forcing himself to stay grounded.

When he opened his eyes, the workshop seemed different— smaller, somehow, the ceiling closer, the tools and clutter on Rasmira's workbench distorted, the angles all wrong. He shook his head, trying to clear the fog. The world tilted precariously with each movement. He reached out, his claws scraping against the stone floor, the sound alien to his ears.

Elazar huffed out a breath. The world finally settled around him.

"If this is too taxing, you may benefit from a break," Rasmira suggested.

"No." Elazar wanted to figure this out. "And the shift back to human has gotten easier, at last." It didn't cause the vertigo like his drake shift.

The power came easily now, surging through him at his command. Rasmira had fixed that, at least. He gritted his teeth, seeking that elusive pocket dimension. And there it was—an ephemeral space that seemed to exist just beyond his grasp. He strained, reaching for it, but it was like trying to snatch something from a passing airship.

A heartbeat later, the world snapped back into focus. He was standing upright, his clothes miraculously back in place, though he was breathing hard. Elazar glanced down, tugging at the hem of his shirt, a shaky laugh escaping him.

"Well, that's...progress." Asher nodded. "Your shirt's unbuttoned, but it's definitely a step in the right direction."

"The bar was admittedly low." Though Elazar couldn't suppress the surge of triumph that coursed through him. He had a shirt. Trousers. Who cared about buttons? He'd snatched clothing from the chaos of his pocket dimension, pulled it through the veil of magic and transformation. A win was a win.

He ran his fingers over the fabric of his shirt, nostalgia washing over him. "How...how is this even possible? These are the clothes I was wearing...back when..." He trailed off, shaking his head, warding off the memory of Cailan throwing him over the side of the *Tempest*. "A long time ago."

"Ah, yes." Rasmira's face lit with understanding. "As your control over your shifting grows, you'll find you have access to a variety of garments stored within your personal pocket dimension. With practice, you'll be able to select specific items, choose what you wish to bring through with you."

Elazar nodded slowly, his gaze lingering on the familiar

fabric, the feel of it soft against his fingertips. So much had changed since that fateful day on the *Tempest*.

He smoothed the fabric of his shirt, then turned to Asher. "What about the chimeras? Could a nexus chain help them with their shifting?"

"It's possible—" Rasmira began, only to be cut off by Asher's sharp interjection.

"The chimeras will *not* be given nexus chains," the elder drake snapped. "Nexus chains are for *drakes*."

Elazar frowned, his frustration rising. "But they were *sensed* as drakes when we arrived," he argued.

"As did your *airship*," Asher pointed out, his tail lashing behind him. "And that is *hardly* the case, is it?"

Elazar's jaw tightened. "You're being unfair to them," he insisted. He paused, then added, "And to the *Tempest*. You're hardly one to talk with your stone golems."

"My golems are not *alive*," Asher shot back, his voice dangerously low. "I command them. *My* will is *their* will. Your magic surely isn't that different from mine." He shook his head, his expression hardening. "And that is the last I wish to hear about the chimeras from you, Elazar. Do I make myself clear?"

"What?" Elazar whirled on his father, unable to contain his anger, and not wanting to. "I came here to *help* them. To help all of us."

"You came here at the behest of the *Jade Empress*," Asher countered, his voice soft, almost silken, but armored with a steel that made Elazar's breath hitch. "A *tyrant* whose will I no longer bend to. And neither will you. That is not up for discussion." He shook his head. "Do not test me on this, Elazar."

"But—"

"No." Asher's gaze pinned him in place. "You are a drake now. And I will *not* let Belen manipulate you. Not anymore." A shadow of something unreadable crossed his face—pain? Regret? Elazar couldn't be sure.

"What happened to taking their plight into consideration?" Elazar asked, his voice tight. "To showing compassion?"

"Their fate is still being deliberated," Asher ground out. "A verdict will be announced in due time." He drew in a breath, composing himself. Then, his tone shifting abruptly, he said, "Now, on a more auspicious note. We are holding a celebration in your honor in two days. For both you and your brother, of course."

Beside them, Rasmira nodded enthusiastically. "It will be a grand affair! Festivities unlike any we've seen in years!"

Elazar swallowed, overwhelmed by the conflicting emotions that warred within him—anger at Asher's refusal to help the chimeras, confusion at this sudden announcement. "Oh," was all he managed.

"Indeed. And you'll be expected to attend as a drake," Asher continued, his gaze sweeping over Elazar, taking in every detail. "Though you're passable, I must say, your scales could use some attention."

"My scales?" Elazar blinked, utterly bewildered.

Asher sighed, the sound long-suffering. "Yes. I'd forgotten you have much to learn." He nodded to himself, a decision made. "I'll arrange for one of our stylists to attend to you before the festivities begin. Consider it a welcome home present."

23

PLAY THEIR GAME

Danelor

As Dane slipped down the hallway, his thoughts were a jumbled mess.

Tiberia still hadn't come back to their room. He'd asked a frazzled-looking drake attendant to look for her, and she'd promised to get back to him. She'd kept her word, but all she had to report was that no one had seen Tiberia. No one knew where she was.

Fatigue had clung to him all day. Aside from that one brief inquiry about his sister, he'd stayed in their room and slept. Maybe he'd stayed up too late with Cailan, or maybe his body was failing him right when he needed it most.

At least he felt rested for tonight's meeting with Cailan. The memory of their parting kiss sent a flush through him, cheeks warming as he recalled his own boldness. He'd just... leaned in. Kissed Cailan. It was so unlike him to do something so impulsive, but with Cailan...he'd felt this pull, this spark. Or maybe he'd misread everything, and it was just his dragon side taking over, that primal urge to claim what he wanted.

Cailan had been startled. Upset, even. That hadn't been Dane's goal at all. He'd just thought maybe the opal drake needed someone to lean on, a safe harbor in the storm that seemed to surround him. How foolish he'd been to think *he* could be that for Cailan. After Dane's close call with him on the *Tempest*, after seeing how sharp and guarded Cailan was, he knew better. He should steer clear.

But despite his misgivings, Dane was excited to find Cailan already in Iaxis's nook, going through a ledger. Dane had feared that the kiss might have kept Cailan away, but the opal drake had kept his word.

Dane cleared his throat as he entered. "Sorry, I didn't realize you were so far ahead of me."

Cailan looked up, a smirk playing on his lips. "Figured one of us had better get to work." Then his expression softened. "I've only been here a few minutes, so don't worry." He paused, his gaze lingering on Dane. "I didn't see you at dinner."

Wait. Cailan had noticed his absence? Warmth spread through Dane, banishing his anxiety. He moved closer, unable to hide the slight limp that plagued him today—his left thigh was throbbing with a dull ache that radiated down to his knee. "Slept right through it," he admitted. "Wasn't feeling my best."

Cailan nodded, pushing a thick, leather-bound ledger across the desk toward Dane. "Maybe we'll have better luck if we both have a look." When Dane accepted the volume,

Cailan's gaze met his, a question in the depths of his golden-brown eyes. "That whole *not feeling well* thing...that happens a lot, doesn't it?" He winced, as if realizing he'd overstepped. "Sorry. You don't have to answer that."

Dane hesitated. It wasn't something he liked to talk about, but a part of him—a traitorous, hopeful part—wanted Cailan to understand. He opened the ledger, his fingers tracing the worn leather. "I'm always in pain. Some days are better than others."

"How can you live like that?" Cailan's voice was filled with a genuine concern that surprised Dane.

"What choice do I have?" He shrugged, trying to make light of it. His neck and shoulders, at least, were cooperating today. "Healers, physicians...they've all tried. It's just part of who I am now."

"Do you think it's a side effect of the dragonfruit? The corruption?" Cailan's voice was low, a thread of fierce determination running through it. As if he could somehow will a solution into existence if he just tried hard enough.

"We thought that, at first," Dane said, turning a page in the ledger. The first few entries had yielded nothing promising. "But none of the other chimeras experience this. So, it seems unlikely."

The memory of the Jade Court dragons' reaction to his condition—their barely concealed disgust, the thinly veiled suggestions that his very existence was an affront...it still stung. He suspected, privately, that his resilience was seen as a threat. A challenge to their dominance.

Cailan's jaw tightened. "That sucks. So, even if we find what we're looking for, you'll still be..." He hesitated, his gaze darting away, as if searching for a word that wouldn't offend. Dane had heard them all: *broken, flawed, incomplete.*

"The pain will always be with me, yes," he confirmed, his

voice even. Then, desperate for a change of subject, he gestured to the parchment in Cailan's hand. "You've already got a few notes. Find anything interesting?"

Cailan pushed the scrap across the desk, a wry grin crossing his lips. "This is my list of...questionable relics. The ones with names that make absolutely no sense. See this one? Soup Taper."

"Soup Taper?" Dane echoed, tilting his head. "Show me?"

Cailan flipped open the ledger, tapping the relevant entry. It was easy to see why he'd been confused. Whoever had penned this section of the ledger had handwriting that resembled a drunken spider's frantic crawl.

Dane squinted at the cramped script. "Actually, I think it's Soul Taker."

"Soul Taker..." Cailan repeated, testing the weight of the words. He made a face. "I definitely preferred *my* version."

Dane chuckled, a warmth spreading through him at Cailan's humor. He couldn't disagree. The image of a Soup Taper, whatever that might be, was far less ominous. He leaned closer, his shoulder brushing against Cailan's. "So, what else caught your eye?"

Cailan flipped through a few pages. "There's one called the Scales of Balance. Supposedly has the power to restore...equilibrium, I guess, to magical beings." He tapped the page with his finger. "Could be useful for the chimeras, maybe even those wingless dragons."

"Interesting." Dane nodded, scanning the entries in his own ledger. "I found something called the Essence Amplifier. It's described as enhancing innate magical abilities." He frowned, a note of concern in his voice. "Though there's a warning about...potential side effects."

"Worth investigating, maybe." Cailan's eyes gleamed with a speculative light. "Oh, here's another intriguing one—the

Arcane Resonator. Said to harmonize conflicting magical energies within a being."

They continued their search, the silence punctuated by the rustle of turning pages, the soft scratch of Cailan scribbling a note on parchment. But the memory of their last encounter remained on Dane's mind. He cleared his throat. "Cailan," he began, his voice a little rough, "about that kiss. I wanted to apologize. It was...presumptuous of me. I shouldn't have done that. Not without asking."

Cailan looked up, his eyes wide with surprise. For a moment, he simply stared at Dane, his expression unreadable. Then a slow smile spread across Cailan's face. "No one's ever kissed me before," he admitted. He paused. His voice was edged with amusement as he added, "Though, to be fair, I've spent most of my life around dragons, and they don't exactly kiss. "

Dane chuckled, relief washing over him. Dragons had their own mating rituals. Not exactly something he could replicate in his current form. "That's true. But I'm sorry if I made you uncomfortable. I honestly wasn't sure you'd even show up tonight."

Cailan glanced up from the ledger before him. Now there was a sizzle of intensity in his golden-brown eyes. "I'm a little surprised, too—partly because you scare me. But I said I would be here."

Dane's brow furrowed. "*I* scare *you?*"

Cailan huffed out a laugh, though there was a tightness around his eyes that belied the humor in his voice. "Not like you think." Cailan paused before explaining. "You scare me because I protect myself by not liking *anyone*. By not letting anyone get too close." Which, Dane suspected, wasn't working out well for him with how tangled he'd become to the *Tempest* crew, Chandra, and now the Forgotten Library. "For most of my life, it didn't matter. I wasn't exactly surrounded by people worth liking."

Aside from Chandra, Dane thought, though he wisely kept the observation to himself. The Seer was clearly a sore subject for Cailan. So, was he saying...he *liked* Dane? Or at the very least, *tolerated* him?

"You don't want to be vulnerable," Dane guessed, the words leaving his mouth before he could stop them. It seemed to fit with everything he'd observed about the opal drake—the sharp wit, the guarded heart, the constant need to be in control.

Cailan pushed the ledger aside, his full attention focused on Dane now. "I don't," he confirmed, his voice rough. "And you, with your winds-blasted *cheerfulness* and that ridiculous smile...you make me want to tear down all my walls, let the whole damn fortress crumble." His gaze swept over Dane. "And my traitorous brain finds you *alluring*, for reasons that defy all logic and reason."

Dane laughed, a genuine, startled sound. "*Wow*. I'm not sure if that's a compliment or an insult."

A sardonic smile touched Cailan's lips. "Maybe it's both."

It was odd to think that something as simple as Dane's positivity could eat away at Cailan's defenses. But it was clearly something the other man was still grappling with, so Dane let the issue rest, for now. "We should probably get back to work."

"Yeah, probably," Cailan agreed, though his tone suggested otherwise. Regardless, he bent back over the ledger spread open before him.

The words on the page before Dane seemed to swim. He rubbed the bridge of his nose, fatigue wearing at him again. It was probably time to head back to his room—

Oh, no. How could he have forgotten?

Cailan noticed Dane's sudden tension. "You okay?"

Dane shook his head. "I'm feeling fatigued and need to go

but…" He mentally kicked himself for his muddy thoughts, his Cailan-fueled distraction. "Have you seen Tiberia?"

Cailan blinked, clearly surprised by the question. "What?"

"She hasn't come back to our room," Dane explained, his worry resurfacing. "I asked one of the drakes to look for her, but no one's seen her."

Cailan's jaw clenched, a muscle jumping in his cheek. "You should have said something sooner, feather-brain."

Dane winced. "Probably. It's hard to think sometimes." He sighed, rubbing at the persistent ache in his temple.

"Sorry. Shouldn't have called you feather-brain." Cailan's apology was almost sheepish. "But no, I haven't seen her. She hasn't been at any meals. Honestly, I hadn't even noticed. Because…"

"Because she's Jade Court?" Dane supplied.

"No. Because she's not *you*," Cailan corrected, his gaze meeting Dane's. Then, as if chastising himself, he added, "Winds, I'm a terrible marshal. Should have been doing head-counts, making sure everyone from the *Tempest* was accounted for." His shoulders slumped, and Dane saw a flash of genuine self-reproach in his expression.

Dane hadn't expected that—the concern in Cailan's voice, as if Tiberia's disappearance was a personal affront. He reached out, placing a hand on Cailan's shoulder, hoping he wasn't overstepping. "There's been a lot to think about. Will you help me try to find her?"

Cailan nodded, the shadows beneath his eyes deepening with worry. "Of course." He glanced at the scattered ledgers, his jaw tightening. "But first, let's get these back where they belong. Wouldn't want to arouse suspicion."

Cailan did most of the work, carefully reshelving the heavy volumes. Dane watched him, admiring the effortless grace of his movements, the way the muscles in his arms flexed beneath his linen shirt.

They were just about to leave when the distinct sound of approaching footsteps echoed from the corridor outside. Dane's breath caught in his throat as Cailan cursed.

"Winds take it," Cailan hissed, his eyes darting around the room, taking in the lack of cover.

Dane's stomach dropped. There was nowhere to hide. No conveniently placed closets, no heavy drapes to conceal them, no desk large enough to duck under.

Cailan stepped over to Dane, his sudden nearness a confusing but not unwelcome invasion. "Just go with it," he whispered urgently, his arms snug around Dane.

Before Dane could process his words, one of Cailan's hands shifted to cup the back of Dane's neck, fingers finding their way through his long hair. His other hand moved to Dane's waist, drawing him closer, their bodies pressed together in a suddenly searing embrace.

Cailan's lips found his. He didn't press in, but instead traced the seam of Dane's lips with his tongue. Dane parted his lips, meeting the touch, and Cailan deepened the kiss. Cailan's hand on Dane's waist roamed, exploring the curve of his hip, tracing a line down his side. Dane's world narrowed to the feel of Cailan's body pressed against his.

The study door swung open with a groan, and Dane heard a startled cough. Cailan didn't release him, but he angled their position. Just enough to see Iaxis standing in the doorway, his blue-haired Elven form radiating disapproval and a touch of something that looked suspiciously like embarrassment.

"What, *precisely*, do you two think you're doing in here?" Iaxis asked.

With a huff of reluctance, Cailan pulled out of the kiss, though his eyes gleamed with satisfaction. Dane's mind blanked. He opened his mouth to speak, to offer some kind of explanation, but the words wouldn't come.

Cailan, however, seemed utterly unfazed. He shrugged, his arm tightening around Dane's waist. "It looks like exactly what it is, *Archivist*," he said, his tone challenging.

Iaxis pinched the bridge of his nose, looking as though he'd rather be anywhere else. "I would appreciate it if you would relocate your romantic endeavors elsewhere," he said, his voice strained. "This is a place of *scholarship*, not a lover's retreat."

"Fine, fine. Guess we'll just have to pick up where we left off later. Thanks for the interruption," Cailan grumbled, somehow managing to make it sound like *Iaxis* was the one at fault. He released Dane from the embrace, but swept an arm around to keep him close. Cailan arrowed a final annoyed look at the Archivist before walking out with Dane, leaving a speechless Iaxis in their wake.

"I thought you said I scared you," Dane whispered once they were a safe distance away.

"I decided to face my fears," Cailan said with a lopsided grin. He shrugged. "Besides, we needed some sort of ruse to cover for our questionable choice of location." His grip around Dane loosened, but he didn't let go. "Come on. Let's get you back to your room. You need to rest."

Dane allowed Cailan to lead him away. So that was all it had been...a ruse? Cailan proving to himself that he wasn't afraid of what Dane offered? Had the kiss meant *anything* to Cailan?

Cailan

HE'D BEEN TEMPTED, SO *VERY* TEMPTED, TO ASK DANELOR if he could stay. To make sure the chimera was all right, of course. Certainly not because he found the cheerful, infuriating man fascinating and the thought of another kiss, this time without the threat of discovery, sent a pleasant shiver down his spine.

Instead, he'd settled for walking Danelor back to his room, making sure he got there safely. Tiberia was missing, and the guilt weighed on Cailan, another reminder of his failings. He'd do a proper headcount of the *Tempest* crew in the morning. He *had* to.

At breakfast, he scanned the faces gathered around the tables of the dining hall, relief washing over him when he saw all the familiar faces. All except Tiberia's. And Danelor's. He'd made a quick detour to their room, finding Danelor awake but groggy, a flush of embarrassment coloring his cheeks when Cailan caught him in such a weakened state.

Cailan understood the need to hide, to project an image of strength, even when your body was betraying you. He'd been teased mercilessly for his size, back when everyone had assumed he was a runty dragon, not a drake. It had left a scar, a deep-seated distrust of others. What if others saw him as weak, as less? He'd learned to keep his toughness at the forefront.

"Cailan?" Elazar's hesitant voice broke through his thoughts.

He turned to face his brother, noticing the way Elazar fidgeted, his gaze darting around the hall as if he were afraid of being overheard. They hadn't spoken much since that *enlightening* conversation with Asher.

"What's up?" he asked, keeping his tone casual, though curiosity pricked at him.

"Do you have a few minutes?" Elazar glanced nervously over his shoulder again. "Somewhere more private?"

Elazar's attempt at clandestine maneuvering was almost comical. The poor drake didn't have a sneaky bone in his body. Intrigued, Cailan pushed away from the table. "Sure, I've got a few minutes."

He followed Elazar out of the hall. They wound their way through the maze of corridors, the air growing cooler, the scent of old paper and leather giving way to something fresher. Finally, they emerged into a secluded garden. Sunlight filtered through a canopy of lush foliage, casting dappled shadows on moss-covered stones. It was surprisingly tranquil.

"All right, out with it. What's so secret?" Cailan asked, crossing his arms and leaning against a weathered stone pillar.

Elazar glanced around nervously, as if expecting a drake assassin to leap from the foliage, before lowering his voice to a hushed whisper. "I don't think they're going to help. The drakes, I mean. They're not going to help the Jade Court."

Cailan snorted. "That seems pretty obvious, doesn't it? You saw how Asher reacted."

"That's just it," Elazar insisted, frustration edging into his voice. "That was the whole reason I agreed to come here. To find a way to help them, to fix things."

Cailan studied his brother's face, his features creased with worry lines. "I get it. You want to make things right," Cailan said, softening his tone. "But these drakes—especially Asher— they've got some serious bad blood with the Jade Court. They're not inclined to be charitable."

Elazar raked a hand through his hair, his frustration growing. "But why? I don't understand. This place...it's incredible. Full of power, knowledge..." He hesitated, then blurted, "Did you know our nexus chain helps with shifting? With channeling magic?" His fingers brushed the gold chain at his neck.

Cailan's hand went to his own chain. "No, I didn't." But

Chandra had always insisted he wear it, keep it close. She'd *known*. Another truth she'd kept hidden.

Elazar blew out a frustrated breath. "I asked if the drakes would consider letting the chimeras try them. See if it helped. Asher flat-out refused."

Cailan rubbed his chain, a thoughtful frown creasing his forehead. If the nexus chains really *did* have that kind of power...Elazar's idea had merit. "So, it's easier for you to shift now? Using the chain?"

Elazar sighed. "Sort of." He explained the problematic vertigo. Cailan had never experienced anything like it, so he was at a loss for suggestions. Except...

"Have you asked Gretchen?"

Elazar blinked, surprised. "No. I...it didn't seem like something she could help with."

Cailan snorted. "It's about your *health*, idiot. Of course, it's something she could help with."

Elazar's expression shifted, thoughtful. "Actually, that's not a bad idea. I'll talk to her." Then, his voice dropping to a near whisper, he asked, "Should I speak to Chandra? She's the one who said I needed to come here. But if the drakes won't help... doesn't that mean it's all been a waste? A failure?"

Chandra. Cailan carefully schooled his expression, keeping his reaction neutral. He was grateful the drakes had found a secluded space for the Seer, far from the rest of the *Tempest* crew.

"You're reading too much into it," Cailan said. Elazar hadn't grown up steeped in the maddening vagaries of prophecy, hadn't learned to parse *every* syllable, *every* inflection, for hidden meanings. That was the problem with prophecies—people twisted them to fit their own narratives. Just because something *sounded* profound didn't make it true.

"I don't understand." Confusion clouded Elazar's eyes.

"Did Chandra ever actually *tell* you to come here?" Cailan pressed. "Or did she just hint at it? Make suggestions?"

Elazar winced. "I think...she asked if I'd find the Forgotten Library. If I'd mend the past." He rubbed his forehead, his expression pained as he struggled to recall the exact words. "I don't remember the rest. Sorry."

Cailan took a breath, forcing down the frustration that simmered within him. Elazar hadn't been trained to memorize a Seer's every utterance. "It's fine. But what I'm saying is, *mend the past* doesn't specify *whose* past. Or *what* past." He shrugged, hoping to make Elazar see the flaws in his logic. "What if she never meant the chimeras? Or the Jade Court?"

Understanding dawned in Elazar's eyes. "Oh."

"Exactly." Cailan let out a humorless snort. "And it's a little late to go back and ask for clarification, wouldn't you say?"

But the thought lingered, a burr beneath his scales. The more he considered it, the more bothered he felt. Especially considering the horrors Iaxis had revealed—the Forgotten War, the devastating power unleashed upon the world. Maybe he was being too pessimistic. Maybe *mend the past* simply meant rectifying those ancient atrocities, honoring the memory of those who had died.

But something about that didn't sit right. It felt incomplete. He needed time to think, to see what patterns emerged. He did his best thinking when he wasn't actively *trying* to think, when he let his instincts guide him.

"Have you seen Tiberia recently?" Cailan asked, shifting the conversation, though the chimera's disappearance *was* a genuine source of worry.

Surprise ghosted across Elazar's face as he searched his memory. Cailan could practically see the gears turning in his brother's head.

"I can't remember," Elazar admitted. "Why do you ask?"

"Danelor said she didn't come back to their room two nights ago." Cailan kept his voice even, careful not to betray his own growing apprehensiveness.

Elazar's eyes widened. "That long? We have to find her! We should ask around, see if—"

Cailan held up a hand, silencing his brother's rising panic. "Hold on. We need to be careful. We don't want to tip off the wrong drakes."

"But—"

"I'll handle it," Cailan cut him off, his voice firm. "I'll do some digging, see what I can find out. *Discreetly.*"

Elazar nodded, though his reluctance was clear. He understood the need for caution, but inaction clearly chafed at him.

"Good. For now, just act normal. I'll let you know if I find anything," Cailan said.

Elazar shifted from foot to foot, his gaze darting to the path back to the library. "Did you know they're planning a celebration for us? Tomorrow night?"

Cailan frowned. "No. But then, Asher hasn't exactly warmed up to me the way he has to you."

Elazar winced. Unfairly, Cailan knew, but he couldn't help the bitterness that rose in his chest. "Well, you're included, too. They want us both to attend...as drakes."

"I'm not a drake," Cailan grumbled, defensiveness hardening his voice. Dragons might be a part of his past, but he'd be damned if he'd embrace the label of *drake.*

"You know what I mean." Elazar sighed. "They want us to not look human."

"Why?"

"Because they're *drakes,*" Elazar said, as if that explained everything.

It didn't, of course. But it didn't really matter. A slow smile spread across Cailan's face. This celebration. It might actually work to their advantage. "Fine. I'll play their game. For now. I'll keep looking for Tiberia. And if we don't have answers by tomorrow night...well, that might be the perfect opportunity to ask."

Alarm flared in Elazar's eyes. "What do you mean?"

"Think about it," Cailan said, his voice low. "If we ask about Tiberia now, in the shadows, they can lie to us. Dismiss us. But in front of an audience—during their precious celebration—they'll have to answer."

"You think something bad happened to her?" Fear shadowed Elazar's features.

"I don't know." Cailan met his brother's gaze. "But they won't be able to ignore us, not then. We'll force their hand."

Elazar nodded, accepting Cailan's logic. "Okay. We can try that. But what about the chimeras? The Jade Court? What about helping them?"

Cailan grinned, his gaze sweeping over the imposing edifice of the library. "Remember what you said before? About this place being full of magic and promise?"

"Yeah?"

"Danelor and I...we've been doing some research." *And kissing*, he added silently, the memory sending a rush of warmth through him. But that was his own business. Not something he was going to share with his brother.

Elazar's eyes widened. "When? How?"

"Late at night." Cailan glanced around, making sure they were still alone, then stepped closer to his brother, lowering his voice to a conspiratorial murmur. "You know about the history of this place, right? The Forgotten War? All that messed-up history?"

Elazar nodded. "Max filled me in."

"Good. We found ledgers. A complete catalog of every

book, every artifact, in this place. We're already *way* ahead of you."

"Can I help?" Elazar's eagerness was almost endearing.

The thought of Elazar intruding on his research sessions with Danelor wasn't appealing, but realistically, the more eyes scanning those ledgers, the better their chances of finding something useful.

"Yeah, all right," Cailan conceded after a moment's hesitation. "I'll show you where to go tonight."

24

HEAVY HEART

Elazar

Tiberia's absence unnerved Elazar—and he felt awful that he hadn't even realized she was missing until Cailan had asked. He shook his head, frustration mixing with worry as he made his way back to the *Tempest* crew's assigned accommodations. He had enough on his mind, he reasoned—the Forgotten Library, his newfound parentage, the challenges of mastering his shifting, Maxine...

But still. Tiberia was a friend. He should have noticed. And Cailan had been adamant—they couldn't alert the drakes. But he hadn't said anything about asking their own crew.

Gretchen. Cailan was right—she was the best person to

consult about the vertigo. And maybe she'd have some insights about Tiberia, too.

He headed for the room she shared with Aunt Josephine, but found it empty. Frowning, he tried to recall where else they might be. Then it hit him: the Brew Nook. He and Max had discovered the marvelous coffee machine a few days ago, and knowing Gretchen's fondness for strong beverages, it was a safe bet Max had shared the location with her.

The rich aroma of freshly brewed coffee greeted him as he approached the Brew Nook, a comforting scent that momentarily eased his anxiety. He found Gretchen and Aunt Jo seated at a small round table tucked into an alcove, steaming mugs in their hands.

"Elazar!" Aunt Jo's face brightened as she saw him. "Come join us. This contraption...it's a marvel of engineering. Have you seen it?"

Gretchen nodded in agreement, taking a long, appreciative sip from her mug, her eyes closed in contentment.

Elazar managed a weak smile. "Yeah, Max and I found it the other day. But that's not why I'm here."

Aunt Jo's smile vanished, replaced by a worried frown. "What's wrong?"

Elazar hesitated for a moment, then said, "Actually, I wanted to talk to Gretchen about something."

Gretchen set down her mug, her gaze focusing on him with an intensity that always made him feel a little like she was peering into his soul. "What's troubling you, Elazar?"

"Well..." He ran a hand through his hair. If he'd had a tail at the moment, he was sure it would be twitching. "Every time I shift into a drake, I get this awful vertigo. It's really intense, and I was hoping maybe you might have some ideas?"

Aunt Jo's eyes widened in alarm. "Vertigo? Elazar, why didn't you say anything?"

"I didn't think..." He sighed, wishing he'd come to Gretchen sooner. "Because it was related to shifting, I didn't think it was something a human or a mage could help with."

Gretchen's lips pursed, but a spark of understanding lit her eyes. "Vertigo isn't magic, Elazar. It's not even a condition, really. It's a *symptom*. Like a sore throat, or a headache." She tilted her head, studying him with a clinical eye. "Tell me more about it. When does it happen? How long does it last? What does it feel like?"

Elazar did his best to describe the sensation, the way the world twisted and spun, the nausea that rose in his throat, the disorientation that clung to him like a shroud. Gretchen listened intently, occasionally murmuring soft sounds of understanding. Aunt Jo sat beside the Healer, her expression tight with worry, but she didn't interrupt.

When he finished, Gretchen nodded, her gaze thoughtful. "Most cases of vertigo are caused by issues within the inner ear." She tapped a finger against her temple. "There are tiny crystals, you see, both in human ears and dragon ears. And drake ears, in your case." A small smile touched her lips. "When those crystals are knocked out of their normal positions, it can trigger vertigo. I suspect that when you shift, those crystals are...well, quite *dramatically* rearranged. It's likely taking them some time to settle back into place."

"But why hasn't he experienced this before?" Aunt Jo asked, her voice laced with concern.

Elazar knew why. Or suspected, at least. "Because every time I shifted before, I wasn't the one in control. It was always *traumatic*. I was usually unconscious for a bit afterwards."

The explanation did nothing to ease his aunt's worry. Her eyes narrowed, expression fierce. "Elazar!"

"Love, he's only telling the truth." Gretchen patted

Josephine's shoulder reassuringly. "It's a logical explanation, given the circumstances."

"But can I do anything about it? The vertigo, I mean." Hope swelled in Elazar's chest.

Gretchen nodded, taking another sip of her coffee, her gaze thoughtful. "If it's those pesky inner ear crystals causing the trouble, a series of specific head movements can sometimes alleviate the symptoms."

Something that simple? Elazar frowned, skeptical. "Really?"

Gretchen chuckled. "Oh, it's not as easy as it sounds. Don't underestimate the complexity of the inner ear." She rose, her mug still in hand. "But my morning's free. If you're willing to put in the work, I'm happy to guide you."

"I'd like that, actually." The prospect of relief from the dizziness was incredibly appealing. Then another, more pressing worry resurfaced. "But first, have either of you seen Tiberia lately?"

"No..." Aunt Jo's gaze was troubled. "I assumed she was in her room. She didn't seem particularly happy with the drakes. Not that I blame her."

"She's *not* in her room?" Alarm lit Gretchen's eyes.

Elazar shook his head. "Cailan said Danelor hasn't seen her for two days."

Aunt Jo cursed. "*Two days?* Winds above, we have to find her. We need to start searching—"

"No," Elazar interrupted, finally understanding Cailan's insistence on secrecy. "Just wait, please. Cailan's looking into it. He said it was better if we didn't alert the drakes."

Aunt Jo nodded, accepting his explanation. "Knowing Cailan, he probably didn't want you to tell anyone about this. But I expect regular updates, Elazar. Understood?"

He couldn't help but laugh. "You know him pretty well,

don't you?" He sobered, nodding. "Don't worry, Aunt Jo. I'll keep you informed."

Gretchen smiled. "Now that that's settled, where do you want to practice these maneuvers? We'll need some space."

Elazar glanced around the Brew Nook, taking in the vaulted ceilings. It was spacious enough to accommodate his drake form, but too public. The memory of his botched transformations, the sudden lack of clothing... He shuddered. "My room, maybe?"

The Healer chuckled. "Very well. Lead the way, Elazar."

Cailan

Dressed in dark clothing, Cailan slipped out of his room. He was on a mission. Find Elazar and head to Iaxis's study. He needed to know more about those artifacts that were scattered throughout the library.

He hadn't expected to find Asher waiting for him. His father leaned against the wall in human form. He straightened as Cailan stepped into the hallway.

"What do you want?" Cailan asked, crossing his arms, his tone guarded.

"Hello to you, too," Asher said with a ghost of a smile, pushing away from the wall. "I was hoping I could speak with you. Just the two of us." He swallowed. "I know I've been spending a lot of time with your brother, and I don't want you to feel left out."

"It's a little late for that, isn't it, *father*?" Cailan shot back, a bitter edge to his voice. Winds blast it! Why now? He had things to do, secrets to uncover. A traitorous part of him *wanted* to have this conversation with his father, to mend the rift between them. But Cailan ruthlessly pushed that sentiment aside. He'd been abandoned. He wasn't about to let that happen again.

Asher ran a hand through his long, pale hair, his gaze pleading. "I know you're angry, and your anger is justified. But—"

"Damn *right* it is," Cailan growled. "You've made it pretty clear how you feel about me. Starting with the fact that you didn't even bother to check on your own whelps."

Asher took a step back, his nostrils flaring. Cailan knew it had been a savage blow, but he didn't care. He wasn't going to be gentle.

"I'm trying to make things *right*, Cailan," Asher said softly. "I'm trying to be the father you deserve. And you won't even give me a chance."

"I'm cynical like that." Cailan narrowed his eyes, then made a shooing motion with his hand. "Keep on with Elazar, though. He's clearly desperate for someone like you in his life." Okay, maybe Elazar *wasn't* desperate, but Cailan was running out of ways to get rid of his father.

Asher's shoulders slumped, his expression pained. "Fine. I'll leave you alone. If that's what you want. But I hope that someday you'll see that I really *do* care about you." He turned on his heel and strode away, leaving Cailan to watch him go.

Yeah, I'm really an asshole, he thought, a sigh escaping his lips. Cailan shook his head. He wasn't sure who he was more irritated at: his father or himself.

Danelor

Dragging himself out of bed had been a monumental effort. Dane cursed his treacherous body—why did it have to fail him now, when time was so precious? At least the day spent resting had helped. The fatigue remained, a leaden weight in his limbs, but he was mostly functional.

He'd expected to find Cailan alone in Iaxis's study, but as he slipped through the door, Dane blinked in surprise. Elazar stood beside Cailan, hunched over the open ledger as he scanned the neat rows of spidery script. Maxine was there, too, eyeing a shelf of books. She waved at Dane.

Both brothers looked up at his entrance. Elazar offered a distracted smile and a mumbled greeting before returning his attention to the ledger. Cailan, however, straightened, his gaze fixed intently on Dane.

He cast a quick glance at Elazar, then crossed the room, his footsteps silent. "How are you feeling?" His voice was low.

The genuine worry in Cailan's voice eased the tension that had knotted Dane's shoulders. He smiled, grateful for the attentiveness. "About the same."

Cailan shifted his weight, a small nod of acknowledgement. "Hope you don't mind. Elazar wanted to help with the search, and he decided to drag Max along."

"I wasn't dragged along," Max corrected, glancing over. "I *wanted* to come and help."

Dane didn't mind. Not really. More help was always welcome, but he'd been looking forward to spending time with Cailan, to exploring this connection that had sparked between them. But this was probably for the best. They might actually make some progress with more eyes scanning those ledgers.

"No, it's a good idea," he agreed, forcing a brighter smile. "The more the merrier, right?" He hesitated, then asked, "Any news about Tiberia?"

Cailan sighed, running a hand through his hair, his frustration clear. "No luck. I poked around today but came up empty." He paused, his gaze hardening. "If we haven't found her by tomorrow night...I'll bring it up at the celebration. Publicly."

The celebration. Right. Dane vaguely recalled someone mentioning that. He was invited, of course. But his heart sank. Every hour that passed without news of Tiberia increased his worry. Where was she? What had the drakes done with her?

Cailan's expression was the most sympathetic Dane had ever seen him use. "I know you're worried. But we have to play this carefully."

Dane understood, but it did little to ease his anxiety. "I know." He forced a smile, turning his attention to the ledgers spread across the desk, hoping to lose himself in their secrets. "Find anything useful yet?"

Cailan let out a snort. "Elazar found the schematics for that fancy coffee machine in the Brew Nook."

Dane couldn't help but laugh, the tension momentarily broken. "Well, glad to see someone's got their priorities straight."

Elazar shot him a sheepish grin. "Sorry. It was the first non-magical gadget I came across. I couldn't resist."

Dane settled into a nearby chair, pulling one of the ledgers closer. The script swam before his eyes, and he blinked, trying to focus. He'd barely made it through two pages when fatigue surged through him, his limbs growing heavy, his eyelids drooping.

"This one mentions something called Soulchains," Elazar said, his voice colored with fascination.

Cailan leaned over his brother's shoulder, peering at the entry. "That sounds ominous. Any details?"

Dane tried to listen, to follow their conversation about Soulchains and whatever arcane properties they might possess, but their voices seemed to come from a great distance, distorted. He rubbed his eyes, willing himself to stay awake, but it was no use.

"Sorry," he interrupted, his voice slurring slightly. "I hate to do this, but I need to call it a night."

Cailan looked up, alarm flashing in his eyes. "Already? Are you sure you're all right, Dane?"

He nodded, though the simple movement made the room tilt precariously. "Just tired. Some sleep and I'll be fine."

Cailan stood, moving toward him, his hand outstretched as if to steady him. "Let me walk you back to your room."

"No, no, I'm fine." Dane pushed himself to his feet, swaying for a moment before finding his balance. "Really. You three stay. This is important. We need to find those answers."

Cailan hesitated, torn between concern for Dane and the urgency of their research. Dane offered him a reassuring smile, hoping it masked how he truly felt. "I'll be fine. Promise. Just need some sleep."

After a moment, Cailan nodded, though his reluctance was clear. "Fine. But if you need *anything*, anything at all, you call for me. Understand?"

"I will." Dane managed another smile before turning to leave. As he left the study, he heard Cailan and Elazar pick up their conversation, their voices fading as he walked down the corridor.

Each step was an effort, his body protesting. Fatigue weighed him down, but it was the worry for Tiberia that kept him moving.

He knew he shouldn't press the drakes for information—Cailan was right, caution was paramount—but what if Chandra knew something? She was a Seer, after all. Maybe she could offer some reassurance, ease his fear.

As he neared Chandra's quarters, his pace slowed. He ignored his body's aches; finding Tiberia was all that mattered.

Dane knew from their time on Outcast Island that Chandra kept odd hours. He tapped on her door, hearing her muffled invitation to enter.

He pushed the door open. The room was sparsely furnished, allowing the dragon ample room. Chandra was curled on a pile of huge cushions in the corner.

A soft whimper drew his attention to Vesper, nestled beside her. The aralez thumped his tail weakly, a half-hearted greeting, his soulful eyes darting between Dane and Chandra.

Chandra's head lifted, her pale eyes finding his. "You carry a heavy heart, young one," she said, her voice a low rasp.

Dane swallowed, uncertainty churning in his gut. Exhaustion made his thoughts sluggish, his words clumsy, but the worry for Tiberia burned through the fog. "I need your help," he said, taking a hesitant step further into the dragon's room.

The Seer's eyes seemed to glow in the dim light. "Tell me, what's wrong?"

The words tumbled out. He told her about Tiberia, about her disappearance, about the utter lack of information, about the dread that had settled over him like a choking cloud. Chandra listened, her expression unreadable, nodding occasionally as if acknowledging his concerns. Beside her, Vesper whined, his unease growing with each passing moment. The aralez rose, padding silently across the room. He curled up near the door as if seeking an escape.

When Dane finished, Chandra sighed, her breath a soft rustle in the quiet room. "I understand your worry. And I'm afraid your fears are not unfounded."

Dread coiled in his stomach. "Do you know where she is? Is she...is she all right?"

Chandra nodded slowly. "I know where she is. And Tiberia is safe, for now."

Relief flooded him, so potent it almost made him weak.

"Where is she? What have the drakes done with her?" Then her words, *safe, for now*, hit him with a jolt of fear. "Wait. What do you mean, *for now?*"

The Seer rose gracefully from her cushions, stretching like a cat waking from a long slumber. Her tattered wings unfolded, then mantled once more. She turned to face him. "It means precisely what I said." Chandra's voice was edged with a chilling finality. She lifted her right foreclaw, uncurling the talons.

Tendrils of darkness, like inky smoke given life, rose from her outstretched claws, snaking toward Dane with a terrifying speed. He couldn't react, couldn't even cry out, before it enveloped him, coiling around his entire body. The icy touch seeped into his skin. He gasped, his vision blurring, his limbs growing heavy. Horror flooded Dane as the dark tendrils tightened. He fought against the shadowy bonds, but they held firm.

"Chandra!" he rumbled, his voice raw with terror. "What are you doing? I thought you were going to *help* me!"

The Seer's eyes glowed, twin points of eerie light. "But I *am* helping you, Dane. Don't you remember? I promised to end your pain."

Icy fear threaded through him. This wasn't what he'd expected, not at all. He'd trusted her, believed in her wisdom, in her kindness. Now, trapped by her magic, he felt a wave of nausea rise.

"This isn't what I meant," Dane pleaded. "Please, Chandra, let me go. We can talk about this. There has to be another way."

But Chandra simply shook her head. "I'm afraid it's too late for that, young one. I made a promise. And I *always* keep my promises."

His mind raced, struggling to make sense of this betrayal. How could he have been so wrong about her? How could the promise of relief, the desperate hope for an end to his pain, have blinded him so completely?

Then, he remembered his kiss with Cailan—not the heat, but what Cailan had called it. *A ruse.* That's what Chandra's promises had been, too. A deception to cover her true intent.

The Seer approached, her shredded wings unfolding behind her like a shroud. She extended a clawed hand, pressing it against his forehead. The world dissolved into darkness.

25

Family Feud

Cailan

"Did you know this was a thing?" Elazar asked. He sat obediently in the middle of the drake salon, his copper scales gleaming under the practiced ministrations of his assigned stylist.

"Not a clue," Cailan admitted, tilting his head back to give his own stylist better access to the scales beneath his jaw. He hadn't been prepared for this—the drakes' meticulous grooming rituals.

"Proper scale care is essential!" Altira, his stylist, declared, waving a polish-laden brush at them. The drake, who adopted an Elven form with silver hair, cast a critical eye over Cailan's opal hide. "How could you let them get so *frayed?*"

"Hard use," he muttered, shifting uncomfortably as she resumed her fussing. Elazar, at least, had the good fortune of being assigned a stylist who preferred to work in silence, aside from answering questions. Cailan still didn't quite understand the importance of all this preening and polishing, but it was clear the Forgotten Library drakes took great pride in their appearance.

Elazar, however, was lapping it all up. His eyes shone with fascination as his stylist—a stocky, taciturn drake in a Knossan form—explained the different polishes and brushes and the intricacies of proper scale alignment. It made sense, Cailan supposed. Elazar had spent his life surrounded by humans, and humans, in their own way, were just as obsessed with appearances.

"There! All done!" Altira stepped back, admiring her handiwork. "Now for the shaping."

Cailan tensed as Altira stepped forward, brandishing a wicked-looking metal rasp. "Shaping?" he echoed, eyeing the tool with wariness.

"Of course! We can't have you looking unkempt for the festivities." She clucked her tongue disapprovingly, tapping the rasp against one of his opal scales. "These need some *serious* attention."

"I like them just fine," Cailan grumbled, but she was already back at work. He tried to ignore the rasping sound as she smoothed and shaped his scales.

"You have so many split ends!" Altira exclaimed, as if he'd committed some unforgivable fashion crime. She paused, stepping back to survey her work, a satisfied smile blooming on her face. "There! You'll both look magnificent. Everyone will be so impressed!"

Cailan grimaced. The last thing he wanted was to impress anyone. The Conclave had flat-out refused to assist the Jade Court, and he was still furious that he hadn't been able to find any trace of Tiberia.

"Perfect! You're both ready." Altira beamed, clearly pleased with her efforts. "Just in time, too. The celebration is about to begin!"

Cailan exchanged a look with Elazar, who met his gaze with a nervous spark in his eyes. "Well, let's get this over with," he said, shaking out his wings, enjoying Altira's gasp of dismay at the movement. He hadn't spent the last hour being meticulously groomed to stand around like a statue.

"You really enjoy irritating people, don't you?" Elazar asked, following Cailan out of the salon.

"It's a gift," Cailan replied with a grin, his mood lightening.

"When are you going to ask about Tiberia?" Elazar's voice was hushed.

Cailan paused in their walk down the corridor. "I'll play it by ear. We don't know what they've got planned for tonight. I need the right opportunity."

Elazar nodded, his gaze troubled. "And what if they refuse to tell us anything? What if they deny any knowledge of her disappearance?"

Cailan's jaw tightened. He hated that those were distinct possibilities. "Then we take matters into our own claws." He glanced at Elazar, a mischievous glint in his eyes. "It sounds like every drake on the island will be here tonight. Which means... it's the perfect opportunity to explore some of those restricted areas mentioned in the ledgers."

"What?" Elazar stopped short, his eyes widening in alarm. "What are you talking about?"

Cailan had been turning this plan over in his mind all day, the seed of an idea growing into a tangled, thorny vine. "Think,

Elazar. If they're hiding Tiberia, it's likely in one of those off-limits sections. And even if they're not...we've got a list of relics worth investigating. Relics that might be *useful*."

"Useful?" Elazar blinked, confusion clouding his features. "You mean you intend to *take* them?"

"Exactly."

The copper drake shook his head, aghast. "But that's *stealing*."

Cailan snorted, remembering that Elazar, in his naiveté, was unaware of the debt hanging over the *Tempest*, the pressure to return to Gibson with something of value. He'd been compiling his own list of potential targets—artifacts that seemed less horrifying and dangerous than others, though perhaps he was misjudging their true nature.

"Look, you want to help the Jade Court, and the drakes have made it clear they won't lift a claw to assist them." He fixed Elazar with a steady gaze. "You helped me with the research, remember? What did you think we were going to do? Ask nicely? Bat our eyelashes at Asher and beg him to let us borrow a few relics from the Forgotten War?" He let out a harsh laugh. "Get real, Elazar. You know they'd never agree."

Elazar winced. "There has to be another way."

"I'm all ears," Cailan said, though he doubted there was a better option.

"I just wish we had more time." Elazar sighed.

"Yeah, well, wish in one hand and—"

"Don't even finish that sentence," Elazar cut him off. "I'm just frustrated that you're right. And frustrated that the drakes are being so stubborn."

Cailan nudged him with his shoulder, offering a rare gesture of comfort. "I get it. But sometimes, you've got to make your own luck."

Elazar nodded, accepting the harsh truth. "So, how do we do it? Search those restricted areas, I mean."

"There's no *we* in this one, brother." Cailan shook his head. "The more of us involved, the higher the risk of getting caught." He saw the annoyance in Elazar's eyes and added, "But you still have a role to play. The drakes seem to like you, for whatever reason. Keep them occupied. Distracted. You can handle that, right?"

Elazar grimaced. "I can try. But charming a room full of drakes isn't exactly my forte."

"You'll be fine. Just talk to them about arcane engines and pistons or...whatever." Cailan straightened his shoulders, his gaze fixed on the doorway ahead. Music and laughter spilled into the corridor, beckoning them towards the heart of the festivities. Elazar trailed behind him, his steps hesitant.

"There you are." Asher's deep voice rumbled, halting their progress. Cailan turned to find his father striding towards them. His scaled form cut an imposing figure. Cailan's gut tightened instinctively, but the drake's expression wasn't one of anger. In fact, his golden eyes gleamed with a warmth that Cailan couldn't quite decipher.

"*Father,*" Cailan acknowledged cautiously, dipping his head in a gesture of minimal respect, though the word felt foreign on his tongue. Beside him, Elazar straightened, offering Asher a tentative smile.

Asher's gaze swept over them, lingering for a moment on Cailan's freshly polished scales. "You both look presentable," he said, approval lacing his baritone.

Cailan resisted the urge to fidget under his father's scrutiny. He still wasn't sure what to make of Asher. The drake was trying, he'd give him that. But the wounds of abandonment ran deep, and trust, once broken, wasn't easily mended.

"Thank you," Elazar murmured, sensing Cailan's discomfort. "We're honored to be honored." He coughed as the words came out stiff and awkward.

"It is a proud day for our family." Asher spread his wings, drawing both Cailan and Elazar into a surprisingly warm embrace. "You have both overcome much to reach this place. I'm proud to see you standing before me. I only wish your mother could be here to share in this moment."

Cailan blinked, caught off guard by the raw emotion in Asher's voice. He opened his mouth to speak, unsure what to say, but a sudden commotion from within the Celestial Hall drew their attention. The rhythmic beat of drums echoed through the hallway, urging them onward.

"It seems the festivities are about to begin." Asher released them. "Go on. Enjoy yourselves." His gaze lingered on them, and for a fleeting second, Cailan saw something that looked suspiciously like pride in his father's eyes. "I will be watching over you both."

With that, Asher turned and strode back toward the entrance. Cailan watched him go, the tightness in his chest easing slightly.

"Well," Cailan said, squaring his shoulders, a spark of defiance rekindling. "Let's get this party started."

Elazar nodded, drawing a deep breath, and together they stepped into the Celestial Hall.

The room was alive with light and sound. Countless drakes, a kaleidoscope of colorful scales, milled about. In one corner, a group of drakes, their secondary forms a mix of Elven grace and Theilian ferocity, played a melody on an array of exotic instruments—flutes carved from crystal, drums fashioned from hide, and stringed instruments that seemed to hum with an otherworldly power. Cailan watched, mesmerized, as the musicians coaxed out a melody that thrummed through his very being, urging him to move, to *dance*.

He tapped a claw against the stone floor, keeping time with the music, resisting the urge to join the throng of dancers. Clusters of drakes engaged in animated conversation, their voices an indistinct murmur that blended with the melody. Cailan caught snippets—the latest gossip, the merits of different polishing techniques, the shared woes of molting season.

The center of the hall was a graceful ballet of scales and wings. Drakes wove in and out, their movements synchronized. Cailan couldn't help but admire their effortless grace, the way they anticipated each other's movements.

Envy needled him. He'd never truly been a part of this world. Even now, standing among his kin, he felt like an outsider, a pretender masquerading in a borrowed form. He might be a drake, but this wasn't his world.

Cailan glanced at Elazar, who stood beside him, his eyes wide with a mix of awe and uncertainty. Cailan knew his brother felt it, too—this sense of displacement, of being caught between two worlds. This was a world they'd never imagined, a world that both beckoned and repelled them.

"There they are," Elazar murmured beside him.

Cailan followed his gaze, spotting Captain Jo, Max, and the rest of the *Tempest* crew gathered on the far side of the hall. They'd all dressed for the occasion—silks and velvets that shimmered in the light. Clothing that the drakes had provided, most likely.

"I don't see Danelor." Cailan halted, glancing around in case he'd simply missed the chimera in the crowd. Was he still asleep? Or had he chosen to avoid the festivities altogether?

"Maybe the noise is too much for him," Elazar said.

"What?" Cailan blinked.

"He had trouble with all the noise on the *Tempest*." Elazar gestured in the approximate direction of the airship.

"I didn't know that," Cailan muttered.

A subtle shift rippled through the crowd, a hush falling over the revelers. Cailan noticed Asher striding toward a raised dais he hadn't spotted before. The elder drake mounted the dais, his pearlescent scales bright, and let out a roar that silenced the music, drawing every eye to him.

"Drakes of the Forgotten Library," Asher began, his voice booming. "Today is a day of great joy. For years, I have mourned the loss of my whelps, believing them stolen from me, lost forever." He turned, his gaze warm as it settled on Cailan and Elazar. "But now...they have returned. My sons have come home."

A chorus of roars and trills erupted from the assembled drakes, a wall of sound that vibrated in Cailan's very bones. He felt Elazar stiffen beside him as hundreds of eyes turned on them.

"It is with immense pride that I welcome Elazar and Cailan into our community," Asher continued, raising a claw to quell the excited din. "They are of our blood. And I'm pleased that they'll remain here, with us. To learn the ways of the drakes, to reclaim their rightful place."

Wait. What? Cailan bit back a growl, his hackles rising. He wanted to shout, to tell them all that he'd agreed to no such thing.

Asher's voice softened, but the steel beneath the words remained. "The Forgotten Library has been our sanctuary for generations. And now it will be a home for my sons as well. Like us, they will take up the mantle, becoming guardians of the wonders and the power entrusted to our care."

Anger coiled in Cailan's gut. This was happening too fast, spiraling out of control. He opened his mouth to object, but a thunderous roar of approval from the crowd drowned him out.

Asher raised a claw, silencing the clamor once more. His gaze met Cailan's, a challenge and a promise in those golden depths. "To my sons," he declared, his voice ringing with pride, "Elazar and Cailan. Welcome home."

"What in the four winds was that?" Cailan hissed to Elazar, his voice tight with barely suppressed fury.

"I have no idea," the copper drake murmured back, his eyes wide with alarm. "But we have to play along. For now."

"No other choice." Cailan forced a smile, baring his fangs in what he hoped resembled a pleased grin as he met the expectant looks of the surrounding drakes. Asher's sharp gaze was fixed on them. With dismay, he realized their father was playing the same sort of move Cailan had intended—forcing them to agree to something before a crowd. It was infuriating. But perhaps this was something he could exploit later.

Satisfied with their apparent acquiescence, Asher turned back to the crowd. "Now," he called, his voice resonating through the hall, "let the feast begin! Celebrate the return of my sons!"

Servers in bipedal forms wove through the throng, bearing platters piled high with delicacies. The air swam with savory aromas—roasted meats seasoned with unfamiliar herbs, platters of glistening candied fruits, baskets overflowing with warm bread that smelled of honey. Cailan's stomach rumbled appreciatively.

Asher gestured towards a large trough that had been brought to the center of the hall, its metal sides shimmering with an iridescent sheen. An amber liquid filled the trough. "And what celebration would be complete without our traditional Ember Ale?"

The drakes surged forward, eager to partake, dipping their snouts into the trough. Cailan watched as they drank deeply.

Asher turned to Cailan and Elazar, hoisting a chalice made of silver and crystal. He dipped it into the trough. "My sons, try this. It is a tradition, a way to welcome you properly to the Forgotten Library."

Cailan narrowed his eyes, his gaze fixed on the ornate chalice. Several chalices and goblets were listed among the artifacts in Iaxis's ledgers, each with its own unique properties. Was *this* one of them? "That's a pretty fancy cup you've got there," he said, his voice deceptively casual.

Asher smiled, a proud gleam in his eyes. "This is Eletheria's Blessing. It's a great honor to be offered a drink from this chalice."

Liar. Asher was a liar. Whatever this was, whatever game he was playing, it was a trap. Cailan had seen the entry for Eletheria's Blessing in the ledger. Anyone who drank from it lost their memories, their minds becoming as malleable as clay.

"Don't drink from it," he hissed to Elazar. The copper drake shot him a confused look, but there was no time for explanations. Cailan tilted his head, feigning disinterest, his gaze sweeping over the chalice with exaggerated disdain. "Yeah, not really feeling the whole *communal drinking* thing." He took a step back, his nostrils flaring as if offended by the very idea.

Asher's smile vanished, replaced by a shadow of annoyance. He turned to Elazar, his expression expectant. "Perhaps you have better manners than your brother."

Winds damn it. How could Elazar refuse without arousing suspicion? The copper drake froze, clearly struggling to find a response that wouldn't betray their suspicions. Cailan knew he had to act, had to neutralize this threat, and quickly.

"You're in no position to criticize my manners," Cailan snarled, letting outrage fill his voice. His wings snapped open, the spines along his back bristling. Cailan stalked toward Asher, his smaller size irrelevant. He'd make up for it in sheer aggression. He lashed out with a taloned hand, slashing the chalice from Asher's grasp. It clattered to the stone floor, the tinkling music of shattering crystal echoing through the sudden silence.

Every eye in the Celestial Hall turned on them. Asher's face contorted with fury. "You've done nothing but defy me and disrespect this library since you arrived!" he roared, his voice shaking. "Show some respect, whelp!"

"Or what?" Cailan challenged, meeting his father's rage head-on. "I'm not your puppet, Asher. I'm my own dragon. And I'll do as I damn well please."

Without another word, he spun on his heel and stormed out of the hall. He didn't care what Asher thought, what the entire Conclave thought. He was done with them.

And maybe, if the winds were with him, this outburst would buy him some time. Because whatever game Asher was playing, whatever trap he had set, it had just become a lot more dangerous.

What other artifacts were the drakes planning to use against them? And *why*?

Elazar

ELAZAR WATCHED CAILAN GO, STARTLED BY HIS BEHAVIOR. Cailan's unsettling warning about the chalice echoed in his mind, especially concerning since he had no idea what made Eletheria's Blessing so dangerous. The not knowing...*that* was the worst part.

He had to make the best of this. Maybe Cailan's outburst would buy the opal drake some time, give him a chance to search for Tiberia. Elazar dipped his head, offering Asher a placating smile. "I apologize for my brother's behavior. He's not always the best in social situations." He glanced at the shat-tered remnants of the chalice, scattered across the stone floor like fallen stars. "I'm truly sorry about the cup." But he was also incredibly grateful for Cailan's impulsive act of destruction.

Asher sighed, his anger momentarily forgotten as he surveyed the broken chalice. He waved a dismissive claw. "It's not your fault, Elazar. And Eletheria's Blessing can be repaired. Though it will take Rasmira longer than she'd like, no doubt."

Even as he spoke, Rasmira hurried towards them, her Theilian features creased with dismay. She knelt beside the shattered chalice, carefully gathering the fragments into a soft leather pouch.

"A day or two, Asher, and it will be as good as new," Rasmira assured him, her gaze meeting his, silent meaning passing between them.

Asher nodded curtly.

A day or two. Then they would try again. Use the chalice on them. But for what purpose? Elazar shuddered, pushing the thought away. He didn't want to know.

"I'm truly sorry for Cailan's outburst," he said again, hoping to appease his father. He leaned closer to Asher, keeping his voice low. "But we never agreed to stay here."

Asher's scaled brows rose, surprise bright in his golden eyes. "But why wouldn't you? You'd be among your kind, Elazar. Safe. Welcomed. You'd learn our ways, embrace your heritage."

It was a dangerous question. Elazar had to tread carefully. The wrong answer could set off alarms. He shrugged, letting his wings brush against Asher's in a gesture of casual affection. "It was just a bit unexpected, that's all. Maybe give us some time to consider the idea?"

Asher nodded, seemingly mollified. "Of course, of course. You're right. I allowed my enthusiasm to get ahead of me. I should have consulted you both first." He smiled, his fangs glinting. "Perhaps the best way to help you decide is to experience all the Forgotten Library has to offer! Why don't you mingle? Meet some of the other drakes? You haven't had much opportunity to socialize."

Socializing wasn't exactly Elazar's strong suit. He much preferred quiet conversations, tinkering with gadgets, or losing himself in the pages of a technical manual. But he nodded, seeing a potential opportunity. A little distance from Asher would give him time to think, to process this sudden turn of events. And maybe, if he played his cards right, he could glean some information about Eletheria's Blessing. Perhaps one of these drakes, distracted by a moment of celebration, might let slip a crucial detail.

"Sounds good," Elazar agreed, letting himself be steered toward a group of younger drakes. They looked around his age, their gazes alight with curiosity.

A female drake with sleek silver scales stepped forward. "So glad you could join us! Tell us about yourself. What was your journey like?"

Elazar hesitated, unsure how much to reveal. These drakes, for all their welcoming smiles and friendly chatter, were still strangers. "It's been...eventful," he said carefully, choosing his words with caution. "I'm still trying to make sense of it all, to be honest."

The silver drake nodded sympathetically. "We understand. Discovering your true nature can be overwhelming. But you're among friends now. We're here to help, in any way we can."

Elazar felt momentary gratitude for their kindness, but it was quickly eclipsed by his other more conflicted feelings. These drakes spoke of friendship, but they weren't the family he'd found on the *Tempest*. He still felt like an outsider, even in this place that was supposed to be his home.

"What do you all do here?" he asked, hoping to steer the conversation away from personal matters. It was time he got some information from someone other than the Conclave.

The silver drake grinned. "Depends. Some of us have specific duties within the library itself." She gestured around them with her tail. "But the island is large, as you've seen. Some tend the land, cultivating crops, raising livestock. We need to be self-sufficient, after all."

That made sense. The Forgotten Library, hidden behind its veil of storms, was a world unto itself. "Does anyone ever leave?" Elazar asked, unable to keep the curiosity from his voice.

An orange drake snorted, his laughter a harsh sound. "*Leave?* Why would we? The world beyond the Eye is a treacherous place. Full of hardship and cruelty. Full of those who would exploit us, as the Jade Court did."

"And besides," the silver drake added, her voice firm, "our duty lies *here*. Protecting the Forgotten Library. Preserving its secrets."

Elazar frowned. "But the world...it's huge. *Beautiful*. There's so much to see, so many different cultures, so many different people."

"There are some drakes who venture into the wider world," the silver drake said. "And others out there who have never known of the Forgotten Library." She shivered. "I can't imagine the hazards out there!"

The orange drake raised a skeptical brow. "I was under the impression the Jade Court enslaved you."

"I wasn't a *slave*," Elazar retorted with a flash of anger. He'd been a prisoner, certainly. Just as he was here. Just as everyone he cared about was now. The cage might look different, but a prison was a prison. His jaw tightened, tempted to voice his concerns, but he bit back the words.

"Regardless," the silver drake said, her voice softening, "you should be grateful you're here now. Safe. Protected." Then she winked, a mischievous glint in her dark eyes. "And it's always nice to have another handsome drake as a potential mating option."

Her words caught him off guard. Elazar blinked, completely flustered. "Um, yeah. Thanks." *Mating?* That was the last thing he was thinking about right now. Then he spotted Max across the hall, leaning against a pillar. Her arms were crossed, her lips pressed into a thin line as she watched him.

Oh, no. She and Aunt Jo must have heard Asher's little speech about him staying, about becoming a guardian of the Forgotten Library.

He swallowed, his throat suddenly dry. "Thanks for talking. But if you'll excuse me, I need to..." He cast about for a plausible excuse. "Go...elsewhere." It wasn't his most convincing performance, but he slipped away, heading toward Max.

Her posture didn't soften as he approached, and her eyes narrowed, a storm brewing in their depths. "You're staying here?"

He winced. "Can we talk? Please?" He needed to explain. To make her understand that this wasn't his plan. He hadn't agreed to any of it.

Max worried her lower lip, then nodded curtly. "Fine. Later. Meet me at the Brew Nook?"

He shook his head, panic rising. He had no idea what else Asher had planned, and he couldn't spend the rest of the evening pretending he was on board with this. "No. Now."

Her brow rose, and she glanced back at the celebrating drakes, their laughter echoing through the hall. "You're probably not supposed to abandon your own party."

"It's my party and I'll leave if I want to." Then a wry

chuckle escaped Elazar's lips. "Besides, that didn't stop Cailan."

A smile ghosted across Max's face. "Nothing stops Cailan." She pushed away from the pillar, her gaze meeting his. "All right, let's talk."

The celebration, Asher, the drakes...*none* of it mattered right now. All that mattered was setting things straight with Max. And maybe, once that was done, he'd find Aunt Jo. He hadn't seen her, or any of the *Tempest* crew, since Asher's grand announcement. He wouldn't blame them for walking out, for believing he and Cailan had chosen these strangers over the family they'd built together.

"We'll take as long as we need," Elazar said. He gestured toward a nearby exit, an archway that promised escape from the noise and the suffocating expectations of the celebration. "Come on."

Elazar relaxed as soon as he stepped into the empty corridor, the sounds of revelry fading behind them. He let out a breath, glancing at Max. "Give me a sec."

He closed his eyes, summoning his shifting magic. It flowed through him, effortless, a comforting warmth that spread outward from the nexus chain at his chest. Unlike the turbulent rush of his drake transformation, the shift back to human form was...peaceful. But he still had to concentrate on—*winds*, he couldn't let his mind wander right now! He reached into his pocket dimension, grabbing blindly for the first set of clothes he could find, afraid to open his eyes, afraid of what he might have pulled through. Afraid that maybe he'd failed to grab anything at all.

He heard Max's sharp intake of breath, but no cool breeze touched his skin. Only the soft feel of fabric. He opened his eyes, finding Max's eyes fixed on him, a smile curving her lips.

"You clean up nice," she murmured, her voice teasing.

"Yeah, I doubt Altira's going to appreciate this," Elazar said, a rueful laugh escaping him. "All that work, and I undo it in a heartbeat." Then, "Max, about what Asher said—"

He didn't get a chance to finish. Max touched an index finger to his lips, silencing him. Then she edged closer, her gaze meeting his. It was a look that promised a world beyond their current reality.

Before he could even think, her lips were on his. It was a kiss that stole his breath, a sudden surge of heat and need. She didn't explore, didn't linger, but pressed her lips hard against his, demanding his attention, making him forget everything else. Her touch was strong, her fingers digging into his hair, pulling him closer, deepening the kiss.

She pulled away, breathless. Elazar gazed at Max, his cheeks flushed. There was so much he wanted to say, a torrent of emotions surging within him, but all that came out was a gasping, "What was that for?"

She crossed her arms, a playful smirk curving her lips. "To convince you not to stay here. Seems like a decent enough reason, don't you think?"

Elazar laughed, a surprised sound. Max shot him a mock-glare. "But that's exactly what I wanted to talk to you about." He glanced over his shoulder, the sounds of revelry echoing from the Celestial Hall, and decided a more private setting was in order. He took her arm, gently guiding her towards the main library. "Come on."

"Where are we going?"

"Away," he murmured. He didn't stop until they were well away from the noise, standing beneath the soaring stained-glass windows that depicted the horrors of the Forgotten War. The Eye of the Storm rested on its pedestal nearby. He took her hands in his. "Everything Asher said back there...it was a lie.

Cailan and I have no intention of staying here. Of becoming guardians."

Max's lips pursed thoughtfully. "Then why did he say it? He clearly wants you to stay, Elazar. He wants you to be a part of...all of this." Her gesture encompassed the library.

"He does." Elazar whispered, understanding the yearning in his father's heart, even if he couldn't share it. "But there's something else going on here. Something wrong." He quickly filled her in on Tiberia's disappearance, his voice dropping to a hushed whisper. "And there was something off about that chalice Asher offered us. Eletheria's Blessing. Cailan warned me not to drink from it."

"Is that why Cailan threw a fit?" Max asked, her eyes widening.

"It was a calculated fit," Elazar confirmed, a grudging admiration for his brother's quick thinking creeping into his voice. "I just...I don't know *why*. What was so dangerous about that chalice?" His gaze drifted to the shadowy corridor that led to Iaxis's study. He was tempted to take Max there, to delve back into those ledgers, but...if they were missing from the celebration for too long, someone might come looking for them. And that would be the worst possible place to be discovered.

Lost in his thoughts, he'd momentarily forgotten Max. When he turned back to her, what he discovered was alarming. Her gaze was distant, unfocused, as if she were staring at something only she could see. He'd seen that look before, at Ship's End, back when she'd been ensnared by Selene's siren song.

"Max?" He touched her arm, his voice sharp with concern. "What's wrong?"

"It's calling to me," she whispered.

"What?"

She pulled away from him, her movements jerky. "I have to take it. I have to *claim* it."

Too late, Elazar realized where she was headed, her path a direct line to the pedestal where the Eye of the Storm rested, pulsing with arcane energy. "Max, no! *Stop!*"

She reached out, her fist closing around the gemstone. A distant rumble of thunder seemed to shake the foundations of the library.

The stained-glass windows above them exploded, a cascade of shattered rainbows raining down.

26

ƧYE OF THE ƧTORM

Cailan

The moment he was out of sight of the Celestial Hall, Cailan shifted back to human form. Being a dragon had its advantages, but when it came to stealth, humans were far more subtle.

He ducked into his room, retrieving the list of potentially useful artifacts he'd hidden beneath his mattress. It had been a risk, stashing it there, but it was the best option he'd had at the time. The only safer place would have been aboard the *Tempest*, but making frequent trips to and from the airship would have raised suspicions. He wasn't part of the crew assigned to maintenance duty.

He scanned the list, his lips twisting into a frown. He didn't know the locations of the restricted vaults. The ledger had listed designations for each one and he'd seen similar labels on some of the doors as he'd explored the library. But the place was a maze, and he'd need more than cryptic names to navigate its depths.

Cailan would get nowhere if he just stood around fretting, though. He changed into darker clothing, slung an empty bag over his shoulder, and tucked the list of artifacts into a secure pocket. His cutlass was in its scabbard, strapped to his back. Cailan hoped he wouldn't need it, but it was better to be prepared.

He slipped out of his room. The muted sounds of revelry drifted from the distant Celestial Hall, a reminder that most of the drakes were preoccupied. This was his chance.

Asher was likely still fuming, but Cailan had made a spectacle of himself. It should buy him some time. At least he *hoped* so.

He consulted his notes as he walked. The vault designations were jumbled, with no discernible order, but then again, not every room with a fancy name was of interest.

Cailan found his first target sooner than expected. The Vault of Whispers. He approached cautiously, his senses on high alert, scanning for any sign of watchful drakes or errant partygoers. But the corridor was deserted, the silence broken only by the distant echo of music and laughter.

He tested the door handle, expecting resistance. To his surprise, it turned easily, the heavy door swinging open with a soft groan. Cailan hesitated for a moment, then stepped inside. The scent of aged parchment and a sharp, citrusy tang—the unmistakable aroma of potent magic—washed over him. It was a scent that permeated the entire library, woven into its very fabric, but here, in this enclosed space, it was almost overpowering. Shelves lined the walls, each one laden with a collection of artifacts, and each object labeled with a small card.

"I *do* love a good organizational system," Cailan murmured with a grin.

He pulled out his list, comparing his notes to the neatly printed labels. Most of the objects appeared to be trinkets: rings, bracelets, pendants, some tarnished with age, others gleaming as if newly crafted.

This was a good start. Small, easily transportable—ideal for slipping back to the captain. He frowned, scanning his notes. He wished he'd had more time to compile a detailed list. There was no way to know what these trinkets *were*, what kind of magic they held. Innocent baubles, or instruments of destruction?

He'd have to come back later, do a little more research, but for now...he snagged a pendant that had caught his eye earlier— a shimmering blue fire opal, set in a delicate gold frame. It matched his scales, which was a bonus, but more importantly, it possessed a type of magic that might prove useful. The ledger had called it the Shroud of Shadows, mentioning something about rendering the wearer invisible.

Cailan held it in his hand, turning it this way and that, but felt no different. A quick glance in a nearby hand mirror confirmed he was still very much visible.

"Useless piece of costume jewelry," he muttered, disappointment pricking at him. He was about to return it to its velvet-lined shelf when a thought struck him. Elazar's pocket watch-slash-compass had to be activated. Was this the same?

He examined the pendant once more. Elazar had mentioned that their nexus chains could channel and amplify magic. Nodding to himself, Cailan attached the opal to his own golden chain, letting it settle against his chest. The fire opal rested against his breastbone. It felt warm. As if a spark had ignited within the gem, a faint hum of energy resonating outward.

Cailan closed his eyes, focusing his will, drawing on that familiar wellspring of power within him, the same energy he channeled when he shifted between forms. A tingling warmth spread outward from the opal, racing across his skin.

He opened his eyes, glancing down at himself, expecting to see...something. Or rather, *nothing*. But nothing had changed.

"Garbage," he muttered, reaching up to unclasp the pendant's chain, ready to toss it back onto its shelf and move on.

Then, as Cailan shifted his weight, something—or rather, the *lack* of something—caught his eye. He froze, staring at the spot where his foot should have been. There was...*nothing*. Just the empty floor.

Understanding flooded him. The Shroud of *Shadows*. It wasn't just a flowery name—it was literal. Cailan stepped fully into the shadow cast by a nearby bookshelf, watching in fascination as his body seemed to dissolve, blending seamlessly with the darkness. A slow grin spread across his face. This was perfect. With this, he could move through the library, a ghost in the shadows.

He stepped back into the pool of light cast by one of the magical orbs, his body reappearing as if by magic. Cailan touched the opal pendant, a thrill of excitement coursing through him. "Maybe you're not so useless after all," he murmured.

The door to the Vault of Whispers closed with a soft *whoosh* as Cailan slipped out. It was time to see what else awaited in the off-limits sections of the library.

A few wrong turns, a muttered curse as he backtracked, and Cailan stood before another vault door. He double-checked his notes, confirming this was indeed the Chamber of Infusion.

And, just like the previous vault, it was unlocked. He pushed the door open, wincing at the protesting creak of unoiled hinges.

The room beyond was larger, grander, than the Vault of Whispers, crammed with objects far more imposing than mere trinkets. Some resembled machines—cogs and gears intertwined with glowing crystals, metal armatures that pulsed with a subtle energy. Elaborate contraptions that blended technology and magic. Elazar would have loved this.

Cailan moved through the collection, his gaze sweeping over the bizarre assortment of relics, when a pair of black granite slabs positioned at the rear of the room stopped him short. It wasn't the slabs themselves that sent a jolt of alarm through him, but *who* rested atop them.

Tiberia and Danelor.

His breath caught in his throat. He hurried toward them, his pulse quickening with dread. Their skin was pale, almost translucent in the dim light, a waxy sheen clinging to their features. For a heart-stopping moment, he feared the worst, but the gentle rise and fall of their chests confirmed they were alive.

"Danelor!" Cailan hissed, kneeling beside the slab. The chimera didn't stir, his usually animated face slack. Gods, he wanted to see that stupid smile more than anything. Cailan considered shaking him, attempting to prod him awake, but what if whatever force held Danelor captive lashed out? Snagged him, too? He took a step back, activating his magical sight—a skill he hadn't used much within the library, given the sheer amount of ambient magic that saturated the air.

The room exploded with light, a dazzling brightness that momentarily blinded him. Cailan squinted, honing in on Danelor. Fine threads of obsidian magic bound the chimera to the slab, coiling around his limbs, seeping into his skin. The same tendrils held Tiberia captive, as well.

He let his magical sight fade, the room returning to its normal state. Anger surged through him. Why would the drakes do this to the chimeras? It made no sense.

This confirmed his suspicions: the drakes were up to something. Something sinister. Cailan had to get back to Elazar and Captain Jo. Warn them. Together, they'd figure out how to free Tiberia and Danelor, how to escape this prison disguised as a sanctuary.

"I won't let them have you," he whispered to Danelor, his gaze shifting to Tiberia's still form. He wouldn't abandon either of them; not if he could help it.

His mind raced as he hurried back towards the Celestial Hall. The discovery of the trapped chimeras had left him shaken, anger roiling in his gut. He had to tell Elazar and the captain, but how? How could he get them alone without raising suspicion?

He rounded a corner, and the sound of familiar voices brought him up short. Asher and Oriana. He didn't hesitate. Activating the Shroud of Shadows, he melted into the darkness along the edge of the hallway.

Asher and Oriana came into view, their expressions taut with concern. Cailan held his breath, scarcely daring to move as they passed.

"We've searched everywhere, Asher," Oriana was saying, her voice strained. "Maxine is nowhere to be found. Not in the library, not in the gardens, not in the dormitories."

Cailan's gut twisted. Why were they looking for Max?

"Search again," Asher commanded, his voice sharp. "The mage must be here somewhere. Perhaps she's with Elazar."

"That's just it," Oriana replied, frustration creeping into her voice. "We can't find Elazar, either. It's as if they've both vanished."

Cailan's blood ran cold. Max and Elazar...*missing?* What in the four winds was going on?

The drakes' voices faded, their footsteps echoing down the corridor, but Cailan remained hidden, his mind reeling. First Tiberia and Danelor, and now Max and Elazar? He had to sort this out and fast. Something was very, *very* wrong.

Maxine

MAX BRACED HERSELF, HER HANDS HITTING THE GROUND before she could faceplant. Pain shot up her arms as her palms met the uneven surface, a jagged expanse of stone that felt like shards of broken glass. She hissed, scrambling back into a crouch, then slowly rose to her feet, her gaze sweeping over her surroundings.

Elazar stood a few paces away, his copper scales gleaming in the harsh sunlight. Hadn't he been human? Gods, what had happened? Fragments of memory danced through her mind—anger at Asher's pronouncements, Elazar taking her away from the celebration, the insistent pull of the Eye of the Storm...

She'd *touched* it.

A bitter knot of guilt twisted her stomach. Whatever had happened...it was *her* fault.

"Max?" Elazar's voice was laced with concern. "Are you all right?"

She bit her lip, the metallic taste of fear flooding her mouth. "I'm fine," Max lied, the words hollow. "But Elazar...you're a dragon again."

He looked down at himself, confusion crossing his draconic

features. "I don't...I don't remember shifting. And there's no dizziness. No vertigo." His gaze met hers. "Did we almost die?"

Max wished she had a better answer. "I don't think so." She swallowed, her throat dry. "Where are we?"

Elazar moved closer, his presence a reassuring warmth beside her. "This looks like the island. The one the Forgotten Library is on. Except there's no library."

Maxine's gaze sharpened, taking in the details. He was right. They stood between a rocky island cliff and a dense jungle, the air thick with humidity. But the library was *gone*.

"What now?" she asked.

"We need to figure out where we are," Elazar said, his tone practical. "Then...maybe we can find a way back."

Before they could discuss further, a deafening crack of thunder split the air, vibrating through the ground beneath their feet, making Max jump.

Leaves rustled nearby, the sound too deliberate to be the wind. Max whirled, wishing she had a knife with her. A figure emerged from the dense foliage, striding toward them with effortless grace. His skin was a rich brown, his presence radiating an aura of power that sent a shiver through Max. He was tall, his physique impressive, a chiseled jawline framed by high cheekbones and tightly coiled black hair that brushed his forehead. His eyes glittered with sharp intelligence. This man looked like he belonged to another world entirely, one where legends walked among mortals.

He smiled, a flash of perfect white teeth against his dark skin. "It's been a long time since I've had visitors." His voice was a deep, resonant baritone, ripened with amusement.

Max blinked, forcing herself to find her voice. "Who are you?" she asked, her tone steady despite the whirlwind of emotions.

His smile widened slightly, a hint of something predatory

in the curve of his lips. "An interesting question. In my time, names held power. True names, I mean." He gazed at the distant horizon, a hint of longing in his eyes, before turning back to them. "You may call me The Shaper. And now, perhaps you can tell me how you came to be here. On my island."

Max glanced at Elazar. He, too, seemed taken aback by The Shaper's sudden appearance and enigmatic words. Elazar dipped his head, the movement somewhere between a bow and a show of nerves. "We didn't mean to intrude. We were transported here, somehow."

"Indeed," The Shaper agreed, his lips pressing into a thin line. His sharp gaze settled on Max. "You possess power. That much is clear. But not enough to *Traverse*." The way he uttered the word, the weight he infused it with, told Max it wasn't a simple matter of walking, sailing, or flight. This was something else. Something *magical*. "It has been centuries since a sorcerer of sufficient strength to *Traverse* walked this earth."

Max's jaw dropped. "Sorcerers?" The word came out as a squeak, a pathetic sound that made her cringe.

"Of course." The Shaper spread his hands, a gesture that encompassed the island and the sky. "What else would I be?"

"Not a..." She shook her head, unable to even voice the word.

"That term carries a certain *unpleasant* connotation in our world," Elazar explained, a silent apology in his eyes.

The Shaper's expression eased, mirth crinkling the corners of his eyes. "I understand. I can't fault the world for its misunderstandings." He shook his head, a hint of sadness in the gesture. Then his attention shifted to Elazar, his gaze filled with wonder. "The dragonkin endured. I'm pleased."

Elazar blinked, utterly bewildered. "What?"

The sorcerer chuckled. "I *created* the dragons. Your ancestors began as lizards. Little tiny lizards, this big." He held up his thumb and forefinger, the space between them barely an inch. "I always enjoyed transforming the insignificant into something magnificent."

Max exchanged a bewildered look with Elazar. This man—if they could believe him—was the progenitor of dragonkind. "Can you tell us where we are?" she asked. "And more importantly...how do we leave?"

"The first question is one without a true answer. I have been..." The Shaper hesitated as if searching for the right word. "...*gone* from the waking world for a very long time. Asleep in the bones of the Forgotten Library."

"Is this Perdition?" Elazar's voice wavered. "Are we *dead?*" The thought clearly did not appeal to him.

Amusement rippled across The Shaper's expression. "I think not. But tell me...how did you find yourselves here?"

Max winced. "I think it was my fault." She held up a hand, silencing Elazar's protests before they could even form. She *knew* it was her fault. It had to be. "I couldn't...I couldn't help myself. There's this gem. It's called the Eye of the Storm. Do you know it?"

The Shaper's expression remained neutral, but he nodded, gesturing for her to continue.

"It was...*calling* to me. I tried to fight it, but the next thing I knew, I was holding it."

The Shaper drew in a sharp breath. "The Eye of the Storm *claimed* you?"

"What does that even *mean?*" Elazar interjected, his voice sharp with worry.

"It didn't...I mean..." Max felt heat creep up her neck.

The sorcerer chuckled, raising a hand to quell their anxieties. "Calm yourself, Storm's Daughter. You can hardly be blamed if an artifact *recognized* a potential wielder."

Confusion flooded Max. She exchanged a bewildered glance with Elazar. "But what happened? What does it mean?"

The Shaper sighed, his shoulders slumping slightly. "It means *several* things." He held up a hand, ticking off the points on his fingers. That gesture, in her experience, never boded well. "First, it means you are descended from a line of sorcerers. A lineage of immense power."

"But I'm a *mage*," she protested, bristling at the label. *Sorcerer* was a dirty word, one with which she wanted no association.

The Shaper nodded. "Indeed. Your current abilities are *modest*. Not enough to warrant the title of *sorcerer*." Max winced. That stung, a little. But before she could retort, he continued. "However, if a relic of such power—a weapon of the Forgotten War—has *chosen* you, it means there is a need for the great power of your lineage."

"So, what's the reason?" Elazar pressed, his gaze fixed on the sorcerer.

"Because they are trying to return," The Shaper said, his voice an ominous rumble, a hint of warning in it. "The sorcerers. They are trying to break free."

Max shuddered. The images from the stained-glass windows flashed through her mind—the devastation, the casual cruelty, the sheer overwhelming power. "But...*how?*" she asked, her voice sharper than intended. "There have been no sorcerers for centuries, right? You said so yourself. They're all...*dead.*" She gestured to the island, to the empty sky, as if that somehow explained the impossibility of it all.

The Shaper regarded her with a patient, almost indulgent air. "Some perished during the Forgotten War, yes. Some, like me, were *absorbed* into the fabric of the Forgotten Library. Others were banished. Imprisoned in arcane realms beyond the reach of this world. But you clearly cannot grasp the true nature of a sorcerer, child." He clucked his tongue disapprovingly, shaking his head. "The inconvenience of death is merely a temporary setback."

Max exchanged a look with Elazar. *Temporary setback?* That wasn't terrifying at all. "What do you mean?" Elazar asked, echoing her own thoughts.

The Shaper sighed. "Precisely what I *said.* Not even Faedra, in all her glory, could truly destroy us. It took *us* to stop ourselves." He shrugged, his expression turning grim. "Do you truly believe the bonds of death would hold a sorcerer for eternity?"

"Well, I'd certainly *hope* so," Max said, honesty the best policy, even when dealing with a being who could probably turn her into a toad with a flick of his wrist. "That's how it works. Or how it's *supposed* to work."

The Shaper's smile vanished. "You still don't understand. You're incapable of comprehending the scope of it all." Max bristled but held her tongue. She saw a flare of indignation in Elazar's eyes, as well. "These obstacles you speak of—death, banishment, imprisonment—they are mere inconveniences. Challenges to be overcome, given sufficient time and will."

It still didn't make sense, not entirely, but then again, Maxine hadn't expected her entire understanding of reality to be upended today. She drew a deep breath, deciding to accept the sorcerer's explanation, for now. There were more pressing matters at hand. "Okay," Max said, "I get it. Sorcerers are resilient. So, what does that mean for us? What do you want us to do?"

The Shaper smiled, a slow, congenial curve of his lips. "Why, stop them, of course."

Elazar let out an exasperated sigh. "How are we supposed to *stop* a sorcerer? You just told us they're practically invincible!"

The Shaper chuckled, their alarm apparently a source of entertainment. "I'll endeavor to explain in a manner more conducive to your understanding." He paused, his gaze sweeping over the surrounding jungle, the lush foliage rustling softly in the breeze. "Imagine the sorcerers of the Forgotten War as trees in a vast forest. The war itself, a raging fire that consumed most of those trees. Some were utterly destroyed, their essence extinguished. Others might yet return. Perhaps from the roots of those fallen giants. Or from seeds that require the heat of the fire to germinate."

Max exchanged a wary look with Elazar. "So, we're going to be facing a lot of them?"

The Shaper sighed, rubbing his forehead in exasperation. "Do not fixate on numbers, Storm's Daughter. Focus on their state. Their vulnerabilities."

"I don't know what you're talking about!" Max snapped, her patience wearing thin. A crackle of lightning, a surge of power she hadn't consciously summoned, accompanied her outburst. She blinked, startled, glancing upward. The sky was clear, a serene expanse of blue. That shouldn't have been possible.

The sorcerer cocked his head, his dark eyes studying her with renewed interest. Then, a slow smile spread across his face. "*You* are one of the seeds."

Before Max could fully process that unsettling statement, Elazar seemed to grasp The Shaper's meaning. "You're saying it will be easier to...well, to weed them out, I guess? Because they'll be weaker? Less powerful, while they're still sprouting?"

The Shaper clapped his hands together, delight radiating from him. "Precisely! Clever drake! You understand."

That actually made sense. Max nodded. "Okay. That's a little less terrifying." Though, she still wasn't thrilled about the prospect of facing down a sorcerer, no matter how weak their powers might be. "But there were so many sorcerers. With different abilities, different goals... How will we know who this one is? Where to find them?"

The Shaper spread his hands again. "If you are here, Storm's Daughter, it suggests one of these nascent sorcerers is already at the Forgotten Library. Seeking a conduit back to this world. They likely intend to use the artifacts to regain their full strength." He paused, his expression turning thoughtful. "And if that is the case, I may be able to determine their identity."

"You can?" Hope surged within Max. "That would be amazing."

The Shaper held up a finger, silencing them. "A moment." He closed his eyes, and Max felt a wave of power wash over her, a tingling pressure that made her ears pop. His eyes snapped open, alarm replacing the earlier amusement. "This is not good."

"What is it? Who is it?" Fear coiled in Max's stomach.

The Shaper paced, his movements agitated. "The Grief-Eater. She was one of the most formidable sorcerers I encountered during the war." He shook his head, the gesture heavy with a remembered dread. "A powerful sorceress, made even stronger by her children, who fought at her side. A son and a daughter. The Flameweaver and the Soulcaller. The Soulcaller, in particular—she revolutionized the methods of soul preservation to cheat death, to return from the long walk to Perdition time and again."

"How did you defeat her?" Elazar asked, his voice hushed.

The Shaper shook his head, his expression grim. "I wasn't present for their final confrontation. I cannot tell you. But this much I know." He held up a finger, emphasizing the point. "Only the Grief-Eater's presence is detectable. And it's weakened. She is vulnerable, but she is also *cunning*. Weaken her further and you may destroy the foothold she has on this life."

Elazar and Max exchanged worried glances. "How?" Elazar asked, his voice edged with desperation. "How do we even *do* that?"

"Use this." The Shaper tapped his temple. "And this." His hand moved to his chest, resting over his heart. He turned his gaze to Elazar, a new intensity in his eyes. "The Storm's Daughter now wields great power. But your magic, young drake, while commendable, may not be enough." He stepped closer to Elazar, his presence radiating warmth and power. "So, I will grant you an echo of my strength, to aid you in the struggle to come. Use it wisely."

Before Elazar could protest, The Shaper placed a hand on his shoulder, just below the joint of his wing. A blinding flash of white light engulfed them, and then...

Max and Elazar were falling.

27
Never Guests

Josephine

A throbbing pain pulsed behind Josephine's eyes, a dull ache that reminded her of long-ago hangovers from her youth. She forced her eyes open, her vision swimming. The world was a blurry mess of colors and shapes. This wasn't her cabin. Not the familiar warmth of the *Tempest*, not the gentle rocking of the airship. Unfamiliar stone walls sent a jolt of alarm through her foggy mind.

"Gretchen?" she croaked, her throat parched.

A groan answered her. "Jo? Where in the Abyss *are* we?"

Josephine pushed herself upright, her limbs uncooperative.

As her vision cleared, she made out Gretchen, Galatea, and Isaac, sprawled on the cold stone floor around her.

"Captain?" Isaac's normally steady voice wavered, confusion lacing his words. "What...what happened?" He rubbed his forehead, his expression pained.

She racked her brain, but her memories were fragments, a jumbled mess of impressions and half-formed thoughts. "I don't know. The last thing I remember...we were at the Forgotten Library. There was a...celebration."

Galatea sat up, clutching her temples, her face pale. "The drakes were hosting us. There was music...dancing...and then..." Her voice trailed off, her gaze distant. "It's all...blank."

The drakes. Josephine's stomach twisted. Asher's declaration echoed in her mind—Elazar and Cailan staying, becoming guardians of the Forgotten Library. There'd been that drink, that...traditional brew. Cailan had made a scene, refusing it, and a drake—Oriana, she thought—had pressed a cup into Josephine's hands, urging her to try a variety brewed especially for their guests. She hadn't refused. She'd wanted to appease them, to buy herself time to find Cailan, to understand what had sparked his outburst. His behavior had screamed danger, though anyone else might have seen it as rebellion.

"The drink," she whispered, realization dawning.

Gretchen cursed, her voice venomous. "Winds take them all. They drugged us."

"But why?" Galatea asked with a whimper. "They welcomed us. Treated us as *guests.*"

Josephine swallowed, a knot of fear tightening in her throat. Tiberia's disappearance, Cailan's fruitless search, Asher's declaration, and now this. Pieces of a puzzle, a terrifying picture emerging.

"We were never guests," she said, her voice a ragged whisper.

"Then what are we? Prisoners?" Isaac's gaze swept around the chamber, taking in the stone walls, the heavy iron bars that crisscrossed the single narrow window high above.

"Let's hope so," Josephine said. "Because that means we still have a chance."

Confusion clouded Isaac's face. "What do you mean?"

"If we're not prisoners, Isaac, we're prey. And that's a far worse fate." She pushed herself to her feet, her legs unsteady. How long had they been unconscious? How much time had they lost?

"Prey?" Isaac sputtered, his eyes widening in alarm. "You think the drakes are going to eat us?"

"Not the drakes." Gretchen's voice was grave. She seemed to understand the direction of Josephine's chilling thoughts. "Something much worse."

Frustration etched Isaac's features. "Speak plainly! What are you talking about?" He caught himself, his expression softening slightly. "If you please."

"If I knew what we were up against, I would." Josephine closed her eyes briefly, trying to sort through the chaos of her memories, to find a thread of hope in the tangled mess. Could she count on Elazar and Cailan? Had Elazar already succumbed to the allure of his newfound family? And Cailan... Cailan was a wild card. There was no guarantee he would help, not when he was so deeply distrustful of...well, of everyone.

But Maxine...Maxine wasn't with them.

The Stormcaller. She might be their only hope.

Cailan

The Eye of the Storm was gone.

Cailan had been hidden in the shadows, weighing his options, when alarmed shouts reached him, echoing from the direction of the Celestial Hall. Drakes—some in their scaled forms, others in their secondary visages—came pouring out, their voices raised in fear.

"The Eye of the Storm is gone!"

It took him a moment to realize they weren't just talking about the gem itself, but the protective barrier that had shielded the Forgotten Library for centuries. Curiosity piqued, Cailan slipped out of his hiding place.

He found a vantage point on one of the library's balconies, high above the throng of drakes who had gathered on the beach below. The night sky stretched above him, an endless, inky expanse dotted with a million glittering stars.

The perpetual hurricane that had shrouded the island since their arrival—the protective eye wall, the distant swirling clouds, the crackling lightning—was gone. The air was still, the silence almost deafening, broken only by the gentle breath of a tropical breeze and the distant crash of the tide against the shore.

The moon hung low on the horizon, casting a silver path across the water, transforming the sea into a shimmering mirror that reflected the star-dusted sky. It should have been a beautiful sight, but a cold dread coiled in Cailan's gut. After witnessing the carnage depicted in the stained glass, he understood why the Forgotten Library had been hidden. Why its secrets had been so fiercely guarded.

"Just peachy," he muttered, leaning against the cool stone balustrade, his gaze drawn to the partially obstructed silhouette of the *Tempest*, her balloon-sails luminous in the moonlight.

The storm's absence meant escape was now a possibility—a simple matter of setting sail, riding the winds to freedom. But a quick check of their assigned quarters revealed the rest of the *Tempest* crew was missing. Even if he wanted to flee, he was alone.

There was only one person left to turn to. One person he could...*maybe*, possibly trust.

Chandra.

He didn't *want* to ask her. Cailan knew this reticence was ridiculous, childish even. He needed to get over his hurt, bridge the chasm that had opened between them. But it was hard. Harder than he'd expected.

He sighed, exhaustion settling over him like a shroud. The night's events—the celebration, the confrontation with Asher, the discovery of the imprisoned chimeras, Max and Elazar's disappearance—it was all too much. He needed time to think.

Cailan found a secluded alcove tucked away in one of the library's lesser-used corridors—not ideal, but it would have to do. Settling into the shadows, his back against the cool stone wall, he closed his eyes, letting the silence of the library envelop him. Exhaustion claimed him, pulling him into a restless slumber of roaring storms and shattered chalices.

Pale morning light filtering through a nearby window roused him. He stretched, his muscles stiff and aching from sleeping in a less-than-ideal position. Cailan gathered his thoughts, steeling himself for what he had to do.

Taking a deep breath, he emerged from his shadowy sanctuary, heading for Chandra's quarters. As he reached her door, he hesitated, fresh resentment washing over him. He hated that he needed her, hated the vulnerability that came with seeking her help. But this wasn't about him. Not anymore. His crew, his family, Danelor and Tiberia...*they* needed him.

Squaring his shoulders, he rapped sharply on the door. Chandra called for him to enter.

Cailan pushed the heavy door open, stepping into the

room. The Seer herself sat upright upon a mountain of pillows, her attention fixed on him as if she'd been expecting his arrival. Vesper was curled in the corner, only lifting his head and offering a single thump of his tail at Cailan's entrance.

"Cailan. What brings you here?" she asked, her voice warm. *This* was Chandra, the dragon who had been his confidante, his teacher, the closest thing he'd ever had to a *mother*, for all those years. Surely, she would help him, if he could just swallow his pride and banish his hurt.

Cailan fought to keep his expression neutral and hide the conflicting emotions that churned within him. "There's a problem," he began. His voice was tight, each word forced. "The Eye of the Storm is gone. The barrier surrounding the island has vanished." He paused, drawing a breath, the words tasting like ash in his mouth. "And that's not all. I found Tiberia and Danelor trapped by magic in one of the vaults. The rest of my crew...they're missing, too. Something's wrong here, Chandra. Something bad."

He watched her, searching for a reaction—alarm, concern, *something*—but her expression remained impassive, as if he'd merely commented on the weather. "I see." Her voice was soft. "And you've come to me for guidance, I presume?"

Cailan nodded curtly, shame burning in his throat. "I need to know what's going on. Where are they? Where are my friends?"

A sad smile touched Chandra's lips. "Oh, Cailan." She sighed. "You have no idea the danger you've stumbled into. What you've found...it's but a glimpse of something far greater, far more terrible than you can possibly imagine."

Gooseflesh prickled his arms, and he took an instinctive step back. "What do you know? What have you Seen, Chandra?"

She tilted her head, studying him with those unsettling

eyes. With rising alarm, Cailan realized she was no longer squinting at him, as she'd always done before. "Now you're asking the right questions." A glimmer of approval in her gaze. Then she rose from the pillows. Out of the corner of his eye, Cailan saw Vesper rise as well, on alert. Trembling. "But," she continued, her voice hardening, "you're also asking the *wrong* question, Cailan."

Tendrils of darkness, like inky smoke given form, seeped from beneath her tattered wings, reaching for him with a terrifying speed.

Vesper moved before Cailan could even blink. The aralez snarled, lips peeling back from gleaming fangs, a guttural growl ripping from his throat. He launched at Chandra, jaws clamping down on her foreleg. His teeth sank into scaled flesh.

"No!" Chandra shrieked, her voice raw with pain. But Vesper clung to her, growling, shaking his head, his powerful jaws unrelenting. The tendrils of dark magic faltered, dissipating like smoke in a strong wind, receding back into her. The Seer thrashed, swinging her injured leg, trying to dislodge him. But Vesper held firm until she slammed him against the wall. Again. And again.

The aralez fell to the floor with a soft yelp, loose feathers blowing free from his wings.

Cailan watched in horror, his mind rebelling against the scene unfolding before him. This wasn't Chandra. Vesper would *never* have attacked her.

Never.

Finally free of the aralez, Chandra whirled, fury contorting her features. Her wings snapped open. A volley of dark magic surged from her, coiling outwards, seeking him.

Cailan bolted, hoping that breaking line of sight would block the attack. He rounded a corner, gasping for breath, and activated the Shroud of Shadows.

That's not Chandra. That's not Chandra.

He squeezed his eyes shut, the mantra a desperate prayer against the rising tide of horror. He'd felt it all along, hadn't he? That unsettling *wrongness,* her delayed revelations. And Vesper had sensed it, too. Tried to warn him. But Cailan had dismissed those feelings as his own mistrust, his wounded pride. He should have listened to his gut.

Tears pricked at his eyes. The Chandra he'd known, the dragon he'd loved...she'd truly died at Belen's claws. Whoever this was, this creature who wore Chandra's skin and spoke with her voice...it was an imposter. A puppet mimicking its master.

The *real* Chandra had warned him about the Jade Empress, about the danger of her finding the Forgotten Library. That advice had changed.

The brutal truth slammed into him. Whatever was happening, it was centered here. In the Forgotten Library.

Belen

THE STORM WAS GONE. THE JADE COURT WAS ON THE wing.

Sunlight warmed Belen's scales, her metal wings singing against the wind as she soared behind her vanguard. Their mechanical wings winked with every powerful beat.

She had waited so long for this, for the Seer's prophecy to come to fruition. When Chandra had declared that the Eye of the Storm would falter, that the hurricane would vanish, Belen had almost dismissed it as yet another deception. She had thought the ferocious storm hiding the Forgotten Library from the prying eyes of the world would remain in place forever.

But this morning, this *glorious* morning, the storm was gone.

And now, the Jade Court had its chance. They would strike at the heart of the drakes' treachery, exacting vengeance for lives lost, for futures shattered. It wouldn't erase the grief, but it was a start. With the drakes defeated, she would plunder the library, claim its secrets as her own, searching for a cure for the wing rot that plagued her kind, for the blight that had claimed her whelps.

And maybe, just maybe, Belen would find an artifact that could bring her mate back to her.

"Jade Court!" she bellowed, her voice a clarion call that echoed across the windswept sky. "Attack!"

A chorus of roars answered her. Airships, their engines thrumming, fanned out beside them, cannons gleaming, ready to unleash their fiery vengeance. The time for whispers was over. The time for retribution had arrived.

28

THE GRIEF-EATER

Elazar

"What the—hey!" Cailan yelped, his cry cut short as Elazar crashed into him, a tangle of limbs and startled curses. Fortunately, he'd somehow shifted back to his human form—clothing and all—but it didn't make the impact any less jarring. They tumbled to the ground in a heap, Max landing on top of them a heartbeat later.

"Get off me!" Cailan growled, though Elazar and Max were already scrambling to untangle themselves.

"Sorry," Max gasped as she found her feet, Elazar's hand steadying her elbow. "We weren't expecting that."

"Yeah, well, neither was I." Cailan pushed himself upright,

glancing over his shoulder, his eyes wide with alarm. He was trembling, and Elazar knew it wasn't from the fall. "Where have you been? I heard you were missing! Both of you!"

Raw fear sharpened his voice. A shiver of apprehension ran down Elazar's spine. He exchanged a look with Max, a silent question passing between them. "It's a long story. A weird story." He swallowed, his throat suddenly dry. "What's going on, Cailan? What happened?" He hesitated, then added, "Did something happen with your search?"

"You have no idea. Too much to explain now, but...Chandra's not Chandra anymore. I found Danelor and Tiberia. They're trapped. Imprisoned by magic." Cailan didn't give them a chance to respond, the words tumbling out in a rush. "And Max...the drakes were looking for you. And the *Tempest* crew are all missing."

The news hit Elazar like a physical blow. The *Tempest* crew...Aunt Jo... He had to find them!

"Found them!" a triumphant voice called from the corridor. Oriana. "The mage is here, too!"

"*Winds!*" Cailan cursed. "We have to get out of here. *Now.*" He didn't wait for a response, bolting down the corridor.

Elazar and Max sprinted after Cailan. Elazar struggled to keep up—he wasn't as agile as his brother, and his body felt sluggish after the abrupt shift back to his human form.

They rounded a corner, nearly colliding with a towering bookshelf. Cailan ducked into a narrow alcove, its shadows concealing them. Elazar pulled Max in after him, their bodies pressed against the cool stone wall.

"What's going on?" Elazar hissed. "What do you mean, Chandra isn't Chandra? And the crew...they're all gone?"

Uncertainty lit Cailan's golden-brown eyes. "I don't know how, but someone's taken her place. They've got her memories, her mannerisms...but it's not her." He shook his head, his expression grim. "And the crew has just vanished. I can't find any of them. I overheard Asher and Oriana talking. They were specifically looking for Max."

Max's grip tightened on Elazar's hand. "But why? What do they want with us?"

"I don't know," Cailan admitted, frustration lacing his voice. "But it can't be good. And there's more. The Eye of the Storm is missing."

Elazar's stomach plummeted. He exchanged a guilty look with Max. "About that..."

Cailan's eyes narrowed, suspicion replacing the worry. "What did you *do?*"

"It wasn't intentional," Elazar started to explain, but Max cut him off.

"I touched it," she said, her voice flat. "It claimed me, somehow. We were transported to this other version of the island. We met a sorcerer. He called himself The Shaper."

Cailan's jaw dropped. "You *what?*"

"Long story," Elazar said, waving a hand dismissively. But as he spoke, a chilling realization took root in his mind. "I think this is all connected." He'd tried to convince himself that the encounter with The Shaper had been a dream, a hallucination, a trick of his mind. But what if it was real? What if the sorcerers were truly returning?

"No kidding. Spit it out, Elazar. We need to figure this out. *Now.*" Cailan's voice was sharp, edged with urgency.

Maxine jumped in, giving Cailan a concise, chillingly surreal account of their encounter with The Shaper. To his credit, Cailan didn't bat an eye as the tale unfolded, simply absorbing the information, his expression hardening with each passing detail. His calm acceptance and utter lack of disbelief only fueled Elazar's growing apprehension.

"The Grief-Eater," Cailan murmured, his lips pressing into

a thin line. Then his face contorted with anger, his fists clenching. "*That's* who's taken over Chandra. *That's* who's behind all of this."

"But how?" Max asked, echoing Elazar's own bewilderment.

"Because Chandra was supposed to die to Belen. She told me as much," Cailan said, his voice hoarse. "I thought Vesper had saved her. Healed her." His voice cracked on the aralez's name, a shard of grief piercing the anger. "I should have known that kind of healing...it's beyond anyone. Even an aralez."

"You couldn't have known, Cailan." Max's hand settled on his shoulder. "You were hurt."

Tension returned to Cailan's frame, his shoulders stiffening. "Yeah. I let my anger cloud my mind and I didn't see *any* of this." Guilt twisted his words, making them sharp.

"It's not your fault," Elazar insisted. "But we need to figure out—"

He was cut off by a sudden commotion, distant shouts echoing through the library's echoing spaces. They fell silent, listening.

"Dragons!" a voice cried, the words full of panic. "The Jade Court is attacking!"

"The Jade Court?" Max's eyes widened. "Why would they attack here? Why attack the Forgotten Library?"

A cold, sickening certainty flooded Elazar. He closed his eyes briefly. "Grief," he whispered. "It's because of grief."

Cailan

"Great. Because we need *more* chaos in our lives," Cailan muttered, shaking his head, his frustration mounting. He pushed away from the stone wall.

"Wait!" Max called out. "What are you doing?"

"It's too late to hide," Cailan said. "Whatever we're going to do, it's now or never. We've got to be proactive." He ignored the frantic thump of his heart.

Elazar hesitated, clearly torn, before nodding. He understood the logic, even if it was reckless. Max, however, didn't seem convinced. She frowned, her gaze wary. "But we can't fight the Jade Court, the drakes, *and* this sorcerer. It's *too much*."

"What if we didn't have to fight the Jade Court?" Elazar suggested, his tone hopeful.

It was a brilliant idea—but *completely* unrealistic. "And how do we manage that? Even if we're not directly targeted, we're still vulnerable." Cailan frowned.

There was a gleam in Elazar's eye that meant the gears of his mind were turning, fast. He shook his head. "Grief. It's *grief*. That's what they have in common."

"Grief?" Max asked, clearly as exasperated as Cailan. "Grief is what *who* has in common?"

Elazar blinked, then his gaze locked with Cailan's. "Our father and Belen."

Cailan's mind clicked into place. He understood. Or at least, he *partially* understood. Belen mourned her mate, her ruined court, the loss of her whelps. Asher mourned his mate, and for a while, he'd thought his sons were lost as well. "Okay, but I don't think you're going to convince them to sit around and have a little heart-to-heart," Cailan said, unable to contain a note of cynicism. "So, what's your point?"

"It *matters*," Elazar insisted, his voice softer now, as if he were still teasing out the details. "It matters because they've never had a chance to heal. To move on. Because the Grief-Eater won't *let* them."

"What?" Cailan blinked, his expression incredulous.

Elazar stabbed an index finger outward, his gesture vaguely encompassing the entire library. "It's not their true nature. All this anger, this resentment, this festering *hate*...it's not who they are. It's the Grief-Eater's influence."

"So, what do we do about it?" Max asked, her tone weary. "I hate to say it, but Cailan has a point. I don't think we're in a good place to fix that."

Elazar swallowed, his brow furrowed. "What has the power to weaken grief? To combat it?"

Cailan and Max exchanged puzzled glances. "I don't know," Cailan admitted. It wasn't something he'd considered before.

"Hope," Elazar whispered, his voice soft, but his eyes held a new, determined light. "Joy. That's how you weaken the Grief-Eater. That's how you fight back against her."

They were lovely, *idealistic* ideas, but again, not at all *realistic*. Cailan sighed. "Elazar, we—"

"I know what you're going to say," Elazar cut him off, his gaze shifting to Max, something unreadable in his eyes. "But I have to try."

"Try what?" Cailan *really* wished his brother would get to the point.

"I think I really *can* help the Jade Court," Elazar said, his voice firm. He took a step forward, then paused, his gaze settling on Max. "I know I promised I wouldn't leave you behind, but I think Cailan needs you. More than I do."

"Need her *why?*" Cailan asked, annoyed.

"Because you and I have to stop whatever the Grief-Eater is planning," Max said, her tone resolute. "While Elazar does his part."

Cailan wasn't sure how they intended to pull any of this off. But it was time to act, to save Danelor and Tiberia from the creature that had stolen Chandra's form. "Fine," he said, accepting the challenge. "Let's do this."

He wasn't looking forward to another encounter with the creature that called itself Chandra, but at least now he knew what he was dealing with.

29

TRANSFORMATION

Asher

"Why?" Asher muttered to himself, the question a bitter echo in the stillness of his study. Why had he attempted to force Elazar and Cailan to stay? He'd known, in his heart, that such a move would only push them further away.

And that relic, Eletheria's Blessing. He'd never use it on his own sons. Never. So *why* had he been so eager to force it upon them, to bend them to his will? It was almost as if...

"Dragons!" A terrified shriek rippled through the library's corridors. "The Jade Court is attacking!"

Asher snapped to attention, every muscle in his body taut.

Belen. Hot, searing rage flooded him, a wave that threatened to drown all other thoughts. He could dissect his own motivations later. Right now, he had to protect the library. And possibly, *finally*, end the Jade Court.

He whirled, heading for the nearest exit. The Forgotten Library drakes were already gathering on the beach, readying themselves for the battle they knew was coming.

But they were ill-prepared. Years of isolation had lulled them into a false sense of security. The library, hidden behind its veil of storms, had shielded them from the dangers of the outside world. They were untested. Vulnerable.

Nothing to be done about that now. They would look to him, the Guardian, for direction. He wouldn't disappoint them.

Asher launched into the air with powerful wingbeats. He landed with a soft thump on the sand, the tide washing against his tail. The gathered drakes relaxed as their eyes settled on him.

"What do we do?" a younger drake asked, his voice trembling. A ripple of fear spread through the assembled drakes.

Asher's gaze hardened. "We fight," he declared, his voice a low rumble as he scanned the incoming forces. There she was. Belen. Leading the charge, her wings gleaming with an unnatural metal sheen.

"We cannot allow them to breach the library's defenses," Oriana said, taking her place beside Asher, her expression grim.

Zark nodded, his dark scales absorbing the sunlight. "The knowledge within these walls is too dangerous to fall into their claws."

"Take your positions!" Asher barked. "Fight with fang, claw, and magic. Defend this library with your lives!"

The younger drakes hesitated for a moment. Then they spread their wings, taking to the air in a flurry of brilliant scales against the bright blue sky. They were brave, but young. And so inexperienced.

Their inexperience doesn't matter, a cold, insidious voice whispered in the back of his mind. *Only their deaths matter. The library is all that matters.*

Asher shook his head. Where had that come from? He didn't want any of them to die. He knew, with a cold certainty, that many would be lost today. But that didn't mean he *wanted* it.

He dismissed the thought, focusing on the task at hand, the grim reality of the situation. He called on his power, and with a rumbling groan, the two massive stone golems pulled themselves away from the structure, their stone bodies gleaming in the sun.

"These dragons think they can take what we protect!" he bellowed, his wings flaring behind him. "But today we will show them the true meaning of might. The might of the small, the brave, the *drakes!* For the Forgotten Library!" He vaulted into the air, leading the charge.

Elazar

HUFFING FOR BREATH, ELAZAR RACED THROUGH THE library corridors, hoping he was right. Hoping his idea wasn't as absurd as it sounded. He skidded around a corner, his boots screeching as he nearly lost his footing.

The scene that greeted him as he burst through the massive entrance doors sent a surge of dread through him. Dragons and drakes circled each other, their roars echoing, the air thick with anticipation.

His throat went dry. What if he was wrong? What if his plan failed? The consequences could be catastrophic. The drakes, outnumbered and outmatched, would be crushed. And the library, with its trove of knowledge, would fall into the clutches of the dragons.

A familiar squawk pierced the din. Elazar turned to see Sprocket swooping toward him. She landed on his shoulder, her metal claws digging into his shirt.

"Ouch," he hissed, wincing. "Glad to see you, too, Sprocket, but I've got a situation here."

Wait. He'd left her on the *Tempest.* The mischievous cogwing had escaped, probably been wandering the library. He shook his head, trying to dismiss the thought. "You need to get back to the airship," he told her, pointing away. "I can't worry about you, too."

The cogwing stared back at him, her mechanical eyes unblinking. Then, with a whirring of gears, she launched off his shoulder. But she didn't leave. She hovered in the air, zipping from side to side like a hummingbird, her wings a blur of motion. Then, she circled him in a wide loop before giving him an insistent look.

"Sprocket, please," Elazar said, attempting to sidestep the determined cogwing. "I don't have time for this right now. Can't you see what's going on?"

Sprocket responded by grabbing his shirt sleeve with her beak and tugging hard. Her eyes, usually filled with a mischievous glint, now flashed with an urgency that gave him pause.

She wanted him to follow. He sighed. "Fine, but hurry."

Sprocket took off. Elazar ran after her, his breath catching in his throat as they descended a staircase. The air grew cooler, musty, and the scent of old paper and aged leather was heavier. This part of the library felt older than any he'd explored before.

Sprocket darted around a corner, almost disappearing. He

quickened his pace, rounding the bend and finding himself in what looked like a storage area. Dusty crates, their surfaces covered in cobwebs and grime, towered over him, creating a maze of haphazardly stacked boxes. The space was crammed with old furniture—a cracked mirror, a rickety armoire, a wooden chest that looked as though it might be filled with treasures.

He wove through the clutter, following the insistent squawks, when he heard muffled voices, *familiar* voices, echoing from the other side of a wall.

"...can't believe they actually *drugged* us," Aunt Jo said, sharp with indignation.

"Shhh," Gretchen's voice cautioned. "I think I heard something."

His heart leaped. He hurried forward, stumbling over a broken chair. "Aunt Jo? Gretchen?"

"Elazar!" Josephine's voice rang out, stronger now, closer. "We're in here!"

Sprocket led him to a heavy wooden door, its surface carved with a dusty pattern of vines and flowers. He tested the handle, but it was locked. He pressed his ear against the wood. "Are you all okay?"

"We're fine," Josephine answered. "But we can't get out. The door's locked from the outside."

Elazar examined the lock. It was old but sturdy. He glanced at Sprocket. "You know what to do. Open it."

The cogwing bobbed her head. He watched as she inserted her beak into the lock. Sprocket was keyed specifically to open Elazar's sea chest, but with a bit of tinkering, he'd expanded her capabilities. She could now pick most locks, though he'd added a safety measure—she had to be given a direct command before she could act. Otherwise, Elazar was certain she'd let herself in places she was meant to stay out of.

A satisfying click echoed through the room as the mechanism gave way. Elazar yanked the door open, revealing his crewmates.

Aunt Jo emerged first, her eyes blazing. She reached to embrace him, but he held up a hand, his heart aching at the necessity of the gesture. "No time for reunions," he said, his voice tight. "The Jade Court is attacking the Forgotten Library. We need to move."

Isaac stepped out, rubbing at his temples. "Good," he growled. "Those backstabbing drakes deserve everything they get."

Elazar shook his head vehemently. "No, you don't understand. If the Jade Court takes the library, it could be catastrophic. I have a plan. But..." He looked at each of them, their faces etched with bewilderment and distrust. "I want the *Tempest* ready to defend the library. If it comes to that."

Aunt Jo's eyebrows shot up. "*Defend* the library? Elazar, these drakes *drugged* us, locked us in this room. Why would we help them?"

"Because the alternative is far worse," Elazar insisted, urgency rising in his chest. "Trust me. We need to get to the *Tempest* right now."

Gretchen stepped forward, her gaze sharp. "You've got that look, boy," she said, a hint of a knowing smile in her voice. "The one that says you're about to do something potentially foolish."

Elazar couldn't help but laugh. "Probably. But it might be our only chance."

Josephine's jaw tightened, a fierce glint flaring in her eyes. "Elazar, I don't want to see you hurt again! Not after what happened before."

He understood her fear. He wasn't eager to face more danger, but... "I know. But I won't leave you behind this time." He worried at his lower lip, his gaze meeting hers, a plea in his eyes. "I'm asking you to have my back. If my plan doesn't work. If things go wrong."

His aunt's shoulders slumped. "We'll always have your back, Elazar. You know that."

He led the way out. Aunt Jo and the rest of the crew followed close behind. Sprocket trailed them, whistling as they walked.

As they emerged into the open air, the sounds of battle above them intensified. Roars and screeches filled the sky, punctuated by the occasional pulse of magic or boom of a cannon. Elazar forced himself not to look up, knowing that every second counted.

They reached the *Tempest*'s mooring, but as they approached, he noticed something was off. The airship seemed to shiver. Her ropes strained against the moorings, as if the ship was trying to break free.

"She knows," Elazar murmured, placing a hand against the *Tempest*'s hull. He felt a thrumming energy beneath his palm.

Aunt Jo barked sharp orders and the crew sprang into action. Elazar helped where he could, but his mind was already racing, planning his next move.

As the last mooring line was cast off, he turned to his aunt. "Keep her ready, but hold back. Stay out of the fight for now. I need to try something first."

Josephine's worried gaze met his. "Be careful, Elazar. We'll be here if you need us."

He drew a breath, steeling himself. He focused inward, calling upon the drake within. The transformation began, his body elongating, red-gold motes of magic dancing across his skin. As his form shifted, dizziness rippled through him. The world tilted, disorienting him. He stumbled, newly formed wings flaring to regain his balance.

"Remember your positions!" Gretchen's voice cut through the haze of chaos.

He remembered. The head movements. The specific angles Gretchen had taught him. He sucked in a calming breath, angling his head just so, going through the series of motions until the dizziness subsided, the world returning to its proper axis.

"Better now," he said, gritting his teeth, his voice a rasp against the wind. "Thanks, Gretchen."

"What's your plan?" Aunt Jo demanded.

Elazar winced. "No time to explain. Just trust me." He wasn't eager to lay out his plan—a gut feeling, really, more intuition than strategy—but he also didn't have time for a full briefing.

He tapped the arcane engine at his chest. The metal augments at the leading edges of his wings slid into place with a satisfying hum. He launched into the air, his wings snapping open to catch the stiff breeze, the rush of wind a welcome distraction.

"Elazar!" Aunt Jo's voice followed him. She was probably furious. He'd left her in the dark again.

Please trust me. He had to be right. If she didn't trust him, if she ordered the *Tempest* into battle, it would be catastrophic.

Elazar soared, the wind whipping past him, carrying the acrid bite of smoke and the metallic tang of blood. He scanned his surroundings, a confusing vortex of bright scales and wings, searching for Belen's distinctive emerald sheen.

There. A flash of green amid the tangled mass of dragons and drakes. He angled his wings, pushing himself towards the Jade Empress.

As he drew closer, he saw one of Asher's massive stone golems locked in a brutal struggle with Belen. Its granite fists smashed down upon her. But the Jade Empress was a formidable opponent, her hardscale hide deflecting the blows. Asher himself, a blur of pearly scales against the azure sky, circled the pair, seizing every opportunity to aim for her softer areas.

To his left, Elazar caught sight of Asher's second golem. Its fists were wrapped around the tail of a thrashing dragon, dragging the creature down into the sea. The dragon roared, but its voice was cut short as it vanished beneath the surf, the frothy waters claiming it.

Elazar steeled himself. He was almost there, within range. Now was the time to act.

But before he closed the final distance, Asher's voice cut through the din. "Elazar! Get away from here! *Now!*"

Elazar faltered, his wings missing a beat, a moment of hesitation that cost him dearly.

Belen spotted him. "*You!*" she hissed, venomous. "You won't betray me again, drake. Your usefulness is *over.*"

She surged forward. Her jaws gaped, closing around Elazar's torso before he could react, fangs piercing his leathery scales, drawing blood.

He screamed as her jaws clamped down, crushing, threatening to *end* him.

No. The world narrowed to the terrifying reality of Belen's jaws surrounding him. Elazar reached up, talons clattering against his arcane engine as he frantically traced another rune.

"*Tenomaru,*" he whispered, voice shaking.

Metal plates whispered out of his nexus chain, sliding into place over his body, armoring him from head to tail. The plates wedged themselves between his scales and Belen's fangs, earning a surprised rumble from the Jade Empress. He gasped, relief racing through him. The armor was in place. Elazar was wounded, but he was alive.

Belen spat him out, lowering her head to glare. "*What is this?*"

Dazed, Elazar landed in the churning water with a resounding splash. He began to sink but spread his wings wide like a raft to increase his buoyancy and keep himself afloat. Sprocket swooped down to circle him, screeching. "I'm fine," he called to her, trying to sound more confident than he felt. "Make sure the *Tempest* doesn't attack. Not yet."

Fine was a stretch, but the truth wouldn't help anyone right now. He lifted his head, glancing at Asher's golem, which was now battering Belen. One of her mechanical wings was clutched in its stony fist, pulling the Jade Empress down. She roared in surprise, a desperate cry that made Elazar's breath catch.

"No," he whispered. If Belen died now, this desperate gamble would be over.

His consciousness was flagging, the power of the sorcerer's gift waning. He *had* to act. Gathering his strength, he surged out of the water to hover in the air. Elazar pulled on that unfamiliar magic, the echo of The Shaper's power, and funneled it outward, toward the dragons.

Elazar closed his eyes, focusing his will, and golden tendrils of magic flowed from his body. Then his eyes snapped open once more.

Asher's golem released Belen, taking a giant step backwards, its stone form trembling as if struck by an unseen force.

Elazar watched, awe washing over him, as the magic enveloped Belen first. Her emerald scales gleamed beneath the golden light, her movements slowing, her rage fading. The threads of magic wrapped around her mechanical wings, seizing them, and a surge of energy pulsed through Elazar, an echo of that same power, guiding him.

Merging The Shaper's creation magic with his own Gearweaving abilities, Elazar *focused*. He envisioned intricate metal gears, those gleaming plates *transforming*. Becoming living tissue. And, to his utter astonishment, it happened. The mechanical structures morphed before his very eyes. The golden magic pulsed around him, a warm, energizing current that vibrated through his veins. Elazar felt a deep connection, an inexplicable bond, to this transformation, this act of creation. Metal softened, reshaped itself, forming delicate bones and sinews. Gears melted away, replaced by muscles and tendons. Shimmering plates dissolved, giving way to a delicate membrane that stretched between the newly formed bones.

As Belen's wings completed their metamorphosis, Elazar turned his attention to the other dragons. The tendrils of golden magic expanded, encompassing more of the Jade Court. One by one, their mechanical wings began to change, following the same miraculous process.

Elazar's body trembled with the effort, the pain of his own wounds momentarily forgotten as he poured all his energy, all his will, into this task. He felt the dragons' emotions—surprise, disbelief, hope—course through the magical connection.

He didn't stop there. Elazar sought the chimeras. He found them—some were on the airships. Tiberia and Danelor were somewhere hidden within the library. He sent the same inexorable magic towards them.

The chimeras were a puzzle, their bodies forever changed at a molecular level. But the essence of their dragonkind remained, locked away by the corrupted dragonfruit. He sent his power to burn away the barrier.

A triumphant roar erupted from one of the Jade Court airships, a sound that cut through the chaos of battle. A dragon —no, a *chimera* in dragon form—took to the air on silky wings.

Exhaustion pulled at him. The Shaper's magic was fading, but there was one last thing he had to do.

Elazar felt the lingering shadow of grief that clung to both Belen and Asher. He'd been right. The Grief-Eater had sunk her claws into them, feeding on their pain, twisting their emotions, denying them the solace of time and healing.

This wasn't a physical wound that could be mended. Elazar reached out gently, opening their minds, helping Belen to truly see the restoration of her court, the chimeras soaring around her, their wings whole and strong. He reminded them both that it was time to let go. To let their lost mates rest. To stop clinging to the shadows of the past.

A gusty sigh escaped Belen, a sound of surprised relief. She surged away from the battle, her gaze sweeping over the dragons, truly *seeing* their restored wings. She stared at the young chimera soaring before her.

The last whispers of magic fled. Elazar sank down into the surf.

"Elazar!" Asher swooped down. "Drakes, retreat! It's over." He abandoned the fight, hovering above his son. "Elazar!"

The next few moments were a blur, a hazy recollection of being gently lifted by Asher's golem, carried back to shore, and settled on the sand, the tide playing at his feet.

"Elazar." Asher's voice was a plea. "What happened? Where is Cailan?"

Elazar swallowed. Everything hurt—his body, his mind. He'd almost died, hadn't he? That usually triggered a shift, but... "I think...I think I've finally figured out how to control my shifting," he mumbled, his words slurring.

Belen landed nearby with a splash, sending a new tide rolling ashore. Asher growled, a deep rumble in his chest. Elazar braced himself, expecting another attack. But the Jade Empress shook her head like a dog shedding water, a confused, almost bewildered expression on her face.

"You've done enough! Stay back!" Asher snarled.

The emerald-scaled dragon bowed her head. "I was not... myself." Her voice trembled, the raw emotion radiating through the air. "Tiberia...Danelor...my *children?* Where are they?"

Wait. Tiberia and Danelor were her *children?* Suddenly, everything fell into place—Tiberia's unwavering loyalty, Danelor's surprising survival. Elazar groaned, the effort of recalling Cailan's words too much to bear. "Inside the library. Trapped."

Belen exhaled a gusty breath. "I must go to them." She turned, her renewed wings mantling at her sides as she strode toward the library.

Asher watched her go. Then he turned to Elazar, his expression somber. "You're hurt." He turned, seeking someone to help. "This is all my fault."

Elazar blinked, confusion fogging his mind. No, this wasn't Asher's fault. Not entirely. But he was too injured, his mind too fractured from the exertion of wielding the sorcerer's power, to explain. And there wasn't time.

"Cailan," he rasped, a new fear gripping him. Max was with Cailan. Even if Belen found Tiberia and Danelor...would it be enough? "Help him. Against...Chandra."

"*Chandra...*" Asher repeated, as if an old memory stirred. He blinked, his gaze distant.

"We've got him," Gretchen announced, racing toward them. She and Aunt Jo dropped to their knees beside Elazar, their faces filled with concern. "Go. Help Cailan."

Asher nodded, his expression grim, and bolted toward the library.

"Elazar!" Aunt Jo's voice shook. "Oh, gods, Gretch, there's blood everywhere..."

"Yes, our boy is very good at bleeding," Gretchen agreed, her tone dry. She tapped a finger against his armor. "Clever, though. Can't beat a dragon, so you join them, is that it?"

He released a shaky laugh, pain throbbing through his body. "Yeah..." He groaned. "Shift. I need to shift."

"No," Gretchen murmured, her tone soothing. "There's no need. But if you can, remove the armor. That would help. Otherwise, we can—and will—pry it off you."

Elazar sighed, his claws trembling as he traced the rune. With a whisper of magic, the armor slid back into his nexus chain, vanishing from sight, leaving his scaled body exposed. He heard his aunt's sharp intake of breath.

"We've not hunted dragons for months, and you've gone soft. Forgotten what they can do!" Gretchen scoffed.

"I *never* forgot. But I hate seeing the reminder on my nephew," Aunt Jo shot back, her voice tight.

Elazar sank into unconsciousness.

30

Sob Story Serpent

Danelor

"Soon, my loves. Soon you'll both be mine again." The words, whispered with a chilling, possessive affection, sent a shiver down Dane's spine.

He blinked, his vision blurry. Where was he? The ceiling overhead was unfamiliar. Not the rough-hewn caves of Outcast Island, not the ceiling of his room at the Forgotten Library. He was certain of that. He was lying on something cool and hard. Stone, Dane thought. But he couldn't move. His entire body was frozen.

He tried to piece together what had happened, the events

that had led to this. He remembered leaving Cailan in the library...

"Do you feel it?" The voice wrapped around him like a caress. "The drakes and the dragons...they are falling, their life force fueling the spell that will bring you to me."

A figure materialized into view, the light filtering through a hidden skylight illuminating her. Chandra. But something—a deep, instinctive fear—told Dane that this wasn't quite the Seer he knew.

He remembered. He'd gone to her, seeking word on Tiberia. And she'd taken him. *Betrayed* him.

"Hey, Sob Story Serpent." Cailan's defiant voice echoed through the chamber. "Stop whatever shady business you're up to and release Danelor and Tiberia. *Now*."

Chandra whirled, a spark of rage flashing in her eyes. "You! I didn't expect to see your face again. After you tucked your tail and ran." Dane heard the click of claws on stone as she approached Cailan.

"Yeah, well, strategic retreats are a thing," Cailan shot back. "Especially when it comes to getting reinforcements."

Chandra sucked in a sharp breath. "No! I won't let you stop me. *You won't stop me!*" There was a flurry of frantic claws, a scraping sound, a pulse of energy. Out of the corner of his eye, he saw Chandra moving towards a massive artifact shaped like a vase that stood between him and Tiberia. She did something to it, and a volley of cold, dark magic rippled through the air, seeping into his bones, claiming him.

You are mine now, a malevolent presence whispered.

He couldn't even whimper, couldn't call out for help. He was trapped, his will dissolving, his identity fading beneath its influence.

Maxine

LEAVING ELAZAR WAS THE LAST THING MAX WANTED TO do, but she had to trust him—and trust her instincts. But the creature standing before her and Cailan...Max didn't need a sorcerer's insight to know the truth. Chandra was the nascent sorceress, the Grief-Eater, that The Shaper had warned them about.

And Max and Cailan were too late.

Tiberia rose from the dark slab, her eyes glowing with an unnatural light. She smirked, the expression haughty, and everything about her, from the way she moved to the tone of her voice, betrayed the fact that this wasn't the chimera Max had known. This was something far more terrifying.

"More willing souls for us," Tiberia purred.

No. This wasn't Tiberia. This was the Soulcaller. And the Grief-Eater was bad, but dealing with her *and* the Soulcaller was much, *much* worse.

Cailan, still in his human form, pulled his cutlass from its scabbard. He grinned, a gesture of bravado, but Max noticed the tremor in his hands. "Nothing *willing* about us," he said, standing firm. "But I look forward to sending you back to the Abyss. Where you belong."

Maxine's pulse raced as she assessed the situation. Tiberia —or rather, the Soulcaller inhabiting her body—stood before them, radiating an otherworldly power. To Maxine's left, Cailan clutched his cutlass, but she knew conventional weapons would be useless against such an entity.

Her mind raced, desperately searching for a solution. How

could they possibly defeat these ancient sorcerers without harming Tiberia and Danelor?

The Grief-Eater's voice cut through Max's thoughts. "Finish your brother's return," she commanded, her gaze turning toward the Soulcaller. "I will deal with this *interruption.*"

Maxine watched as the creature wearing Tiberia's face nodded, turning back to the dark slab where Danelor lay. Chandra—no, the Grief-Eater, Max reminded herself—strode forward, a darkness that seemed to seep out from her saturating the air, making the very atmosphere thick.

"Cailan," Max whispered. "We can't hurt them. They're still in there, somewhere."

Cailan's jaw clenched, his expression grim. "Danelor and Tiberia, maybe. But Chandra..." His voice softened, a raw ache in his tone. "I was one of her sentinels, you know. She wouldn't want this."

Max's heart ached for him. "She's got so much power. I don't think you can fight her. Not alone."

"That's where you come in." A pleased smirk played on his lips, his eyes gleaming with a confidence that bordered on arrogance. "Keep her busy."

Max nodded, though she didn't have the foggiest idea where to even begin. Cailan slipped to the side, his form dissolving into the shadows. Max did a double-take, then forced herself to focus on the dragon sorceress.

"You're not the only sorceress here, Grief-Eater," Max declared, though the word *sorceress* left a bitter taste in her mouth. It was right, though, wasn't it? Lightning traced a blistering path up her arms before receding into the depths of her being.

The Grief-Eater exhaled, her eyes narrowing. "Don't flatter

yourself, girl. Not a sorceress, no. You dabble in powers you don't understand."

A flare of dark magic rose from the Grief-Eater, a suffocating darkness that assaulted Max, weaving through her mind, tugging at her vulnerabilities. Memories she'd tried to bury surfaced—the gut-wrenching grief of Elazar's supposed death, the harrowing memories of being sold by her own family as if she were livestock, never feeling truly loved, the remembered pain of the devastating storm she'd created in her desperate attempt to escape her abusive marriage.

What fights grief? Hope. Joy. Elazar's words echoed in her mind. She remembered her first glimpse of the *Tempest*, the hope it kindled in her heart, the promise of a new life. She recalled the moment she'd found Elazar alive, transformed into a dragon. And then their kiss.

Max's eyes snapped open, and she ducked, rolling just in time to avoid the dragon's slashing claws. The Grief-Eater had tried to paralyze her, to break her, by exploiting her deepest wounds.

The Grief-Eater growled, her tail lashing. This time, tendrils of dark magic snaked out toward Max, seeking to subdue her. But the moment those tendrils touched her skin, a coating of crackling lightning erupted, rippling across her flesh. The tendrils recoiled as if scorched.

The Grief-Eater's eyes narrowed, and another wave of dark power surged outward. Shadowy tendrils lashed out and Maxine's lightning shield faltered, weakened beneath the relentless assault.

The Shaper had been wrong. She *couldn't* do this. Winds above, she could barely even control her own Stormcaller magic. It was like trying to ride a bolt of lightning, to tame its sheer force, to command it with her will. *Impossible.*

But give up? Surrender? That was unthinkable. Not just

for her. For everyone. For Elazar, for Danelor, for Tiberia, for Cailan. For everyone threatened by the Grief-Eater's insidious power. Her muscles trembled, her body ached, but she pushed on, drawing on the last reserves of her strength.

With a mighty effort, she summoned a powerful bolt of lightning, a white-hot energy that crackled through the air. She unleashed it towards the Grief-Eater, hoping to give them some breathing room, but her hope vanished. The sorceress deflected the attack with a casual flick of her wing, the gesture effortless, a terrifying display of their disparity in power.

Maxine staggered, trembling from exhaustion, her vision blurring. She couldn't keep this up. Not for long.

"You're out of your depth, mage," the Grief-Eater said, a sneer twisting her lips. "But it's adorable that you thought you could actually challenge me." Dark power crackled around her, a serpent coiled, ready to strike.

Then a blur of motion, a flash of steel, caught Max's attention. Cailan dove out of the shadows toward the Grief-Eater. He slid between the dragon's forelegs.

The Grief-Eater let out a guttural roar of pain and fury as Cailan's blade found its mark, piercing the vulnerable spot where her foreleg met her chest.

Maxine's instinct screamed at her to attack, to press their advantage, but she held back. Cailan was too close. Any strike could easily hit him instead. She watched in horror as the sorceress, seemingly ignoring the cutlass embedded in her chest, pinned Cailan to the ground, her powerful claws digging into him.

"You were right to flee the first time," the Grief-Eater snarled.

Cailan was covered in blood—his or Chandra's, it was hard to tell—but he didn't react. He ignored the pain, the sting of the dragon's claws. His gaze locked with Max's. Unwilling to yield.

As Maxine watched, a glimmer of magic pulsed around him, the familiar transformation taking place. Cailan shifted, his human form dissolving, his drake form taking its place.

He was still smaller, still lacking the raw power that the Grief-Eater wielded, but Max knew from experience that very little stopped Cailan. He writhed, his tail lashing, his claws scraping against the ground as he thrashed. Cailan's hind legs kicked up into the sorceress's chest, the motion driving the blade deeper.

The Grief-Eater hissed, drawing back instinctively, giving Cailan precious seconds to scramble to his feet. To Maxine's horror, he wasn't unscathed. His right side was scored with deep talon marks, his wing hanging crooked, unable to close fully. It must have gotten caught beneath the dragon's claws during the transformation.

The sorceress gathered her magic. A foreboding vortex of darkness swarmed around her, preparing for another attack.

Danelor

HE HAD NO CONTROL OVER HIS BODY, BUT HIS EMOTIONS remained his own. And panic flooded him as he saw Cailan ready to challenge Chandra.

You're still here? the malevolent presence that had hijacked his body asked, its voice laced with a touch of frustration. *You should be making the walk to Perdition now. Like your sister.*

Tiberia? Dane would have growled if he could, if he could *do* anything but endure this assault on his mind and body. He dug in, refusing to yield. If this invader wanted him gone, there would be a fight.

Never mind. I'll be rid of you soon enough. The presence dismissed him as if he were a gnat.

He felt his body rising, pulled from the slab, a puppet on a string. The invader flexed its fingers, testing its new vessel. A rush of foreign energy rippled through Dane's form.

What is this? Confusion colored the invader's mental voice. *These pains...I do not recall experiencing this in my previous existence as the Flameweaver. This body...it is damaged.*

Dane would have smirked if he could, if he could *control* his lips. His chronic pain, the bane of his existence, was now an unwelcome surprise for this intruder.

Oh, that? Dane asked. *It's nothing. You're having a good day right now. It gets much, much worse, sometimes.*

He felt the invader measure his words, its mental focus intent as it gauged the veracity of his claim. Dane split his attention—one part focused on the unwelcome presence within him, the other drawn to the scene of chaos unfolding outside, the battle between Maxine and Chandra, and where was Cailan...?

Suddenly, a new sensation surrounded him. Warmth. A soothing, almost radiant energy that flowed through his body. Dane would have preened beneath it if he'd had any control. It felt *good*. Wait. Had this power somehow dampened his chronic pain? His pain, which had become his only advantage against this invader?

The Flameweaver grumbled again, his hand rubbing at his shoulder. No. Whatever magic had touched him, that strange energy hadn't impacted the sorcerer. It was a powerful force, but it had targeted *him*. Dane studied the sensation, a sense of *completeness* he hadn't experienced before. As if he'd discovered a part of himself he'd been missing.

His dragon.

But even with that piece of him unlocked, even with a

surge of primal power coursing through him, he wasn't sure he had a chance against this sorcerer, this *thief* of his body.

Then he saw Cailan leap from the shadows, his cutlass flashing, aiming for Chandra. The next moment, he was slammed to the ground, the sorceress's claws pinning him. Cailan bucked, his form shifting. His drake form emerged, blood staining his gleaming opal scales. He was a fighter, a formidable one, but he had no chance against a dragon fueled by dark magic.

He was going to die.

A roar built in Dane's throat, a primal cry of defiance. He had to fight back and help Cailan! Digging in, Dane pushed everything he could against his intruder. The Flameweaver struggled, but the sorcerer was disoriented, his concentration broken by the unrelenting pain coursing through his body.

Dane felt the Flameweaver's grip loosen. He pushed harder, clawing his way back, fighting for every inch of his own being. The sorcerer lashed out, his magic a barrage of burning pain, a desperate attempt to subdue Dane's consciousness. But Dane's determination burned brighter. He wouldn't allow this invader to use him as a puppet. He wouldn't stand by while Cailan, Tiberia, Elazar, Max...all of them were in danger.

As he wrestled for control, he felt that warm energy again, the surge of power he'd glimpsed earlier. His dragon. He reached for it, grasping at the magic that had always been denied him.

No! This body is mine! The Flameweaver's mental voice shrieked, panic and rage crashing against Dane's consciousness.

But Dane was done being a passenger. With a roar, he seized control, forcing the sorcerer back, the unwelcome presence retreating from his mind. Dane gasped, air filling his lungs. He was back. He was in command.

Dane didn't have time to savor the victory. Cailan was still in danger, though he'd freed himself from Chandra's claws. He reached deep within himself, tapping into that newfound source of power. His body began to shift, bones rearranging, muscles rippling, growing. The transformation was unlike anything he'd ever experienced. His body expanded rapidly, his skin hardening into gleaming amethyst scales. Wings unfolded, stretching wider and wider, their edges catching the light, a shimmering purple. He grew larger and larger, his form quickly outgrowing the confines of the vault.

The ceiling above him cracked, the stone groaning as his head and back shoved against it. The walls buckled, the stones crumbling under the pressure of his massive dragon form. Dust rose in a thick cloud, obscuring the chamber, threatening to collapse the entire structure. The library, built to house knowledge, to protect secrets, was no match for the power surging within him.

And now, he wasn't just a danger to Chandra. He was a danger to *everyone*.

Chandra, her eyes wide with disbelief, took a step backward, her talons scraping against the crumbling stone. "What... what is this?" The walls behind her trembled, a cascade of stone tumbling down.

People were going to die because of him!

Max was closest. He scooped her up, his foreclaw cradling her against his chest, his powerful body a shield. Dane hoped he wouldn't crush her. But Cailan...he couldn't move closer to the opal drake without further risking the collapse of the library. He had to do something.

Dane opened his jaws and lunged. He snapped Cailan up, his fangs closing around the smaller drake like a cage. He felt Cailan's weight against his tongue, tasted the tang of his blood.

The rest of the library fell around them.

Belen

Belen charged into the library. She wished she had time to think—to untangle the twisted threads of her own mind, to understand how she'd been so easily manipulated—but her children were in danger. She'd failed to save her mate all those years ago, a wound that had festered. Then most of her whelps had perished, lost to the insidious effects of the corrupted dragonfruit. All except Tiberia and Danelor. She couldn't lose them, not now.

The corridors of the library, deceptively narrow, seemed to expand to accommodate her form—proof of the magic that imbued this place. It would have been both humbling and terrifying, had she time to reflect, but she was on a mission. The entire structure reeked of magic, a potent mixture of arcane energies that sent a shiver down her scales.

"Wait!" a voice called behind her.

Belen slowed. Asher was racing towards her. "My quarrel, at the moment, is not with you, drake," Belen growled.

"I know," Asher said, his voice taut with worry. "But Chandra...she's got my whelp, too."

"Chandra?" Belen repeated, the name a bitter echo in her mind. Chandra, the dragon who had manipulated her, poisoned her mind, led her down a path of untempered vengeance. Her sister.

"Yes," Asher confirmed. "But not the Seer you knew."

She didn't understand, but it didn't matter. Whatever was happening, her focus remained. She had to get to her children, to save them, and then she would deal with Chandra.

"Follow me. I think I know where they are." Asher jerked his head towards a corridor branching off to the right.

Belen hesitated for a moment. She didn't trust the drake, but this was a gamble she had to take. Asher broke into a run, and Belen, with her longer strides, easily kept pace.

They burst into the vault, the scene before her a chaotic nightmare. Chandra—or something wearing her form—had Cailan pinned beneath her. The human mage, Max, rested against a broken bookshelf. Tiberia stood at the far end of the room, and though Belen's instincts screamed this creature wasn't her daughter, she saw a shadow of Tiberia's spirit in those dark eyes. Perhaps she wasn't lost.

And Danelor...he was there, rising to a sitting position atop a dark slab, his face contorted in pain. His fists tightened, his body tense. Then...

He *changed*. His form twisted and warped. Deep purple scales bloomed, wings burst from his shoulders, a monstrous transformation taking place before her eyes.

The walls trembled, cracks spider-webbing across the ceiling. Chunks of stone rained down. Belen's wings spread instinctively, but she knew that wouldn't offer any protection against the collapsing structure. She was going to die here, crushed beneath the weight of this ancient library. After all she'd endured, after finally regaining her ability to fly...this was how it would end.

"No!" Asher's cry cut through the rumble of collapsing stone.

The floor beneath them shuddered, and for a moment, Belen thought it was just another tremor. But then, two massive forms erupted from the stone itself—golems, easily twice her size, their bodies a patchwork of rock and crystal.

The golems moved with surprising speed, positioning themselves over Belen and Asher as the ceiling gave way completely. Masonry and debris rained down, but they didn't flinch. The air filled with choking dust. Belen coughed, her lungs burning.

As the dust settled, the golems retreated. Belen turned to Asher. "You saved my life."

The drake's attention wasn't on her. "I may have only delayed the inevitable."

Danelor stood nearby, as still as a statue, as if fearing any movement might trigger another collapse. Chandra and Tiberia emerged from the rubble, their forms dusted with debris, but otherwise unharmed.

Magic. They'd used magic.

"I don't know how either of you slipped your leash," Chandra said, stepping toward them, her eyes gleaming with an unsettling light. "But I'll make sure you find a new use. A more *permanent* use."

"Why have you done this, sister?" Belen demanded.

"Sister?" Chandra laughed, a cruel, unnatural sound. "Your sister is *gone*, little wyrm. Like you, she was nothing more than a tool. A means to an end."

The chilling words rooted Belen for a moment. In their youth, she and Chandra had been inseparable. But in adulthood, they'd grown apart. Their bond had fractured. No, Belen realized, it wasn't fractured. It was *poisoned*.

"I'm no one's tool!" Belen growled, her claws spread defensively. She glanced at Tiberia, her heart clenching. Her daughter had been fully claimed by this evil.

"You're playing right into her claws," Asher's voice cut through the tension, his tone filled with a quiet determination. "Just as we have for so many years." He swallowed. "We have to end this. Here. Now."

"I'm ready," Belen said, her gaze fixed on Chandra.

31

SOULCHAINS

Cailan

Ending up in a dragon's mouth hadn't been part of the plan. Even if that dragon was Danelor.

Cailan's world was suddenly very dark, very wet, and uncomfortably toothy. One moment, he'd been facing down Evil Chandra's claws and dark magic; the next, he was engulfed in what could only be described as a fleshy cave.

"Well, this is just *fantastic*," he muttered. "Survived a psychotic, grief-eating sorceress only to become dragon chow. Just peachy."

But as the initial shock subsided, Cailan realized something wasn't quite right. If Danelor—and he was *certain* it was

Danelor—had wanted to kill him, he'd be in considerably more pieces by now. And probably a lot further down his throat.

A deafening crash reverberated through the dragon's skull, a sound that made Cailan instinctively curl into a tighter ball, bracing himself against the rough, moist surface of the dragon's tongue. The vibrations of falling debris and shattering stone surrounded him.

Oh. Now it made sense. Danelor had gone *huge.* His impromptu transformation had taken its toll on the library, shattering walls, undermining the foundations. Apparently, even magical buildings couldn't withstand the pressure of a dragon suddenly sprouting to epic proportions within their confines.

"Did you have to save me in such a disgusting way?" he demanded, his voice colored with both annoyance and amusement. Danelor's tongue quivered beneath him, the world's slobberiest carpet. The dragon turned his head, and Cailan tumbled onto his side, hissing as the movement jarred his damaged wing. It was impossible to maintain his balance without digging his talons into the dragon's flesh.

He felt the disorienting sensation of movement again as Danelor lowered his head. Then, a moment later, he was dumped unceremoniously onto the broken floor, the impact jarring, the dragon's breath a warm gust in his face.

Cailan blinked rapidly, trying to clear the dragon saliva from his eyes. His head spun, the world a whirlwind of dust and shattered stone. Chunks of the library's ceiling lay scattered around him in broken shards. Dust hung thick in the air.

Cailan stumbled to his feet, his injured wing protesting the sudden movement. He saw Belen and Asher mere feet away, their postures tense, their eyes fixed on the creature that had stolen Chandra's form. Instinctively, he crouched lower, though his injured wing quickly reminded him he wasn't in the best shape.

Danelor, the truly *massive* amethyst dragon, gently deposited Max on the ground beside him.

"Max!" Cailan hissed, his good shoulder bracing her as she staggered. "Are you all right?"

Max nodded, her eyes wide, taking in the scene. "I'm fine. Mostly. But what in the four winds is going on?"

Cailan shook his head, his gaze darting between Belen, Asher, and the sorceress. "I'm not entirely sure," he admitted, the truth hanging heavy in the air.

But it didn't take long for him to understand. Chandra surged towards Belen. The emerald dragon reared up, her wings snapping out in a defensive posture, talons extended. A chilling sensation struck Cailan. It was an echo of the last battle he'd witnessed between Belen and the Seer.

"*Chandra*," he whispered, voice hoarse.

"It's not her," Danelor rumbled from above.

He was right. This was not the same. Chandra was supposed to die, *had* died, during their last encounter. This was something else. Something far more terrifying.

"She's a sorceress!" Max shouted, her voice barely audible above the roar of the battle. Her gaze met Asher's, her expression filled with a desperate urgency. "She's not a dragon at all. She can't be killed so easily!"

Asher stepped closer to them. He was about to respond, but first Tiberia struck.

With a flick of her wrist, she unleashed a spell. Spectral roots erupted from the ground like grasping fingers, binding Danelor's limbs, head, and neck. The roots drew taut, pulling him down to the ground. Cailan and Max barely had time to scramble out of the way, narrowly avoiding being crushed beneath the amethyst dragon.

Tiberia stalked toward them, a chilling smile playing on her lips. Her gaze was fixed on Cailan. "You *won't* interfere with my brother's return."

For a short-lived moment, Cailan thought she meant Danelor. Then he realized, with a sickening certainty, that the woman before him wasn't Tiberia. She hadn't wrestled back control. And if this pretender had her way, the same fate would befall Danelor. He would be lost as well.

"Don't count on it!" Cailan yelled, launching himself at the creature. Then he froze as more spectral roots broke from the ground, wrapping around him. His muscles locked in place, his body refusing to obey.

"No!" Danelor's voice, a plea filled with anguish, echoed across the rubble. "Leave him alone. Please."

Maxine

MAXINE SLUMPED AGAINST A SHATTERED BOOKSHELF. SHE had nothing left. No magic to shield herself or anyone else. No way to fight back.

She turned to Asher. "Do you know how to kill a sorcerer? Not just *stop* them, but truly destroy them. For good?"

Asher sighed. "I don't know. This is what we were trying to avoid."

But it had happened. It had already begun. From what The Shaper had said, it was inevitable that some of them would return. That the seeds of the Forgotten War would sprout once more.

"There is a way," a new voice declared. Max turned, her heart leaping as she saw Iaxis striding towards them in his

Elven form. He clutched a pair of burlap sacks against his chest, their contents hidden.

Max's eyes widened as she saw Vesper limp in behind the Archivist. The aralez's wings hung at odd angles, and much of his fur was stained with blood, but his tail swayed in a gentle wag. His dark eyes filled with a solemn concern as he watched his possessed mistress battle the Jade Empress. Cailan, trapped by Tiberia's spell, spotted the canine as well, a strangled sound escaping his throat.

"How?" Asher demanded.

Iaxis set down the sacks, then crouched, dodging the swing of a dragon tail by sheer luck. "First," he said, reaching into one of the sacks and pulling out a long chain, its links crafted from carved bone, "we must bind them. To a host."

"Bind them to a host?" Max repeated. Chandra and Belen still clashed, their forms a blur of sapphire and emerald. Tiberia was working her dark magic on Danelor, wispy forms that looked suspiciously like dragon and drake souls flitting around him.

"Yes," Iaxis said, his voice almost distracted, as he tossed the chain to Asher. The drake shifted to his human form in a heartbeat to catch the bone chain. The Archivist reached into the other sack and pulled out another object. "And then, they must drink from this."

Max's eyes widened. It was the same chalice. The one Cailan had shattered. It appeared to have been repaired, though the evidence of a rush job was clear—a few hairline fractures still visible.

"Eletheria's Blessing?" Asher narrowed his eyes, suspicion in his gaze. "That will wipe their memories."

What? Max's breath caught. She understood, finally, why Cailan had been so angry, so horrified by that chalice. Such an act...it was unconscionable.

"In a mortal, yes," Iaxis said, his voice taking on the measured tone of a lecturer. "But for a brief moment, while the Soulchains are in place, the sorceress's essence will be dominant. And we have evidence in our records that this method has been used to neutralize sorcerers in the past. "

"How did you know to come?" Max asked. Was this more manipulation? Would this gambit be their doom?

The Archivist nodded toward Vesper. "The aralez was rather insistent. He brought the chains to me himself—I don't even know how he got into the vault where they were stored. And then—"

"That will be enough, thank you." Asher held up his free hand to forestall further explanation. "The more important thing is, how do you know this will work?"

Iaxis nodded, then gestured to Maxine. "This is precisely how her lineage came about. The sorcerous spirit was bound to a host—usually a human—and then the chalice was used to sever the connection. In essence, it destroys the sorcerer, leaving behind the host with an echo of their power. It's a dangerous gamble." He gestured grandly, his hand sweeping over the ruins.

"Dangerous?" Asher repeated, a hint of concern in his voice.

"Yes, anything involving sorcerers is *dangerous*." Iaxis waved off the concern. "But we must proceed. Now. While we have a chance."

"Fine. How?" Asher grimaced, his gaze fixed on the clashing dragons.

Iaxis outlined their plan. "I have three Soulchains. We must wrap them around our targets: Chandra, Tiberia, and Danelor. The Soulchains will not only hold the sorcerer at the forefront but also nullify their magic, giving us just enough time to administer the chalice."

"Problem." Max pointed at the battle raging between Chandra and Belen. Both dragons were bleeding, covered in dust, but neither looked close to backing down. "How do we get a chain around that?"

If Danelor, the massive amethyst dragon, could regain control, he would be the key to neutralizing Chandra. But he was still trapped, bound by Tiberia's magic.

"I'll take care of it." Asher's chin lifted, his golden eyes ablaze with determination. The twin golems shifted, their stony gaze settling on the battling dragons.

Iaxis nodded. "I will handle the chalice. I... "

The Archivist was cut off by a desperate scream. Cailan had somehow broken free from the sorceress's grasp. He lunged towards Tiberia.

Cailan

THE SOULCALLER'S MOMENT OF DISTRACTION, HER FOCUS entirely on the delicate task of reestablishing the Flameweaver within Danelor, cost her.

Cailan rammed into her, the impact sending them both sprawling across the cracked marble floor. The Soul Taker clattered away from Tiberia's grasp. He shifted mid-collision, fluidly transitioning from drake to human, prepared for the struggle.

"Get off me, you overgrown lizard," Tiberia snarled.

Cailan pinned her arms, his muscles straining against the sorceress's supernatural strength. "Not a chance, you possessed harpy."

Suddenly, Tiberia's body went limp beneath him. He

frowned, confused by the change. Then he felt it: a cold, slithering presence seeping into his mind, a whisper of darkness, a touch that chilled him to the core.

"What the—?" he gasped, his mind reeling.

Tiberia's eyes cleared, the eerie glow fading, replaced by genuine fear. "Cailan! Watch out! She's—"

But it was too late. The Soulcaller's essence, a dark tide of magic, poured into him, filling every crevice of his being. It seeped into his thoughts, his memories, his very soul.

My, my, an amused, silken voice purred in his mind. *What a strong vessel you are. So much potential. Far more promising than that chimera.*

Cailan gritted his teeth, refusing to yield. *Get. Out.*

The Soulcaller's laughter echoed through his mind, a sound that made his blood run cold. *Oh, I don't think so, little wyrm. You are mine.*

He felt his control slipping away, his limbs moving of their own accord. He tried to shift, to return to his dragon form, hoping to dislodge the sorceress, but he found himself trapped.

None of that, now, the Soulcaller chided, her voice smug in his mind. *I am in command.* She shifted him, his dragon form taking shape. His muscles involuntarily flexed, his claws scraping against the fractured floor.

You and I, she whispered, her voice seductive, *we are going to do great things together.*

Not if Cailan had anything to say about it. He remembered Iaxis's plan, the Soulchains, Eletheria's Blessing...a terrible, desperate plan. He'd hoped to avoid it by securing the Soul Taker, but...so much for *that.*

Cailan scrabbled for control, and for a heartbeat, he had the upper hand. Finding his voice, he yelled, "Chain me! *Now!*"

Maxine

MAX GRABBED THE SOULCHAIN, ITS BONE LINKS COLD AND smooth against her skin. She darted towards Cailan, a statue carved from defiance, his sides heaving as he fought a battle she couldn't see. Max had no doubt that the Soulcaller was attempting to fully claim his mind.

Frantically, she wrapped the Soulchain around Cailan's legs, her fingers clumsy and damp with perspiration. Her gaze darted to Asher, who was battling towards Chandra. Belen's tail lashed out, nearly tripping him as he struggled to loop the chain around the sorceress's neck. His golems loomed nearby, appearing to wait for an opening to assist their creator.

Tiberia and Vesper had reached Danelor, the pair working together to wrap a Soulchain around the huge dragon's legs. The amethyst dragon remained frozen by the Soulcaller's magic, so he offered no resistance.

Max struggled to interlock the links of the chain, her fingers slipping. Her gaze darted back and forth between Cailan and Asher. One of Asher's golems held a thrashing Chandra by the wing, pinning her in place. Belen had her claws hooked into the Seer's other side, her tail lashing with the effort. Asher finally managed to loop the chain around Chandra, his face set in grim determination. Max held her breath, urging him onward. For a moment, it seemed as if he might succeed.

"Oh, no you don't," the Soulcaller growled in Cailan's voice.

Before Max could react, the chain slipped away, the bone links clattering to the ground. She cried out, reaching for it, but Cailan was on the move, shifting back to his human form. He lifted his hands, darkness coalescing in his palms as a black, pulsing energy. He sent a shadowy bolt towards Asher.

At the same time, Chandra, the Grief-Eater, unleashed a burst of brutal magic against the Jade Empress. Max watched in horror as Belen crumpled, her body seemingly boneless. The Jade Empress' furious roar was cut off as she fell.

Asher hadn't seen the bolt coming. He was almost upon Chandra, the Soulchain ready, when it struck him. The dark magic hit him with a force that sent a shockwave rippling out, a wall of energy that seemed to touch everything in its path. Asher gasped before the darkness consumed him. The air vibrated with the intensity of the attack.

The chill of death brushed against Max before settling on Asher. "*Macawi,*" he whispered, eyes widening. His body convulsed as the life was ripped from him. The golems collapsed into rubble.

A strangled cry ripped from Cailan's throat. "*Chain me now!*" His eyes blazed with a fierce spirit that was all Cailan.

Trembling, Max grabbed the chain, her fingers working frantically as she secured the loops. It was easier now, with his human form. But...*oh, gods*...the Grief-Eater was free.

Tiberia, a blur of determined movement, broke away from Danelor, dodging past Cailan. She screamed, "For the Jade Empress!" as she snatched up the chain that hung loose around Chandra's neck. Her nimble fingers, fueled by vengeance, worked swiftly, snagging the links into place.

Chandra roared, her dark magic sputtering. Then Tiberia shifted, her human form expanding, transforming into a magnificent midnight-blue dragon, a creature that might not rival Danelor's imposing size, but was still slightly larger than Chandra. Her claws slammed against the sorceress, forcing Chandra down.

"*For my mother,*" Tiberia snarled. She tightened her grip on the sorceress, her gaze falling on Max for a split second. "For the Jade Court!"

"Iaxis!" Max yelled, her voice ragged with desperation. "We're running out of time!"

The Archivist, still in his Elven form, was already moving. He raced towards Chandra, and though the Grief-Eater tried to resist, Iaxis forced her to drink from Eletheria's Blessing. Chandra convulsed, coughing as if trying to expel the evil within her.

Maxine watched anxiously as Iaxis approached Cailan with the chalice. Her grip tightened on the Soulchain, determined to keep her friend secure. Cailan's eyes were wild, unfocused, as Iaxis pressed the chalice to his lips.

The moment the liquid touched Cailan's tongue, his body went rigid. Then, without warning, he began to thrash violently. Max barely dodged a flailing arm that came dangerously close to striking her face.

Just as suddenly as it began, the thrashing stopped. Cailan slumped to the ground, unconscious. Max's heart raced as she checked his breathing, relief washing over her when she felt the steady rise and fall of his chest.

She looked up to see Iaxis shifting, his Elven form dissolving. Powerful drake wings unfurled as he took to the air. He soared toward Danelor, the chalice clutched carefully in his claws. Max watched, her breath catching in her throat, as Danelor drank.

The massive dragon's reaction mirrored Cailan's. Danelor convulsed, his huge form making the ground tremble. Then, just as abruptly, he, too, fell still, head slumped.

Worry gnawed at Max's insides. Were they okay? Had the chalice worked? Or had it only made things worse? She longed to check on Danelor, but she couldn't bring herself to leave Cailan's side. Tiberia had abandoned Chandra, standing beside her brother, her expression torn between the fallen Jade Empress and the unconscious Danelor.

Vesper, limping, made his way towards Chandra. The aralez whimpered softly, gently licking the azure dragon's muzzle.

As Max watched, Chandra's breathing grew more shallow. The Seer rolled her eyes in agony. Then, softly, she said, "I'm sorry, Vesper. I failed you and Cailan both. I failed everyone." She gasped, her claws flexing. "But I'm taking the Grief-Eater with me."

The great dragon's eyes dimmed. With a final, shuddering breath, Chandra's body went still.

32

Consciousness is Overrated

Elazar

Elazar sat on a log, his gaze fixed on the horizon where the sea met the sky. In the distance, the partially destroyed ruins of the Forgotten Library stood like a shattered tomb. Most of his wounds had healed, but a few lingering bruises served as a reminder of his close call with Belen—a reminder that his future held no guarantees.

He'd needed to get away for just a little bit. Elazar had found a cove on the island, one that gave him the space he needed. The gentle lapping of waves against the shore did little to soothe his mind. He felt a deep conflict for the sacrifices Asher and Belen had made. They had stopped the sorcerers, saved countless lives, but the cost was steep. Elazar couldn't shake the feeling that there might have been another way.

He thought of Asher, the father he'd only just met, who'd risked everything to protect them. He thought of Belen, their enemy turned ally, who'd ultimately chosen to stand against her own corrupted sister, to choose her children over vengeance.

Elazar swallowed a lump in his throat. He hadn't been there for his father, in the end. And while he doubted his presence would have done anything to lessen the blow, he couldn't help but think things might have been different.

A seabird's cry caught his attention. He turned to see Max approach, threading her way through toppled masonry.

"Hey, Max. Any news?" he asked as she drew near.

Max nodded, a hint of relief easing her features. "Danelor woke up a while ago. Gretchen said he'll be fine. Cailan's stable."

Elazar ran a hand through his coppery hair. "Good to hear." He shifted on the log, making room for her to sit beside him. "And the others?"

Max shrugged, her expression hesitant. Elazar nodded, understanding. The unnecessary battle had left its mark. Many had perished, drakes and dragons alike. He knew everyone would bear scars, physical and emotional, for years to come.

Two days had passed, a strange blur of time that felt like both the blink of an eye and an eternity. The Jade Court airships had settled onto the sea, bobbing like a flotilla of pelicans as they awaited whatever came next. Elazar couldn't quite fathom what the future held. From the little he'd seen, the dragons were torn—horrified by the death of their Empress, by the realization that her mind had been poisoned by a sorceress, but also overjoyed by the return of their wings and the restoration of the chimeras.

"How are *you?*" he asked, turning to Max, who settled beside him on the log.

She seemed lost in thought. "I don't know," she said at last. "Part of me is relieved it's over. But another part..." She shook her head, unable to articulate her emotions.

Elazar nodded, understanding her conflicted feelings all too well. He'd been grappling with similar emotions since the battle ended.

Max turned to face him, her eyes searching his. "I keep replaying everything in my mind. I never imagined I'd be part of a battle like that." She paused, swallowing hard. "But then I think about what could have happened. What if we hadn't stopped them? And I know...we did what we had to do."

Elazar reached out, taking her hand. "We did," he agreed. "It doesn't make it easier, but we saved a lot of lives."

Max nodded, a small smile touching her lips. "And we survived. *You* survived."

"I never would have heard the end of it if I hadn't," Elazar said with a chuckle.

She bumped her shoulder against his. "You're right. I'm sure there's an artifact here that would allow me to pester you even in Perdition." They both laughed.

Elazar's thoughts were interrupted by the unmistakable sound of wings cutting through the air. A large, midnight-blue dragon descended toward the beach, powerful wings stirring the waves.

"Tiberia," Elazar whispered. Max had told him about her transformation, but he hadn't seen it with his own eyes yet. He watched as a dusting of magic coated the dragon, revealing the woman he knew a moment later.

Tiberia approached them, a smile curling her lips. "Elazar," she greeted, her voice carrying weariness, but also a strength he hadn't expected. "Maxine."

Elazar stood, offering her a nod. "Tiberia. I wasn't expecting to see you...*scaly*." He gestured vaguely, his words failing him.

She grinned, a flash of warmth amid the sadness. "I understand I have *you* to thank for that." She tilted her head, studying him with a thoughtful gaze. "It seems the Dragon Who Isn't really *was* the key, wasn't he?"

Elazar shrugged, deciding to avoid the complicated tale of The Shaper, the sorcerer's gift, the power he'd channeled. "Looks good on you, though. Do you like it?"

Tiberia laughed, a sound full of mixed emotions. "I'm not sure I can answer that. It just feels as if a long-lost part of me has come home. Fallen into place." She glanced back toward the destroyed library and seemingly beyond, to where Belen had battled Chandra. "Though the cost was high"

"I'm sorry," Elazar said, his words a hollow echo. It was hard to muster genuine sympathy for a dragon who'd ruled with such cruelty, but he understood now that Belen, like Asher, had been corrupted into something other than herself. And despite it all, she was Tiberia's and Danelor's mother. She'd *loved* them. She'd died protecting them.

Tiberia sighed. She moved to sit on the log. "Thank you, Elazar. That's part of what I came to tell you. It's complicated." She swallowed, her chin lifting, her expression determined. "I'm the new Jade Empress. The Jade Court will leave once Danelor has fully recovered."

Elazar and Max exchanged surprised glances. "Congratulations, I think?" Max said, her voice hesitant.

The chimera smiled, a bittersweet expression. "It's not something I ever expected. But fate has a way of surprising you."

"I have no doubt you'll lead them well," Elazar said, sincere. He'd seen the strength and compassion within her.

Vulnerability flared in Tiberia's eyes. "I appreciate the vote of confidence, Elazar. But it won't be easy. I know that." She rose, rubbing her upper arm. "I also wanted to let you know that you and any other drakes are welcome on Jadefire Island. Under my reign, the Jade Court will treat you as equals. As friends."

Elazar knew the significance of her words. If she kept her vow, it would heal old wounds. He smiled. "Glad to hear it." He squeezed Max's hand, a reassuring gesture. "I plan to stay with the *Tempest*, but it's good to know I've got options."

He watched as Tiberia stepped back, a flash of brilliant cyan rippling over her skin. In an instant, she was gone, replaced by the magnificent blue dragon, her scales gleaming in the late afternoon sun.

"I have much to do. But I wanted to make sure I spoke with you before we departed. Goodbye, Elazar. Maxine." Though she was much larger, her voice was still Tiberia's, the chimera Elazar had known. "May the winds always be at your backs."

With a powerful beat of her wings, she took to the air, sand and sea spray dusting them as she climbed, her form silhouetted against the brilliant blue sky.

Elazar followed her flight path, watching as she maneuvered towards one of the Jade Court airships. Tiberia's wings spread wide, her descent graceful. She landed with ease on the deck of the largest vessel.

Even from this distance, Elazar could see the crew's reaction. Some bowed their heads in deference, while others cheered, their voices a joyous chorus that carried across the water.

As he watched the scene unfold, Elazar felt a mix of emotions. Relief that the conflict was over, hope for a better future between dragons and drakes, and a twinge of sadness for the losses they had all endured.

"It's really over, isn't it?" he murmured, his gaze still fixed on the distant airship.

Max leaned against him, her warmth a balm. "This part, yes," she replied. "But I have a feeling our adventures are far from over." Max rested her head against his shoulder, a soft sigh escaping. Elazar hesitated for a moment, then swept an arm around her. She glanced at him, a smile touching her lips. "So, what's this I hear about you having *armor?*"

He chuckled at the question. Honestly, Elazar had almost forgotten. Magical exhaustion and healing from the puncture wounds caused by Belen's fangs had taken their toll. "It was a little something I worked on while I was in captivity. I never had a chance to test it, though, so I'm lucky it worked."

Max raised her brows at that. "I'm *very* glad it worked. Can I see it?" She paused. "That is, if you're up to a shift."

Elazar grinned, drawing his arm from around her before rising. He couldn't resist sharing his creations with Max. "I'll show you."

Thanks to his functional nexus chain and his vertigo-quelling tricks, a moment later Elazar stood before Max as a dragon. He reached up, sketching the required rune on the engine's casing. His augments slid into place along his wings, followed a beat later by the rasp of metal plates locking into place around Elazar's body.

"Wow," Max whispered. "That's incredible. You really did it." She rapped a fist against the armor on his chest.

"Yeah, though looks like it needs some repairs." Elazar noticed dents and scratches from Belen's fangs. Then he withdrew the armor back into the nexus chain. Repairs would have to wait. "We should probably head back before someone looks for us. Want a ride back?" He dropped his shoulder in invitation.

"Don't have to ask me twice," she said with a grin. Max's

hands found a secure grip on his scales, and she pulled herself up.

Elazar glanced back, ensuring she was settled. He spread his wings, the air catching beneath them, and took to the sky.

Cailan

Consciousness, as far as Cailan was concerned, was overrated. Being awake meant facing the brutal reality of Chandra's corruption. How long had she been like that? Had it happened only when she'd been meant to die, or had it been festering for far longer?

And Asher. He'd killed his own father. Sure, the sorceress who'd been determined to commandeer his body at the time was *really* the one responsible, but Cailan't hadn't stopped her. *Couldn't* stop her. But it didn't matter, because the result was the same. Cailan had failed someone again.

The Soulcaller no longer had free rein of him. One of the Forgotten Library drakes who specialized in possessions (and it was disturbing *that* was even a thing) had studied him alongside Gretchen, declaring the sorceress was fully nullified. But that darkness...it wasn't entirely gone. Cailan could feel it, a faint whisper of magic still lingering within him. And it was *his* now.

He didn't know what to make of it. He didn't know what to make of anything anymore.

"I know you're awake," a warm voice said. "But you can keep your eyes closed if you want. I'm not in a hurry."

Cailan opened one eye out of spite, a playful smirk sliding onto his lips as he met Danelor's gaze. At some point, the chimera had shifted back to his human form, his vibrant purple scales gone, replaced by a simple cotton shirt. They were both in sick bay aboard the *Tempest*, but it felt strangely comforting. Danelor lay on his side, watching Cailan.

"Just what I wanted to wake up to," Cailan said. "The world's most optimistic dragon. How are you going to turn this whole mess into sunshine and roses?" He raised an eyebrow, a teasing challenge, but the truth was, he desperately wanted to *believe* in that sunshine, to cling to that hope he knew Danelor would deliver.

"We survived," Danelor said plainly, his voice even.

"You realize you've set the bar incredibly low, right?" Cailan assessed his own body, feeling the tightness in his muscles, the uncomfortable echo of the Soulcaller's magic that still pulsed within him. It would take time, a *lot* of time, to adjust to that. "We survived. But the extra baggage we're hauling around now...*dead sorcerers.*" He made a face, his expression grim.

"*We survived,*" Danelor repeated, unwavering. As if to emphasize his point, he rose to a sitting position, though he winced slightly as he did so. "The bar is higher than you think, Cailan. Not only did we survive, but we'll get to see sunsets. Rainbows. We'll get to see each other." He paused, his gaze meeting Cailan's, a hint of something vulnerable in his eyes.

"Oh yeah, *there's* the sappiness I was waiting for." Cailan allowed himself a leisurely eye roll, though Danelor's words warmed that cold place within him. "So, who said I wanted to wake up and see *you?*"

An amused look flashed across the chimera's face. "I think you were sleeping, but you murmured my name a few times."

Cailan's cheeks warmed. "I did not!" Had he? Really? "You must have imagined it."

Danelor paused, a ghost of hurt crossing his features. "Do you really dislike me so much?"

"*Winds*," Cailan muttered, biting back his own frustration. Then, softer, he said, "No. And you know it." He closed his eyes, exhaustion pulling at him, his thoughts a jumbled mess. "It's just...we've been through so much. So much pain, so much loss. I don't think I can trust anyone again." Or love anyone. He'd loved Chandra and look where that had gotten him.

Danelor was quiet for a moment, his gaze fixed on the ceiling as if searching for an answer there. Then he nodded, understanding. "When I was with the Jade Court," he began, voice thoughtful, "I was alone. *A lot*. Not just because of what I am, but because of my pain. It made me too vulnerable, especially when I was younger." He wet his lips. "I could only trust my sister and my mother. It's a hard life, when you don't have others to rely on. Others who care." He spread his hands, a gesture of helplessness. "But you have people here, Cailan. People who care about you. Who would do *anything* for you. You shouldn't turn your back on that."

Cailan wanted to argue, to tell the chimera *exactly* what he could do with his advice. His gut reaction to anyone, *anyone*, telling him how to think or feel was to fight back. But the chimera was right, wasn't he? And a troubling thought rose within him: if he closed himself off, if he allowed himself to retreat into his shell of cynicism and distrust, he risked succumbing to a different kind of poison. The Grief-Eater might have died with Chandra, but her legacy could live on.

He couldn't allow that. He wouldn't. But trusting others, loving others...it was hard. Risky. But maybe it would be worth it.

Cailan cleared his throat, breaking the silence between them. "So, I guess you're going back with the Jade Court. Now that you've got your *dragon thing* sorted out." He made an expansive gesture with his hands. "I didn't think there was anything larger than a leviathan dragon. But you *you* were something else. You were gargantuan. No one's going to mess with you anymore, Danelor."

"I'm not going back with the Jade Court," Danelor said, shaking his head. "And you can call me Dane, by the way. Less formal."

"What?" Cailan blinked, utterly surprised.

"Dane," the chimera drawled. "It's a nickname."

"I know what a nickname is." A rush of uncertainty flooded Cailan. "You're...staying with the drakes?"

Dane raised his brows, amusement dancing in his eyes. "You're missing the obvious, aren't you?"

"Give me a break. I'm still getting over a nasty case of sorceress," Cailan grumbled, trying to hide his embarrassment. "Tell me."

"I'm staying with the *Tempest*," Dane said, a smile curving his lips.

Oh. Cailan blinked, surprised. "Didn't know that was an option."

"I spoke with Tiberia and Captain Jo a little while ago." Dane's smile widened. "While you were *legitimately* sleeping, I might add."

"Right." Cailan gingerly pushed himself upright, hoping he was hiding his eagerness at the news. "Well, you weren't exactly a disaster on the airship. Guess the captain's desperate for anyone to help."

Dane rolled his eyes at Cailan's obvious attempt at a barb. Then, he cleared his throat, his expression serious. "I have a question for you. About the sorcerers."

"Yeah?" Cailan swung his legs over the side of the cot, his feet hitting the floor with a thud.

Dane swallowed, a hint of nervousness in his gaze. "Have you felt any effects from it?"

Cailan tilted his head. "Maybe? What do you mean?"

The chimera pursed his lips, then shook his head. "Not the best place to show you. Not right now."

Dane's cryptic words only intensified Cailan's curiosity. He would have pressed, but Gretchen entered the room. She checked their vitals before declaring that they were in good enough shape to make themselves nuisances elsewhere. She released them from sick bay.

As they left sick bay, the rest of the crew enveloped them. Max wrapped them both in a tight hug. Elazar, his arm circling Cailan's shoulders, muttered something about *cocky dragons* that made him snort.

The rest of the day was a blur of activity. The surviving drakes had invited the *Tempest* crew to share a meal in one of the library's few undamaged sections.

The Celestial Hall, though no longer the grand space it had once been, had been repaired hastily, make-shift tables and chairs replacing the elegant furnishings. But the atmosphere was surprisingly light, a cautious hope clinging to the air. Cailan sat between Dane and Elazar, picking at his food. He caught snippets of plans for rebuilding, discussions of new alliances between drakes and dragons, and whispered concerns about the lingering effects of the sorcerers' magic.

As the meal wound down, and the drakes dispersed, Cailan seized his chance. He caught Dane's arm as the chimera rose to leave, his voice low. "Hey. Maybe now?"

Dane nodded, a silent understanding passing between them. They slipped away from the gathering.

"Okay," Cailan said, crossing his arms, his gaze fixed on the chimera. "Spill it, Dane. What did you mean earlier? About the effects?" He had to admit, now that he'd finally said it aloud, the name felt *right*. More intimate.

Dane pulled a face, his expression hesitant. "It's probably nothing."

Cailan raised an eyebrow, a slow grin spreading across his lips. "You realize that means it's *definitely* something, right?"

The chimera rubbed the back of his neck. "I just don't want to alarm anyone. But..." He glanced over his shoulder, as if expecting to find someone eavesdropping. "Let's go somewhere a little more secluded. Out on the beach, maybe? Where I can show you what I mean."

Cailan's curiosity intensified, fueled by concern as he considered the chilling magic in his core. He followed Dane out of the library, the scent of the sea air refreshing. The chimera led him down a winding path through the dense foliage that surrounded the library. He glanced back occasionally, as if to ensure they weren't being followed. Cailan resisted the urge to make a snarky comment about Dane's paranoia. Whatever this was, it had the normally cheerful chimera on edge.

They emerged onto a secluded strip of beach. The trees formed a natural barrier between them and the library. The sound of the tide lapping against the shore filled the air, masking their voices.

"Great," Cailan said, crossing his arms, his gaze fixed on Dane. "We're here. Now get on with it. What's got you so worked up?"

Dane took a deep breath, his gaze fixed on the horizon. Then, without warning, he began to shift. Magenta motes of magic danced across his skin as he transformed. A heartbeat later, a massive dragon stood before Cailan, amethyst scales lit with a rich iridescence from the setting sun, so large he dwarfed the surrounding trees.

"I already know you can turn into a dragon, feather-brain," Cailan said, raising an eyebrow. "Is that what all this secrecy was about?"

Dane shook his massive head. "Not exactly."

Before Cailan could come up with a witty retort, the

amethyst dragon turned toward the sea. He braced his forelegs against the sand, his back straightening, his neck arching. Dane opened his jaws, and Cailan at first thought he was preparing to roar, but...

A gout of searing flame erupted from the dragon's mouth, so intense that blistering heat chased over Cailan before dissipating into wisps of dark smoke that danced over the water.

Cailan stared, his eyes widening in disbelief. The Flameweaver...*he'd* done this to Dane. Made him Danelor the Firebreather.

Cailan quickly schooled his features, forcing a mask of nonchalance onto his face. He leaned back on his heels, as if he hadn't witnessed something extraordinary and terrifying. "Well, well," he drawled, his tone dripping with sarcasm. "Looks like someone had a bit too much spicy seafood at dinner. I told you those pepper-crusted shrimp were suspicious."

Dane's head swung around to face him, smoke still curling from his nostrils, an incredulous look on his face as if he couldn't quite believe Cailan's response.

Cailan continued, determined to maintain his facade of indifference. "You know, there are easier ways to deal with indigestion. Have you tried mint tea? Much less dramatic than setting the ocean on fire."

Inside, Cailan's mind raced, piecing together the implications. Dragons in this part of the Dragon Latitudes *didn't* breathe fire. Legends spoke of dragons in the East, fiery beasts that could scorch entire countries, but not *here*. Dragoneering vessels would have *never* succeeded against creatures like this. Not without more protections.

"This is serious, Cailan," Dane said, shifting back to his human form. His voice was ripe with worry that Cailan couldn't ignore.

"Oh, I'm being *perfectly* serious," Cailan retorted, arching an eyebrow. But then, he closed the distance between them. "And yeah, I feel it, too. Something different...but nothing like *that*." Now, he understood why Dane was so reluctant to return to the Jade Court. He'd already been seen as an outsider, a freak. This new ability...it only made him more of a threat.

Dane swallowed, his expression troubled. "I don't know what to *do*."

Cailan didn't think there was any simple solution. They'd just have to figure it out, learn to live with their new, unconventional abilities. He placed a hand on Dane's shoulder, hoping to offer some reassurance. "Don't worry. You *can* control it, right? No randomly setting the *Tempest* on fire. That would be a problem."

Dane allowed himself a small chuckle, his usual sunshine breaking through the darkness. "Yes. At least, for now, I feel in control. It's just...*there*. Burning inside me."

Cailan nodded, a wry smile playing at his lips. "Good. Guess I should be glad you didn't pull that trick when you were trying to eat me."

Dane frowned. "I was trying to *save* you!"

Cailan rolled his eyes, his smirk widening. "Yeah, I know, you big lug. Just teasing."

He was tempted to pull Dane into another kiss right then and there—if only to forestall any questions about the traces of the Soulcaller's magic that still pulsed within him. But unfortunately for his potential distraction, a resounding bark drew their attention.

Vesper trotted toward them, his tail wagging, his movements stiff, wings bandaged but clearly on the mend. Cailan relaxed at the sight of the canine. He smiled, scratching behind Vesper's ears. "Been thinking about you," he murmured. Then, for Dane's benefit, he added, "Vesper's the only reason we made it out of that mess alive. Or at least, without ending up as meat puppets."

Dane chuckled. "Sounds like Vesper deserves a steak. Or several steaks."

Cailan agreed, his heart softening. Vesper deserved all the treats in the world. But something nagged at him... "Yeah, but I've been thinking. How did Vesper *know?*" He met the canine's intelligent brown eyes. "Vesper knew about the Grief-Eater, I think. And no one listened." No one understood the warnings.

Dane blinked, his expression one of surprise. "Really?"

"Yeah." Cailan sighed, guilt washing over him. Vesper's uneasiness around Chandra, his reluctance to be near her, should have been a sign. He'd been so focused on his own drama, so blind to the aralez's silent warnings. "And I keep thinking...from what I was taught, there's always supposed to be a Seer. Usually one of the aspirants, trained by the previous Seer."

"Okay," Dane hazarded, his tone uncertain, clearly not following the logic.

Cailan knew the chimera had no idea what any of it meant. But he peered into Vesper's eyes, his certainty growing. "All the aspirants are dead. And it's certainly not *me.*" He swallowed, the realization settling heavy in his gut. "I think *Vesper* is the Seer."

Vesper's tail thumped against the sand in an affirming wag.

Josephine

THE *TEMPEST*'S BALLOON-SAILS SNAPPED IN THE BREEZE AS the airship pulled away from the Forgotten Library. The sky overhead was clear, leaving the island exposed to the world.

Josephine glanced at navigation—the strange pocket watch-turned-compass was still at work, projecting a spectral map of the area. It was going to take time to get used to that being a normal part of their life on the airship.

Things would be different, that much was certain. The white aralez, Vesper, stood at the bow, his head poking through the aurora, the wind ruffling his ears. Cailan had insisted the canine accompany them, and Josephine saw no reason to deny him.

Everyone she cared about was here. Gretchen was reorganizing her supplies in sick bay. Elazar was somewhere down in the bowels of the ship, attending to routine maintenance. And Cailan, who Jo counted as family, too, stood vigilant near the bow, watching Vesper.

She inhaled a calming breath. Things wouldn't be easy. She still had that monstrous debt to Gibson. But maybe, just maybe, the treasures she and Gretchen had liberated from the library in the chaotic aftermath of the battle would help win them free from the financier. At least, that was her hope.

"We've faced down sorcerers and corrupted dragons," she murmured. "We're due for a break."

"Did I hear you say *break?*" Gretchen asked, coming onto the bridge. She waggled her eyebrows, her expression mischievous. "I got the coffee maker set up. Just need someone to test it out with me."

Josephine paused, a smile spreading across her face. "Is that what you've been doing?"

The Healer gave her an innocent look. Her eyes twinkled. "Tending to my *supplies*, of course. And coffee, my love, is *absolutely* essential. A vital part of any Healer's arsenal." Then, before Josephine could offer a retort, Gretchen added, "Come on. Enjoy a cup with me. You can even bring it back up here if you want."

Josephine smiled. That sounded wonderful. It was time to embrace the small joys, the simple pleasures. Because sometimes, it was those small things that made the biggest difference.

PLAYLIST

Music that inspired *Dragon Meridians*.

El Capitan - Zayde Wolf
Children of the Sky - Imagine Dragons
Eye of the Storm - Watt White
Fight Till the End - Shangrii-La
Vengeance - Neoni, Saint Cardinal, & Silverberg
Higher Than High - Zayde Wolf
Sound of War (feat. Fleurie) - Tommee Profitt
All or Nothing - Theory of a Deadman
The One to Survive - Hidden Citizens

Also by Amy Campbell

Tales of the Outlaw Mages

Breaker

Effigest

Dreamer

Persuader

Songbinder

Heartseeker

Airship Dragons

Dragon Latitudes

Dragon Meridians